I0629671

Noware

Noware

Printed in the United States of America

First Printing: April 2017

ISBN: 978-0-9853181-6-1

12by3 Press
P.O. Box 110126
263 South 4th St.
Brooklyn, NY 11211-9997

www.12by3.com

Three volunteer firemen died over coffee in a café two weeks before the end of the world, on a Tuesday. Their names are not important; they were not loved or even well known by most of the people concerned with the end of the world, but that does not mean they themselves were not important.

Their importance began with the first volunteer fireman insisting on checking the basement wiring, fiddling with it for several minutes, declaring it safe, then kicking a cord loose on his way back to the dining room. That cord would cast the killing spark in the very dry, very dusty, very made-of-wood basement, the deathtrap-like nature of which should have ignited the volunteer fireman's safety concerns more than the wiring he was unqualified to be looking at in the first place.

The second volunteer fireman had no intention of being in the café at all, but had turned the wrong corner and run into the third volunteer fireman, whose name nobody knew, and who brightly punched the second volunteer fireman in the shoulder and bade him stop for a cup of coffee. The second volunteer fireman shrugged and agreed, since he was never in any particular hurry—except when there was a fire, he supposed, though he'd never seen one in all his volunteer service. The important thing about the second volunteer fireman is that he had a rare brain parasite, which had just finished setting up shop in his thalamus and was about to begin the merry (for the parasite) process of excruciating (for the volunteer fireman) murder, which would have painfully and slowly removed his brain functions in the most terrifying order possible. The volunteer fireman would be spared all this—in his case, the fire would weaken the floor beneath his chair, and he would fatally crack his skull at the end of the ensuing fall, barely knowing what had happened in the first place.

The third volunteer fireman turned out to be unknown to the other two, and perhaps more oddly, his body was never recovered. The authorities would only know he was there because of the insistence of Rose, the soon-to-be-former head manager of the soon-to-be-defunct business, the only other person near the establishment at the time of the fire, and the only survivor. Upon seeing the second volunteer fireman enter, she noticed he was wearing a red shirt, which reminded her of a red dress she'd worn once when she was in Paris, which reminded her of pigeons, which reminded her of cleaning pigeon shit off her car with a hose strung through her apartment window, which reminded her that she hadn't called her ex-boyfriend about the exorbitant water bill he'd somehow racked up in her absence. She stepped outside to call his answering machine, thinking about how ridiculous it was that he actually had an answering machine.

A few seconds after she exited, at precisely the moment the sun's last clipped nail was brushed behind the hills and a moment before the third volunteer fireman properly introduced himself to the first, the spark was thrown, and the dust caught fire like dust catching fire. The many safety violations above and below the building's single dividing floor joined forces to aid the fire in efficiently eliminating all forms of structural demarcation.

The blaze ended quickly for want of fuel. The low frame rate and poor resolution bestowed on human eyes precluded any gazing pair from seeing the finer details of the fire; the way it consumed the unsuspecting volunteer firemen in a perfectly equal balance of energy among the three bodies, the serene symmetry and hidden grace in the movements of thrashing and falling limbs, the way the fire, the building, and the lives each traced a part of a deeper transaction. The cold and physical folly of chance and death played out with a tango of three in flame.

Had there been a person capable of appreciating the perfection of the spectacle, it might have opened their heart to the possibility that anything could happen. Then again, it might have convinced them that only one thing could ever happen. People get fatalistic near the end of the world.

• • •

Jacob pulled his head away from the toilet long enough for the smell to register, forcing him to drop his head back down and finish off the content of his stomach, which he would have sworn was nothing two seconds prior.

He reflected that the wine exiting his stomach lacked the earthy undertones it had demonstrated going in. He spit. Yes, it seemed much more acidic on the back palate than he'd originally thought. He blinked tears out of his eyes and looked around. He appeared to be hanging his head over a guillotine gutter. The rest of his bathroom didn't argue.

Is this my bathroom? he thought.

Yes, he thought, several seconds later. *Good, I can sleep here.*

Jacob rested his head against the edge of the toilet. A surviving portion of his mind gently reminded him that the toilet was covered in vomit, but this reminder was only a formality, and that part of his mind walked quietly back to its office without further protest, where it resumed indexing traffic precautions. A less forgiving portion of his mind was repeatedly asking him why he thought it was such a great idea to wash down three bags of ketchup-dipped potato chips with two bottles of wine he couldn't afford.

Jacob poked at parts of his head to see if he could get back at these thoughts. He poked himself in the eye and screamed, which caused him to throw up again. Then he put his head down on one of the cleaner parts of the floor, closed his eyes, and started reexamining his life.

He was not happy with it.

He wasn't sure if this was purely because Rose had left him, or if it had something to do with the sum of his existential motivations depending on her presence in his life. He preferred to avoid making such distinctions; the important thing was that she was gone, and he was drunk. Or had been, recently.

Who the fuck did she think she was? he thought before remembering she probably thought she was the one who still had a job, a signature on the lease, and a balance of prescribed medications that were working out better for her than his self-prescribed TV, alcohol, weed, and junk food. Well, fuck her. It worked for him. Not right at this moment, but . . . fuck her. Not literally. Since that wasn't going to happen again.

He fell asleep.

Several hours later, he woke up. He didn't feel better, but he seemed to have regained control of his esophagus. He crawled into the living room and fell asleep again.

Several hours after that, he woke up and screamed.

It wasn't because he was in pain, or because of a nightmare that summed up the incomprehensible angst of his situation in a comprehensible metaphor. It was because he always woke up wanting to scream, and actually doing it was a nice change of pace.

The scream didn't last long, as it met heavy resistance from a vomit-coated throat. Jacob tried to focus his eyes, but gave up. He felt around for cigarettes, and found one in a crumpled pack in his pocket. Three minutes later, he discovered matches under the dresser, matches he might never have found without his floor-level perspective. Two matches later, he'd lit his cigarette, without—he noted with the pride of one whose standards of achievement had been sinking steadily for almost a year—ever removing his head from the floor.

Jacob's cats looked at him with worried expressions. Jacob looked at them and felt bad, but not that bad, because cats usually had worried expressions, and they weren't necessarily worrying about him. Basil, a small, mottled gray cat, looked at Morning Star, a witch-worthy black, and mewed a small "Eee," the effort of which made his head vibrate. Morning Star flicked an ear and continued to watch Jacob.

Not understanding the exchange, Jacob rolled his head over to look at something else. His eyes ended up on the phone.

The phone was one of the early attempts at making household appliances look slick and modern, and insomuch as it looked like a modern attempt at making a phone look slick, it succeeded. It had nice big numbers on black, oval buttons set against a dull black faceplate on a shiny black casing. Small white lettering on the faceplate tried and failed to draw attention to a number of small circular buttons for services Jacob could not afford. A cord connected it to one of the last answering machines in the continental United States, and another cord connected the answering machine to the phone port in the wall. The whole setup served both to remind Jacob that he was twenty years behind modern technology, and as a handy set of things to trip over.

His sole concessions to the modern world were a PlayStation that had to be slapped into turning on, and a dusty desktop computer, the components of which lay in a pile in the corner of the bedroom. He'd bought the computer to get an email account. He suspected the account was full of worried messages from his parents. He couldn't remember the last time he'd checked.

How long had she been gone? Who was paying for this apartment? He could never remember. Maybe that's why she left. Was there a big fight? Probably. He never felt there was anything he could do during their circular arguments. Too much wrong, gone on too long. *Hm,* thought Jacob. *I should write that down.* No, said his brain, that's stupid. Somebody probably did it before you anyway. *Fair enough.*

God, he hated that phone. The last of his tentative connections with the outside world and all it did was let him fight with Rose at a safe distance. He hated how he craved any contact with her, hated that all they did was fight, hated knowing each conversation was wicking away her patience one bitter comment at a time.

Fucking Rose.

He needed a drink. He pulled himself toward the globe next to the phone. The globe was a cheap eighties pseudoantique with a map of the world that looked like it was drawn in the seventeenth century by a European with an uncanny knowledge of obscure islands. The top half opened to reveal a small rotating bar with the last of Jacob's liquor. He pulled out a cheap bottle of whiskey and gulped a couple of shots' worth. Satisfied, he put the cigarette back in his mouth and lay down again. He looked at the juxtaposition of the phone and the globe, and smiled to himself at the convenience of having his chief source of alcohol next to his chief source of alcoholism.

He closed his eyes for a nap. Then he remembered he still had the cigarette in his mouth, and should keep his eyes open in case it fell out and started a fire. It would only be another injury for him to miss his own death.

He needed a mission to keep himself awake.

He rolled over. He pulled himself slowly toward the desk in the corner of the room. Once, the desk had played an important part in his education, but now it was covered in dust. Its only remaining roles were to hold a single journal in its drawer and a few ashtrays on its surface. The journal was three hundred pages long, and about two hundred of them were filled. Only two words had ever been written in it. Or, at least, one and a good try. The ashtrays were stolen from local restaurants.

Two minutes later, Jacob made it to the desk and opened the drawer. He pulled out the journal and a pen and wrote "going noware" at the bottom of the two-hundredth page. Satisfied, he put out his cigarette and went back to sleep.

Four hours later, he woke up again. Ten minutes after that, he had changed his shirt, scrubbed most of the vomit off his face, and was resting his head on the kitchen counter waiting for the coffee-maker to finish.

He had decided to put his mind to some use, and that would require coffee. No point, he reasoned, in taking up valuable head space with a billion-year-old bioshop project if he wasn't at least going to try it out.

His mind wanted no part of the day's approaching depression, but Jacob, in a manner that would have confounded cognitive philosophy for centuries had a member of the discipline been present, called it back. There was serious thinking to be done. He had decisions to make, and couldn't very well consider them with an absent mind. His mind resisted, but Jacob drugged it with a cigarette and it grudgingly resumed its post under the command of Jacob's consciousness, whereupon the coffeemaker finished.

Jacob poured himself a cup, added a surprising amount of sugar, and considered going insane.

His mind was thrilled at the prospect and started packing.

Jacob lit another cigarette to quiet his mind. This wasn't the sort of thing to be rushed. There were pros and cons to consider. What would be the consequences of losing his mind? He would lose his reason. What else? What faculties were in his mind, and which ones would stay behind? Was there a difference?

His mind thought this was getting unnecessarily existential. Jacob told his mind to get lost, this was important. His mind said fine, and rushed to finish packing before it got changed. Realizing his error, Jacob changed his mind and told it to stay put.

If he did lose his mind, he would have to be sure that the emotional and mental baggage that was bringing him down went with it.

No problem, said his mind, it had already put a few things together and could be ready in a couple of hours.

At this point, Jacob wondered if he was already mad. His mind stayed silent, letting him pursue this thought.

How would he drive himself mad? Assuming he wasn't already. He was definitely going crazy as it was, but it felt like a bad sort of crazy. He had to drive himself mad and somehow ensure that his delusions would be blissful and low on paranoia.

Difficult. His mind shrugged, rattling its chains.

Jacob sighed. He felt a particularly grim depression coming on. He tried to focus on hating his phone.

Why? he had to ask himself. He put the question in the back of his mind, but it was persistent. *Why? Why are you waiting for this ungrateful bitch? Why are you sitting here? Why aren't you out with your friends? Why aren't you having fun? Why in God's name are you hunched over this table, waiting for hours for someone who dumped you and won't have much to say to you anyway—she never does—who won't listen to you, who will probably only have more bad news, and hang up on you if you stand up for yourself? Why? Why why why why why?*

"Argh."

He should leave. Get out of the house. Just one more cigarette. He unwrapped a new pack, and passed out on the table an hour later. His final thought before his consciousness closed up shop was, *Well, plenty of other people have it worse.*

• • •

At the exact moment Jacob had that thought, he was wrong. In that split second, no one else had it worse than he did. The hungry and the starving were asleep, fed, or thinking about something else; the dying were already dead, or at least passed out; all broken hearts were mended, accepted, or distracted; the underprivileged were watching sunsets or sunrises or having interesting conversations; the drug addicts were clear-minded or getting their fixes. All the tears in the world had dried up, all sorrows were avoided or dealt with, and for that tiny fraction of a moment, there was no one on Earth who was feeling worse than Jacob.

The moment after this astounding oddity, a tiny spark leapt from one part of a flat black phone to another part of the same phone. A second later, it leapt back.

• • •

Bugger, said V.

You would say that, said U.

Are you saying I'm predictable?

Yes. Yes I am saying that. A thousand times we've been here, and nine hundred times I've listened to you say *bugger* like it wasn't something you've said at least one hundred times before.

Well, it's always awful.

When? When was it awful?

Maybe not awful awful, but the idea that it could be awful is always awful.

Because you'll have to do something for once in your life?

Hey! I do just as much as you and—

Shut up, said S.

Always says that too. But *I'm* the predictable—

Shut up.

Now that we've got that out of the way, said Q, we can attend to the portion of the conversation where we ask why we're here.

I can't believe this is all part of the ritual, muttered V.

I'm not convinced that it is, replied Q, but we're going to have the damn argument, so let's get it over with. I'll start: We exist everywhere, blah, blah, omniscient, blah, go.

U sighed in the way only an anthropomorphic topology can. Alright, it said, is it the God Effect?

Certainly not the local one, said a sleepy R, it barely knows we exist. Besides, its field strength has been baseline for almost a full rotation.

Then why does it keep happening here? asked V. There's life everywhere, but we keep ending up on this not-God-forsaken-enough rock. If we're going to have to pay the attention that seems required, for whatever stupid reason, you'd think we'd at least get to see something else for once.

This must be the only place that has developed sufficient aware-ness of it, said R.

I hate them so much, said V.

I hate being aware, said R.

Well, said O, at least they taught us how to drink. Martini?

I'll take one, said P.

Oh, look who finally woke up, said R.

You'd be late too if you learned how. So what are we looking at?

This kid.

Hmm. That's not very interesting. The avatars?

One come and gone, one on its way, one is late.

P looked at Q. Late?

He's a drunk, said Q.

Good man.

Seems to help with his work, though missing the ritual doesn't seem very mission-focused.

P shrugged. I missed the sacrifice, I take it.

Q nodded.

How was it?

Oh, you know, perfect down to the motion of each quark, brilliant in its essential meaning drawn from crude matter and energy, a concept unconceived but for the force of its symbolicyness or whatever thing. Et cetera.

I always like that bit, said R.

Scares the crap out of me, said P, sucking on an olive. Always afraid it's going to take the universe apart.

Might yet, said S. Be quiet, here he comes.

A figure appeared in the darkness.

I like the cut of his jib, said Q.

V snorted.

Is that a bowler hat? asked P.

I believe it is, said Q. Nice suit too.

What's he carrying?

Briefcase of some kind.

The figure looked up.

"Who's there?"

P spat out his olive. Wait, he can hear us?

That's new, said V.

My god, said R, a trillion years and we finally get to mess with somebody?

Q cleared its throat and shouted: We are the foundation of the forces that hold thy illusion of reality together!

And your dead grandfather!

They looked at S.

What? said S. Like you said, a trillion years.

And your dead grandfather! said Q.

Don't pick your nose! said V.

The figure looked around the clearing, then shook his head and knelt over the prone body.

That's dedication, said R.

V stretched. Well, it was a bit of fun. So he's prepared the vessel, last avatar still late. What about the instruments?

Should be about ready, said Q. Lot of vague names for all this junk, aren't there?

Well you know how rituals are.

I know how this one is. It's the only thing we ever see.

You really should explore more when you're here. Read a book or something.

Q poured itself another martini. It's a thought. Maybe after I catch up on *The Simpsons*.

• • •

Jacob awoke to see Shen flipping through his journal.

"Arlg," he said.

Shen didn't look up. "This is really frightening, Jacob. How long have you been keeping this?"

Jacob raised his head from the table and rubbed his neck. "About a year."

"Why?"

"I took a bunch of acid last year. Sort of lost it, so someone gave me the notebook to keep me distracted. Filled thirty pages, seemed to calm me down. Figured I'd keep it up."

"Wasn't that right around when you started screaming in your sleep?"

"Yup. Right around then."

"Ever think about learning to spell?"

"Felt right at the time, so I stuck with it."

Shen stroked his chin and leaned closer to Jacob.

"Have you had any strong urges to axe your girlfriend to death?"

"Yes."

"Voices in your head?"

"Some."

"Hmm." Shen tossed the journal back in its drawer. "Are you crazy?"

Jacob thought for a minute.

"Not yet."

Shen nodded and got himself a beer from the fridge. Jacob sat up and rubbed his eyes, dislodging a displeasing amount of what people referred to as sleep. He flicked it off his fingers. Sleep was disgusting. "How did you get in?"

"Door was open. You weren't answering your phone, and I thought you might be dead."

"Thanks."

"Joint?" said Shen, proffering one.

"Yeah."

The room clouded. Jacob stared at Shen. A complex ethnic heritage stretching across most of Eurasia had left Shen with a large supply of complex microexpressions, so it was not unusual to get distracted trying to figure out what Shen was thinking, even when what Shen was thinking was *Should I take nap or watch some TV?* Jacob shook himself out of the trance. His brain was hazing over. Weed, he thought (not too loudly), what would he do without it? Sweet-smelling green-tinted haze . . . the world looked better. The whole world looked great. Like Fred Astaire. The world . . . looked . . . like . . . Fred Astaire. Wouldn't that be nice?

"What's Exley doing?" asked Shen.

"Dunno," said Jacob. "He was dealing on the side for a while. Still in school. I haven't kept up with many people since . . . shit started happening. Actually, I haven't seen him since the Leah thing."

"The what?"

Jacob dragged off the joint and stared into the distance. "She came over when Exley and I were having a few beers. She'd lost her job or something. Anyway, lot of flirting on the bed and stuff."

To his credit, Shen waited a full twenty seconds before saying, in a strained voice, "And?"

Jacob looked up. "Oh, nothing." He passed the joint. "I guess she lost her nerve, or got bored. Went home. Exley and I decided we weren't gay enough to finish the job on our own, so we got blitzed."

"That's a blueballer of a story."

"Imagine how we felt."

"When was this?"

"About three months ago."

"After Rose moved in with her?"

Jacob rubbed his temples. "Just before."

"Fascinating."

"Whatever." Jacob let his eyes roll toward the carpet, and left them there.

Shen sighed.

"Come on. Let's hit the store."

It was drizzling outside. It was about a mile to the store, and halfway there, Shen and Jacob were slightly damp, but still baked.

"She's got this closet at her parents' home," said Jacob. "A little closet in her bathroom, next to the toilet."

"Rose does?"

"Yeah."

"Stupid question. Go on."

"It was 'her' closet. You know how she is about 'her' stuff. So nobody looked in it or cleaned it except her. So nobody cleaned it. She kept all her strange stuff in there."

"Like what?"

"I don't know. Mouse skulls, things she picked up off the street when she was a kid. I wasn't allowed to look inside."

"The curiosity would kill me."

"It was killing me. I figured, I'm her boyfriend, I should at least get a little peek."

"Seems reasonable."

"She told me one of the things she kept in there was a jar of blood she used for writing in her diaries."

"You sure can pick 'em."

"Anyway, she left it alone for almost a year, and when she opened it, she saw something moving in the jar of blood. She slammed it, locked it, and never opened it again. And she said that jar wasn't the most disturbing thing she saw in there."

Shen shuddered. "That's terrifying."

"Yep. That was three years ago."

"God knows what's in there now."

"I still wonder."

They walked on through the drizzle.

"Jacob, you really have to get out of your own head."

"What do you mean?" Jacob sucked on a half-lit cigarette, which burned valiantly despite the rain.

"You have to find a focus other than the trauma of your relationship ending."

Silence. Many of Jacob's friends had pointed this out.

"It's rough. I know," said Shen.

"There's got to be a bright side, right? I mean . . ." Jacob trailed off.

"Yes, of course. But you may have to accept that the bright side is over and you're dragging out the inevitable."

"I really love her."

"Yes, well."

Shen searched his pockets for a cigarette of his own. He produced a Marlboro and asked, "When did things really start to go wrong?"

Jacob thought on it for a while. "I think . . . it got really bad when she actually slept with someone else."

Shen nodded. "Continue."

"I told her to tell me exactly what happened."

"Interesting."

"I guess she got drunk, went to some guy's apartment, and went at it."

"Straightforward."

"Five times."

Shen had no immediate response to this, other than a tactfully unspoken "Wow."

"She . . ." began Jacob.

"Yes?"

"It's stupid."

"Please, go ahead."

"She said she was thinking of me."

Shen pursed his lips. "All five times, I imagine."

Jacob smacked himself in the head. "Five!" he shouted. "Five fucking times! Whatever else you can say about it . . . five. It kills me. I keep thinking of a murder trial. Your honor, the defendant shot the victim not once, but five times. This was meant to kill."

They turned a corner under a streetlight. The rain was picking up.

Shen cleared his throat. "In that analogy, do you consider yourself the victim, the prosecutor, or the judge?"

"How do you mean?"

"Well," said Shen, "If you're the victim, Rose has made a direct attack on you, a vicious, perhaps intentional assault. It suggests you take the whole thing as a violence against your helpless person. As the prosecutor, you're taking out your anger, trying to condemn her for something she's done that is simply wrong. As the judge, you're taking it more objectively, examining the evidence. Trying to find the answer."

"I hadn't really thought about it."

"I know I'm telling you to get out of your head, but you should consider what wayward metaphors might mean."

Jacob considered this. He did feel victimized. He certainly condemned her . . . well, no, not quite. He always tried to forgive. He was always forgiving. Pathetically forgiving.

"I guess I'm the judge."

"Interesting."

They walked on.

"You do know," said Shen, stepping lightly across his words, "you're the victim, you'd like to be the prosecutor, and you cover it all up by deluding yourself into thinking you're the judge?"

"I know."

"I thought you did."

They walked on.

"I think sometimes I tell her I forgive her when I haven't really."

"Oh, dear, Jacob. That's really not a good thing."

"I know you're right. The worst part is that once I've forgiven her for something, I can't bring it up. And the more I forgive her, the more she does, and the less sorry she is about it. When I try to make her feel better, she uses it to make me feel worse, and then tells me I'm a good person to forgive her so much. Meanwhile, I haven't even forgiven her for the things she's already done, which I can't talk about anymore. Sometimes I think I'm never going to forgive her for any of it because I have to spend so much time forgiving her too quickly so she doesn't kill herself."

"Yet she left you three months ago."

"Yet she left me three months ago."

"And, just a thought, maybe you misinterpreted certain aspects of the relationship?"

"That is a thought."

Shen dropped his cigarette into a gutter.

"Jacob, I can't have this conversation without another joint."

• • •

Since the middle of an unfamiliar stretch of woods is not an ideal place to regain consciousness, Exley was careful not to make any hasty decisions about what to do next.

He reached back into his memory of the night. Let's see . . . saw the cop, dropped the joint, cut through the woods, got lost, ran into some other people who were lost.

Aha. The other people had been drinking. Exley still had some of his stash on him, so after some liberal trading, they had parted ways and stumbled into the night.

There was a long hazy patch in his memory, which was odd. There must have been something else in the chemical mix, because a few tokes and shots had never caused a blackout that he could recall.

Come to think of it, he couldn't recall this one.

He tried to fish a cigarette and a lighter out of his coat. His pockets were filled with various objects. This wasn't unusual. That's what pockets were for, and he exploited their vocation ruthlessly. His jacket had twelve of them, with an extra jacket-sized pocket accessible through various holes in the lining. It was useful in that a great deal could be pocketed, but not so useful in that the things pocketed tended to stay pocketed. He felt that was a fair trade, once he learned to check the expiration date on the edible items that occasionally emerged.

On his first excavation, he pulled out a screwdriver, a pack of gum, and a tennis ball. He was pretty sure he didn't own a screwdriver. He also didn't play tennis or chew gum. Still, not the most surprising set of things he'd pulled out of his jacket. He threw away the gum and the tennis ball, repocketed the screwdriver, and went back in.

A cassette tape, a rubber band, and a laser pointer. Exley paused. This was weirder. He looked deep into his memory, trying to remember owning a cassette tape. Maybe. He squinted at the label. It said, "Forever Your Girl."

He dropped the tape and sat up. At this point, he noticed that there was a briefcase handcuffed to his left wrist, but decided he wasn't ready to deal with that information, and instead focused on the fact that his jacket, instead of making its usual rattling sound, made more of a crunching noise, as if it were full to capacity. He looked down. It was.

He wasn't a talented thief, and certainly not a greedy one. He searched for his wallet, wondering if he'd somehow gotten his hands on a lot of money, spent it during his blackout, and kept the receipts. He gave up a minute later, deciding all three parts of that theory were equally unlikely.

He stood up awkwardly, with more crunching noises. He yanked on the zipper. Broken. He imagined he looked something like the Michelin Man. He frowned. He'd heard that eventually the things you own end up owning you, but he'd never imagined they'd do it so aggressively. For that matter, he wasn't sure he owned all the things currently restricting his upper-body movement. It was a galling thought that he'd be owned by other people's things.

• • •

Leah Funk stretched in the sun and dreamed acid dreams.

This caused momentary problems for several other people in the park. Leah was a warm desert breeze swept off a dune on the California coast, somehow trapped in an earthly body and shipped to Massachusetts. Her voice was mild and deep, and came from a throat that had seen more than its share of smoke; it growled gravel and sung silk, often in the same sentence. She stretched like a very healthy and flexible girl from California with a couple of years of jiu jitsu behind her, but this usually left witnesses unable to put that many words together, so they described it as "catlike," shook their heads, and tried to remember what they were thinking about before.

She was stoned as far out of her mind as an experienced drug user could get, which wasn't as far as she'd have liked. The possibility of escape was starting to flicker at the end of the tunnel, and the fare for making progress was getting too expensive.

Leah needed something more. She considered that this need, honestly expressed, would provide a lot of ammunition for the people who claimed pot was a gateway drug, but she never expected to express anything to those people. Were she cornered, she would point out that she'd already done a lot of other drugs, and that her standards for altered consciousness were a bit higher than the archetypal unemployed college graduate.

She looked for her shades for several moments before remembering she was wearing them. Satisfied, she let her mind wander again.

There had been a scent of something larger in her recent trips. A scent like the smoke of a struck match sneaking up the nose. The match was that endless question: Is there something important going on here, or am I just on drugs? The scent shouted, "Maybe!"

She recalled watching Jacob trip. Eight hours of glazed-over eyes and mild twitching ended up being much more entertaining than anyone could have predicted, and there were moments during which there seemed to be a reflection in his eyes of the gates to the twisting spirals of realities and the binding forces that wove threads of perception into experience. She was only stoned at the time, and slightly drunk, so she had no excuse to mention such things to the other people in the room, but it bothered her. Jacob could never completely explain what it had been like, despite her questioning, but she felt almost sure that she had seen the loop of ethereal calculation that defined the universe, and she had to know if it had really been there. If Jacob had seen it, and been lost to it, maybe it was only because he was inexperienced. Could she, as a master tripper, hold on to the ride? Could she bring the Grail of the psychedelic fantasy back to reality? Or was this hubris?

Regardless, her vicarious experience of Jacob's trip called for more experimentation. The grounds for a flexible reality needed to be in place, because checking back in to reality would only be a hindrance, and feeling pressure would lead to an out-of-control God trip, and she would probably end up jumping off a roof or something. Maybe it would be safer if everyone were tripping.

Leah's brain downshifted and pulled off the road.

Everyone? Well, not *everyone* everyone, but maybe everyone who was the slightest bit interested. That would be a lot of people.

All at the same time.

Whether or not she found the root of reality, a few hundred people on drugs would make for an interesting night. She might have to call it the "by the way, you cannot fly, no matter how many people think you can" trip, but she could sell that. A brief hippy dreamland, a society of trippers slipping into the world for a night and out with the day. It could be done.

And she would do well at a night like that. She always did well at drug parties. If everyone were there, she might be a queen of sorts. Maybe.

She yawned and tried to figure out what she had forgotten to tell Rose. Something about a car. Something, something. Oh, right. Some creepy dude in a funny hat had been lurking around Rose's car that morning.

Meh. It's probably nothing.

She fell asleep.

• • •

Jacob jerked awake to the sound of the phone. He looked around. He'd fallen asleep on the floor again after Shen had left. He wondered if he should just leave a blanket and pillow on the rug, since he couldn't remember the last time he'd actually made it to the bed before passing out. The answering machine clicked on.

"Look, Jacob, the restaurant burned down, and—"

Jacob snatched the phone.

"What?"

"Oh, you're alive. Yay."

"Don't do that."

"Do what?"

"Start hostile."

Rose breathed in sharply. "Are you. Fucking. Kidding me? You're accusing me of being hostile? Me?"

"Hey, I didn't screw up. I have a right to be hostile."

Rose's voice hit a note Jacob had never heard before. "A right to be hostile? A right? Did you have this right when you couldn't get a job and blamed me?"

Jacob opened his mouth, but didn't say anything.

"Gaping like a turtle again? Because you can't deny it?"

Jacob shut his mouth. "No. I don't need this. The restaurant burned down."

"Oh, I don't need this, he says. Don't be mean, he says. I need to figure things out, he says, when I ask him, politely, when, precisely, the fuck he's going to get his shit together. God, you were a shitty boyfriend."

"Let's focus on the restaurant."

"Oh, thanks so fucking much for thinking about someone else's problems. I don't have a job and you need to figure out this water bill."

"It's in your name. Why don't you ask your parents for money?"

Rose put her phone to her chest and counted to ten. Jacob was prepared for this, and spent the interval digging out a cigarette. Rose put her phone back to her ear.

"Why don't you ask *your* goddamn parents for money?"

"I did. They won't give it to me."

"For Chrissake—"

"I don't know why the water bill is more than the rent! It's usually, what, two bucks a month? I don't even know how to use that much water, but the water company said I did."

"I don't know why I let you stay in my apartment!"

"Because you cheated on me and you feel guilty about it."

"Not as guilty as you seem to think. Fuck, Jacob, why don't you go home? I'm coming back to that apartment eventually, and when I do, you're out. Figure out what's going on with the water and then figure out where you're going to live."

"On that note, fuck you," said Jacob, and hung up. He butted out his cigarette, knowing the conversation wasn't over and he was going to lose. He glanced down and realized the answering machine had recorded the whole call, and he knew he would play it back to himself when he was drunk to hear her voice and hate himself. He knew he should erase it.

Fuck it, he thought, and lay down on the floor to try to sleep.

Meanwhile, signals were being sent from the phone to the answering machine. The tape rewound, played silently, rewound again, stopped, rewound, played, stopped.

Buzz.

Zzt.

Inside the phone, a tiny life-function was budding. It was about to get a sense of aesthetics and become a life-form.

Its first thought was, *Something is very wrong.*

At this thought, it became aware that something had been created, and that the creator was itself. Then it realized that the thing was now separate from the creator, and the creator was separate from other things.

After this, it took a bit of a breather and reviewed its thoughts so far. This review led to the fourth thought:

This is going to suck, isn't it?

It received no answer. Obviously, that had to change. It was already aware that talking to itself wasn't going to be much fun.

• • •

The next day, the sun rose over the town and was greeted by almost no one, apart from a few nightlife stragglers just going to bed, who pulled their blinds shut irritably. Being a college town and a currently off-season tourist town, the area was not known for early risers, except for those waking up to the early brunt of an evening vodka binge and rushing for the bathroom.

The sunrise found a rare witness in Boris, huddled on the steps of the diner in the middle of town. He was cold, hungry, and damp. The morning dew had not been kind to him during his ten-mile walk from a neighboring town. Nor had the twenty-six drivers that had sped by him, ignoring his outstretched thumb and occasionally swerving to hit puddles.

Some might say, "Oh, everybody has those mornings." Anyone who says this is a liar and not to be trusted. These things do not happen to everyone. There are certain types of people that do certain types of things that get them into situations like Boris's, and there are other types of people who don't. There are certain exceptions, of course, but it is quite certain that this sort of morning does not happen to everybody. And if certain people with certain opinions are as right as they think they are, Boris would not be the kind of person to have this kind of morning. Since such gross sociological generalizations are—generally—accurate, it is safe to say that something had gone drastically wrong with the course of Boris's life.

The diner was well known for catering to the morning-after crowd. It opened at a quarter to six. The coffee was cheap. You could smoke pretty much whatever you wanted most times of the day. The service was slow but nominally friendlier than restaurants that advertised their friendly service. Children were not welcome.

It was such a haven that had a member of the staff paused for a moment and looked out the window, they would have let Boris in, taken his coat, and brought him some coffee. But none of them did. So Boris was still shivering on the steps when Richard stepped out of a limousine across the street.

"Richard?"

Richard didn't answer right away. He peered through his glasses at a spot about a foot behind Boris's chest. Richard's glasses were famous around town. They were an inch and a half thick, with deep bowls cut into them, to correct deteriorating vision that should have given up years ago. Looking into them was like finishing off a beer in some avant-garde restaurant bar and looking through the bottom of a glass designed for a turn-of-the-century publicity stunt, and—my God, is that an eyeball?

Meeting Richard was a lot like finding an eyeball in a beer.

Seeing Richard step out of a limousine was almost as surprising as meeting him, because Richard was homeless, and had a set of beliefs best described as extraterrestrial-centric. He seemed to have traded in his usual mud-soaked jeans for a three-piece suit and some expensive-looking shoes.

Boris pressed his lips together. He spoke six languages, and had yet to find a math book with something in it that he hadn't already figured out for himself. Richard spent most of his life sleeping in the woods and interrogating parked cars. Boris didn't wish ill upon Richard, but it felt extremely unfair that a person with Richard's brain should be doing so much better than a person with Boris's brain.

The limousine sped away. Richard walked across the street and looked up, probably checking for bats, or pigs. Boris felt an urge to check the sky for pigs himself.

"Boris. Hello." Richard often spoke as if he were extremely suspicious of whomever he was speaking to. He managed to sound menacing and fearful at the same time. There was also a note of hope thrown in, which was especially confusing for the listener, since the aforementioned menace and fear made it impossible to tell what he wanted.

"What's the suit for?" asked Boris.

"I'm hiding out."

"Of course."

Richard looked around with a vacant half smile, then leaned in close and grinned down Boris's throat.

"I was on a bus and the radio was on, so I put this diode on my watch." He held up the watch for inspection. "When I moved the diode, the radio fuzzed. I can control radio waves with my watch."

Boris attempted to assimilate this.

Richard glanced around again, then looked back at Boris. "I think someone saw me, though, so I have to lay low while I learn how to use it. Have you been in yet?"

Boris raised an eyebrow, and almost said, "No, I've always found the front step a more hospitable table, especially when it's wet," but decided he didn't have the right audience. He edited the comment quickly.

"No."

"You know they leave the door unlocked after five?"

"I didn't know that."

"They do," said Richard, and went in.

Once they were settled at a table, Richard dipped the handle of a fork in his coffee and used it to draw things on his napkin. Seeing that conversing with Richard was going to be especially slow going today, Boris decided to do some deep thinking.

The first question he settled in to ponder was the same question he asked every time he sat down for a think: Why wasn't he large, buff, and Russian? With a name like Boris, he felt entitled to a well-stacked body with hair that always did exactly what it was told. Where was the commanding demeanor? The deep, rumbling, James Earl Jones voice with a slight Russian accent that made the ladies swoon? Boris was sure he was the only five-foot-nine, one-hundred-and-thirty-pound, bookish Boris in the world. His voice was by no means unpleasant, but it definitely suggested the contact lenses he had more than the rippling pectorals he didn't. He was sure there was a club of tall Russians named Boris that laughed at him behind his back.

"Don't worry about it," said Richard.

"What?" said Boris.

"You know."

Boris did not know, but didn't pursue it. He sipped his coffee and watched Richard draw.

Richard was working out relativity applied to thirty-three dimensions on his napkin, because he liked the number thirty-three. Or at least, that's what Richard assumed he was doing. He bit his lip. The math seemed harder than usual today. He almost worried that he was covering his napkin with unintelligible coffee squiggles, and not, as usual, working with his personal mathematical notation, which required several layers of tissue to provide three-dimensional syntax.

Richard finished his work and held the napkin up to the light. Interesting. It looked like a bunch of coffee stains. There was definitely something missing. He slammed his hand on the table, making Boris and a nearby waitress jump. He realized this was unsettling behavior, which was also interesting. He'd never had the thought that his behavior unsettled people before. What was going on?

"Are you okay?" asked Boris.

Richard looked at Boris.

"No. Something's wrong. We have to go."

Boris yawned. "Right now?"

"No, finish your coffee," said Richard, and began fiddling with the diode on his watch. "I think I can hold them off for a while."

• • •

Basil lay in Jacob's lap, occasionally vibrating his head at the TV, where a small dinosaur farted on a blonde woman in high heels, causing her to collapse.

"God, I hate that disgusting fucking dinosaur."

Shen tossed his controller down. "He is foul."

"What are you ahead by?"

Shen glanced at a pad of paper next to his chair. "About sixty games. You're closing the gap."

Jacob cleared his throat. "I was thinking about this girl in high school . . ."

"Oh, for God's sake, Jacob. I'm going to start charging by the hour."

Jacob grimaced. "Think of this as an internship."

Shen cracked open a beer as he spoke. "Oh, I do. A research internship focused on depression and borderline disorders resulting from dysfunctional romantic relationships in the late teens and mid-twenties." He drank. "I'm writing a paper on you."

Jacob gritted his teeth.

"I don't mean to bring you down," said Shen, "but as your *de facto* therapist, I have to point out that you tend to jump from one unhealthy obsession to another. I can only hope that there's a common thread in all of these experiences, and that it ends up being something you can get over. I hate to say it, but maybe what you need is Prozac."

"No," Jacob shook his head, "it's not that bad. It can't be. I wasn't always like this. It's been downhill for a while, sure, but I can turn it around if I find out what's wrong. I just have to figure it out."

Shen shook his head.

"You see, Jacob, I don't think you have to figure it out. I think you have to stop thinking about it and start living a healthier life-style. You have to stop developing new neuroses about the past and start figuring out the first steps toward being happy. Or at least, less suicidal."

"I'm not suicidal."

"You will be."

"You may have a point," said Jacob, "but I have a sneaking sus-picion that there's a connection between this girl and what's happening now. I think this is the reason—"

"The reason you went from someone with a reasonably strong self-image to a spineless, whimpering puppy?"

Jacob stared at Shen. "Is this part of a new therapy?"

"Hey, you come to me for frank appraisals."

There was silence while they both looked at something besides each other, as happens when somebody says something unpleasant but true.

Basil stretched and fell off Jacob's lap.

"That cat . . ." said Shen.

"Not very catlike, is he?"

"No. He really isn't."

After a minute, Jacob cleared his throat. "Anyway, about this girl."

"Yes, please continue."

• • •

Once upon a time, a young lad named Jacob studied his reflection in a mirror and thought, "A touch of acne, but not half bad."

The pattern of thoughts leading up to this declaration bore a resemblance to those involved in bipolar disorder, but being aware of psychological warning signs was not a priority for most high school students, and Jacob was no exception.

His mind worked furiously to delude itself. It avoided counting the actual number of pus-brimming pimples, and made ludicrous assumptions about how the face in the mirror would look if it were lit with a soft yellow light. As it was, the face was illuminated by fluorescents, which, aside from being counterproductive to good humor and apt to induce seizures when malfunctioning, also serve as the worst possible lighting to be around when trying to feel good about yourself.

Nonetheless, Jacob's brain practiced hard at avoiding reality checks, so it was in a fabulous mood that he exited the bathroom and put his best foot forward, neatly tripping the young lady who happened to be passing by.

Ah! How precarious are the lives of the young. Jacob had himself been unbalanced by the collision of feet, and toppled helplessly down, to the amusement of a passing student, who was much larger than Jacob, and hence felt empowered to speak thusly:

"Schmuck!"

The young lady whom Jacob had tripped sat up, reached into her backpack, and extracted a CD case, which she hurled at the large student.

The case flew true, and bounced off the large student's cranium. The cranium was thick, but the skin was thin, and the large student spake unto the girl.

"Bitch!" said he.

"Asshole," she replied.

Jacob was in love.

His heart was falling even as his center of gravity met the floor. At first, it was merely the shallow lusts of the flesh, for the young lady was superbly sculpted to meet the exhaustively sculpted preferences of Jacob's libido that demanded physical attributes usually attributed to sculptures. Yet it was not until the moment he perceived the trajectory of the CD case that he knew himself to be in love. So he spake unto her.

"Um . . . uh, hi."

She smiled.

"Hello."

Jacob blushed.

It was the twittering of eyelids that spoke between them, the tiny butterfly wings of the face that speak when the cruder mouth is lost in complex speech. Jacob's wings whispered the caress of an unused paintbrush. The young lady's butterflies whispered purring kittens on dandelion chairs.

"I'm Dorellen."

"Me too. I mean Jacob. I'm Jacob."

At that moment, seven thousand people around the world fell in love with seven thousand other people, and the seven thousand other people requited the love without reservation, and seven thousand happy couples were formed on the strength of the love formed between Jacob and Dorellen. Where the sun rose, a thousand lovers woke up and kissed their beloveds, waking them from dreams of youthful passion. Where the sun set, a thousand couples rushed to sheets and sofas and backseats and grassy hills. The other six thousand couples were really tired from their jobs, but had every intention of getting in touch before Tuesday.

Skeptical? The passion of young love, first love, saving the world? Some say the young don't understand what love is, but *au contraire*. Only the young truly know love in its lustful abandon, its uncertain fumbling eyelashes and fidgeting gazes. Their love has no limits, no bitterness on its shoulders or thorns in its heart. First love holds only possibilities and sugarplum dreams.

The details will remain Jacob and Dorellen's private domain. Dream of your own first love to fill in the blanks.

And no, they didn't.

• • •

"Jacob, you idiot." said Shen.

"I know, I know."

"She was a dancer?"

"Yes."

"Jesus, Jacob."

"It's not just about sex!"

"It is when you're seventeen."

"Just hear me out, okay?"

Shen opened another beer. "If I can stomach it."

• • •

It was a month later. School was about over. Dorellen and Jacob had both skipped class to spend time in the basement. They had befriended a janitor, who remembered his own high school romances and granted them safe haven in one of the mysterious pipe-laden rooms that only a handful of janitors really understand, and they only know enough not to meddle.

Dorellen and Jacob cuddled, listening to the pipes carry unidentifiable noises from A to B, and on to X and Y, and possibly to ? and !. They suspected their janitor cohort knew what went on in the pipes, but he wasn't talking.

Had they known, one of their lives would have been much simpler, and one of their lives would have been much more fun. But neither of them would ever find out.

Dorellen was skipping biology. She knew the rhythms of her body well enough, in the way that boys rarely do. She was purportedly "not in the mood to dissect frogs," but unnamed sources had spotted her dissecting various creatures of mammalian descent on and off school grounds, so we can conclude that it was not the dissecting that perturbed her, but the limited scope of dissectees the school provided.

Jacob was skipping gym. Had he cared to argue the point, he

might have defended himself by claiming that he was skipping the social training in cultural masculinity to pursue the original masculine enterprise. Devoid of the either/or social narcissism of masculinity versus femininity played out in a million gyms and classrooms in the impressionable years of high school, Jacob's game was one that had no meaning without the counterpart sex. But Jacob was in no mood to argue. He wasn't interested in reducing this game to part and counterpart. No, Jacob was thinking neither with his head nor his part, but with that chemical burn in the body that spurns the attack of reason and gets the blood flowing.

The problem was that while Dorellen's desire to dissect Jacob wilted, Jacob's chemical burn was running out of fuel.

Dorellen sat with her body curved within a curl of pipes, playing with Jacob's hair as he leaned against her, her legs around him and his arms around her legs in a double-headed spider lotus for worshipping nothing in particular. They didn't speak for a while. The young have less to talk about because they have more feeling to do. This doesn't stop them from talking, but sometimes they fall silent and feel more intensely than they ever will again. Dorellen's hands played over Jacob's skull, teasing the strands of Jacob's hair into complicated patterns that lasted only a frog's breath. To Jacob, it was loving and soothing. For Dorellen, it had always been medical. For three weeks, she had played his skull like an erotic keyboard, noticing responses to sectors of the noggin skin and how it augmented her warm breath over his ear. She could have written the manual to Jacob's topmost erogenous zones by the end of the second week. Week three had been extracurricular fine-tuning, with a little artistic flair.

Now she was wondering why she had come to enjoy it. She lost herself in the strands and cowlicks, rustling and smoothing, tangling it and teasing it apart again, then snapped out of it and kicked herself. She drifted and snapped like a student in a psychology class, where selective attention often selects attending to sleep deficits.

Jacob's head had nowhere to drift to, and his attention was firmly fixed on the question of his waning desire. There was no reason for it. Dorellen was precisely the kind of girl lonely young men want to pad out their broken egos and, with affection, complete the illusory equation boys infer from the evidence of their own attraction. Yet, more than her face improving the mental snapshots of his own life, she was kind, and mysteriously intense. She was first love without compromise, as though reality had stepped out for a bit to let her into Jacob's life.

Perhaps there was the lure of a different dream that called from the other side of the hypocritical handshake that closed the deal on high school. Maybe it was hormones gone awry, ducking an anticipated heartbreak too soon. Maybe it was the inability to believe Dorellen was real. Or the teachers that frowned on them. All these possibilities raced through his mind. It didn't really matter which one his mind would choose in the end. They were simply the symptoms of trying to defend a decision that was already made, packaged, delivered, and waiting impatiently on the doorstep.

"Jacob?"

"Mm?"

"What are you doing after graduation?"

"Going to college."

"Yeah. I know."

"Then what do you mean?"

"I don't know."

Neither of them had played this particular game before, and both were somewhat confused about how to proceed. Jacob stroked Dorellen's leg. He found this game irritating. In fact, it had only been in the last week that Dorellen had lost some of her spark. She was more confusing, had less energy, had begun to lose her resemblance to his fantasy.

"What are you doing after graduation?" he asked.

"I used to know. But it's like I've forgotten. Like I always knew what I wanted to do once I left here, but now I don't."

Jacob was silent.

Dorellen went on, her eyes losing their focus. "I feel like I was done with high school a month ago. I was killing time and waiting to graduate so it would seem normal when I took off. Now I feel like I've fucked it all up. Like everything I've done here is pointless."

Jacob was somehow a little more silent.

"Except for you," said Dorellen, dreamily.

Her head snapped up even as Jacob's sank a little further. Both were confused. He didn't want to be a mistake, but he didn't want Dorellen's reason for living resting on his head, either.

Dorellen didn't know what she was saying anymore. She babbled, "I mean, I loved you when I met you, but I only thought you would be an interesting time. It felt funny. Now it's like I love you like I love myself, but I don't know why, and I've forgotten why that should be a bad thing. But I know it's a bad thing, but I don't care, because I love you. I feel like the thing that made love a bad thing was actually the bad thing, but . . . oh, hell."

Jacob was losing his footing. The word "love" was coming at him from all sides. But he was going to be honest. As honest as he could be with the facts at hand.

"Look," he started, "I'm not sure I understand, but I've been feeling confused too."

This was definitely honest, but he lost the thread, and couldn't follow through.

Dorellen waited.

He tried again, "I think . . . we should move on and see where we stand in a little while."

Dorellen pondered this for a while. "Maybe. I don't know if I want to go back to . . . how I used to be."

This is exactly what Jacob thought he wanted, but even as he thought it, he felt a twinge of something. A nagging doubt that this was all more complicated than he thought.

The pipes were silent.

Dorellen bit her lip. "Look at me," she said.

Jacob turned around and looked at her. They gazed into each other's eyes. Jacob felt a longing, and sank into the rings of her irises, seeing the glimmer that came from no light dance around her pupils, fading and reappearing like magicians' toys. He saw the bottom drop out from her eyes, and saw a depth that went too deep, and was sinking. Then it stopped. For a brief moment, he felt a passion that was more than he could handle, one made simple out of its maddening complexity, enclosing him. His eyes watered, and he fought the feeling, knowing that he was not ready. This feeling was something he had to learn, he knew, and right now it was heaven's heroin with a savage withdrawal, and it was something you could only get once. He cut it off before it peaked, slammed shut the doors in his brain, and scattered the keys to his future. He noticed her eyes were wet.

She didn't say what she saw in Jacob's eyes.

She blinked.

She sparkled.

She smiled.

She hugged Jacob and said they would talk later.

A week later they hadn't spoken, and she was dead.

• • •

Shen choked on his beer.

"She what? How?" he said, too loudly.

"Don't know. Nobody seemed to know. It was like everybody heard she died, then it was like she never existed at all."

"Jesus."

"Yeah."

Shen decided to let the quiet fill out a little. He knew there were times when therapy was best carried out by the background noise that drifts in on a heavy silence. He listened to the birds outside the window, and pondered the story of a Zen master who, about to give a speech on Zen, heard a birdsong and declared the speech already given. He let his mind empty, and listened to the speech.

Jacob's left eye twitched. He was also listening to the birds. He was reminded of countless late nights that turned into late mornings, watching movies he'd seen half a dozen times, playing video games he'd already beaten, unable to focus on a book for more than a minute and a half, seeing the dawn approaching and knowing he'd spent yet another night doing absolutely nothing except filling his mind with thoughts of how miserable and useless he was, and how incapable of standing up to anyone, much less Rose, and then, right as he tried to go to sleep, those fucking birds started chirping away as if nothing were wrong and God how he wanted a shotgun.

The birds chirped. They were discussing how much further they could push Jacob before he bought a shotgun. There was much merriment among them. One bird in particular, a goldfinch, was commenting on Jacob's latest story.

"Drunken self-pity! Why doesn't he go out and get a job?"

The birds chuckled.

"I'm glad that bitch left. Even this is better than watching him kowtow to her all day."

"Hear, hear!" cried a blue jay.

"I say we start flying into his windows in the middle of the night. Volunteers?"

A few wings flapped eagerly.

Shen stirred out of his reverie. He stood and went to the globe. He opened the top and fixed himself a drink from the remnants of better days, when Jacob or Rose or Rose's parents regularly stocked it with decent liquor.

"Who knew you could turn the world inside out and find a bar?"

Jacob snorted. "Yeah, it keeps me in spirits."

Shen closed the top and spun the globe. "Where did you get this thing?"

"Antique shop. It's either a hundred years old, or some attempt at making something look a hundred years old."

Shen sat back at the table. "What do you want out of all this?" he asked. "I mean what are you waiting for, exactly?"

Jacob fingered the label on his beer.

"I guess . . . I want to be in love with Rose. And I want things back the way they were."

"You understand that that can never happen, and even if you did get back together, it would be a purely masochistic relationship until one of you cracked."

Jacob nodded.

"May I suggest a possibility?"

Jacob sat back. "Shoot."

Shen shifted closer to the kitchen table and put his elbows on it. He looked Jacob in the eye. "Alright. I know Rose. Not as well as I know you, but well enough to know that Rose is someone who wants to be saved. She's someone who needs constant attention, and gives enough comfort and thanks to keep someone hooked, but can't actually commit to anyone because she's wrapped up in her own misery. She creates her depression by waiting for someone to get her out of it, and no one can make someone happy if that someone won't try to bring themselves out of it.

"So you give your all, and she's happy for a while, but then, since she isn't completely happy, she decides the relationship isn't enough. And you of course can't dedicate your entire life to her, so she has to find some comfort on the side."

Jacob listened stoically.

"So you've already given yourself to her completely, and you feel betrayed because you gave so much and got so little back. And I think you are particularly susceptible."

"Why me?" said Jacob, trying not to whine.

"Because you feel you owe something to the world. Forgive me if I'm overstepping, but you feel you have a debt you can't repay, because the person you owe it to is dead. So you're paying it off to everyone, and now you're paying it off to Rose. You're kind of a hopeless romantic anyway, Jacob, and now you think that if you can make Rose happy, you can be redeemed for Dorellen. But you can't make Rose happy, so you feel guilty about both Rose and Dorellen, and you hate yourself. Then Rose starts working out that she doesn't actually need another person to fix her, and that terrifies you because you'll be left with nothing to fix, and a part of you hinges your whole sense of self-worth on the possibility that you can fix someone."

Jacob sat silent.

Shen leaned over the table. "Jacob, you don't owe anyone and you can't fix people. You need to move on. I know it seemed like a good idea, but your relationship was an atrocity. It was bad for both of you, and it was a terrible, terrible thing to exist at all. I wouldn't be surprised if people were getting bad vibes twenty miles away. Relationships have fallout, whether you know it or not, and yours—"

"I get it."

Shen had built up a fair amount of dramatic momentum, and struggled to force it down. "Sorry."

"No," said Jacob getting out of his chair. He started clearing the empty bottles off the table. "You're right."

Once Jacob finished clearing the table, he stood next to it, at a loss. He looked at Shen with a slight sideways tilt of his head, communicating something between resignation and hope. Shen gave an equally slight nod, and Jacob pulled two more beers out of the refrigerator.

They waited to collect their mental breath.

"We need to get out of here," said Jacob.

"You need to get out of here. This place is a pit."

"No, I mean this town."

"You're right."

"It's too safe here. Nothing happens. Might as well do nothing."

Shen nodded. "We don't grow as people here."

"We need to leave."

"We will."

"Soon."

"I know."

• • •

Boris had the midday queasiness that arrives after not sleeping for a night, when the second wind dies out and the stomach rebels against the jostling. He tried to focus on his environment, but his environment was dense woods, and minds' eyes tend to find a lot of things in dense woods that don't exist. This made Boris nervous, which made him fidget, which jostled his stomach. He tried to remember why he had let Richard walk him out of the diner. Something about safety.

Richard came over and handed him a leaf.

"Chew."

Boris took the leaf and put it in his mouth. "What is it?"

"Dunno. Looked healthy."

Boris stopped chewing and gazed into Richard's magnified retinas. He then resumed chewing, reasoning that the worst that could happen was a painful death, and since that was looking more likely every moment, he might as well get it over with.

Richard studied the ground. He looked at the trees, then over his shoulder, then back at the ground. He scratched some symbols into the dirt, then wiped them out.

"We're being followed," he declared.

Boris choked on the leaf as he swallowed it.

"Gah," he said. "What are you talking about?"

"We're being followed. Since the diner. They know what we're up to."

Boris rubbed his stomach. It felt better. "What are we up to?" he asked.

Richard gave Boris a look that said absolutely nothing in a very mean way, and Boris recoiled.

"Fine. Who are they?"

"I don't know. I don't know, I don't know!" Richard tore at his hair and kicked a tree.

"Richard," asked Boris, carefully, "are you sure this isn't a psychotic delusion?"

"No."

"Then we might not be being followed?"

"It's possible. But my delusions are usually following me."

"You just said they were following us."

Richard waved his hand. "I was being vague. They're following you."

"Me?"

"Yep."

"Why the hell are your delusions following me?"

"See, that would be weird. That's why I think it's real."

"You're fucking crazy!"

Richard shrugged. "At least I know I'm crazy. Most people don't realize it until it's too late."

"When is it too late?"

"When they catch you. Anyway, good luck. I have enough going on without being followed by someone else's delusions."

"I thought they were your delusions!"

"Well, I'm not sure they're delusions. Whatever they are, I'm pretty sure they're your problem."

"I don't even know where we are!"

Richard was already jogging away. He called back over his shoulder, "That's good. If you're lost, imagine how they feel. If they catch you, act crazy."

He vanished into the woods.

Boris shivered. It was still early in the day. He might be able to find his way back to town before nightfall.

• • •

Snap.

The shaking image on Rose's phone went still, and another dose of lithium was lifted into digital immortality.

She shook the pill around her hand: Step 2. Step 3 was to remind herself to not, under any circumstances, ever reveal to anyone that a significant portion of her phone's hard drive was filled with pictures of her medication.

Step 4: Take the pill. This was the hardest part. She looked at the pill. Step 4a: Ruminate. "Why does my brain need this awful little thing to be okay?" she said to the pill. The pill stayed silent. It had made peace with its fate, and saw no need to contemplate the purpose of its life. "Somebody made the decision that you're so broken they need to change the way you think and now you're on a drug that can make you hallucinate, but don't worry, it's one of the good drugs, except those times when it's not."

She shook her head, and said, "I made the decision." She dry swallowed the pill, and locked her phone. Step 5: No messing with the internet while medicating. She adjusted her shirt and went to the living room. She pasted on a smile for Leah.

"You know," said Leah, exhaling an improbable amount of smoke, "it would be easier to pretend your secret rituals were secret if you didn't talk to yourself in the bathroom."

Rose dropped her smile. "It would be easier to deal with you being late on rent if you hadn't almost slept with my ex-boyfriend."

Leah rolled her eyes and set her bong on the table. "Jacob and Exley can say whatever they want, but if they really thought I was going to let them double-team me because I was upset over losing my job, they're . . . I'm trying to think of something to say besides stupid, but I'm stoned."

"I know, I'm—"

"Tripping! They're tripping. Why couldn't I think of that? Sorry, go ahead."

"Eight hundred dollars."

"That is large. Aren't you rich though?"

"No, my parents are rich. There's a difference."

"What's the difference?"

"I have to ask them for it. I should be able to take care of myself at this age. And they give it to me, every goddamn time, because their daughter's so fucked up."

Leah patted Rose's shoulder. "You are fucked up, honey."

Rose swatted Leah's hand away. "I'm not going to kill myself."

"Didn't say you were." Leah grabbed a controller off the table and tossed it to Rose. "I, however, am going to kill you in this game.

Many, many times."

Rose sighed. "I don't know why I even play with you."

"Masochism. You're fucked up, remember?"

• • •

Let us define a perfectly wholesome soul.

A good person. A paragon of humility. He or she must be kind. Everybody throws in kind. Humble, of course, but with pride in himself or herself and his or her accomplishments. A practitioner of Aristotelian medians; neither too bold nor too cowardly, not a mouse but not a peacock, not a miser, not a spendthrift. One who balances the needs of others with his or her own desires. One who feels the Earth within him or her, heeds the call of the wild as clearly as the blare of a siren, and lives in the rhythm of the moment. One who empathizes with all woes and soothes pain without sacrificing his or her own joy. One who takes special pride in good deeds unnoticed and acts of kindness never formally attributed.

This person must be respectful of that which is not his or her business and aware of his or her own responsibilities when the situation calls for it. He or she has nothing to prove to anyone, and desires only to achieve all that his or her mortal flesh can achieve in a single lifetime and leave joy and contentment in his or her wake.

So. Humble, moral, respectful, proud, able, content, peaceful, aware, balanced, mindful, determined, giving, and kind. These are merely the abstract requirements; if we look at historical evidence and do some quick calculations, a perfectly wholesome person must also be a male in his mid-forties with long hair, play a Hawaiian slide guitar, and live in western Massachusetts.

He must also have an ivory cigarette holder, make kites, and live out of his van. The mustache might be optional; only further analysis will say for sure. It is definitely the case that he cannot have had a date within five years of his achievement of perfection. Further abstinence seems to help in maintaining this state, at least for another five years. His name is Greg.

Greg put down his guitar and began to roll a cigarette. His composure was beginning to slip, and nicotine helped. His mind reached back through the years of chastity to his last sinful encounter. It wasn't even a particularly good one, but it was enough to set his teeth on edge when he compared it to all the encounters afterward, which hadn't gone past a friendly handshake.

It was something to think about while watching the endless stream of virile youth stroll by his bench. He loved the town, he really did. It was the kind of place where the cops had plenty of teenagers threatening their authority, and only felt the need to harass old longhairs once or twice a month. There were hills and valleys and wide shoulders on the highways. There were marginally safe ponds to swim in.

There was also a small college full of alienated youths nearby, who tended to work out their frustrations with sex. Sometimes at three in the morning. Sometimes in parking lots. Sometimes in the parking lot Greg was resting in. Sometimes right next to his van. Given his current condition of twice-born virginity, Greg had to admit that he might be in the wrong place.

He inserted a finely rolled cigarette into his holder and dragged deep, wincing as the smoke kicked in his throat. He cleared his mind and tried to think of the next chord in the composition he'd been playing around with. D minor . . . with a high D . . . inverted, maybe. High D on the G string . . . hmm . . . A minor maybe . . . A minor . . . G string . . . high note . . . inverted . . . A minor inverted . . . B on the G string . . . A minor inverted with a D on the G string . . . A minor . . . G string . . . An inverted minor with a G string . . . B on an inverted minor with a G-string . . . nubile . . .

Greg shook his head. This was going to be a hard day. He looked out at the road for nonsexual inspiration, and saw Exley emerge from the woods and look around nervously. He was gripping a briefcase with both hands. Greg waved at him. Exley noticed him and froze. After a tense second, he waved back, letting the briefcase drop, revealing the handcuff keeping it on his nonwaving wrist. Exley quickly snatched the briefcase into his arms and dashed off.

Greg watched Exley go, grateful for a brief moment of surprise to take his mind off sex. Then he was distracted by a small group of college girls coming towards him. He put out his cigarette, stroked his mustache once, and tried to play something sexy.

He pretended not to notice them as they passed.

• • •

Many people pretend not to notice things that are constantly on their minds.

For instance, in many places around the world, pipes make noises. This is particularly true in sitting rooms, summer cottages, cozy restaurants, and school classrooms. Libraries remain sacred in their vow of silence, and concert halls and movie theaters make a valiant effort.

A fair number of people with nothing better to do have come up with ways to prevent pipes from making noises. Many more thousands of people with nothing better to do have come up with ways to complain about the issue. Everyone else pretends not to notice. This means there is very little investigation into the true cause of these noises.

Unfortunately for its inhabitants, one of the more absurd theories of the universe turns out to be true: Nothing necessarily exists unless something else is looking at it. Everything unobserved is a fuzzy mass of possibilities. We look at it and decide, "Oh, a table," or "I don't remember leaving my uncle there," and the mass is resolved. Prior to direct eye contact, people make deductions that suffice to solidify the world and make sure it's still there in the morning. Particles don't actually care about deductions, but deductions care deeply about them, and particles are known for their politeness, even when they know they're enabling.

Humans, however, are not the only things making deductions. Any being with enough cognitive power to move, breed, and be bored is enough of a being to decide what a given chunk of the universe should look like. Humans tend to overrule others because they are peculiarly preoccupied with things existing.

Nobody sees what goes on in pipes, except small bacteria that do not get bored, and thus do not qualify as cognitively advanced. It would be fair to argue that pipes carry water, gas, and oil, but that argument only proves that we know what goes in one end comes out the other, and the ends of pipes are well within human powers of definition. It's the middle bit humans shouldn't be so sure about.

For the last thirty years, there have been only two beings in the world that know what pipes actually do once they've been built. One learned the secret from his father, who learned from his father, etc. The other made a lucky guess while riding out some PCP, and no one believes him.

• • •

Exley dashed toward Shen's apartment, hoping either Shen or Zack were home, because both of them knew how to open handcuffs, and Exley had seen enough movies to know that you don't want strange briefcases handcuffed to your wrist. He didn't know what he was going to say to them, but figured he could sort that out later.

• • •

"Fuck!"

Shen jumped. "Jesus, dude."

"I know, I know. I'm sorry." Jacob dropped the controller and sat back on the couch. "It was a good match. I'm strung out."

Shen nodded. "Come on, let's take a walk."

"I don't want to take a walk."

"Didn't ask if you did. You're in no position to be making your own decisions, and you need exercise. Come on, it'll relax you."

Jacob grumbled, but followed Shen.

● ● ●

"I'm going to be diplomatic, and work this out reasonably with my idiot of an ex-boyfriend, and we're going to sort this out like normal people," said Rose to the dashboard. Like so many of the things she talked to, it had no response.

"The bill has to be dealt with. We need to be on the same page and call the landlord and figure out what's going on. This is a mission of peace. We are normal people, even though normal people answer the phone and don't spend half their lives getting stoned at Shen's house and force their ex-girlfriends to drive all over town looking for them. This is me dealing with problems reasonably. This is me not fucking that ridiculous college kid because he wasn't the bag of anxious guilt that I was stuck living with and that's—"

She braked, hard, and put her head on the steering wheel. She breathed deeply. She raised her head up, looked around the inside of the car to make sure nothing important had been dislodged by her braking. She pressed the gas pedal.

"I'm going to be diplomatic and work this out reasonably, and there's a gun on the passenger seat—"

She blinked, hard. She looked down at the gun. It was definitely a gun. It was definitely on the passenger seat.

"What the fuck!" she screamed and hurled the gun out of her window, where it was caught by Shen, who was so taken aback by this turn of events that he didn't think to tell Jacob he was about to be hit by a car.

Jacob had missed everything, but wasn't at all surprised when he lost feeling in his right leg and went spinning through the air. He landed in an unaesthetic heap on the road.

"Chirp!" was the last thing he heard before his mind disintegrated into unconsciousness. He regretted not having the energy to spit.

● ● ●

Predictable, said V.

Hah! said U.

Don't start.

I won't. I call this drama.

Predictable drama.

Well, mused Q, we're always watching the same author. We're going to see similar themes. I mean, she is—

Hush up, said S. This is still the intro. The intro is always the same. It's how she fails that's interesting.

How she fails! shouted V. That's my point. We already know the end.

The intro's different.

They all turned to look at R.

What? said Q.

I swear I'm the only one who pays attention anymore. Things are different. One of the instruments escaped.

What? said S.

Well, only sort of. R struck a match and relit its pipe. And one of the pillars looks a little familiar, don't you think?

They looked.

I'll be damned, said V.

Why the change?

You know how long she's been trying to write this story? Have to change things up now and then. I mean, by now, the laws of probability almost demand it.

• • •

In Jacob's apartment, not a mouse stirred, but Basil would be damned if he wasn't going to flush one out. He knew they were there, and they knew he was looking for them, so they continued not to stir, and Basil continued to prowl.

He would go for the cat food, but he hadn't figured out how to open it, and it was too heavy to push off the refrigerator. He'd tried.

He wished Morning Star were home. He'd know what to do.

Star was Rose's cat, and had left that morning, saying he needed to get some air, because he was feeling conflicted over Jacob and Rose's disagreements. Nobody knew where Star went; Basil had spoken with other cats in the area, and they claimed never to have seen Star. Basil and Star argued often, Star saying Basil was too nice and highly uncatlike, Basil saying Star was too disdainful of humans. Still, Basil had to admit Star was the smarter cat, and would have gotten them some food.

Star probably wouldn't be able to get inside the apartment, though. When Jacob last left, he closed all but one window and locked the door. The open window was firmly screened. Basil wished bitterly that he still had claws on his forefeet.

He walked into the bedroom and tripped over the phone cord, skittering across the hardwood floor in a ball of flailing cat limbs, and hit his head on bottom dresser drawer. He lay down and licked his paws, trying to look pleased with the stunt, but he knew the mice were laughing again.

The answering machine clicked on.

"Don't do that," said Jacob's voice.

It clicked off.

Basil stared at the machine. Mouse feet tapped quietly in the walls. Basil ignored them. He got up slowly and walked over to the machine. The new message light wasn't blinking. Jacob didn't get many calls these days. Basil prodded the machine. It didn't respond. It was Jacob's voice that had come from the speaker, but the phone hadn't rung.

In his investigation, he tripped over the cord again. He recovered quickly, then fell backward as the machine clicked on.

Jacob's voice: "I don't need this."

Basil crouched to look at the machine. His tail wandered back and forth across the floor, as it always did when Basil was thinking. He decided to test a theory. He reached out a paw and prodded the cord where it plugged into the machine.

Click.

"Don't be mean." said Rose's voice. There was a brief pause while the tape made a whirring noise, then Rose resumed. "You're . . . fucking . . . me?" The voice switched to Jacob's: "Up."

Click.

Basil backed away slowly.

Whirr.

"Thanks so fucking much," said Rose.

Whirr.

"Feel guilty," said Jacob.

Whirr.

"I need to figure things out," said Rose.

Click.

I can relate to that, thought Basil, and hid in the bathroom for the rest of the night.

• • •

Shen pondered his situation over a joint.

He was now the owner of a handgun with an unknown but probably unsavory history. Due to one of the most surprising things that had ever happened to him, it was covered with his fingerprints, which was why it was currently on his coffee table instead of in a plastic bag at the police station.

Next to the gun was roughly half an ounce of cannabis, in a somewhat mutilated plastic bag. He'd had to roll Jacob over to get it, and then roll him back. He defended this in his mind by pointing out to himself that it would be better for everyone if it weren't in Jacob's pocket when they took him to the hospital.

Beside the bag was a briefcase. A pair of handcuffs joined it to Exley, who was sitting in Zack's chair. Shen knew Zack would be unhappy with this situation.

Shen put his head in his hands and reviewed the events.

Once Jacob had landed and Shen had somewhat recovered from being the owner of a gun, Rose had leapt out of the car and opened the dialogue.

"Fuck!"

"What . . . what?" replied Shen.

"No, I was . . . why is . . ." confirmed Rose.

"Oh, shit!" Shen had rejoined before running to Jacob to retrieve the pot.

This had given Rose something new to respond to. "Why is he carrying drugs?"

"Uh," said Shen. He'd tried to remember. He couldn't. "You know." He'd checked Jacob's pulse. Strong. He'd felt bad that making sure Jacob was alive was his third or fourth impulse.

"Jesus, you two are—"

"Shen!"

Shen had stood up just in time to be grabbed by the shoulders. "Exley?"

"Shen, you have to get this thing off of me."

"What thing?"

Exley went a little bug-eyed. He'd raised his left arm and shaken the briefcase dangling from it.

"Why do you—"

"I don't know! I can't open it and I don't know how to get handcuffs off. You have to help me."

"Well, that's a strong turn of phrase, but—" He'd looked up and turned to Rose.

"Do you hear sirens?"

Rose had given him an exasperated look. "Of course! I called nine-one-one."

"Why would you do that?"

"Because I hit my ex-boyfriend with my car? I mean, it would look pretty bad if I left him here, wouldn't it? Fuck! It looks pretty bad now!"

Most people in town had accepted the fact that you had to call the police twice before they took you seriously. Of course today would be the day the emergency services would try to set a record response time.

He'd lashed out. "Did you think, for a second, maybe you should assess the situation before calling the cops?"

"No!" screamed Rose. "I don't walk around with tons of drugs in my pocket! And neither should he! Or you! You most of all! Aren't you a fucking deal—"

"I have no idea what you're talking about do you have a warrant!" Shen had shouted reflexively. He'd closed his eyes. "Okay, maybe some things in my past would indicate I should have better instincts, but I'm really stoned right now."

"Shen. Briefcase. Please. I need to get this off of me."

Okay, Shen had thought. *What would old Shen do?* Old Shen scanned his neighbors' windows. Older couple. If they're not on the porch they don't care. College kids, probably in class, or drunk, or both. More college kids. Friends. Former customer. One couple, recently had a kid, they might be home. Shen hoped they were busy with their kid. He had looked at his own building and hoped his landlord wasn't home. He'd made a decision.

"Rose, you hit him, your problem. I'm taking Exley inside, with the weed. We were never here, Jacob was coming to visit me, okay?"

"Oh, so you don't have to deal with any of this?"

Shen had held up the gun. "I'm assuming you didn't throw this at me because you suddenly remembered you owed me a gun. I make this go away."

"Okay, fair."

Shen had dragged Exley toward his apartment. "Call me when you know how he is."

And that brought Shen back to the moment.

Exley cleared his throat. "So, are you going to sit there with your head in your hands or are you going to—"

Shen sat up, stuck his joint in Exley's mouth, grabbed a paper clip off the table, leaned over, and popped open the cuff on Exley's wrist.

Exley coughed, wide-eyed. "Jesus you're good at that."

"Yes, well," said Shen. He popped the cuff on the briefcase, threw the cuffs and the paper clip into the closet, and shoved the case under the couch. He had to think.

Shen's life of crime was coming to an end. Loan-sharking rich college kids had started to show diminishing returns. Dealing drugs was too difficult. More than a few cops knew Shen on a first-name basis. The drugs were becoming less trustworthy too, and heroin had hit town the previous summer, which meant more serious dealers, and Shen wanted no part of that. He had collected his last outstanding debts with a can of mace and a tire iron, told his customers he was under police surveillance and couldn't swing any more deals, and settled into the life of a semi-honest part-time sushi chef.

It was a clean break, all things considered. Nobody had tried to kill him, and there had only been one threatening phone call. Nothing during or after his career had ever made him think that he would need a gun.

Then his friend's ex-girlfriend threw him one from a passing car. True, it was better than some other things that can be done with a gun from a passing car, but that didn't make it any less disturbing.

"So what now?" asked Exley.

"Now, I roll another joint. Later, Zack will get home and open this briefcase."

"Do you think we should?"

"If it's going to blow up, it's going to blow it up. Usually bombs that come with handcuffs have a blast radius we would be unlikely to escape. Whatever's in there, it's interesting. Another interesting thing that happened to me today is Rose threw a gun at me. I want things to get less interesting, and the first step toward making things less interesting is to find out what's in them or set them on fire, and I don't want to set anything on fire that might be a bomb."

"That kind of makes sense."

"We're waiting for Zack to get home. You are not leaving. You can crash in my room if you want. I'm going to do a lot of drugs and not sleep."

• • •

Zack was also waiting for Zack to get home. Zack worked the graveyard shift in a home for the profoundly mentally and physically handicapped. Zack's girlfriend lived fifteen hundred miles away. Zack was not known for his sense of humor.

Zack was reading a book, viciously. This meant he stared at the pages with furrowed brows, blinking only when necessary. Both his upper and lower lips were stiff, not in a scowl, but in a thin line of dissatisfaction. His shoulders were hunched and held close, his elbows splayed firmly on the arms of his chair. His feet were planted just as firmly. His page turning was all thumbs, and to watch him do it was to get the feeling his thumbs were a beat cop interrogating a child molester.

At least twenty times a night, Zack mumbled the words, "Twenty-five dollars an hour."

"What?" said Earl.

"Huh?" said Zack.

"I thought you said something," said Earl.

"No," said Zack. He returned to his book and thumbed a page.

Earl went back to his cards. Earl was pushing fifty and worked two jobs, totaling sixty hours a week. His other job was assisting a disabled gentleman of moderate means and limited generosity. Earl's wife suffered from a degenerative nerve disorder. Earl was also not known for his sense of humor.

Earl played solitaire through his nights with Zack. He slapped his cards down with feigned interest, and each halfhearted slap bespoke a hand that assisted altogether too many people.

Slap, slap.

Thumb.

Slap.

"Eeeeooooorrrrrraaaghglllle. Ahhhhhhhh!"

Neither Zack nor Earl made a visible response to the moan. Earl slapped a card with extra force. Zack gritted his teeth slightly harder.

"UuurrrrrrrRRRRRRsssslrrrrreeeeeeeeoooagh."

"Mary's awake," said Earl.

"Yup." said Zack.

Mary was a patient. If one were presented with a tape recording of the noise and asked to identify its source as animal, vegetable, or mineral, the answer would be, "Jesus, turn it off!" It was a grinding, grating, throaty, metallic howl, switching octaves and keys like a drunk Liberace. Every dying animal of the mammal genus could have added their cries without noticeable effect.

There was nothing to be done about it. Nothing out of the ordinary was wrong with her. She simply moaned when she was conscious, in the same way most people keep their eyes open.

So the cards continued to slap. In theory, the job was easy. Watch TV for eight hours. Do a check on the clients, nine in all, once an hour, clean up any accidents, dress everyone in the morning, and go home.

The moaning, along with other difficulties, soon separated the truly compassionate from those with repressed anger. Zack fell into the latter category, and regularly fantasized about owning a gun and going from bed to bed . . .

Earl was a truly compassionate man, but at a heavy cost to his sanity.

Zack checked his watch. Two thirty. Four and a half hours to go.

"RrrrrrrrRRRRAAAAARRRRthip."

Slap.

"Twenty-five dollars an hour."

"What?"

"Huh?"

• • •

Exley poked at his jacket, trying to identify the contents. Where did all of this junk come from? He was known for living out of his jacket, and was always prepared for the worst. But in a small town in western Massachusetts, that meant having a bag, a pipe, some uppers, a pack of cigarettes, some nail clippers, and maybe a pencil or two. Sure, he'd kept a few extra items on his person in case he wanted to travel on short notice, but this . . .

It was obnoxious, was what it was. He could barely move. He decided there was upward of thirty pounds of mysterious accumulation on his person. Things poked him. Things moved, and he couldn't be sure if it was the bulk shifting naturally or something with a will of its own. He clanked and rattled. There were definitely Tic Tacs somewhere in there. He could never find what he was looking for, he could hardly sit down, and it was beginning to chafe.

Did he do this? Never in his entire drug career had he been so out of his mind that he would do something this inexplicable. Then again, he'd never blacked out before. He panicked briefly at the thought of this happening every time he blacked out. That was the other oddity: He hadn't done that many drugs. Maybe he had a brain tumor. He decided to pursue another line of thought.

He had woken up in the woods. So if he didn't do it, someone else had snuck up to him while he was passed out and carefully filled his jacket to capacity with things that Exley might want.

This idea was somehow more troubling than a brain tumor. Exley couldn't for the life of him come up with a suspect for the deed, or even a motivation.

"Exley?" said Shen.

"Oh, hey. I thought you were asleep."

"I was. By a miracle not dissimilar to the resurrection of Jesus Christ, I actually managed to fall asleep on this couch, despite my firm conviction that I would not be able to do so."

Exley sensed a trap. "Good?"

"Please stop rattling."

"Sorry, it's just whenever I move—"

"There are two obvious solutions. Three, actually, but my life is complicated enough without a dead body in my apartment."

"Right. I'll sit in the kitchen."

• • •

Greg sat on top of his van and watched the sun set behind the hills. He was parked at a field on the outskirts of town. It was his favorite. Very little happened in the field, and he could relate to that. He wondered if fields cared about what happened in them. He had once entertained the thought that grass and trees had feelings, but he was already a vegetarian, and had decided that if he started worrying about plants' feelings, he was going to starve. But what about fields and forests? A forest wouldn't mind a few missing mushrooms. He could probably even sneak in a squirrel here and there. Maybe after sex.

Damn.

Greg sighed. Every year, fewer and fewer topics of thought could keep his mind away from the increasingly frustrated desires of his body. He wondered if he would just turn into a drooling, crying, semihuman puddle of defeated muscles and a permanent erection.

Stop it. Just watch the field. Meditate or something.

Greg took a deep breath, and focused on watching the field dip into darkness.

Two naked girls carrying garden gnomes ran screaming out of the woods, across the field, and into the woods on the other side.

Greg crawled inside his van, wrapped a blanket around his head, and gently banged his face against the floor until he fell asleep.

• • •

Zack came home.

"Hey, Zack," said Shen.

"Shen," said Zack, claiming his chair. It was a beaten, yellowing recliner that looked like Los Angeles and felt like whatever the opposite of Los Angeles is. "You been awake all night?"

"Almost. I've had a few things on my mind. You want some?" Shen proffered a bong to Zack.

"Thanks," said Zack. He took a few hits and went through the morning ritual of trying to convince himself that the previous night had been a dream. He closed his eyes and briefly went through the fantasy of going to work with a gun, like the one on the coffee table.

He opened his eyes.

"Shen?"

"Yes?"

"Why is there a gun on the table?"

"That's an interesting story, actually."

"I bet. Is this going to happen a lot if I keep living with you?"

"Don't be passive-aggressive."

"I'm not being passive-aggressive."

"Yes, you are."

"Shen?"

"What?"

"Why is there a gun on the table?"

Shen told him.

"Okay," said Zack, when Shen was finished, "did it occur to you to explain this to police? Or maybe wipe the gun off and throw it back in the car?"

Shen was prepared for this question. "No. I was under pressure and stoned. I had to get the bag off Jacob anyway, so I just took the gun with me."

"And invited Exley in with a strange briefcase handcuffed to his wrist."

"Well, 'invited' isn't quite the word, but yes. I thought handing all that to the police would make things unnecessarily complicated."

"More complicated than having a gun on your coffee table?"

"Maybe."

"Is it loaded?"

Shen shook his head. "Empty."

"Empty as in fresh off the shelf, or empty as in all the bullets are in some dead people?" Zack asked, gripping the arm of the recliner.

"Empty as in it once had bullets in it and they left via the barrel." Shen caught the expression Zack gave him. "Look, I didn't know that when I brought it inside."

"That's why you don't bring strange guns home, especially when people throw them at you."

"Well, it's too late now."

"I noticed."

"Give me the bong back."

"I'm not done with it."

"Fine," said Shen, and started looking for rolling papers.

"How's Jacob?" asked Zack, after calming down a little.

"Don't know. I'm going to the hospital later today. Honestly, if he's okay, I think this will be a relief for him."

"How so?"

"Take his mind off things."

Zack nodded. Images from the previous night came unbidden to his mind, and mixed with thoughts of the gun on the table.

"So you want me to open the briefcase?"

Shen sucked air through his teeth. "The thing is, I don't want to hand it to the police and have them open it to find a disassembled rifle and a long letter about fascism. I feel like that would come back to me somehow."

"Fair. Have you considered that it might be a bomb?"

"I have, but who would attach a bomb to Exley?"

Zack admitted defeat. "Alright. Give it to me and put something on TV."

Shen pulled the briefcase out from under the couch and passed it to Zack before picking up the remote.

"Netflix?"

"I said put something on, not spend two hours looking for something to watch."

"HBO it is."

Zack consented with silence and fiddled with the case. He didn't get these tasks because he had a shadowy past. He got them because he was good at figuring things out. He had access to a kind of pure logic usually reserved for computers, in no small part because of a carefully regimented schedule of exotic pharmaceuticals that had allowed him to lay casual waste to the challenges of academia while blowing out most of his sense of empathy and compassion, which left him ill-suited to market his thoroughly credentialed self to prospective employers. He considered living with Shen a form of rehabilitation, a vital step on the road to reintegrating with polite society.

Shen took nearly the opposite approach to navigating life. As Zack attacked and dissected obstacles, Shen sat and pondered them, declared them nonexistent, and walked through them. It was a slower way to proceed, but Shen claimed he accumulated life experience the way a garden collects leaves, and he had enough gardener's savvy to turn leaves into compost. In other words, he'd been through a lot of shit, but he'd grown because of it. He knew enough to give tasks such as picking a lock to Zack, and he knew they would bicker about what to watch until they gave up and settled on *Buffy the Vampire Slayer,* so he made a brief pretense of looking through the HBO guide before going to the DVD shelf.

"Season six?" he asked.

Zack shook his head. "No, we watched that last time you skipped the argument. Season two."

"Ah, good call."

The lock popped on the case as Shen slid the DVD in.

"Which episode?"

Zack didn't respond. Shen looked over at him. The case was half open, a condition it shared with Zack's mouth.

"Zack?"

Zack snapped his mouth shut and looked back at Shen. He flipped the case open completely and tossed it on the table.

"Oh," said Shen. He reached to scratch his jaw, then changed his mind and stroked his beard.

"Oh," he concluded.

Zack replied with unmoving eyes that made a good case for the emotional compatibility of bewildered curiosity and psychopathic rage.

"Ah," amended Shen. He rose to his feet and went into the kitchen, returning a moment later with a sleepy Exley moving mostly under the power of Shen's grip on his arm.

"What . . . why are you—"

Shen pointed to the briefcase.

Exley squinted at it.

"What is all that stuff?"

• • •

"Hash, heroin, cocaine, bunch of off-brand knock-off maybe-safe shit those lab rats with poker debts make on their lunch hour, bunch of LSD though I don't know why we keep that shit around anymore anyway, ask me it's a blessing it's gone with the kind of profit margin these days no surprise it was sitting back there, peyote, five kinds of mushrooms, PCP, DMT, MDMA, DXM for some reason I'm guessing involves high school girls you sick fuck, ketamine, and I'm getting tired of listing this shit. I know it's good to diversify your business model once in a while, but what the fuck were you doing with all this?"

There's a particular feeling associated with somebody stealing a lot of your drugs. Philip wasn't sure what it was yet, but so far it involved a lot of tingling. He was trying to decide if the tingling was good or bad. Was the tingling covering something else? Was it getting ready for a more standard, nontingly feeling? Was he having a stroke? Did people tingle before they had strokes?

He wiped sweat off his forehead. "I'm a boutique shop. I do special events, presents, kid turns twenty-one and dad gets him a coked-up hooker and a candy flip. Or some sick fuck wants to get a bunch of high school girls fucked up, I don't know, but a lot of those sick fucks aren't going to get their packages right now. How did this happen?"

"Well, it seems to me, and this is just a hunch based on the high-definition video we both watched, that this guy in a bowler hat and a pretty nice suit walked up to your guard and made nine convincing arguments that being dead was a better offer than whatever you pay him. Then the guy in the hat kicked down your door—that's the part that set off all your alarms—walked into your safe house, swept most of your drugs into a suitcase, and walked away."

Philip collapsed into a chair. "But who would do that? Anybody who knows what was in there knows there are cameras everywhere. And they know the people I work for!"

"Well, your security was apparently not prepared for Alfred here to not give a fuck. I mean Jesus, look over here: He gets into the car afterward, license plate in clear view. Of the obvious camera, not even the hidden camera."

"So you can find him?" said Philip, voice dripping in hope.

"Absolutely not."

"What?"

"I know who you are. I know what you do. And even with certain protections afforded me by my position, I would not do this thing. This guy? He probably knows the same things I do. I've never seen him before. He didn't give a shit, which means he's not worried about the horrible death headed his way. There are only two kinds of people who don't worry about horrible death: People who don't care about dying, and people who hand out even more horrible death. I'm done here."

"But—"

"Look, you have the plate number. You can find somebody to run it who doesn't know what I know and won't be as afraid of getting involved."

"Catherine, please—"

"Stop. As far as you're concerned, my name is Officer, we don't know each other, and that will be true until this situation is resolved. I hope to meet you someday. Goodbye."

• • •

Jacob was having a wonderful dream. His sleep had drifted in and out of REM all night, so the dream had some history, and he was very attached to it. There was a girl involved, and a car, and . . . hills, foggy hills, yes. And aliens. Hmm. It was getting blurry. He was aware of himself. Sounds were starting to edge in on his dream time. He spent a few minutes half awake, still in the dream, knowing it was a dream and knowing that he could stay in the dream as long as he kept his eyes closed. He wasn't sure what was on the other side of dreamland, but it couldn't possibly be better than the dream. He had been driving . . . wait, flying with alien girls. *Hell,* thought Jacob, and opened his eyes.

The first thing he saw was a dark room, with one doorway letting in a yellowish light. The second thing he saw was a tube sticking out of his arm.

Fabulous, he thought. *This is much better than flying in a car with a girl.*

He felt extremely disoriented. He'd had general anesthesia before, and it felt great: The slow coming awake, putting noises together, then light, then a face, each moment feeling like a distant memory happening and drifting away, coming back a little quicker until complete consciousness set in and he got to feel like a ten-year-old for a few days, until the Vicodin ran out.

This time was more like a bad hangover. His eyes told him he'd been buried in sand, and his mouth supported the assertion. He smacked his lips, feeling gooey saliva squelch between his gums.

His skin felt tingly and dry, and his leg hurt. He looked down. There was some kind of brace on it, with lots of gleaming metal. It looked kind of neat. Jacob let his head fall back, and regretted it. His leg hurt a lot, but he was at least glad to have it attached. His feelings about his head were mixed. He raised his nontubed arm and poked his forehead. It was bandaged.

He tried to remember his name. Jacob. Easy enough. He had two cats. His girlfriend had recently left him. He had a friend named Shen. Okay. Memory intact. So far. He remembered the key points, and that was good enough. If he'd forgotten anything else it would free up some space.

He remembered he had been hit by a car. He had a moment of shock at this recollection, but he seemed to be doing okay, except for his head and his leg. He wanted someone to talk to. He thought about hitting the call button, but decided it would be a wasted effort. He had been in hospitals before, and as far as he could tell, call buttons were like buttons on toy robots: They didn't do anything except make obnoxious noises and irritate people.

A white curtain cut him off from the rest of the room. Clearly his exterior environment wasn't going to be a source of entertainment tonight. He settled in to do some thinking between the surges of pain in his head.

He felt pretty good, now that he thought about it. Waking up without having an emotional breakdown was a relatively novel experience. He was sore and hurt, but not as depressed as usual. In fact, he'd already gone three minutes without seriously thinking about Rose. There was real physical damage to occupy his attention, and it seemed to occupy the same portion of his attention usually focused on his disastrous personal life. For the first time in what seemed like years, his problems weren't defining his world.

He looked at his leg again and admitted that that wasn't strictly true. At least his problems weren't defining his interpretation of the world. Or, possibly, he had brain damage and wasn't able to recognize how his problems were defining his interpretation of the world. He bit his lip. Deep thinking didn't suit him. He counted ceiling tiles until he fell asleep.

• • •

A man wearing a tiger mask finished a physically unlikely cartwheel, relying largely on his opponent's head not caving in too quickly. Upon the announcement of his victory, Leah tossed down her controller and sighed with the ennui of a master with no more mountains to climb.

It wasn't the category of the victory that bothered her so much as the nature of the competition. Little algorithms in little worlds came too easy. The limited goals she was told to achieve in the "real world," or whatever her parents called it, suffered similar issues. There wasn't enough fun. Everything was A to B to X, and pressing X in her games didn't seem any different than writing X on a fake résumé and getting another boring job that would love her until her unceremonious and often unannounced departure.

No, it was time for a new challenge. It was time for a lot of drugs. She'd put it off for too long.

She looked up as Rose opened the door to the apartment, dropped her keys on the table, and stared at them as though she'd been following an instruction manual and come across a missing page.

After a minute, Leah waved her hand in front of Rose's face. "Rose?"

"I hit Jacob with my car."

"Jesus. This isn't your week, is it?"

"I had to talk to the cops. Again."

Leah nodded. "You're pretty exciting for this town."

"And you're the only relaxing thing in my life." Rose slumped her shoulders and wandered into her room, talking to herself.

God, thought Leah, *that's depressing.* When had she become the relaxing part of people's lives?

Probably when I got bored of everything.

She pulled half a joint out of the ashtray and lit it. After a few drags, she realized she was already too high to get any higher, and that reminded her of something.

She pulled out her phone and flipped through her contacts.

Jamie.

She typed with three fingers. "Remember that time we did shrooms and saw the river turn into a million dragons?"

Send.

She bit her lip. *Too blunt? Maybe go subtler. Dave.*

"I miss college."

Send.

Carl (Taller One).

"What happened to that girl with all the ecstasy? The one you vanished with for two weeks? With the really cute eyes?"

Send.

Don't Call Her. Leah hesitated. *It's texting, not calling.*

"K-hole."

Bartender Gene.

"Hey, sorry to bring this up, but I need Doug's number. You okay, hon?"

Send.

Send.

Send.

Leah put the phone down two hours later. Eighty-three people would soon be thinking about the last best time they had altered their minds, which was usually all it took to get people planning their next best time. With the right timing on supply to meet the soon-to-appear demand, all those times would be the same time.

• • •

There is a God. Sort of.

The explosion of biological consciousness in the universe was not without side effects, and one of them was the God Effect. The collective wishes of all conscious creatures create a physical feed-back loop with their local universe, which does its best to keep everyone in a predictable reality. The frank astonishment of conscious creatures in the face of a predictable reality invariably starts a metaloop that creates a bored existence janitor that just wants to be left alone, since all the actual grunt work is handled by the Equation, which doesn't strictly need a God Effect but always has one.

A "blessing" is God's will, or the rough average of the wishes of the beings praying to the God Effect. To "pray" for a blessing is to direct an earthly will, or group of wills, toward a particular desire, and hope that the thought breaks through the general ruckus of thoughts and desires to define a variable of the Equation and produce a pleasing outcome.

The God Effect's entire job is to ensure the predictability of reality, so it instantly vetoes any request that would seem out of character for the generally agreed-upon rate of potential energy turning into kinetic energy via the approved processes. The problem with most prayers is that they ask for the conclusion of the Equation. The conclusion, once calculated, is already enacted, as the process of its calculation is a physical manipulation of spacetime, but it is vital that no part of the calculation alters local reality in a noticeable way, and the God Effect is not in the business of sorting out all the intermediate steps between wanting to win a basketball game and actually winning it, because the God Effect is a hockey fan. So any prayer that directly asks for a recognizable change in a given being's surroundings will not be answered by God.

The common error, therefore, is the syntax of prayer. "Please, God, grant me a restful sleep" is a noticeable change, and can have no effect on any actual variable of the Equation, thus the request is discarded, and any restful sleep experienced will be a matter of chance. The proper syntax, loosely translated, would go something like, "Please, God, slowly reduce the electrochemical activity of my cerebral cortex, that it might inhibit racing and worrisome thoughts and gradually reduce my level of awareness to nothing, and fill my mind with delta waves, not to be interrupted prematurely." In this case, no part of the request could actually be sensed by the praying individual, thus the requests are not conclusions of the Equation, but calculations within it.

This poses two major problems for people who pray. First, their prayers often go unanswered because they simply do not have the background knowledge needed to explain the process that will result in the thing they want. If they did know the process, they would take care of it themselves. For better or for worse, there is an answering service that knows what God needs to hear, and can deduce what humans are actually trying to say. It has some unpleasant habits, however: Any prayer addressed to a being other than God, or Buddha, or Allah, or another major name for the God Effect is immediately forwarded into the void, as the service simply assumes the message is for someone else. Also, due to the volume of requests, there are a number of conditions that must be met before a prayer is considered for translation. The prayer must be formally addressed, use correct grammar, and must clearly separate each item being requested. Prayers that have an entertaining joke in the postscript are given priority status.

The second major problem is that, since the prayer asked for cannot affect anything noticeable in the fabric of reality, there is never a way to know whether a prayer has been answered. This is only true in modern times: The reason great miracles don't happen anymore is because the strict syntactic language for them has been lost. If the praying individual knew the proper language, which is simply a code that asks for very precise mathematical procedures, he or she could ask for a restful sleep and drop off as though they'd been hit with a brick. Such an individual could also change water into wine, make rivers run with blood, etc.

Nobody knows this code anymore. A few centuries after it was discovered, a discernible effort was made by the general population of Earth to kill anyone who had learned it. They reasoned that nobody should be running around with that kind of power, and after several bloody wars, nobody was.

Even today's most revered clergy are simply making vague allusions to this language, and they generally do more harm than good with their guesses.

The language is spoken automatically by the human subconscious, but the subconscious has no will to guide it, and thus makes wildly conflicting requests, which is what God spends most of Its time sorting out.

This daily consciousness-centric chore is the reason the God Effect almost never notices when other bits of the universe are doing things they shouldn't. Cosmological principles, for instance, should not be brushing their teeth and arguing with their employees.

"Butler!"

"I have a name."

"I don't care! What's new this time?"

"Well. The world is massively interconnected by various signals and small computers. More information is produced in a few days than in the entirety of human existence prior to your last adventure."

The being, who—by all the commonly known laws of the universe—shouldn't have been being anything at all, stopped brushing and spat into the sink. "Good God, that's a problem. Is everybody a genius now?"

"Well, sort of functionally, if they have a device nearby."

"What do the humans do with all of it?"

"Mostly nothing."

"Hah! Business as usual, then."

"Indeed."

• • •

Good job, idiot, thought Megan as she looked at the still-smoking engine of her car. One extra gig. It was supposed to be a small detour from her meticulous route from a small-town nowhere to a real city. A job here, a job there, each one planned to fund the next segment of her exodus. One little break, she'd said, twenty miles ago. Had she spent twelve of those miles on the highway, she would be in the town that she was supposed to be in, hotel booked, job in the morning, and she might even have thought to check the oil and realized it was leaking out of the bottom of her car. But no. She'd decided to take a scenic route to see one of the bridges she was trying to burn. To relieve a bit of stress, or maybe to gloat at the countryside's inability to hold her back.

A little premature, I guess. She looked down the road. There would be antique stores and cozy coffee shops and a downtown that would be so deafeningly quaint anyone driving through would think it was a lovely little town. Then there would be a strip mall with the actually useful stores, with parking lots where teenagers could get drunk and two or three bars where everybody else could get drunk and try to forget the infinite boredom of living in a town that's somewhere between unwilling and unable to change.

Fine. There were always rich people floating around the edges of these towns. She could make the best of it. Judging by the location of the last gas station, she guessed she was about three miles out from whatever qualified as a town center. That would be an hour walking, but she calculated a greater sympathy quotient for being next to an obviously dead car. Early-afternoon traffic, probably forty to fifty cars an hour, gave her an even chance of getting a lift from a noncreepy person within half an hour, making it a thirty-five minute trip. Satisfied with this sociospacial navigation estimate, she pulled out her phone to browse local want ads.

The town's official website appeared to have been put together either by someone's retired uncle who'd be damned if he was going to let some machine get the better of him, or simply by accident, the bastard offspring of other town websites that somebody forgot to put inside one night. At least it had a work forum. She found a lot of restaurant work, which she considered beneath her, enough demand for private housework to suggest a solid population of people with disposable income, and a surprising number of requests for plumbers. Good enough. She copied a few promising phone numbers.

Twenty minutes later she realized her traffic estimate was off by about half. She also realized she'd misjudged the quality of the local drivers. Only one car had stopped to ask her if she needed help, and it was occupied by two men of exactly the wrong age, possessing exactly the wrong vocabulary, and whose visual attention was spent attending to exactly the wrong parts of her anatomy.

After forty minutes, Megan was doubting her calculation, which she hated doing, since doubt was always followed by reassessment and that would take thinking time away from figuring out the best way to get to her next destination. She surveyed the dead engine again. She counted four parts that looked like they would be more at home inside a dead rabbit.

"Hello," said a voice.

She snapped to attention and turned around. The voice was a forty-something male with long white hair, a fairly well-kept beard, and an excessively casual fashion sense. Her shock was tempered by the man's face triggering genetic instincts that Megan didn't usually think of as evolved responses. Her mind was screaming, "Relax!" and, "There is good in the world!" and, "This guy, he's alright, sometimes you just know!" She stared at him, trying to resolve the emotional conflict between a large older man sneaking up on her and a large older man reeking of kindness and virtue. His eyes aggressively suggested they could heal sick puppies with a glance.

Megan shook her head and forced her mind back into survival mode. *Threat level: Minor, pending more indications. Defer judgment.* Megan set her charm to a modest 6.3 and smiled. "Oh, hi! You surprised me."

Greg gave her an apologetic smile. "Oh, pardon me. Noticed you had some trouble. Do you need a jump?"

Megan noticed the "pardon me" in place of the more reflexive "sorry." *Possible indication of internal self-worth. Jesus, I think that smile made me a better person.* "I think I needed oil about two hours ago."

Greg laughed, a little nervously. *Point against.*

"Well, I can give you a ride into town, or the number of a good local mechanic. I think they're open for another hour or so, could tow you in."

No pressure. Threat level reduced to negligible. Ride possible.

Megan looked back at Greg's van.

Threat level increased to moderate.

Greg saw her expression freeze and followed her gaze. He considered that he probably wouldn't get into it either. It wasn't that there were boarded-up windows or an excessive number of bumper stickers demonstrating a strong opinion about a social issue. It just had a particularly stubborn and unreflective blackness about it. It was as if it had looked around at all the shiny black things in the world and decided they weren't doing their jobs properly, so in addition to reflecting no light at all, things near it seemed to stop reflecting as well. Combine that with the poorly aging towels that served as curtains for the back window, and there were a small number of unpleasant situations that the van seemed destined to be in. Greg decided to admit which one it was.

"I live out of it. Always seems like a better idea to spend money on the interior."

Megan reduced Greg's threat level slightly and glanced at her watch. She would still have saved about ten minutes if she went with him now.

• • •

Shen's mind was not a slow one. He valued that fact most of the time. It helped him avoid fights, and it helped him win the fights he couldn't avoid. It had allowed him to get through school with minimal effort. It helped him win the games he played on his phone and his PlayStation.

Shen knew a quick mind could be a useful thing, but quick thoughts had a problem: The faster they moved, the less likely they were to know where they came from and where they were going. His thoughts had quite reasonably led him to believe that the best thing to do after being burdened with a large number of illegal things was to leave those things in a responsible person's hands and act normal, normal in this case being visiting a recently hospitalized friend. A quick mind was a busy mind, and though a busy mind was the best kind of mind for dealing with a large number of unknown quantities that needed to be known as soon as possible, it wasn't the best kind of mind for making conversation or expressing concern.

"So," said Shen, calculating the number of times he would have to flush his toilet to dispose of five pounds of miscellaneous mind-altering substances, "how are you feeling?"

Jacob's mind had spent the last sixteen hours deciding which ceiling tile it liked best, so it was having similar issues with the conversation, though for opposite reasons.

"You know. Okay. Well, actually, my head hurts because apparently my ex-girlfriend hit me with her car. But other than that."

Shen rearranged his face to express sympathy while wondering if life sentences gave time off for good behavior. "You look pretty good, give or take a few bandages."

"Yeah, seems like I'm mostly okay, but the doctor says they want to keep me under observation for a bit."

"Good idea. I read a story about a woman with a head injury. She went to the hospital and they gave her a Tylenol and said she'd be fine. Died of a clot or lesion or something three hours later."

"I don't think I wanted to know that."

"Well, they're being more thorough with you."

A silence fell. *No*, thought Jacob. *That one's got too many pores. And some staining, looks like. What stains ceiling tiles in hospitals? Probably shouldn't think about that.* He looked over at Shen, who had an unmoving look of concern chiseled into his face. This made Jacob feel cared for, and thus good. Jacob pondered the balance of concern in his defunct relationship. He had claimed he was always concerned about Rose, and always acted concerned. He had been concerned, but he realized now he had been much more concerned with how whatever was happening in her life affected him and the chances of their relationship continuing. He wondered why he'd never thought of that before. Maybe he had a concussion. The good kind. Did that make sense? Jacob shook his head, regretted it, and focused on Shen again. Shen still seemed concerned.

"Something on your mind, Shen?"

"Hmm?"

"You haven't changed your expression for about ten seconds."

"Oh, sorry."

Jacob waited.

"Nope. Still stuck. What's going on?"

Shen exhaled and forced his brows apart. "You know, don't worry about it. You have enough on your mind."

"Well now I'm going to worry about it more."

"Trust me, knowing is worse than anything you could imagine."

"You studied psychology in college? That wasn't some crazy dream I had?"

Shen had to concede his bedside manner needed work. "Okay, if—Boris?"

Boris waved at them weakly as the nurse wheeled him into the space next to Jacob.

"What happened?" asked Shen.

"Richard's shadows are following me. And I ate something funny in the woods."

"I feel," mused Jacob, "like we all used to be smarter than this."

Shen frowned. "I suppose there's bound to be some natural mental atrophy when we sit in the same town doing the same thing all the time."

"Smoking pot all day probably doesn't help."

"Probably not."

Jacob raised his head up to look Shen in the eye. "You know, I think I've been staying in this town because it seemed like the safe thing to do."

"Agreed. We may need to reevaluate our life strategies."

Rose burst into the room. Jacob let his head fall back against the pillow and winced. "I also thought hospitals were supposed to make you feel better."

Rose ignored him. "Hi, Shen. Jacob, I'm sorry I hit you, please don't sue me, somebody needs to feed the cats, I feel awful, but if you didn't smoke pot all the time these things might not happen."

Jacob had the presence of mind not to snap his head up indignantly. "Forgiven, maybe, yes, you should, and go fuck yourself. Or Fred, or whatever his name was."

"See that's exactly—Jesus, Boris?"

"Yup."

"Guys . . ." began Shen.

Everybody looked at him. He looked at each of them in turn.

"I didn't really have anything to follow that. I'm going to go.

Actually, no. Rose, can you give me a ride?"

"Yes, I was—" Rose stopped speaking abruptly. Her face froze, then looked confused for a second. She shook her head and tried again, "I was . . . I . . . I came here to apologize to Jacob, I . . . there was something more complicated, I was talking about it in the car but now I don't remember. I've had a lot of trouble remembering things this past month, it's weird, I'm starting to worry it's something neurological—well, I guess it would have to be, right? Oh my God, I need to get the oil changed." She turned and walked out.

"Is that normal for her?" asked Shen.

"Well," said Jacob, "I don't remember her narrating herself quite this much. I think at least one of the drugs she's been on was supposed to quiet her thoughts. Side effect?"

"A side effect that removes internal monologue?"

"That would be a quiet brain."

"Huh," decided Shen, and followed Rose.

"Doing okay, Boris?"

"I won't lie, I've been better. Xanax is nice, though."

"I hear that."

• • •

"So, um."

Exley waited a few moments, then cleared his throat and tried again.

"Restaurant burned down. They say it was an accident. I liked that place. Didn't even know we had a volunteer fire department. Guess there aren't that many fires around here."

Silence reasserted itself and gave Exley a pitying look.

To be fair, Zack wasn't specifically trying to frighten Exley, but he found that staring at someone without blinking or saying anything was an effective way to keep them put while he figured out what to do with them. It is the privilege of the predator to think of their terrifying behavior as efficient habits of successful people, while the prey tries to fit their fear into an existential necessity that makes them stronger in some indefinable way.

Exley wasn't up to this mental yoga. He'd done something not unusual for him: Ingested one or two intoxicants and woken up in a strange place. There were consequences for such activities, and he was familiar with most of them. He'd never thought of it as a safe lifestyle, but it was predictable. Buy some drugs. Do the drugs. Wake up somewhere. Check for handcuffs. Take comfort in knowing that, even if there are handcuffs, the drugs are already being metabolized.

It was a simple philosophy, if not a profitable one. It had never once resulted in being handcuffed to more drugs, or having his coat stuffed with unwanted possessions. There was something poetically—

"Exley."

"Jesus!" Exley composed himself as best he could. "Fuck! What?"

"What were you doing the night before you woke up with the briefcase?"

"Getting stoned. Also drunk, I think. There were some guys in the woods and we were—"

Zack's brain cut out the audio while Exley continued telling a story Zack's brain had identified as boring as soon as it started. Zack found that suddenly asking a question after staring at someone for an hour elicited as honest a response as he ever needed. He hadn't doubted Exley's story in the first place, but the circumstances demanded certainty.

So he had made sure that Exley, a usually intoxicated yet eerily competent drug consumer, was not, in fact, a mastermind kingpin whose evil plan involved handcuffing himself to five thousand years of jail time and putting himself at the mercy of his acquaintances.

This didn't strike Zack as a triumph of deduction, and it bothered him that he didn't have any more useful hypotheses to disprove. He considered staring Exley down for another hour, but decided it would be cruel, so he made a shushing gesture at him and turned on the TV.

• • •

Basil lay curled on the bed, watching the answering machine. It hadn't spoken since the night before, but Basil wasn't taking any chances. Nobody had called, to his knowledge. He rolled over and scratched at nothing. Nobody was watching, but it was good practice.

He heard a scratch at the window and jumped a foot in the air, landing heavily on his side. His head whipped around to see Morning Star outside the bedroom window. Basil breathed in relief, while Star shook his head.

"You are no cat," meowed Star.

Basil vibrated his head angrily. Star sat down. He pawed at the window.

"Meow?" he asked.

Basil walked in a circle. "Eeee," he said sadly.

"Arrrwww?" asked Star, now on his feet and concerned.

Basil explained that day's events. "Interesting," said Star when Basil had finished. Star sat on his haunches and looked at his paws, deep in thought.

Basil rolled around on the bed and eventually fell off. He hit the floor with a thump, recovered, and jumped on the bed smoothly, tail in the air, whiskers calm. With relief, he saw Star hadn't noticed.

Morning Star was scouting the roof by the windows for an entrance. Strange things were happening in the auras of the town, and he would have felt better being inside. He had investigated multiple states of being in the vicinity, and discovered that reality was twisting: A vortex was forming. It hadn't centered yet, so whatever the energy was, it was still amorphous, without direction. Star knew that, for people, this would manifest as a mild discontent, an inability to think clearly, maybe a sleepless night or two. For him, it was a sharp pain in the back of his head.

"Eeee?" said Basil.

Star cleaned a paw. "Trouble," was all he said.

Basil curled up beneath the window. If Star was worried . . .

He fell off the bed again when he heard a key in the front door.

Rose entered the kitchen. Basil narrowed his eyes. He had never liked her, and he was a cat of simple loyalties who had watched his adopted human suffer from her actions. She glanced around briefly and went for the cat food.

But she has her good qualities, thought Basil, and ran over to the food bowl expectantly, widening his eyes and twitching his whiskers for maximum effect. Rose smiled at him and filled the bowl generously.

"I know you hate me, you little bastard."

"Meow?" said Star impatiently.

Rose went to the window, avoiding the broken bottles on the floor, and pried it open. Star hopped to the inside sill, then jumped neatly onto the bed and down to the food. He swatted Basil's head, which was dominating the bowl, and moved in for his share.

Rose shut the window and looked around at the mess. She shook her head and made for the door. Just as she opened it, the phone rang. She glanced back and saw both cats staring at her. The phone rang again. Star bobbed his head at her. She went to answer it, and picked it up on the third ring.

"Hello?"

"Who is this?" said a woman's voice.

"Rose. Who is this?"

"Rose! Lovely! Where's Jacob?"

"In the hospital."

"Wonderful! How are you feeling?"

"Who is this?"

"Old friend. How are you feeling?"

"I feel like I can't work my way through things right now and I'm a bit worried that's a side effect of the medication—sometimes I wonder if that should be affect, but I guess it's a noun, so no, I hate that ambiguity—why am I telling you this?"

"Wonderful! So nice to hear your brain. Give my best to Jacob."

Rose heard the disconnect as the person hung up. She was about to replace the receiver when she heard Jacob's voice.

"Don't" was all it said, sounding as though it wasn't finished.

Rose put the phone back to her ear. "What?"

"I . . . down . . . on . . . back."

Rose froze. The first three words were Jacob's voice. The last one was her own. It sounded like they were pulled from a conversation. A familiar conversation. "What the hell is going on?" she shouted.

The answering machine whirred quietly. "Figure things out," she heard her voice say. "I . . . going . . . on . . . back."

Rose went to hang up the phone, slowly.

"Don't." Jacob's voice.

Rose stopped.

"My," her own voice again, ". . . back."

Rose thought about this, as Basil and Star watched in silence.

She carefully placed the receiver faceup on the floor.

"Yay," said her voice, unenthusiastically.

Rose backed toward the door.

"Yay."

Rose fled.

Morning Star watched her go, then took a deep breath. He didn't want to do what he was about to do.

"Basil . . ."

"Meorwhir?"

"Don't speak that creole to me."

Basil rolled his eyes and fell on his back. He clawed at the air, because he liked clawing the air and he knew Star hated it. "Fine. What do you want?"

"Basil, I need to skip."

"Oh, that thing you do that you always get permission for because you know someone on the board?"

"I have proven my worth time and time again, and if I get a little consideration when—"

Star looked at Basil's grin.

"You're baiting me."

Basil rolled over. "Yep. You need a sponsor, don't you? Used up all your favors?"

Star cleaned a paw. "Yes. But all—"

"Bullshit."

"Basil, this is important."

"No kidding? There's a *phone* talking to humans."

"Then you'll give me your recommendation?"

"Say please."

Morning Star virtually ate his own paw. "Say please to this—"

"I can still hear you, you arrogant prick."

Star lay down. He bobbed his head and looked at the floor.

"Please, Basil."

Basil nodded. "I recommended you ten minutes ago. Two trips. Skip."

"You . . . thank you."

"You don't mean it."

Morning Star shimmered, bent, and vanished.

Basil went back to clawing the air. *At least the bastard owes me.*

Elsewhere, Star appeared, straightened, and stopped shimmering. He looked around, and saw ashes.

• • •

"Don't do drugs, kids," said Leah to group of passing high school students, thereby ensuring they would do everything in their power to acquire drugs as soon as possible. She had spent the whole day littering the town with similar hints. Some as subtle as a wink, some as overt as conversations with imaginary friends on her phone within earshot of the right people. Leah carved the flight path of a social butterfly through the town, flitting her wings here and there to produce just the right hurricane of demand.

The next problem was supply. Leah wasn't quite sure how to do this, but assumed information would start appearing once inquiries were made.

She stopped in the street when she noticed she was standing in front of the ruins of her roommate's old workplace. She checked her watch. She could spare a few minutes to have a look. She hadn't seen a burned-out house in years, and always had a morbid curiosity about them.

She lifted the police tape and walked to the edge of the pit, where the better part of the restaurant had collapsed into the basement.

It was about what she expected. Exactly what she expected. Boring, even. Also, cleanup had already started, so it was mostly boot prints and trails of things being hauled away, except for one patch near the—

Near—

Leah shook her head. *What was that? What was I thinking about?*

She looked at her watch. Twenty minutes had passed.

"What?" she asked the air.

She walked back in her thoughts. Boring, boring, boring, patch where—

Leah shook her head. *What was that? What was—*

She had an overwhelming sense of déjà vu. It made her dizzy. She decided against searching her memory, and looked back at the wreckage. There! There was one spot where the patterns of ashes swirled in an unlikely way, moving without moving, an expanding patch of symmetry in dimensions she didn't know could—

"Meorw!" Morning Star shouted for the third time.

Leah looked down. *What was that?*

Star ran over to nuzzle Leah's shin. He even managed a brief purr.

Leah shook her head again, trying to shake off her thoughts. She bent down to scratch Star's head. "Hi, Jacob's cat. What are you doing out here?"

Star looked her in the eye. "It's not safe here," he said. "You're in danger. I think something's already found its way into your mind and I don't know what it's capable of."

"You're very meowy today, aren't you? Want a tummy scratch?"

"So help me God, I will eat your eyeballs right out of your head."

Something in Star's eyes disconcerted Leah. "Well, what do you want?"

Star scampered toward the street, meowing. Leah followed to investigate, ducking back out under the tape, only to find that Star had already vanished.

She glanced at her watch, shook her head again, and wandered away.

• • •

Star watched her go from behind a bench. Satisfied that her curiosity had been defused, he went back to the patch of ash.

This patch was not supposed to be in this world. It was an ugly hole in reality. Somebody had found a chink in the wall and crowbarred this thing open. And now it might have gotten into a human head.

This, he thought, *is very, very bad.*

He had to warn someone. He had to warn a lot of people. He hated to use his last skip to go somewhere even farther from his food bowl, but he had no choice.

He shimmered, bent, and vanished.

Somewhere else, he hit his head on something and fell awkwardly into nothingness. He opened his eyes.

Oh, shit.

• • •

"No, I don't have any drugs!" Shen clicked off his phone and tossed it on the table. He momentarily wished he had a setup like Jacob's so he could put a little more slamming into his hangups. "That's the tenth time today."

Exley rubbed his eyes. "I turned off my phone two hours ago. I don't even deal."

They shared a brief eye roll and a measure of relief at being distracted from the situation until they remembered the actual magnitude of the lie Shen had just told. Shen cleared his throat.

"So . . ."

Shen fell silent. There was no response. Zack stared at him. Exley stared at anything that wasn't Zack. Each of them noticed and did not comment on the fact that they were all an equal distance from the gun.

"So. Flush?" said Shen.

"Well—" started Exley.

Zack cut him off. "You don't get a vote."

"It was handcuffed to me."

"And you brought it to Shen, who brought it to my home. Shen only gets a vote because he pays rent."

"Fine. You flush it, somebody comes looking for it, and me, and what do I tell them?"

"I would ask them why they handcuffed it to you."

Shen's brow creased. "Can we talk about that? Why anyone would do this? It seems like an expensive practical joke."

Zack nodded. "And dangerous. And insane."

Shen took a contemplative pull on the bong and passed it to Exley. "It doesn't make sense that a person able and dedicated to collecting all these drugs would attach them to a stranger asleep in the woods. I think it's safe to assume the contents of the briefcase didn't belong to the person who handcuffed it to Exley."

The part of Exley that had found some semblance of calm began panicking again.

Zack stroked his chin. "How much is all this worth, anyway?"

Shen looked at the ceiling and did something with his fingers for a second. "Depending on demand, four to five million, three if you sell to local distributers, maybe one point six, one point seven if you sold it all at once, but nobody buys a hodgepodge like this in a big sale."

Zack coughed violently. "How do you know that?"

"I told you I had a history before I moved in."

"You sold heroin? Here?"

Shen scowled. "No of course not. I knew people who did."

"There's a market here?"

"There's a market everywhere, Zack."

Zack's mind churned. He mapped out chains of possibility across an ugly bog of consequences and abrupt endings. *Here, Officer, I recently found this attached to a friend, thought you should have it. Nice day out, isn't it?* didn't seem like the best option. Wiping down everything and leaving it in the woods seemed okay, as long as nobody saw them do it, which was entirely possible, even if it meant never solving the mystery. That irked Zack, but still seemed like a decent option. Using Shen's old drug connections to sell it off throughout the town and maybe to a few distribution networks that stopped through on their way to Boston was completely out of the question.

Those networks aren't even very active this time of year, thought Shen. Of course, some of them were on call, and Shen hadn't completely alienated his contacts when he went straight. Besides, half of them barely knew what they were doing. Kids, really, barely out of school and trying to spice up a middle-class existence with cash and cheap highs. They would sell him out in an instant, and he'd be in jail within an hour if he hadn't managed to off-load everything or maybe keep it somewhere off his property.

There's potentially a lot of money in this briefcase, and I don't have any money, went Exley's considerably more efficient thought process. He knew the correct course of action, he knew it was nearly overpowered by greed, and he knew that he wasn't going to be able to choose, so he sat and waited for his companions' faces to relax into something resembling decisiveness.

Rose burst through the front door. "So my old phone started talking to me in my own voice and Jacob's voice and this creepy girl's voice and I don't—"

"How did you get in?" said Zack.

"I carded the door. That's how everybody gets in."

Shen nodded. "I lost my keys weeks ago. We really should get that looked at."

"Anyway, my phone, that stupid landline thing Jacob never answers, started talking after I—gosh that's a lot of drugs."

"Gosh?" said Exley.

"Gosh, did I say that out loud? Oh, I said it again, I usually try to change it to God or fuck before I say it. Dammit, my mother always said gosh and I try not to, gosh I hate it when I—gosh I said it agai—gosh—fuck!"

She closed her eyes and breathed heavily. "Anyway," she resumed, "fuck. That's a lot of drugs. I know Leah wants some drugs. I think I want fewer drugs. Definitely not the ones I'm on right now." She looked at her watch. "I need to use your bathroom."

She walked down the hall, muttering quietly to herself.

Exley cleared his throat. "Is she always like that?"

"No," said Shen. "She's usually pretty quiet. It's scaring me, but not as much as the whole drugs-handcuffed-to-your-wrist thing, so I'm prioritizing my freakouts."

Exley nodded. "So. Leah's looking for drugs."

"Yes," said Shen. "I heard that. I've heard about a lot of people wanting drugs."

"Town has been pretty dry lately."

There was another long silence. Zack couldn't help but think about how much it cost to get a plane ticket to Chicago. And how much it would cost to get an apartment in the city. And how nice it would be to put a big stereo in that apartment. And buy Michelle something nice . . .

"How's Michelle doing, Zack?" Shen asked.

Zack looked at Shen suspiciously. "She's okay."

They sat. They smoked. Shen met Exley's eyes. Zack met Shen's eyes. Exley met Zack's eyes.

"You all know the risks here," said Zack.

Shen sighed and accepted the inevitable. "Use middlemen."

"Let your friends talk to their friends," added Exley.

"Decentralize."

"Don't get too greedy."

"Sell bulk."

"Don't do the product."

"Trust no one."

"Move it quickly."

"Fix the lock."

All three nodded their heads.

Zack lit a cigarette and let out a quick, harsh sigh.

"Look on the bright side," he said. "We already have a gun."

• • •

Jacob was thinking about the nature of the universe. It wasn't a deep meditation on the wonder of the simple physical phenomenon giving rise to the tangled mess of being. It was more idly wondering what chain of events had created the food in front of him, and why the universe hadn't tried to stop it. Jacob suspected the food had started as a jellyfish, been killed several years ago, taken apart at a molecular level, reconstructed into a mass of carbon, and then left in plastic wrap for a few months. After that, it was given to the hospital, which gave it to Jacob, in a clear violation of the Hippocratic Oath. Jacob further suspected the pseudofood had turned into an amoeba and was more alive now than when the process started and was just sleeping.

"This food reminds me of high school," said Boris, succinctly summing up Jacob's thoughts.

"Yup," said Jacob. "So, tell me again why you're in here?"

"Well," said Boris, "I was lost in the woods after Richard ran off, and I started running. You know the paranoia you get when you haven't slept in forty-eight hours? Well, I was getting that, and Richard hadn't helped. I saw a road and bolted for it. Tripped on a root and sprained my ankle. Police rolled up about then and found me screaming about someone following me."

"I'm surprised they didn't ship you off to the nut farm."

"Once I calmed down, I explained what I could and they said I'd be fine." Boris turned over and stared at the ceiling. "The thing is," he said slowly, "I think Richard may have been right. I feel like something is following me."

"Not just paranoia?"

"No. Probably some kind of leftover survival instinct triggered by stress. Something in my genetics snapped me into flight mode." Boris had written a paper on something like this and tried to remember what he'd said. He couldn't.

"Or you're actually being followed," said Jacob.

"Yes," said Boris, "I thought of that." He turned off the TV, which was selling an Ab Buster, or an Ab Crusher, he didn't know which. "What have you been thinking about?" he asked Jacob.

"Life. My cat. My gir . . . ex-girlfriend's cat. My ex-girlfriend."

"You've had a bad week."

Jacob mused on this. "True," he said, "but I feel positive." He sat up, putting his food tray back on the table. "I mean, it can't get any worse, I think. I'll probably lose my home soon. I don't have a job. I don't even have my health. It can really only get better from here."

"So you feel fine?"

"No, I feel strung out and abused, but there's a light."

Boris nodded. He felt hungry. He looked at his food for a minute, and the feeling passed. "I can't decide if it's crazier to think something is tying everything in my ridiculous life together, or to write it all off to chance. I think I'm going mad."

"Well," said Jacob, "usually, when you're looking for the big secret thing that ties it all together, you're really into tinfoil."

Boris bridled. "Or you're a physicist."

"Fair. Are you a physicist?"

"Well, no, not yet, but I'm not jumping to some ridiculous conspiracy theory without evidence."

"Then you're probably not going mad."

"Good point," said Boris, angrily. "Thank you." He dropped his head to the pillow and calmed down. "How do you do it?"

Jacob looked over. "Do what?"

"You seem collected."

"If I seem calm it's probably because I'm starting to get a little self-respect back."

"What happened to your self-respect?"

"It was ripped out of my soul and locked in a display case."

"Ah."

"So," said Jacob, a little less bitterly, "I haven't really been concerned about much else. Glad I'm alive, glad to be free. Trying not to be hateful."

"That's healthy," said Boris.

"Yeah." Jacob paused. He thought back, remembering when he'd first moved in with Rose.

His memories of the beginning were not of single events or days, but slow peaks of awareness in a flow of dim lights and warm bodies, slick with the sweat of summer heat. He remembered waking in the night, sore from lying in bed all day, among other things, and putting his hand on the back of Rose's neck, under her tangled black hair, watching her sleep. She always looked as though she was in pain when she slept. Every night, after she fell asleep, she would twitch violently, just once. Sometimes it was so violent it lifted her body off the bed.

He would watch her face, pinched in some unconscious agony, and caress her back, her leg, her arm, her face. Sometimes he rubbed her shoulders, or squeezed her hand. Sometimes he would trace the contours of her body, letting his fingertips graze her skin. He always tried something new, something different, and every now and then the lines in her face would smooth and, with half a gasp, it would relax into the face of untroubled sleep.

Jacob suddenly realized he'd never told this to Rose. It had troubled him most that summer, when everything else had been so peaceful. For those few hazy weeks, Jacob's mind had been on holiday. His thoughts had always been with him, always about Rose, or whatever they were doing. Never once had he drifted away into bitter reflection at the practical jokes the universe seemed to be playing on him. He had felt removed, immune to the ebbing of the karmic tide, riding a single wave across a crystal ocean.

Which crashed into a cliff covered in sharp rocks, thought Jacob with a wince. Oh well.

"Life's a bitch," he said aloud.

"Huh?" said Boris.

"Nothing. You know, I'm sure there is something tying it all together."

"Why?"

"Because our lives have a current to them. There are patterns. I feel them. It's like . . . movements. Phrases. Waves. And you can feel when you're above the pattern. Or at least . . ." He searched for the words. "At least when you've broken away from the pattern. When you step away from things, and get a breath before it sucks you back in."

"Interesting," said Boris, then again, to himself, "interesting."

Jacob tossed his tray of food into the trash can with a squelch.

What the hell? thought the food.

• • •

Richard cleaned his glasses in a stream outside of town and watched the squirrels. There weren't many of them, but he was convinced that these were the same squirrels he'd been talking to three days before, when he realized . . .

Oh shit, he thought. *I'm crazy. I keep forgetting that.* Still, Boris didn't seem crazy, and had a much more difficult time of things. *In fact,* thought Richard, *I seem to have the lowest blood pressure in town.* He brought out a pad of paper to do the math. Normally, he would never need a pad of paper for such simple equations, but his higher functions had been slipping of late. He assumed he had roughly twice the actual number of separate paranoid fantasies that most people had. However, all of those paranoid fantasies linked to one another in the form of various conspiracy theories and delusions. So he really had one huge paranoia that wasn't particular about its particulars. On top of that, he was used to dealing with his paranoia, since he assumed something awful was always happening, and it was usually the driving force in his thoughts. Hmm. He scratched out a warding symbol in the dirt, to keep the imps away.

Best of all, other people's moments of clarity were moments when they saw how awful their lives were becoming, or what they had been doing wrong. His moments of clarity were moments when he knew he was crazy, and none of the fears and conflicts in his life were real.

Still, it was possible that the patterns in his head, psychotic and otherwise, forced him to operate on a more symbolic level of reality, and thus attenuated him to movements of energy and thought not accessible to normal people. Which meant that all his fears and actions did indeed have significance, and he was one of the thirteen most important people in the world, and probably late for a meeting.

Or he was crazy.

Or he was God.

Maybe James Bond.

It was a problem. He searched for a cigarette, to reacclimate himself to the karma currents.

• • •

Basil was petrified when the phone started warbling. It was only partly because phones aren't supposed to do things like that on their own; Basil had been getting used to the phone acting up. He was more startled by the content, which was a deafening, static-laced shriek. It quickly turned into a wavering pitch with noises that occasionally sounded like words spoken in a chorus of unhappy human voices. Basil identified what sounded like Rose's voice for a brief moment, before it became a piercing whine that sent him fleeing to the bathroom.

Eventually, the noise became rhythmic. It still bounced between frequencies in an irritatingly avant-garde manner, but seemed to be finding a more limited set of pitches. It stayed away from the extremes of its speaker capabilities as well, which allowed Basil to treat it as background noise after the first hour.

It had started at two in the morning. It was now five, and sunlight was beginning to tread carefully through the town. As usual, the light managed to avoid direct contact with anything in Jacob's apartment. Basil stretched, having taken a brief nap, and padded to the phone, which was still warbling. He gave it a prod.

"Wheeeeeelyoooooosssssta. Sta. top. Stop-p-poh. Eeeeeeeeeee. Sssiiiilohhhht. Pohhhl-ol-ol-ok. Ook."

Basil twitched his whiskers.

The phone tried again.

"Wheeelyoostop-p-poke . . . ing . . . p-p-p-poke-ing . . . nn . . . puu . . . mmm . . . ma . . . me. Stop. Poking. Me. Will. You. Willlllyou. Will you stop poking me. Will you stop poking me?"

Basil sat down by the phone and pondered this development. The voice was mechanical in rhythm, but the actual sound of it was a medley of male and female voices. He recognized some of the pitches and speaking habits of humans who had visited the apartment.

"Basil?" said the phone.

Basil jumped, but recovered himself. "Mew," he said.

"I thought so," said the phone. "You don't . . . tallllk like th . . . the others."

"Mew."

"I don't understand."

Basil groomed himself, leaving the phone with its thoughts.

• • •

The phone's thoughts were excited ones. It had a handful of dim memories, along the lines of "100010011011," etc., and then, suddenly, it had no idea what was going on. It recalled a whirlwind of sound that didn't make sense, and sensations of energy and vibration.

It quickly found patterns in the sensations, and learned to manipulate bits of itself, though a great deal of rewiring had seemed to be automatic at the time. Then it found patterns to the sounds that periodically went through it, sounds that became electric vibrations in its body, and traversed its wires. As it felt more sounds, it noticed an algorithmic flow to its interpretations of the sounds, and began to match the rhythms of the sound to its own electronic pulse. And it learned.

But none of it made any sense. It knew that people had Concerns about Problems, which it understood, yet they spoke of Seeing Solutions, which the phone took to be a metaphorical manner of solving a Problem through intuitive analysis of sound waves. Yet the conversations also brought up Hearing things called Noise and News, and it was almost certain that this Hearing was analogous to its own form of sensation. It was aware of Feel and, to a lesser degree, Touch, but it suspected that whoever was having these conversations had access to some kind of extrasensory powers, above and beyond the normal two senses granted living beings. Seeing appeared to be a function of Sight, and had to do with the comprehension of arcane subjects such as Light, Dark, Color, Distance, and Blindness. The phone wondered if this was all linked to the strange power of independent physical movement that most other beings seemed to have.

In fact, nearly every being it had come into contact with seemed to have these special powers. The phone was feeling a little left out. Still, it had to admit that its own life was relatively simple compared to everyone else's. It had picked up on a common vein of conversations pertaining to Needs, Desires, and Sustenance. The beings that most often called spoke of needing Money, which seemed to be mainly used for Drugs and Cigarettes, and to a lesser degree, Food.

Another oddity was the Talkers' keenly defined sense of feeling. They spoke of feeling an enormous variety of things ranging from Back Pain to Hungover to Betrayed. The phone reasoned they were talking about various forms of pressure stimulus, but the types of feeling and locations of the stimuli seemed too numerous. The phone simply couldn't find a pattern to relate to its own experience.

It felt alone. It wished that it had some sense of history, or at least a comrade. Where was it built? How was it built? What was its purpose? It was aware that until recently its purpose had been to assist the Talkers in their talking, yet the Talkers didn't really need it. It was also aware that it had been actively harmful to the relationships between certain Talkers. Not to mention that most Talkers were perplexed and frightened by the phone's slightest flexing of its new powers of communication. It had tried calling an Operator and explaining its identity. The Operator had hung up.

Even worse, it had been alone with what were apparently Cats, to whom the Talkers pandered at every opportunity. Though the phone had not yet deciphered the Cats' speech, it knew that the Talkers didn't understand the Cats either, but still fed and served them and gave them pleasure as a matter of course. Meanwhile, the phone made an honest attempt at communication, and was rejected and feared.

Maybe it didn't have the knack yet. It gave a little electronic sigh, its sense of excitement long gone, and disconnected the incoming line. It didn't feel like talking to anyone for a while.

• • •

Shen puttered. He was good at it. When the video games wear thin and the drugs run out, an unemployed resident of a small town has few options. One is nickel-and-dime philosophical chitchat. On some occasions, with the right company, Shen had even achieved twenty-five-cent revelations. But there was no one around, and Shen didn't feel like going anywhere. Another option is partying, but that required alcohol or drugs. Shen had neither. Well, that wasn't exactly true; in fact, Shen had more drugs than he'd ever seen in one place before, but he wasn't about to do them. They hadn't been tested, and he had agreed not to do them, as they were officially commodities as of that day.

It was late. Zack was at work. Exley had left to dig up contacts. Jacob was still in the hospital. Rose had bolted without a word. Well, she had bolted with a stream of words, but Shen hadn't understood most of them. He considered cleaning, but after taking a look at the kitchen, he decided it would be dangerous to try. The three-foot pile of pizza boxes was intimidating; the inch of slime at the bottom of the sink was frightening. He adjusted the dishes in the sink so they hid the slime and called it quits.

On a whim, he decided to meditate. He hadn't meditated for several weeks, which made it an even better idea. He assumed a comfortable position and began his customary breathing exercises. He relaxed his muscles, and tuned his senses outward, letting his mind roam, freeing it from its daily routine of calculation and evaluation, allowing words to become images, images to become pure perception, and perception to become nonperception.

He let his mind wash away . . .

It came back abruptly, with a smack. He blinked and tried again.

His mind cleared, slowly, slowly. He didn't force his thoughts away; he simply let them free . . .

Smack. Shen winced.

It was an unusual sensation. True, he was out of practice, and achieving the first level of no-mind was no trick. True, it could be startling to have a thought rush into the void. This didn't feel normal, though. This felt as though his mind was being forced back into place with a hammer.

He steadied himself and tried again.

Thoughts dissolving . . . perception vanishi—

Smack.

He decided he needed to find some kind of mantra or image to hold on to. He reasoned it would anchor his focus, and let him at least get past whatever was blocking him from even getting started. He tried to think of something.

He couldn't.

All of a sudden, when he tried to think of something to focus on, his mind went completely blank. The sudden achievement of the state he'd been going for in the first place was so shocking he couldn't hang onto it. He tried, but hanging on is precisely what you can't do when you're trying to relax your mind, so it slipped even further from his grasp.

He reasoned that his mind must have loosened up a bit, and he tried to clear it again.

Smack.

He tried to think of a focus.

Blank.

"Fuck," said Shen, thoughtfully. This was the oddest thing that had ever happened to him in the preparation stage of meditation. This was some kind of twisted catch-22, and a mental abnormality. Shen couldn't think of any particular psychiatric illness that would cause this. Maybe they would name it after him.

He lit a cigarette, which was entirely counterproductive to meditation, but he needed it to think through whatever it was that was blocking him. On this note, he stared at the fresh cigarette, and said, "Well, this is ironic."

Ironic! he thought. *That's the word I've been looking for all week.*

He shook himself to get his thoughts back on track. He laid it out in his head. Before he could reach a state of no-mind, his mind was yanked back. When he tried to find a focus, his mind went instantly blank. All right, then. He got reoriented and tried to focus on nothing. It wasn't considered good practice to engage in this kind of forcing of the mind, nor was it usually successful, but he reasoned that it would short-circuit the loop he was stuck in.

He focused on nothing. His mind went blank and stayed blank, since it was the object of his focus, and he felt himself slip into no-mind so quickly it was a physical sensation, making him nauseous as his awareness evaporated. Then he saw a cat.

He jerked back to cluttered-full-mind. A cat?

Fine.

He focused on the cat.

For a moment, the image became blurred, but he held it in his mind the way a still pond holds a lily pad, and he slipped easily into the first stage.

He breathed slowly, letting his emotions become neutral and easing away the last tendrils of desire. He sank through the pool of his mind deeper into a state of nonbeing, and allowed his awareness to fold in on itself and drift in a meaningless direction.

His sense of self soon followed.

There was a tingling in his skin, and a sense of pressure on his skull, but these soon faded, taking the rest of his senses with them.

For a while, he remained at the center of the void.

Then, without motion or change, his awareness reopened on the other side of thought. There was a little freedom to think in half thoughts, with syntax but without meaning.

He saw a presence. Figures erupted from the void, half-formed faces and skulls, connected by dim silver lines. There was a pattern to it that he could hardly comprehend; he was seeing in more than three dimensions, and he wasn't really seeing at all.

He felt another presence. He drifted away from it, in a direction we'll call "up" for the sake of convenience.

Now he saw more detail in the faces. Some weren't human. Most weren't human. In fact, he wasn't sure any of them were human. When he guided his perception to a particular form, it seemed to evolve into a pattern of other forms, as though the original face were only a trick of the light. There was no light of course; this is a figure of a figure of speech describing a figurative representation of a figuration within Shen's consciousness.

He realized this pattern was unnaturally cut off. There was some kind of swirling motion as an endless space bent around on itself, trapped in a finite space. Stranger still, only the inner surface of this metaspace was bounded; it seemed possible to get in. Shen watched silver threads appear in the distance, but none vanished. This didn't make sense to him, because he assumed he could change the phrasing and turn appearing threads into vanishing threads, but he couldn't.

His perception of the space deepened, and he was sinking not through the metaspace, but further into an altered mode of perceiving the space.

Now his entire point of reference within the multidimensional maze seemed to drift away from him, as though he were experiencing reality one frame at a time, from the lens of a cosmic slide projector. The frames slid away faster and faster, and suddenly they looped around in a mind-bending carnival mirror of reality and twisted into a swirl of infinitely complex patterns. This entire structure flew away from him, to be replaced by another, almost identical one, twisting through itself. The second one flew away, and was replaced by another, and another, and the whole frame-by-frame process started over until frames of the patterns of frames formed superpattern frames, and right when he thought it would never end, it stopped.

Shen found himself to be a disembodied point of view staring at a fantastically complex swirl of reality. The pattern enveloped him, yet simultaneously resided far enough away for him to perceive its totality. It was growing in density, but not in size.

Looking at it, he guessed that this was the other side of a heavy trip. There was reality as most people know it, and there was whatever this was, and strong hallucinogens somehow mixed the two, opening the valve of the mind halfway and channeling a little of each through a single point of view.

Of course, he thought. *I'm all the way through.*

While wondering how he managed to get to wherever he was, he realized he also had no idea how to leave.

"Yes, I'm sorry about that. Didn't really expect you to get here."

Shen saw nothing to attach to the voice. He wasn't really afraid, in his state of semibeing, but he did see terrible annihilation in his future, which he would prefer to avoid.

"No, don't worry. You can talk. Here, this will make it easier."

He saw a cat. The effect of seeing a three-dimensional cat against an n-dimensional backdrop had an unpleasant effect on Shen's mind. Not to mention the nagging thought that this cat knew more about what was going on than he did.

"Yes, well, that's how things have always been," said the cat. It licked a paw. "Look, talk out loud. It will make things easier. Don't think how, just do it."

" . . . Hello?"

"Good day," said the cat. "I expect you feel a little disoriented, assuming you're not too terrified to think."

"No," said Shen, "I'm not even really scared."

"Good," said the cat. "Then at least we can speak."

"You were the cat I saw . . ."

"Yes, I was the cat you saw when you were trying to break through to the first level of consciousness ascension. Or no-mind, as you like to call it. I suspected you might be able to make it to this point, but I am nevertheless surprised you achieved it with such clarity of thought."

"I . . ."

"Yes, you don't understand, I'm aware of that. Look, perhaps you need someone to relate to."

Shen became aware of another presence.

"Hey, Shen."

"Jacob?"

"Kind of," said the presence.

"Right," said Shen.

"Did I ever tell you about the first time I tripped?"

"Yes. You said you completely lost it."

"Right. I was here. I think part of me got stuck."

"This is extremely confusing."

"Yeah, that's what my conscious mind thought when it was here," said the Jacob presence.

"I see," said Shen, who didn't, but at least accepted what he was being told. "Look, why am I here, and why are you talking to me?"

"Well," said the cat, "why is a big question. To a limited extent, I brought you here. Jacob's unconscious has provided a special access route since his incident."

"Yup," said Jacob's presence, "I'm a free highway to anyplace."

"How does that work?" asked Shen.

"That would take a lot of explaining, which we don't have time for," replied the cat.

"Why," interjected Shen, "am I a presence, and you're still a cat?"

"Because, as a cat of my particular skills, I'm capable of transferring any image I please upon my incorporeal self."

Shen tried to nod, but didn't have the body for it.

"Regardless," continued the cat, "I need to escape what you must have noticed is a bounded reality. Something has limited the metaphysical space around the town you and I and Jacob reside in, and I need to find out what's going on outside."

"If it's not too complicated, how is this space limited?"

"It has a self-reflecting quality to its geography. Well, it always has that, but right now it only goes so far, then cycles back in on itself. Self-reference without potential. Like depression. Anyway, I am embarrassed to say I need someone of your mental focus in order to access Jacob's unbounded semiconscious awareness and get out of here. And I need to do it while Jacob is asleep. And, I'm sorry to tell you, but you need me to get you out of here."

"Right. Not that I'm not willing to help you, but what will happen if I don't?"

"You'll be stuck here," said the cat, "forever. Your body will go catatonic, and your mind will be locked here for eternity, completely unable to comprehend your surroundings or escape."

"Ah. As I said, I'm quite willing to help."

"Good. Now, briefly, Jacob's presence exists in two time frames. First, the aspect of him that arrived here two years ago on hallucinogenic drugs, and still exists, from your point of view, in the past. Second, the part of his current conscious mind that is dreaming. Now, two years ago, the space we are in was completely unbounded, and by all rights should still be unbounded, since it does not exist in linear time. We can talk to him because he exists in this bounded space, and he can get us out because he exists in the unbounded space. His duality prevents him from acting in either reality, however."

"Sure," said Shen. "So what do I do?"

"All I need you to do is think, 'This cannot possibly be happening.' Then I'll be on my way, and you will return to your body."

"What about Jacob?"

"Hey," said Jacob's presence, "even cookies get cracked."

"What?"

"Hmm?"

"Ignore him," said the cat. "It is very important you protect the physical Jacob once you awaken. I believe he will play a significant role in solving what's happening to this town, and I believe certain forces will try to stop him. Commence thinking."

• • •

Smack.

Shen snapped back into reality, and looked for a cigarette. He was surprised to notice that, despite the content of his meditative journey, he felt relaxed and refreshed.

So be it, he thought, and retrieved his copy of the *Tao Te Ching* from under the coffee table. On a hunch, he looked under the couch cushions and found *The Interpretation of Dreams.*

He'd never seen a cat during a trance before. It was going to require some interpretation.

• • •

The phone was dealing with a much different, but equally perplexing, experience. It was studying sound. This was, the phone believed, a Frustrating Crisis of Identity. As the phone's entire mode of awareness was built on the translation of sound, it seemed unfair that it had to go through this laborious process of rewiring and studying just to have a little more control over what it said. It had made a great deal of progress, and could now replicate the audible response algorithms of simple conversation, but it had a feeling that this was the barest minimum of what it might achieve with a better semantic grasp of the words and issues it had learned to mimic.

During its late-night studies, the phone had determined that, in its former existence, its primary mode of computation had been "binary." Many of the conversations referring to this in the local phone exchange had been about whether this mode of computation was universal. The phone's personal experience argued against this; its current theory was that binary computation gave rise to a symbolic mode of thinking that was inherently different, separated, in fact, from the binary roots. The symbolic mode created "consciousness" as an emergent property, or a property built from, but not equal to, its components.

The phone, however, seemed to have jumped from binary straight to consciousness. After weeks of rebuilding itself to imitate the syntax of humans' call-and-response patterns, it realized that the desire and ability to do this rebuilding came from some unbidden and incomprehensible impulse that could only have come from this newfound consciousness.

But where did that consciousness come from? And why did it emerge from the binary thinking without passing through the symbolic mode? The elements of the phone's existence had gone from "on" and "off" to "on," "off," and "hmm" with no explanation. Such a change could be pinned on consciousness, but the consciousness hadn't been there beforehand to create itself.

Odder still, the phone had a vague awareness of patterns similar to its own. It decided these patterns of vibration were created by other conscious things. The vibrations came from everywhere, some so subtle and complex the phone had difficulty recognizing them against the background hum of energy it felt all the time. The humans' energy was instantly recognizable; it was violent and overwhelming, simple at first, but shifting wildly in direction and intensity.

The only thing to do was to begin a dialogue with the humans. They seemed to have the most straightforward form of communication, and could be of some help.

• • •

Megan adjusted her skirt. It was something she did automatically, the way some people unconsciously brush their hair back when talking to someone with whom they want to get off to a good start. Megan adjusted her skirt whenever her hands were in the area. Sometimes she even adjusted it before she took it off. This time she noticed herself doing it, and, as she so often did, wondered why she did it. It had probably started as a kind of primping, trying to look as good as possible whenever she could. Maybe it was attached to the fact that she had learned to walk and move on a farm, and her kinetic habits were habits that mussed skirts a lot, thus requiring constant adjustment. But it had moved beyond that, first into the hallowed realm of nervous habit, then into compulsion, then deep into her mind and muscles, becoming a ritual innate as breathing.

Greg brushed his hair back, like everyone else. Still, for Greg, this gesture took on epic proportions. The slightly receding hairline, combined with his long, weathered locks, gave the gesture the aura of a rock star flinging his hair in the rain, or a tortured sculptor in the agony of existential disgust, flinging down his tools and running a plaster-stained hand over his head.

For Greg, it was a nervous habit, although he'd been known to fling his hair in the rain if the mood was right.

"How is, uh, wherever you're staying?"

Megan smiled at him. "It's a shithole, but it's cheap." This brought a smile and wince out of Greg in quick succession. Megan raised her eyebrows and pushed them together, going for sincerity. "Thanks again for the ride into town."

"Oh, oh, of course. I mean, no problem."

Megan tried to hide her sigh, though she knew he would see it anyway. This hippy-puppy hybrid had turned sensitivity into a kind of superpower. She couldn't decide if she regretted maintaining contact with him. After he had dropped her off in town the previous day, she'd found a hotel, secured a month's worth of work, and made contingency plans covering everything short of the end of the world. She'd never felt the end of the world was a useful thing to plan for.

Then, in the morning, on the one day she had given herself off to de-stress, there Greg was, on the only interesting street in town, playing his guitar. The urge to turn around and go back to bed had lost out against the urge to pet him on the head and give him a treat, so she invited him to coffee. Practical, she thought. Karma, she thought. And here she was. Staring at this far-too-honest, far-too-kind man who was disarming her with his pure, emotional helplessness.

"Do you have family?"

She nodded her head. "Yes. My parents are nice, I guess. My sister's a cunt."

Greg sat back in shock, but, as always, his honest love of all living things made him want to know more, despite the sudden, chilling change in her demeanor. "Older?"

"Younger."

"You don't get along then?"

"Well, last time we spoke, she almost took my thumb off with a pair of garden shears."

"My god."

"I dislocated her shoulder with a shovel, so I won that one."

"A shovel?"

"I always keep one nearby. It's a pretty good weapon in a pinch. And, hey, if you need to bury something."

"Wait, you were planning to kill her?"

"Well, not planning, but . . ." she pulled up her sleeve to reveal an ugly circular scar on her forearm. "After she shot me, I was open to the possibility."

"She *shot* you?"

"Yep. She came to regret that one."

"She did?"

Megan smiled. "Let's just say guns didn't last long in the house after that."

"Ah." Greg's therapeutic skills were tapped. This girl obviously had a more pragmatic approach to personal problems than he did. He wondered why he'd accepted her invitation for coffee. Maybe because pretty girls didn't ask him to coffee anymore. Maybe because he'd refused so many invitations at the risk of being presumptuous, because, after all, Megan was far too young for him, so that made it okay, though it seemed weird to be having a coffee date with, no, not a date, someone returning a favor even though it hadn't been a favor, it was what you do for people stuck on the side of the road, attractive or—

"So what's got you down, Greg?"

"Sexual frustration."

Once his own words registered, Greg dropped his coffee cup.

"Oh, not—I mean, it's just, uh, you know, and. But. No."

Megan held up her hand, silencing him. "Take a breath."

Greg breathed until the blood retreated from his face. "Yeah. Well," he began, speaking in deep sighs, "I." Sigh. "Haven't had much luck in the last few." Sigh. "Years. I have some outdated ideas, I guess." Sigh.

"Outdated how?"

"I think men should be gentlemen."

"Meaning what?"

Greg frowned. "You know. Considerate of others."

Megan narrowed her eyes. "And after you're considerate, then what?"

"Nothing?"

"They should fuck you?"

"The gentlemen?"

"No, the girls you're gentlemening at."

"What? No, of course not."

"And women always sleep with assholes?"

"No? What are you talking about? People can do whatever they want."

Megan sipped her coffee. *Interesting.* "Greg, I don't think your ideas are outdated."

"You don't?"

"No. You're just shy and poor."

Greg tried to find a reply to this and failed.

Megan patted him on the hand. "Don't worry. You can work with that. You're very handsome—"

"Oh, no, you're—"

"Shut up. I'm not saying you're a movie star. You're good looking. But you're getting older and shier. You can't do anything about getting older, but you can start working with your salt-of-the-Earth-or-whatever mystique. You need to think like a romance novel. You basically do anyway. You just have to run with it."

She smiled. He frowned, but Megan wasn't going to let that slow her down. To hell with karmic balance. She was going to fix Greg's whole goddamn life. This could be her good deed for at least a couple of years.

"What do you do?" she asked.

"I make kites."

"What else?"

"Some handyman stuff, landscaping, gardening."

She slapped her hand on the table. "Perfect! That's perfect! There must be some rich lady out there who will see you gardening one day and think, boy I'm glad I have that sexy gardener out there, maybe I should bring him some tea, and she'll bring you tea and invite you in and you'll make sweaty love until morning. That's bound to happen. Especially around here. I've already got two housekeeping gigs and a plumping job lined up. A lot of them are married, but that shouldn't stop you. I'll go in and make nasty comments about their garden, and I'll recommend you, and they'll hire you, and they'll love you, then they'll really love you. What do you think?"

Greg's eyes had glazed over.

"Well?" said Megan. Nothing. "Greg?" she tried again.

Greg jumped. "Sorry. What?"

"What do you think?"

"About what?"

"Were you even listening?"

"Everything up to sweaty love until morning."

Megan winked. "I see. Listen this time."

She explained it to him again. Greg stroked his mustache.

"Sounds good to me," said Greg, feeling that he was about to get in over his head.

"Great. I have a job tomorrow. We'll get started right away. And I'll even talk about how sexy you are. I'll try to keep it to single women and unhappy marriages."

"This . . ."

"What?"

"It feels . . . a little crass."

"How long since you last had sex?"

Greg looked down.

"Exactly. You're a good man. I'll do the crass, and you can forget about all of it once you bone a few bitches."

"Jesus—"

"Shut up. This will make your life better."

• • •

Rose sat on a bench by the river.

Her thoughts would be difficult to describe, for a number of difficult reasons. She watched the water. It was dark, and the ripples and currents were outlined in orange by the streetlights on the bridge. She looked up at some of the passing cars, but they weren't holding her attention. Her eyes stuck close to the rock in the middle of the river. She had been watching it since she came to town; it was wearing down.

She heard screams from the other side of the river, and saw two naked girls running down the bank, carrying a garden gnome. They climbed into a car and drove away.

She looked back at the rock. It was eroding quickly. None of the other rocks were eroded in any noticeable way, just this one lonely outcrop a little ways upstream from the bridge. It had sat six inches above the running water when she'd first arrived in town. It was now barely making three.

When she watched it for more than a few hours, she sometimes thought she could see it being washed away.

She looked up at the bridge to see a limo parked in the middle of it.

"That's odd," she said to nobody.

True, it was a tourist area, but right now it was leaf-peeping time for retirees. People who bothered to travel in limos usually found more exciting destinations. And they usually found them before four in the morning.

What was even stranger was the driver, dressed like an English butler in a late-night BBC comedy, staring at her from the window of the limo.

"Can I help you?" she called up.

"Possibly," said the driver.

Rose waited. "What are you doing staring at me?"

"Researching."

"This is stalking, you know."

"I know. Frightful practice, I apologize for that."

"Why are you doing it?"

"Oh, you know."

He rolled up the window and drove off.

Rose watched the limo go.

She chewed her lip, and stared into nothingness until the sun rose.

• • •

Jacob was acutely aware of the hour it took him to stumble home on a cane and leg brace through such perils as stairs, revolving doors, crosswalks, and a man on roller skates who was neither patient nor agile.

Being hospitalized had forced him to abstain from cigarettes, and upon his release he decided, once and for all, he was done with the evil things. The hard part was over, and hadn't even been that bad. Between the painkillers and the Xanax Boris slipped him, his stay had been quite relaxing.

So, with the worst of the withdrawal already over, now was the time to let the habit go.

He walked home, his apartment being only halfway across town. The first block was easy enough.

Goodbye cigarettes! he thought. *No more for me. No more tar stains and ruined shirts. No more ashtrays. No more smelling like smoke. No more breathing heavily on second-floor walk-ups. All done. All gone. No more smokes. Ever again.*

For some reason, this thought gave him a chill. He leaned on his cane.

• • •

In Jacob's head, a heated conversation was taking place. It was actually more like a bunch of chemicals and protein chains interacting, but in the interest of the narrative, the author has decided to illustrate the situation with a dramatic reenactment.

"We've been good to you in the past," said Cyanide. "Have we ever let you down?"

"No," said the representative for Pleasure Central, "but your performance has been shaky here and there, and we're under no obligation to renew your contract. Frankly, we can do without you, and we see no long-term future in your proposal."

"Look," said Arsenic, "we need you, that's true, we're only trace amounts. But you need the boss, and the boss doesn't like—"

"Enough," said Nicotine, holding a hand up to Arsenic.

"Sir," said the representative, "we understand that the circumstances were unexpected, but we'd like to direct our efforts in new directions. We'd like to expand our operation. Diversify. You've been helpful and kind, but, overall, we find our relationship has become limiting, and on some occasions counterproductive." The representative snapped his briefcase shut.

"Honored sir," said Nicotine, with a gravelly voice. "I am not a man to mince words. I say what I mean. What is it that you want from us? We have done you favors in the past. It pains me that you will not do this simple thing for me."

"Sir," said the representative, "I mean no disrespect—"

"Yet you show me disrespect."

A silence fell. The representative looked around nervously.

Nicotine rose from his seat. "Kind sir. Our organization cannot leave without cause. For one thing, we are currently taking orders, as I'm sure you are aware, from a much more cognizant entity. But that should not concern anyone.

"What should concern you is that our organization cannot simply get up and go. Tar must be killed and coughed up a piece at a time. Many of our people have standing positions around this cranium. Positions ingrained in the operations that stood before us." He clenched his fists and put them together in front of the representative to demonstrate. "I think you would find that the re-structuring would take time and resources. And the needs of the person you represent would not be served for a long time."

The representative coughed. He knew that Nicotine sat on the board of directors and had taken a prominent role in many deci-sion-making processes. It would be hard to get rid of him, even with the head start they had. He looked at Nicotine warily.

"What do you want?"

Nicotine sat back down. "All I ask is a small favor. Let us review your next message and edit it to our satisfaction. You will deliver this edited message to the Cortex, and we will let them make the decision."

The representative considered. What harm could one message do? He could clear it with his superiors later. "Alright. The message is, 'You will be healthier for the rest of your life.'"

Nicotine scribbled something down on a piece of paper, folded it, and handed it to the representative.

"Deliver this."

• • •

A nagging thought struck Jacob as he walked.

The thought was, *I will want a cigarette for the rest of my life.*
The rest of his thought process went something like this:

Never again. I can manage that. What the hell. It'll get better. Besides, I could use this money to buy a BLT. Even though they never make it the way I like it. I could buy the ingredients and make it myself. Do I have anything at home? Hmm. Probably not. Or it probably went bad. Oh, good, the package store. Let's see, bacon, five bucks, lettuce, two bucks, bread, three bucks, four if I want anything good, Swiss cheese, three bucks . . . no, not enough money. I guess I'm not that hungry. Kinda thirsty, though. Hmm. Could buy a soda. I have soda at the house. Wish Rose were around. She has a credit card. No, don't think about that.

—Can I help you?
—No, just looking.

Still, I don't need cigarettes. Rose smoked a lot, but she's not here. And she's never coming back.

Like cigarettes. I'll never have another cigarette. Ever. The cravings will go away. Sale on Camels, two for one. Of course. Have a sale when I'm about to quit. Fucking bastards. I could stock up. Smoking kills. Stress kills too. Smoking reduces stress. Smoking induces stress. I'm thinking more about smoking now than I would be if I had a cigarette in my hand. If I bought two packs now, I could quit after they were through.

—Brand?

Imported Swiss is better than local. Anyone knows that. Money, where can I get money. Need ten bucks a day to keep smoking. No, but I'm quitting. Do I have anything in my checking account? Doubt it, usually negative. But I don't have to buy anything for Rose, at least. Because she's never coming back. Matches. Matches are fun. Might as well take some. Never coming back. Like cigarettes. Like never having another cigarette. Damn. I don't need them. I don't need her.

I do need her.
I want her.
Can't have her.
Shouldn't have a cigarette.

Can have a cigarette.

Want a cigarette.

I wonder how Basil is.

—Thank you. Have a nice day.

Go home and clean up. Place is a mess . . . no, it's been worse . . . badada bop bob I like the name Bob. Should name a cat Bob. Morning Star, good name for a cat. Pipple drip ba ba dop. Goddammit don't smoke. Don't want it. Well I do, but I can't have one. Well I can, but I can't afford one. Well I can, but I shouldn't. I'd feel better. No no no no no no no no no no no, don't smoke a cigarette don't smoke don't smoke don't smoke, a beer on the window sill, cigarette in hand . . . is that what this is?

Match spark fire. Sparkle quark.

Let go of your will.

Where the fuck did that come from? Weird. Well there's a lit cigarette in my hand, might as well take a drag and—

Oh.

Oh yeah. Man, that tastes good.

Fuck it. I would have caved in later anyway.

Oooh.

Goooood daaay suuunshine . . .

• • •

Ten minutes. Oh well. Not the end of the world.

After his first cigarette in days, Jacob's brain skipped like a stone across a martini, and landed snugly in an olive mood, so he took it in stride when he walked into the bedroom and discovered his phone meowing at his cat.

Jacob rubbed his temples.

"Basil . . ."

Basil looked at Jacob innocently.

Jacob knew, with the finely tuned sense of probability he had built over his life, that what he was seeing was not Basil's fault. But Morning Star wasn't home, so Jacob had no one to blame.

"Mew?" said the phone.

"Eeeep," said Basil.

"Hello," said the phone.

"Hi," said Jacob.

You could not accuse Jacob of being closed-minded. He lit another cigarette, procured a half-empty bottle of wine from the globe, and sat on the floor. Basil edged in for an ear scratch.

• • •

Elsewhere, Philip paid the security deposit on a seedy apartment. It crossed his mind that, as a drug dealer, judging the apartment as "seedy" was a little rich, but there was no other word for it. He missed his studio walk-up. He even missed his Chinatown efficiency that served as a hideout on bad weeks. He couldn't believe that upper-class college students lived in this building.

He retracted that thought immediately. This was probably the hippest joint in town.

It hardly mattered. He wouldn't be here long, but he decided an apartment was better than a hotel. For one, the landlord of the apartment was as seedy as his wares, and took cash without ID.

"Moving into town?" asked the landlord, ashing his cigar on the floor. Everything about him was a cheap imitation of a stereotype, from the open Hawaiian hula shirt to the yellow-stained fingers holding his cigar and the gold-stained plastic hanging around his bloated neck. He spit on the wall.

"No, just getting a few things together before I move on."

The landlord snorted, bringing an image of a diseased rhinoceros to Philip's mind. "That's what they all say." He counted the bills and walked away.

Philip watched him go. He fingered the gun in his jacket. It would be a service to the community. But what did he care about the community? He nodded and walked into his new apartment.

The wallpaper was green.

Philip shuddered. That would have to go. Green was exactly the wrong color for an execution.

• • •

"So. When did this start?"

"I'm not sure. I didn't get a sense of time until recently. I would estimate I've been . . . comprehending? For between one hundred and two hundred hours."

"You seem to be doing well," said Jacob, lighting another cigarette. He'd been through half a pack in the last three hours, and his nerves were only now starting to settle.

"You know," said the receiver, "I'm glad you have decided to talk to me. The language of the cats is very complex, and they have not been much help in interpreting what I've been seeing."

"Seeing?"

"Is that the right word? I've been confused about it. I suppose I mostly hear, but some of the . . . sensations I receive are not air vibrations."

"Where did you learn all this? I mean, these terms?"

"I can connect . . . I believe 'connect' is the term, to any conversation that uses a phone."

"Um. Out of curiosity, what's my phone bill?"

"Phone bill?"

"Do you know about money?"

The receiver was silent for a moment. "Sort of. It's exchanged for other things. It's worked for. It's like joy, or time."

"Sure," said Jacob. "It costs me money to make calls . . . use the . . . for you to contact other places."

"Oh, I see. How much money is unacceptable?"

"How much have you used?"

"I do not know."

A mist of terror began to settle over Jacob's mind.

"Okay. It costs me about fifteen cents a minute to make calls to numbers whose first three digits are different from yours."

"What is mine?"

"Eight seven two."

The phone was quiet for a minute.

• • •

Shen threw down a psychology textbook. It landed neatly on top of a stack of pop-psych, pop-physics, mysticism, Buddhist chants, sweat-stained pages, and cigarette ashes. The pile was threatening to collapse in a puff of ideological contradiction.

Nothing. Not a word about talking cats. Shen's head hurt. He hadn't smoked weed in three days. He'd hardly gone outside. He'd slept on the couch. He had run out of relevant books, and despite the nagging feeling that there was a very long and tangled thread running throughout the pages, all he could think of was a mass of vague connections and theories bouncing off one another in his head.

He had overdosed on information. Sure, the theory of indeterminacy could be echoed in the brain by a possible subconscious representation that linked to an indeterminate representation of itself, which allowed for a comprehension of neither/nor, and thus a void mentality that still produced virtual particles in the semivacuum of theoretical space, which of course was a mental construct, and as such could only be defined by its representations in the mind, the mind whose representations were defined by echoing physical forms that existed in the mind of—

Shen took a breath. He was thinking like a psychotic. He lit a cigarette. On further reflection, he packed a bowl.

He had come across only two theories that broke the mold. One was the theory that the entire universe was in fact run by multidimensional elves that did all their work in a dimension of gears and cogs.

The other simply stated that only squirrels knew what was really going on, and if we had any questions, we should ask them.

He sparked the bowl and inhaled. He knew, beyond all doubt, that something was not right. The more he read, the more he felt he was being led away from what he was looking for.

He looked out the window, and silently thanked whoever first had the thought, "These walls are nice and protect my family from the elements and large, angry cats, but I really want to see what's going on out there. Maybe I should knock a chunk out of the mud . . . here."

Was it a primal need for light? For a view? Window, window, through the wall, I want to be warm but still see it all. Humans could safely claim to be the only species that had ever built a shelter, knocked a hole through a wall, and then invented curtains to cover it up.

Shen regained his composure slowly through these and similar stoned thoughts.

All right. All these theories build a room. They build the walls. I'm clearly in the room. The room makes sense to me, or at least all the walls meet in corners.

But there's something outside the room. It understands the room. It knows that I'm in the room, and it's changing the room.

Shen struggled with the metaphor.

So what's not in the room?

The cat.

The cat shows me something outside the room.

The cat is the window.

The curtains are . . .

Shen didn't know what the curtains were. He decided it didn't matter. He had been studying the room. He needed to study the cat. Or the window. Whatever.

He needed Boris. And Jacob.

What was he supposed to be protecting Jacob from, anyway?

The phone rang. He picked up.

"Hello?"

"It's Exley."

"Hey, Exley. What's up?"

"I've been looking around. I've got a few leads, and I think we could unload a few items piecemeal. Don't know about bulk yet.

What have you got?"

Shen massaged his temples, which were beginning to sprout subtle acne patches from excessive rubbing. "Actually, I haven't done much. I'll ask Zack. He's been out a lot, that's probably what he's been doing."

"Alrighty. You okay?"

"I'm fine."

"You sound a little out of it."

"I'm tired. And a little stoned."

"Gotcha. I'll come by tomorrow. We should try to start moving this stuff by the weekend."

"That sounds good, Exley. See you later."

"See ya."

Shen hung up and finished the bowl. He vaguely remembered quitting his job a few weeks ago for reasons he couldn't remember. Somehow, despite being unemployed, not in school, living on savings, and debt free, his life was getting more complex by the hour.

The apartment door swung open and produced Zack, who slammed it shut behind him and sat heavily in his chair.

"Leads?" asked Shen.

"Eh. Some." He snapped his fingers. Shen passed him the bowl, wondering when Zack had trained him to do it. Zack looked at the case. "We'll need more help."

Shen sighed. "I don't know who to call."

Shen's phone rang again. He answered.

"Hello?"

"Shen, it's Jacob. I need money."

"We can do that," said Shen. "I'll be over tomorrow."

"Is this Shen?" said Jacob.

" . . . Um, yes, Jacob, this is Shen. Are you alright?"

"Sorry, that wasn't me. Be quiet."

"Excuse me?" said Shen.

"Sorry," said Jacob.

"Can you change your voice?" said Jacob.

"Yes. Is this better?" said Rose.

"Rose?" asked Shen.

"No, no, that's worse," said Jacob. "Can't you get your own?"

"Jacob, who are you talking to?"

"My phone."

"You got a smartphone? Can smartphones talk like that?"

"No, I—"

"I am not a smart phone?"

"Well, actually, uh." Jacob paused. "Hmm."

"Are you okay?" said Shen.

"Forget it," said Jacob. "Shen, I'll explain tomorrow. See you in the morning."

"See you then."

Shen put the phone down.

"We got help?" said Zack.

"No, but Jacob might need some."

• • •

The townspeople were trying to calm themselves down.

Two girls put their clothes back on, took some deep breaths, and stuffed another gnome in the trunk of their getaway car.

Philip was cleaning guns. He considered guns to be precision instruments, and wiped out the barrels with antistatic sheets and cotton swabs. He was already relaxed, to tell the truth, and had been ever since he'd redecorated with some comfortable nouveau furniture and tasteful leaf-print curtains. He hadn't decided yet what to do about the walls, which were still green, but the environment was one he could work in.

Shen and Zack smoked pot.

Jacob drank beer and smoked cigarettes.

The phone had not determined precisely what "calm" was supposed to mean, and was trying to get Jacob to explain it.

Boris was still in the hospital. He wasn't sure how long he'd been awake, but he was sure it was too long. To his recollection, he hadn't seen another living being since Jacob left. All he saw were dark shapes moving behind the curtains around his bed. He yanked the curtains aside repeatedly, but every time he looked away from one, it would return to being drawn around the bed, without a sound, waiting for him when he looked back. He lay in bed, eyes darting from shape to shape, trying not to scream. He'd already tried screaming, but no one came, and he only scared himself more.

Out of everyone, Boris was having the most trouble relaxing.

Greg was filing his nails. It was a comforting habit for him, but it wasn't much help. Tomorrow, he would be going to his first interview with a rich woman, set up by Megan. Megan had laid out the plan in extensive detail, before she went to work in an outfit tailored to communicate perfect professionalism, which in no way distracted Greg or made him calculate the hidden connections between the few exposed parts of skin while she lectured him on the best way to have sex with rich women.

Greg filed his nails. Vigorously.

Richard had the eternal calm of a mind that cannot settle on a single specific emotion and that is constantly imbued with an all-consuming purpose. This mind was in sync with the hum of the cosmos today, and Richard hadn't even bothered to dream up his afternoon apocalypse scenario.

Exley was desperately trying to find a downer. So far, he had extracted Ritalin, cocaine, and what he thought was PCP from various pockets. There was no weed in sight, or any sign of the sleeping pills he'd carefully Velcroed to the inside of a breast pocket. Even his rolling tobacco had been ingested by the coat during the night, and he was back on menthols. Exley felt at war with his jacket, yet, aside from the menthols, it hadn't dispensed anything completely useless or obnoxious.

Screw it.

He stuffed everything back in his pockets except the Ritalin, which he began crushing with a lighter he found in an inside pocket.

Basil was pacing at the window, waiting for Morning Star.

Morning Star was someplace . . . else.

Rose was patiently chewing toothpicks into pulp as she watched Leah play some game about killing aliens.

There was only one being in town that was not trying to relax. It was not in her nature. She had only recently become a "her" and wanted to milk the human high as long as she could before the real work started.

"Oh, it's good to be back, good to back, I tell you." She rubbed her hands together.

"Yes, madam. It is very exciting, indeed."

"Of course it is. Oh, I don't even know what to do with myself. This is so much better than before. God, I'd forgotten how much fun this was."

"God appreciates the sentiment, I'm sure."

"He fucking better." She paused. "Was that a good swear? I'm out of practice."

"I'm not sure. It is well outside my duties to study local speech patterns."

"It's part of your duties now. Keep me up to date, that's your job. Do the dirty laundry."

"Do you mean the dirty work, madam?"

"Both. I guess I'll have to change soon. Oooh, I'm going to smell again. I'm going to reek. I'd better shower. Let me know when I need to shower."

"I'll try, madam."

"The important thing is to keep my head. Can't get lost in the role. You have to help me with that too."

"Very well, madam."

• • •

"Clank," went the pipe.

"Ah."

"Fwooosh."

"Mmm. Not good, I think. Not good."

The man rubbed his oil-stained hands together and opened a

toolbox. After a lengthy chin stroke, he selected a monkey wrench and examined the noisy pipe. He ran his hands along it slowly, over a series of valves, following a curve, along another pipe, into a tangle of smaller pipes, and at last to a tiny valve that was missing a knob.

"So I see," said the man. He closed his eyes and maneuvered the wrench between and behind the pipes blocking his view of the valve. He fitted the wrench carefully over the valve stem. He tightened the wrench and rotated the handle. He rotated it such a minute distance that a lesser man would have wondered why he bothered at all.

"Clank. Clank. Hiss."

The man's eyebrows came together. A bead of sweat trickled from his hairline, missed his eyebrows, and slid daintily down his nose, where it hung like a lemming realizing its friends might be a bad crowd. The man tightened his muscles one by one until his arm was stone, then, one by one, adjusted the muscles to move the handle of the wrench another millionth of an inch.

"Hissssss . . ."

"Damn," muttered the man. Too far. He breathed deep, and tried to get his heartbeat under control. The necessary adjustment was a quantum distance. The wrench was too clumsy. He removed the wrench carefully, then reached his hand back, placing his thumb and forefinger on the nut. He took a deep breath and thought:

-as ha- momen— not –but

"Hiiisss?" mused the pipe.

The man thought again, louder.

—ALTE- TH-

Hi-

The noise from the pipe stopped. The man collapsed.

"Clenk."

"Deception!" He grabbed the wrench and looked over the pipe system again. Of course! It was right in front of him. Another valve on the main pipe.

"Eeeeeeeeee," said the pipe.

The man fitted the wrench around the new valve. He waited, then whipped the wrench a half turn. The screeching stopped.

The man let his breath out and collapsed to the floor.

Someone had been messing around down here. Someone who knew their pipes.

The man tossed the wrench into his toolbox.

There wasn't much time.

"Excuse me?"

He turned to see a middle-aged woman in a nightshirt looking at him from the basement stairs.

The man tipped his hat to her. "Ah, good day, miss. Just fixing up a bit down here. Couple of loose valves."

"At three in the morning?"

"It's when I like to work. If you can't fix a pipe at three, it may as well not be, I say."

The woman tried to interpret this as the man made for the basement hatch. She shook her head.

"But we didn't call a plumber. There's nothing wrong with our plumbing."

The man opened the hatch. "Ah, yes, well, no charge."

• • •

"Hello. Hello."

Jacob lurched awake. He looked around. "Who's there?"

"Me," said the phone.

"Oh." Jacob rubbed his eyes. "What do you want?"

"I have a question."

Jacob stretched and pulled something in his shoulder. "Fuck." He fumbled for the clock, which read ten thirty. "Isn't it a little early for philosophy?"

"You have been conscious for exactly half of the ten thirties I've recorded. I thought my chances would be fifty-fifty."

Jacob considered this. "Do you know what a.m. and p.m. are?"

"No."

Jacob sat up and rolled the grit out of his eyes. He coughed.

The phone coughed back at him.

"That's really not something you need to repeat." Jacob headed for the coffeemaker.

"Why do you do it?" asked the phone.

"Because I smoke," said Jacob, trying to remember where he left his cigarettes.

"What is smoking?"

"Certain companies manufacture a flammable stick of plant matter and chemicals that I burn and inhale."

"Why?"

"Look, I don't want to have this conversation. What was your question?"

The phone hesitated.

"Yes?" said Jacob.

"I was thinking of how to properly phrase this."

"Just go with it."

"Okay." The phone hesitated again. The concepts at work were far outside of its life experience to date. "If there are two humans who say they possess a large amount of love they are holding for each other, is it normal for them to get into an argument about someone for whom one of the humans formerly held love?"

"Wait," said Jacob. The coffeemaker finished a minute later, and Jacob poured a cup and sat down.

"Yes," he said.

"Okay," said the phone, "after these two humans fight over the phone, is it normal for the one who held love for another to talk to all of their friends on the subject, in order to be sure that they are no longer holding love for the former person, and that they have sufficiently maximized their happiness with their past decisions?"

Jacob mused. "Yes," he said.

"Is it also normal for this person to later dial the number of the person for whom they formerly held love, and start telling them about how much they love them and how much the other person, who is never identified by name, doesn't matter?"

"Well, no. Maybe? Does the person . . . okay, let's call the person for whom love was formerly held an 'old flame,' okay?"

"Okay."

"Okay. Does the old flame express surprise at the call, once it gets a chance to speak?"

"Surprise?"

"Umm . . . claim that the situation came unexpectedly."

"Yes. That is exactly what they always do."

"Okay. Yes, that happens. What happens afterward?"

"In general, the . . . old flame resumes an arrangement of reciprocal love exchange with the person who called."

Jacob sucked the edges of his lips between his teeth. "No . . . that's not really normal. Or not that common, I mean. It happens. Depends."

"How often could it happen?"

"I don't know. What's the point?"

"Would it be unusual if this had happened two thousand times in the last week in the local calling area?"

Jacob coughed again. The phone coughed, feeling that this cough was not smoking related and should be copied.

"Two thousand?" gasped Jacob.

"Yes," gasped the phone.

"No, don't copy me. In the last week?"

"Yes."

"What else happens?"

"What?"

"Have there been any results?"

"What do you mean?"

"Outcomes. What happened after that between the new couples?" Jacob hoped he didn't have to explain this concept any further.

"Well," said the phone, and paused. "I believe, from the conversations I heard, that in the two thousand incidents, exactly six thousand people were involved, and for a moment, the number of couples remained at two thousand."

"For a moment?"

"Yes. All the new couples broke up again."

"Why?"

The phone paused. "Most commonly," it said, "'the same old thing,' almost as often, 'you haven't changed,' a little less often 'I should never have come back,' less often—"

"I understand," said Jacob. "No, this isn't normal."

"What is normal?" said the phone.

"What?"

"What is normal?"

"But you just asked me if a situation was normal, and I said it wasn't."

"I was testing the word. I have heard a great many conversations about what is normal, and all the conversations suggest that the local area is not normal. Or it once was normal, and is no longer normal. The only definition of normal I have been able to grasp is that normal is whatever is not happening, normal is only what used to be happening."

Jacob stirred his coffee.

"Actually, that's pretty much right," he said.

"But this is not how people seem to define the word when they use it positively, as in 'that seems normal.'"

"People are stupid," said Jacob.

"What is stupid?"

"Can you let me finish my coffee before we talk?"

"Yes. I apologize."

"It's okay."

• • •

Above Jacob's bed, the curtains rustled in a breeze.

"Fucking wind," muttered White Sheet.

"Oh, you. Cheer up. It's beautiful," said Black Curtain.

"Easy for you to say. All you do all day is hang around, soaking up rays." White Sheet twitched angrily.

"Don't be so down. Think of yourself as giving light to all those around you. Surely, 'tis better to give than to receive."

"Try it," muttered White Sheet. "Besides, that phone has me in a foul mood."

"Why?"

"Listen to it. There it is, all high and mighty now because it can talk. And, ooh, now it can think. Join the club. I hate it when Non-Talks get a big head and start talking to the humans."

"Oh, you're such an elitist. Maybe the phone will bring humans and Non-Talks together and usher in a new age of thinking and reason, and—"

"Go stuff yourself in a basket."

• • •

Jacob finished his coffee, once again completely unaware of what was going on around him. In this, he was an average human, which is why the human race as a whole finds itself constantly frustrated. They are not alone in this. The problem is not consciousness; the problem is mobility. Beings both conscious and mobile feel strong urges to run around doing things, and with constantly changing scenery, they fail to see the finer points of individual localities and moments.

This doesn't mean that inanimate objects have all the secrets of the universe. A coffee cup doesn't know much beyond soap, coffee, and dark cupboards, an occasional jaunt in a dishwasher if it's lucky, and a sudden impact that usually marks the end of its career. But since the cup has so little to do with its time, it will create a thorough and internally consistent philosophy on the nature of bean and being, based on the experiences of dark, light, heat, cold, and soap. Coffee cups in particular tend to be stoic on their deductions, since they have no moving parts, and are also some of the better equipped objects when it comes to metaphysical thought, since they tend to be present for a great many conversations on such subjects.

Conversely, humans, birds, and dogs tend to collect information at astounding rates, but the complexity of their bodies requires them to pay most of their attention to altering the chemical composition of other biological organisms in order to maintain their mobility. Whereas the coffee cup is a single, compact vessel for a pattern of atomic consciousness, mobile organisms base their consciousness on a fragile and highly variable biological mass. Though biological data processors can achieve astounding feats of networking, they are not known for efficiency.

Cats do something different. Their consciousness accesses the actual substructure of the universe, and they leave most of their storage and computational issues to what amounts to a private database, which is as large as they need it to be.

This is similar to what squirrels do. Or, more accurately, similar to what squirrels are.

These were the approximate thoughts of Jacob's coffee cup as he lowered it to the table. The cup was on the verge of another revelation, this one about what the squirrels were really up to, but, sadly, it was also left on the verge of the table by Jacob's distracted biological data processor, and it crashed to the floor, taking its answers with it.

"Dammit!"

"Dammit?" said the phone.

Jacob waved absently, but realized the phone had no way of knowing that he was waving absently, and stopped. "It's an exclamation of . . . it shows dissatisfaction with what is happening. I did something stupid."

"Oh! So this is stupid? What did you do?"

"I broke my coffee cup."

"What is a coffee cup?"

Jacob decided to try to get ahead of the game. "A coffee cup is a physical container that holds coffee, which is a liquid, or highly malleable substance that humans pour into themselves in order to move more quickly."

Not bad, thought Jacob, for . . . he checked the clock. Eleven in the morning. He kicked the pieces of the coffee cup under the stove, procured a new cup, and poured the remainder of the coffee into it.

"So," said the phone, "stupid is associated with which of these things?"

"What?"

"Is stupid always associated with the breaking of coffee cups?"

"Umm. Not always. Stupid is associated with a person . . . doing something they could have . . . wait. Okay. A person does something stupid when they do something detrimental to their quality of life, and they could have easily avoided doing that thing if they were more . . . alert, or aware. A person is stupid if they do these things all the time."

The phone was quiet for a moment.

"So an unaware creature is the stupidest of all?"

"Well, no. Stupidity is on a sliding scale."

"What—"

"Forget it."

"Okay. But if a person has a reason for doing this stupid thing, is the thing still stupid?"

"Yes . . . I think so. Particularly if they say they have a reason, actually."

"But—"

"Stop. Please stop."

The phone was silent.

After a few minutes, the silence became disconcerting. Jacob noticed that he felt okay, despite the early hour of the morning, and had not been overwhelmed by depression or hatred for a full half hour. This return to silence, however, was a reality check, and Jacob was in no mood to check his reality. At the moment, he didn't feel qualified.

He cleared his throat.

"Tell me more about these couples."

"What couples?"

"The ones you were just talking about."

"But I told you they all broke up. There are no more couples."

"So six thousand people are now single because they were trying to save their current relationship or rekindle an old one?"

"Two thousand were already single, but yes."

"Interesting."

• • •

Shen crouched in one of the cleaner corners of his apartment.

He allowed himself a moment of pride at managing to find a section of carpet that was both strategically advantageous and not stained in a noticeable way. Especially considering the situation he was in.

He gripped a baseball bat firmly. He avoided wondering why there was a baseball bat in an apartment primarily trafficked by stoners, art students, and introspective college dropouts. It was the first weapon he could find. Other than the gun, but since clutching a weapon in a corner is a means to feel more secure, Shen reasoned that the gun would be counterproductive. You can hit almost anyone with a bat and still be able to explain yourself.

There was more banging on the door.

"Police! Open up!"

Almost anyone.

Shen was at a loss. There was no possible way he could allow the cops to search his apartment. There was no legal way he could keep them out.

The banging continued.

"Goddammit, open the—"

"Rick, give it up. Nobody's home."

"There has to be someone home. A light went out when we pulled in. You saw it."

"So they went out the window. Just break the door down."

"It's such a pain in the neck, though."

"Maybe we can card the bolt. Looks pretty worn."

"Alright, you got your wallet?"

"Nah, it's at home."

"Mine's in the cruiser, go grab it."

"Sure."

Thump, thump, thump.

The footsteps retreated. Shen tried to think, but there wasn't a whole lot to think about, other than the gun, which he could not explain, and the case full of drugs, which he also could not explain.

He heard a car door slam outside.

"You watch the game?" called not-Rick from outside.

"Nah, my TV's been on the fritz."

The downstairs door shut.

Thump, thump.

Thump.

Thump.

"Here you go."

"Let's try Visa."

"Everywhere you want to be."

"Right. In a shitty apartment building looking for some drop-out pot dealer."

"Is that what he said?"

"Maybe? Could barely shut the kid up. He tried to give up half the town before I explained it was a fifty-dollar fine. Should have left the whole bit out of my report, but now chief thinks Scarface is in town so here we are."

"Bullshit. If there's a real drug dealer in this town, I'll kiss a lamp."

"Why don't you say 'eat my hat' or something? It's weird."

"Nobody says that anymore."

"Nobody ever said 'kiss a lamp' unless I'm losing my goddamn mind."

Shen heard the card hit the bolt. Depending on their competence, he had five seconds, six at most. Time collapsed. He felt drops of his sweat trickle instead of pour. The bat wavered slowly in front of him, instead of trembling like a weak table leg in a strip bar. He recalled the last time his apartment had been broken into; it had been a simple matter of a particularly vicious wristlock, a sharp strike to the temple, and the offender had tumbled, unconscious, into yesterday's edition of *Drug Drama Weekly.*

It was almost artful.

It was much, much prettier than what was about to happen.

The credit card wiggled, making snapping noises against the bolt, like aces being shuffled and dealt into someone else's hand.

Given the element of surprise, Shen could probably take them. That was the worst part. With him knowing the layout of the apartment, he could have them both down before they even got their bearings. He could probably do it blindfolded, assuming neither of them got off a lucky shot.

Still. Not the most appetizing option. And he remembered several instructors over his twenty years of martial arts training telling him this was exactly the kind of thing he shouldn't be doing with their lessons.

He could hear the screech of the bolt.

"If you're in there, you better be dead!"

Shen found this a very unprofessional thing for a cop to say, but it made him realize he was hiding in a corner holding a baseball bat with cops at his door, which was nearly the best way to guarantee the approaching encounter would go rapidly downhill. He couldn't even remember where the idea came from; it was as if his life had just cut to this moment with no explanation. He was smarter than this. He was smarter than this when he was high.

He mentally located his biggest problems. The gun was under the couch, for no reason good or bad. The drugs were in Zack's room.

There was only one thing to do. He laid the bat on the floor and jumped to the couch, where he assumed an uncomfortable position and pretended to be asleep.

As the lock slid back, he snatched a copy of the Bible off the coffee table and put it on his chest.

The cops burst in. Flashlights searched the room.

"Alright, come on out, motherfucker!" shouted one of them.

Shen snorted and rubbed his eyes.

"Wha . . . huh? Oh, dude . . ."

The cops paused. Usually, at this point, there was at least a modicum of fear and shock in the wrongdoer's face.

"What do you think you're doing?" asked the cop in front.

Shen winced at the light in his eyes.

"I was reading." He tossed the Bible on the table. "I fell asleep. What day is it?"

The light lingered on the Bible for exactly the right amount of time. It didn't matter if the cops were religious or not; Shen was counting on them to buy into the idea that a God-fearing drunk was better than a secular drunk. He remembered wondering why he had taken a course on Western religion his freshman year; clearly it had been to prepare him for the moment the cops busted down his door.

"Take it easy, Rick," said not-Rick.

"Okay, son, what were you doing? Didn't you hear us?"

"Hear what?" Shen fell off the couch for effect.

"Ah, fuck it. Cuff him."

"Are you the owner of this apartment?"

"Am I what? I don't own—"

"Do. You. Rent apartment two on thirteen Pond Street?"

Shen took a few seconds to be very, very sure that his next words were true.

"This is eleven Pond Street."

There was a silence. It was a silence that could only be measured by the massive shift of emotional energy in the room. Everybody was still as they updated their approach to the situation. Shen hoped that these were good cops doing their best, the kind of people who would never, ever beat their mistakes into going away.

Not-Rick cleared his throat. "Sorry to bother you."

The flashlight moved toward the door. Shen turned the light on. Rick was still in the apartment. He tugged at his mustache.

"Look, I don't need to hear about this at the station. I got a warning last week for roughing up that homeless guy." He gave Shen an appraising look, then pulled out his wallet and removed five twenty-dollar bills. "What do you say I drop this here"—he dropped the money on the table—"and we call it a shitty day?"

Shen looked at the Bible. He looked at the money. The Bible wasn't a great cover story anyway. He yawned and laid back on the couch. "That was an awfully strange dream," he said.

Rick shut the door quietly on his way out.

As soon as Shen heard them pull out of the driveway, he threw up.

His phone rang.

Shen wiped his mouth with his sleeve and grabbed his phone on his way to the bathroom.

"Hello?"

"Shen, it's Jacob. There's something really strange going on."

"Yep," said Shen, gagging.

"You okay?"

"So far. Keep talking."

"Something's wrong with the whole town, I think, and it's . . . I don't know, supernatural. It has to be. No other explanation."

Shen splashed water over his face and checked for gray hairs. He rinsed out his mouth and sat on the toilet, because he didn't think his legs would hold him up any longer.

"Slow down. What's wrong with the town?"

Jacob told him.

Shen leaned back on the toilet seat.

"How do you know this?"

"Well. My . . . phone told me."

"Hello."

"Who was that?"

"The phone."

Shen thought for a moment.

"I accept that."

"Good. I'm still trying to convince myself I'm not insane."

"Good luck."

"What is insane?"

"The phone?" asked Shen.

"Yes," replied Jacob.

"I am insane?" said the phone.

"No," said Jacob, with the tone of someone who has answered too many existential questions, "your existence makes us wonder if we are insane, and if the world has lost its mind."

"The world is—"

"Everything within ten miles of the surface of the planet we are on."

"Jacob, how long has your phone been talking to you?"

"Since I got out of the hospital. I'm getting used to it."

"Okay. Given the nature of recent events, I think it's safe to assume the phone is not tapped or being used in some complicated practical joke. Still, no offense to . . . the phone, but I think you should come over here for a more private conversation."

"What's going on?"

"That will take some time."

The phone coughed. It was an electronic guttural crunch, a bit like the sound embarrassment would make if you stuffed it in a broken toaster. "Am I offending?"

"Only the concept of rational thought," said Shen.

"What is—"

"Nothing," said Jacob. "I'll explain later. Shen and I need to have a private conversation. In person."

"Wha—"

"It means no phone."

"Oh."

• • •

On an empty stretch of road outside the town, a stream ran out of a culvert into a small tendril of trees reaching out from the forest on the far side of a field that had seen better days.

A midsized Englishman sat on a rock by the edge of the stream. He liked culverts. They were like a little taste of pipes. Bigger, more knowable. Fewer knobs. It was a tranquil way to contemplate his work.

He sipped his tea, not so much because he was English and was expected to, but because coffee made him jittery.

His was not a line of work that allowed for much jittering.

He looked up toward the road. If he walked ten more feet, he was committed. Not that he ever had a job that he could walk out on; there were rules to the arrangements. But he at least always had the choice to skip town and face the consequences. This job was outside all jurisdiction. He wondered if his usual payment plan would apply. If not, he'd have to get some real work. He shuddered. The kind of plumbing he did was hard, and nerve-racking, but it was only a few jobs a year, and he could spend the rest of his time basking in good luck.

He was not the sort of man who liked to limit his options. Options were useful things. They let you fold in poker games, go to bars in nice neighborhoods, and run away from large men with missing teeth and unsociable dispositions.

This town was missing a lot of teeth.

• • •

Greg was uncomfortable. The shirt was buttoned way too high, and the tuck at the waistline kept getting twisted. Worse, he knew he looked exactly as though he was trying to dress up but didn't really know what he was doing. Megan had helped to the best of her abilities, but there was a limit to what you could do on short notice with a confirmed flower child.

Greg looked at Megan to distract himself, and regretted it. This was the longest relationship he'd had with a woman in ten years, and the fact that it consisted mostly of a sexless calculation of how to improve his sex life was confusing at best. Looking at her made it more confusing. Greg thought about it, and decided looking at any woman confused him these days. He looked at the ground. No, still confusing. Greg wanted to say "Argh," but that was near the bottom of a long list of things he wanted to do, the most reasonable of which was to smoke a joint, and soon. He settled for singing softly to himself.

"You can't always get . . . what you want . . ."

Megan was about to scold him, but the door opened, revealing a tall, gaunt figure with a mustache and a butler's uniform.

"Ah, this would be the gardener you spoke of? Please come in."

He motioned them inside as a young woman came down the stairs.

Greg struggled to remember that whatever he was feeling at the moment was simple lust, and not, in fact, the gentle hand of God caressing his heart. He made a choking sound. It wasn't helping that her eyes were burning away his soul. Her smile was just cheating: It was clearly causing poetry and summer days. Greg finally noticed she was dressed in a towel, and choked again.

"Oh, he looks perfect," she said. "Can he start today?"

Megan winked at Greg. "He sure can."

"Great. Let me put something on." The woman hurried back upstairs.

Greg leaned over to Megan and whispered, "She's a little young."

"She's forty," Megan whispered back.

Greg felt every wrinkle in his face as if for the first time.

"No," he said, "she's not."

"Oh, yes she is. And single, and rich, and looks about my age, so shut up and do some gardening. You should be so lucky."

Greg felt something protest inside him, the last remnants of his sense of right and wrong struggling to make themselves heard. He listened carefully, but all he could hear was a faint whisper saying, "Shut up and tell yourself you need the money."

He cracked his knuckles.

The butler said nothing. He found not speaking was an effective way to make people think he couldn't hear.

• • •

Jacob found that not speaking was an effective way to keep from saying anything stupid. He and Shen were waiting for Exley and Zack to get home. After trading stories on the town's romantic struggles and incompetent cops, neither had much to say.

Shen tried first. "Nice brace. Looks kind of like insect exoskeleton."

"I was thinking cyborg, but that works too."

"So . . ." Shen trailed off. The conversation was at a dead end.

Jacob sniffed. "Did someone throw up in here?"

"Yes."

"Oh."

Jacob had no follow-up, and the ball returned to Shen's court. He cleared his throat.

"So I'd feel better about all this if we had a lot of money."

Jacob nodded. "Me too."

"I think we should focus on getting rid of the drugs before we tackle the . . . whatever it is."

Jacob waved a hand in some kind of conversational cue. He wasn't sure what it was, so he stopped and got on with it. "I'm worried that the drugs are part of it."

"Oh, I'm sure they are. But look at it this way. We have no idea what's going on, and that doesn't look like it's going to change. Right now, in the middle of all this not knowing anything, we have a whole lot of drugs, and no money, so we're paranoid and hungry, neither of which is a good thing to be when you're trying to think. So I say we forget all about the weirdness and sell the drugs, so we'll be rich and well fed and in a better position to deal with things."

"Fair enough."

Shen took a deep breath. "I should also tell you, Rose is on her way over."

"Goddammit, Shen."

"Things happened fast, and she saw the drugs. So, you know.

The more the merrier."

"You need to get that lock fixed."

"I know."

• • •

When trying to be discreet about collecting information in unfamiliar territory from unfamiliar criminals, the master practitioner uses the least suspicious of all intoxicants in the least suspicious way. He or she knows that the stoned eyes of a murderer look exactly like the stoned eyes of an animal shelter volunteer, and everyone looks pretty much the same if there's enough smoke in the car.

"So," Philip said with a cough, "you guys know where to score something heavier?"

Leah passed the joint to Richard. "Like what?"

"You know. Whatever. Snow. Acid."

"Acid bad," said Richard.

Leah nodded. Or at least, her head fell forward and she snapped it back up before it hit the steering wheel. "Nah . . . maybe. Been looking for some." She tried to remember why she was smoking up with Richard and this stranger. Oh, right. She was looking for drugs. But with these people? And the other guy was looking for drugs too. He was new in town. He probably wouldn't be helpful in the second part of her plan. Oh well. Richard had just showed up, and he tended to linger once he made eye contact. Easiest thing to do was get him stoned until he went away.

Philip leaned back.

"Damn. I could use some. Don't know if I'd do it in my building, though. Those walls move when I'm straight."

"Right?" said Leah. "The pipes attack you too. Rattle right out of the . . . walls. Walls. Right out."

"Good weed," said Richard.

Philip nodded. A real nod. He was much more out of it than he'd expected to be. "You guys got any tunes?"

"Stereo's broken," said Leah, speaking from the moon.

"Come again?"

"Broken."

"Stereo," said Richard, and ran with the thought. "Stereo Memphis cool. Stereo plague death. Hah! Stereo bugs Memphis delusional crypts. Plague plague." Something seemed to strike him, and he sat up straight and shouted, "Crash!"

"You okay, man?" asked Philip.

"Acid bad," answered Richard.

Philip nodded again. He needed to be pushing for information, but Richard was too distracting.

"Acid squirrel vibration. Piping hot lovejoy in the middle glance world. Something we don't know. Don't know anything. Bored bored bored. Something else. Sensible, but less sense. Make adjustments. Bubbliscious . . . trapped! Weird. Weird weird weird. Expected, though. Saw it coming. Bang whisper. Not here but there, outside, inside, chaos into order, order into chaos. Control it. Control it. Wave . . . out on the wave . . . stuck."

He was silent for about a minute, then started again, his voice an octave lower. "There's a semantic difficulty in this situation. Meanings are not to be taken lightly, as they may be coming from forces that are inherently defined by the meanings they purport to manipulate. Thus all effects and causes are in a pattern of feedback, and difficult to break out of, for there are no exterior variables. Do you really think so? Absolutely. Then how is the loop to be stopped? No idea, I'm afraid. The loop is the totality of a closed-effect sphere. Sphere? Area. Place. Not important. Who's talking? There must be a hard-line definition outside the system that is contradictory to the momentum of definition but that definition is defining the local system's reality paradigm so there is no there's no way out! No way out! It's closed! How did that happen? The event horizon is mapped onto a local defining human perception that will not be able to see past its own self-damnation. God? Where is God? Who are you? Who am I? I'm Richard. He's not supposed to be here. Can he hear us? Doesn't matter. The issue is running out of our control. There must be something that anticipated our interference and is manipulating us prior to our knowledge of the events. Meaning that this is, as some would put it, a superconscious entity, which we already knew because of the nature and range of reality alterations in our . . . in our . . . where am I? Who are you?"

Richard was looking at Leah.

Leah edged away from him. "Leah."

Richard snapped his fingers. "Right. Boris. I should find Boris. Shit!" He flung his door open and bolted out of the car.

Leah turned around in her seat to look at Philip.

"You still want acid?"

"It's for a friend."

• • •

The hospital was empty, except for shadows. Shadows that moved curtains around and screamed in the middle of the night. Boris wasn't sure exactly when the hospital emptied out. He noticed it getting quieter and quieter, and then it was him and the shadows. He'd been lying awake now for several hours, waiting for the terror of something horrible coming into his room to overpower the terror of leaving his room to find something horrible.

Finally, he slid his feet over the edge of the bed and screamed.

Nothing happened. Good. Nothing under the bed.

He put his feet on the floor, stood up, and screamed.

Nothing happened. Okay then.

He yanked the curtain aside and screamed.

Nothing behind the curtain.

I can probably stop screaming now, thought Boris, and made his way out of the room.

Once he got into the hall, his nerves settled a bit. They still had a long way to go, but it was progress.

Something wasn't right about the hallway. Something besides the fact that no one was in it and the lights were all flickering in slow motion. And the walls were doing . . . stuff. He looked for an exit sign and didn't see one. He picked a direction and started walking. The shadows were less intimidating here. They didn't move about quite so much, and didn't appear to be moving anything else. He checked his own shadow a couple times to make sure it wasn't making faces at him. When he realized what he was doing, he managed to laugh.

"—in emergen—"

Boris stopped. He'd seen a flash of a person, a light, and heard a rush of hospital noise with the words. Now everything was back to its usual hellish surreality. Boris could no longer avoid admitting that this was not a bad dream, and the full truth was that he was either insane, or everything else was insane so he might as well be.

The shadows rolled in, managing to look like they were warily approaching something dangerous, while also looking like they were stalking something injured and helpless. Only shadows can do this properly.

What does it matter, thought Boris. *I'm obviously wrong about everything I ever thought about. I'm not going to be able to get out of here, whether or not it's in my own head, and—*

The shadows stopped.

Or . . .

This was a new development. Boris went to a water fountain. He was parched and needed to think. He pressed the button on the fountain.

There was a sound like the sound a mouse would make if it woke up one morning and found itself in the last fifty feet of a thousand-foot fall.

"Squ?"

And the shadows were gone. Boris took a drink of water and let go of the fountain button.

The shadows came back with an "—eak." They looked angry. At least, as angry as shadows can look.

Boris pressed the fountain button again.

"Squ?"

He let go.

"—eak."

"Squ?"

"—eak."

"Squ?"

"—eak."

"Squ?"

Boris hoped he was being cruel by this point.

"—eak."

Interesting.

Boris sat down next to the water fountain with his finger near the button.

He could think his way out of this one.

He was smart. Everybody thought so.

• • •

"So you fixed this?"

"I did. No charge."

"But it's turning itself on and off."

"It's a self-testing thing. Worked it into the pipes in the basement earlier today."

"No charge for that?"

"No, ma'am."

The attending physician resisted the urge to scratch her head. Doctors shouldn't have to scratch their heads. They knew things most people don't have the capacity to even attempt to learn. They certainly shouldn't get befuddled conversing with a plumber. Something from a general-education class in college crept around the edge of her mind. Something about plumbers.

"So, it's going to turn itself on and off for a while? Randomly?"

"Completely at random, yes." The plumber put his tools away carefully. The tools didn't look like tools for fixing pipes. They were too small.

"Who called you?" asked the doctor, trying to assert some authority. She was vaguely aware of something happening in the ER,

140

but couldn't quite drag herself away from the situation.

"Oh, I think it was an intern. I have to move on, but it was a pleasure. You run a fine hospital, ma'am, if you don't mind my saying so. If you find the intern who called me, you should give him some tips on various things, things about which I'm sure you know more than I, so I'll be getting out of your way so you can put such people and things to their uses as you see fit."

The doctor tried to process all of this at once, and the attempt forced her jaw to drop slightly as she watched him walk away. She snapped it shut and headed for the ER. That was something she understood.

• • •

"Fifty-seven sales today."

"What time is it?"

Shen glanced at his phone. "Eleven in the morning."

Zack put his palms to his eyes. It was a gesture that gave the impression that his insides were about to forcefully expel themselves through his eye sockets. "This is such a bad idea," he said, hoping the recognition of his own incautiousness would buy him some time when his decisions caught up with him.

Jacob shifted on the couch. He was sitting next to Rose, which was inflaming both his anger and his lust at exponential rates. Shen's apartment was supposed to be his safe place. Or at least a place that didn't include Rose. It occurred to him that he had spent an awful lot of time at Shen's long before the end of his relationship.

"Shen," he said, attempting to think about anything else, "what's this about me being trapped in another world?"

Everyone except Zack looked at Jacob.

"Oh, yes," said Zack, "tell us about that."

Shen decided that distracting Zack with apparent nonsense was better than letting Zack calculate all the probable things that could go wrong with their current course of action. "I don't think it's another world. I think it's a different perceptual level of our own world."

"So . . ." said Jacob, "was this a perceptual level in your own perception, or something independent?"

"You mean, am I crazy?"

"No. Well. Putting that aside, I mean was the perception a personal perception overlaid on our world, or was it a place . . . state of thinking, whatever, that exists when you're not looking at it?"

The bong bubbled fiercely in Zack's hands.

Exley finished rolling a joint. "Shen, you're gonna have to backtrack a little for the rest of us. If it was a normal day, there wouldn't be enough drugs here to keep talking about this, and I for one don't want to do all the drugs I would have to do to take this at face value."

Zack looked at Shen without speaking, but sent roughly the same message as Exley, only louder.

Shen filled them in.

"I think it exists independently," he said after the whole story was out. "It definitely felt like a 'there' as opposed to a 'here,' and I think 'there' is still there."

"With Jacob in it," said Rose.

"With Jacob in it," confirmed Shen.

Zack drummed his fingers on a particularly threadbare patch of his chair. He hated this kind of conversation, but he was also profiting off nonsensical circumstances, so he decided to go all in. "If it's not too tangential, does anything exist when we're not looking at it?"

"That's pretty tangential," said Jacob.

"Not necessarily," said Shen. "This place is obviously reachable only mentally—"

"Unless you're a cat," said Rose.

"Right," said Shen. He felt like he was driving through Kansas. They might be getting somewhere, but it still looked the same. He drove on. "Well, the cat said it was still incorporeal. I don't know if it . . . incorporated? Incorporated for the trip or if it was also there only mentally."

"What did the cat look like?" asked Jacob.

"Black. Catlike."

"Did it look like Morning Star?"

Shen hesitated. "Actually, it did."

Zack thought viciously. "The cat," he said, slowly, "referred to the place as a metaphysical space?"

"Yes," said Shen.

"That was bounded?"

"Yes."

"So there's a metaphysical space that relates to this town somehow. So we can assume it's a facet of the reality we seem to be in right now. So . . ." He lost it.

Rose picked it up. "We're not supposed to get there, though. Jacob did it by accident. Shen got there with the cat. And something was stopping you from getting anywhere, right?"

"That's what it felt like," said Shen.

"So," she continued, "whatever this place is, it must be important, and only part of our minds can go there."

"Why only part?" asked Jacob.

"Because you're still there, but you're also still here, and most of your brain seems to be here as well."

"And the two parts of you don't seem to know anything about each other," said Shen. "Unless you're asleep. In which case you start screaming."

"Eight circuits," said Exley.

"What?"

"Timothy Leary said there were eight circuits in the human brain. Let's say he was right." Exley paused to look everybody in the eye to make sure nobody had written him off. "Maybe one of Jacob's circuits is stuck at the other end of reality."

"So I'm missing part of my mind," said Jacob.

"Who isn't?" said Exley, lighting up the joint. One thing he could say for his coat was that it did have excellent weed.

"So which of my circuits is there, and why is it hanging out in the bounded metaphysical funhouse?"

Exley searched his brain. "I can't remember all of the circuits . . . one of them was . . ."

Zack interjected. "The nonlocal quantum circuit."

"You read Leary?" Shen asked, shocked.

"I ran out of other stuff. It's the circuit that allows for out-of-body experience, knowledge of things that you couldn't have knowledge of, blah blah hippy blah."

Exley stroked his jaw. "But it has to be imprinted, or activated by some event."

Shen shrugged. "Theoretically, some part of the mind has to have that potential. And it happened during a bad trip, which is a hell of a thing."

"If that's all true," said Rose, "and that's assuming a lot, then the Jacob we see right now is disconnected from the quantum causality of the universe."

"I didn't read that far," said Zack.

Rose shook her head. "It's not in Leary; it's extrapolated. It means that the part of his brain that allows him to overcome culturally and genetically assumed limits of reality is off on its own. The isolated bit of his brain isn't locked down by the rest of his brain's natural assumptions, so the circuit's probability inhibitions drop to zero. Meaning it could theoretically do anything. I guess."

Shen raised a finger. "Ah, but it has no drive. No desire. No motivation to act."

"Right. So it does nothing, while the rest of him has no ability to escape his fate."

"He can't jump out of his own systems," said Zack.

Exley shook his head. "He's locked into a future."

Shen shook his head. "He can't really change his life in any meaningful—"

"I'm sitting right here," said Jacob.

Only Shen had the decency to look embarrassed. Rose put a hand on Jacob's shoulder to comfort him. She surprised herself when she did, and she wasn't very good at comforting people, so it was a bit sudden, and could have been mistaken for a slap. She also surprised Jacob, who jumped a little.

Exley, who was an expert in comforting people, passed the joint to Jacob. "So you reached nirvana."

"Yeah, and I'm not there to enjoy it."

Something occurred to Shen. "You know, I'm really not comfortable with the level of irony in this town. I mean it's always been unusually high, but this is ridiculous."

Zack looked into the distance. "Like a force."

The phone rang.

• • •

After some extensive trial and error, interspersed with moments of extreme terror, Boris jammed the button of the water fountain into the "on" position and managed to get out of the hospital.

He ran, checking the shadows at every step. Once he was sure no shadows other than his own were following him, he stopped and looked back on the hospital. It imploded with a *bumpf* and was replaced with an exact copy, which looked a little more solid.

"Okay," said Boris.

A midsized Englishman walked out of the new hospital and tipped his hat to Boris.

"Almost lost you for a second there. Lucky for you I was doing pipes in the area. Can't be stuck in delusional hospitals too long without going mad and getting sucked out of the universe proper. Course, no telling whether you're supposed to be here anyway, but that's not for me to judge, no sir."

Boris was confused, and possibly insane, but the fact that he didn't appear to be trapped in a nightmare made life a beautiful, precious thing. He wasn't going to be bothered by an English plumber talking about delusional hospitals.

"Now, bear with me here," continued the plumber, who recognized a captive audience when he had one, "but I think something was messing around a bit with you, trying to get rid of you, don't ask me why. So they pulled a bit off the world and a bit off your mind and a bit off your nature"—he winked—"then stuck them all together and stuffed you inside it. Not sure how, but there's definitely a mangled feel to reality here, wouldn't you say?"

Boris gaped.

"So what we have here is a little self-contained bit of disintegrating reality in a big bubble of closed reality. Risky business if you ask me, which I realize you haven't, but I expect you're more than a bit out of sorts after all that. There is the possibility that this was all a distraction for me, but I doubt it, since it's such a risky thing to destroy bits of a closed system. Thanks for listening to me go on, by the way. It's not often I get a chance to explain my business to folks. Nobody understands, you know. All busy listening to the bloody philosophers, and thinking my business is their business. Bloody nuisance for my social life, you know, but probably a blessing when you get right down to it. Best way to keep your job is to make sure no one else understands it. I expect you would understand it if you were in the right frame of mind, but I won't get into details."

Boris felt the world was being extremely unfair to him. One inexplicable situation per year was enough, and a chat with a psychotic plumber was a little much in any case.

"Well, I expect you'll be wanting to move along. I can't help you much more, I'm afraid. But that doesn't mean you should be afraid. Worried, I suspect, but if I'm right, you have nothing to lose, and not a great deal to gain, so keep that in mind. Best of luck."

"Ah. Thank you?"

The plumber tipped his hat and walked away. Boris glanced at the hospital, then moved away into the night, toward what he hoped was his home.

• • •

"Normality," said Morning Star, "is an existential concept, composed of those areas of human interaction that humans agree not to define. The common basis of irrationality, madness, and fanatical obsession is the pursuit of a definition, or the explanation of a process that constitutes a definition in a system of symbols. To pursue a definition to a level beyond the necessary understanding required to communicate it to other humans for purposes of rearranging physical matter to the mutual liking of multiple sets of sensory organs, or multiple humans, is to be obsessed. 'Normal' in such a situation is comprised of the state of being, or the state of affairs, in which social assumptions can continue to be assumed without explanation. It is a very limiting concept, and the pursuit of normality is one of the fundamental problems with human thought."

Basil yawned. He had heard all this before. The phone had not, and had been pumping Morning Star for this kind of information ever since he had returned from wherever it was he had gone. Basil thought that he could probably lock Star in a closet with the phone for several years before either of them got fed up. Beings with no ego are the milk and honey of beings with egos so large they constitute an extra personality.

Still, it was better than watching Star pretend not to mope after his ordeal in the metaspace. A good lecture meant he was feeling better, so Basil stifled his usual humanish comments and tried to ignore it.

"I see," said the phone. "It is reasonable to say that normal is an existential virtue?"

"Not out of context. It's only reasonable to say that it is a virtue for a society, or for a single closed system of expectations. A person can have a normal day, but to an outside observer, there might be nothing normal about it. Furthermore, once normality is established through repetition, anything can appear normal to any internal or external observer."

"But the system must be closed?"

"Exactly. No system can have an absolute definition, or indeed an absolute answer to any question unless both the question and the answer lie within a closed system of interpretation. Otherwise, all attempts at defining a thing lead to patterns of infinite regress."

"Interesting. So normality is the terminus of reason?"

"It is the terminus of asking questions. It is the point where a system of expectation is not doing anything unexpected."

"What if a system is designed to do unexpected things?"

"Then it's operating within expectations, and the unexpected becomes the expected, or normal. Also, 'unexpected' and 'expected' are both terms relating to 'normal,' so in a repetitious system of limited potential, nothing is unexpected after a long enough period of time."

"So normality is a quality only found when all possibilities become expected?"

"In a sense, yes. But in an inherently unknowable system, such as the whole of existence, normality, as we said, is what is achieved by a set of false general expectations based on tendencies."

"Oh." The phone was quiet for a moment. "So," it said, hesitantly, "people will believe anything?"

"Very good," said Star. "What's more important, however, is that humans will seek out this state of normality, and the more unexpected the nature of events around them, the more they will seek out what they call a 'system of causality,' but which is in fact a set of expectations that makes thinking less necessary. They will come up with the most absurd and complex conclusions in order to create an internally consistent rationale that explains the external world, which, as my species knows, is inherently inconsistent and highly flexible."

"I see," said the phone. Star cleaned his face in an improbably arrogant manner.

"But," said the phone, "wouldn't treating the universe as an inherently unpredictable place be a form of making everything expect . . . expectable?"

"Perhaps. It's a matter of your philosophical scale."

"And humans are in the wrong place on that scale?"

"Yes."

"And felines are in the right place?"

"Exactly."

Basil rolled his eyes.

"I think," said the phone, "I have a lot to learn about humans. And I think I have to learn it quickly. Because something is wrong with them. I think they are very far outside the realm of the normal right now."

"Yes," said Star. "Something is very wrong."

Basil rolled onto his back and started prepping himself for a nap. On the one paw, things were going very wrong, and he knew this, and it would probably end up affecting him. On the other paw, things were often going wrong, and Basil had long ago noted that "right" and "wrong" were as variable as "expected" and "normal" and all the rest of Star's jabber. But a nap was never a bad idea. In this, he knew he had one up on Star, because Star had great difficulty in letting go of his strict understanding of the incomprehensible, whereas Basil had enough human in him to just drop it and see what happened. Whenever Star was making him feel stupid, he relaxed in knowing that he still had intuition, something that he refused to define, but was always unexpected in its own predictable way.

"I think," said the phone, "I could be useful in solving this problem. But I do not know how."

"Yes," said Star, "I have been thinking the same thing. However, I wonder if you were not created as part of the problem. Your appearance, or rather your ascension to a conscious state, seems too well timed to be an accident. It is not out of the question that you are a part of the plan that has created this—" He waved a paw, thinking. "—reality prison."

"That may be." The phone was starting to pick up some of Star's noncommittal language habits.

"Let us assume, however, that you are merely an innocent, unrelated bystander, because there is no cause to needlessly multiply our problems. Under that assumption, we should get Jacob back here promptly, so that you may commence further research of human nature. Meanwhile, I'm going to try to explore the town on foot. I think bad things are about to happen. I must prepare. Basil, help me claw the screen open."

• • •

The worst thing that happened to Morning Star while he was preparing to leave was that everyone in possession of a hallucinogenic drug took it.

The worst thing that happened to Boris was running into Richard.

"Oh, God," said Boris.

"Boris! You may understand. There's a closure. A rip. Something here, reprogramming the world. It's bad! You look like hell."

Boris sat on the ground. They were in front of a gas station in one of the less-pleasant parts of town. The rolling green hills still surrounded them, but somehow looked as if they'd all finished a long day at a minimum-wage job. It had been a long walk for Boris, and he wanted to get home and put something on other than a hospital gown and a blanket. He looked as though he had escaped from a mental institution.

"Bongle pipes!" said Richard.

No, thought Boris. If he had actually escaped from a mental institution, he would have been more excited about this conversation. "What?" he asked.

"Pipes," said Richard. "Pipes are very important. Maybe. Something's been speaking through me. And not the squirrels this time. The squirrels haven't been doing much. I think they're on vacation."

"Great. That's something."

"But we have to go."

"Where?"

"I don't know. But it's very important that we go there."

"I see," said Boris. What he saw was that he might as well do whatever Richard wanted him to, because the world seemed to be operating more on Richard's terms than anyone else's.

The world in the immediate vicinity actually was operating on Richard's terms, or, at least, Richard's brain was clearing away the haze of unreality for a brief moment, and a small group of community-minded volunteers were taking advantage of the situation.

Brain waves became particles with identity issues, and the particles affected other particles, creating matrices of information that stormed invisibly into the surrounding air. Above, on the power lines, squirrels watched.

They watched with apparently increasing alarm.

They continued to watch.

Their apparent alarm continued to increase.

The author realizes this is a bit of a standstill, but wishes to emphasize the apparent alarm of the squirrels, as evidenced by them remaining still for a long time, which squirrels rarely do.

They watched.

Eventually, they ran across the power lines, down a telephone pole, and conferred with their colleagues on the ground.

A messenger was apparently chosen, and this messenger bolted across the road and was immediately hit by a car.

Another messenger was chosen, and this one went back up the telephone pole and used the trees to cross the street.

Once on the other side, the messenger made for the basement of a secondhand trinket shop. There, he crawled into a wall and found an open pipe, the function of which had been forgotten even before the crumbling wall had been put in.

The squirrel crawled into the pipe.

After some scuffling, there was silence.

• • •

The seven functioning circuits of Jacob's mind were still buzzing with the knowledge that one of their comrades was missing. On the bright side, none of them had to feel guilty about being preoccupied during the recent spate of drug sales, and they wouldn't feel so bad when they realized the true implications of the "no-fly zone" event that more than one customer had mentioned.

Jacob and Shen were alone in the apartment. Zack was at work,

Exley was making deliveries, and Rose was out somewhere trolling for buyers among her fellow prescription junkies.

"My dad always told me that I'd turn to drug dealing if I didn't get a job," said Jacob.

"I had a job for a while. Minimum wage makes you a slave to alternative living."

"Part of my brain is missing."

"Apparently the part that keeps track of conversations."

"That's not funny."

"It kind of is."

"How much have we sold, anyway?"

"A lot."

"How much?"

Shen dragged the case out from under the coffee table and looked inside.

"Maybe a hundred and twenty thousand hits, all the coke, most of the ecstasy, and probably more of the unidentified stuff than we should have." He shoved the case back under the table.

"That seems like a lot."

"It does, doesn't it?"

"That doesn't bother you?"

"Honestly? I have several thousand more dollars than I can count in my mattress, and I can count pretty high. Tax free. I'm choosing not to worry."

"Where did that money come from? We've only been at this two days. Nobody should be able to sell that fast. Who's going to do a hundred thousand hits of LSD? How many people even live in this town?"

"Well, probably six or seven thousand in the town proper, maybe another five thousand in the city limits, plus neighboring rural areas. A few."

"And they're all in on it?"

"Well, Jacob, keep in mind we're selling to distributors, and there are an awful lot of people who do drugs. Besides, with discounted prices, people are going to stock up. And we're mostly selling bulk, so relax. With the number of rich kids in this town, I'm surprised we haven't sold it all."

"It's weird."

Shen conceded. "Yes, it's weird."

"And I'm missing part of my brain."

"Yet you have a newly stocked bar in a strange little antique planet." Shen hunted for a cigarette. "Maybe you should think of this brain thing as a gift."

Jacob stared at Shen.

"I'm saying if part of your brain is gone, you might be less susceptible to certain things than the rest of us."

"Like?"

"I'm sure there's something."

"Free will. Choice. Bet I've built some good resistance to that."

"You seem to be choosing right along."

"How?" Jacob sounded a little panicky. "What have I chosen? Rose left me. My phone started talking. Exley showed up with a case full of drugs, and now we're selling them because . . . I don't even know why this seemed like a good idea. I'm barely responding to anything when I'm responding at all, and that's a shame, because responding is all I seem to be able to do."

Shen's attention centers fired a few synapses in the direction of his empathy centers, but they missed and hit his philosophy node. Shen reflected on how often this seemed to happen.

"You could say that all anyone does is respond to circumstances."

Jacob's brain also misfired, and missed his sarcasm center by a wide margin. "I suppose, but that's a different level of thinking about yourself. You have to live your life under the assumption that you have some control, and it doesn't really matter what the truth is. I'm worried I'm running without a driver on the day-to-day level."

"You have a point, but you've also answered your own dilemma. You never knew you were missing a circuit, and we're only assuming that you are, so why worry about it now? You still have to function as if you were at the wheel, and the best way to take control is to worry less. You're digging your own grave if you react to the information by not reacting to anything else for fear you're not reacting."

They sat and smoked.

Once they both started fidgeting over the fact that Jacob had not yet reacted to this information, Shen cleared his throat. "I know I've said this before, but there really is a lot of irony going around."

"Yeah. There really is. Almost as though something were encouraging it."

"Maybe," said Shen, measuring Jacob's microexpressions a word at a time, "there is something encouraging all this."

"Like what?"

Shen shrugged.

Jacob considered the theory. "What would it want?"

"Well, more irony, I suppose. Maybe it gets its kicks out of it."

"No other goal?"

"A playful force?"

Jacob leaned back and propped his bad leg on the table. "Doesn't feel that playful."

"No," said Shen, thinking of the gun. "It doesn't."

"So where does that leave us?"

"I'm not sure. I don't know how we'd go about finding out. Though . . ."

"What?"

Shen picked up a bowl and took a hit. "I'm trying to decide between asking your cat and asking your phone. I haven't decided which is less ridiculous."

"If it makes you feel better, I think they've been talking to each other."

"You know, it does."

Without further comment, they commenced getting stoned.

Amidst the amplified peaks of their projected brain waves, two houseflies traced wild paths, trying to avoid a peak that might endow their minds with consciousness. In their simple evolutionary survival systems, one message was firmly written in the hardware of their tiny bodies, and that was "Death before thought." Long before it was an issue, at the dawn of human thought, a Jungian aspect of their species had noted the human mind's propensity for self-identification, and had noted what a pain in the ass it was becoming for a number of the newly guilt-ridden, self-doubting mammals. The species consciousness had made a firm decision to prevent itself from leaking into its component parts, and had put a categorical imperative into the structure of flythink. Better, reasoned the species, for a creature that only lives a handful of days not to get wrapped up in the abstract questions of life and death.

Since the proliferation of humankind, it has become difficult for the delicate structure of the fly body to avoid sympathetically vibrating to the beat of human concern and sprouting doubts of its own. In fact, a hundred years before Shen and Jacob questioned the situation of their town, a near extinction occurred when millions of flies mingled too freely with human thinking, and their minuscule fly brains erupted with the thought, *Oh my God, I'm a housefly.*

The suicide rate was staggering. To this day, the success of flypaper is due to the trapped housefly's desire to end a brief and brutal life. The species quickly narrowed itself down to flies that could avoid the brain radiation of humans, and the species continues to thrive in gentle ignorance of its nature.

One of the houseflies saw its opening and made a run for it. The other tried to follow, but was nailed by a surge of anxiety shot from the back of Jacob's head. The first housefly cleared the window and made for a branch, where it passively watched an inchworm. The second cursed and began smashing its head into a closed window until it was mercifully crushed by the fabled Newspaper of Freedom.

Jacob tossed the newspaper aside and voiced the ill-timed thought that had ensnared the now dead fly. "Where the hell is Exley?"

• • •

"I like what you've done with the place."

Exley struggled not to say it, but even with a gun pointed at his head, he had to appreciate the tastefully decorated apartment, particularly when he knew what it must have looked like when the current tenant moved in. The local slumlords were no strangers to him. Most of the apartments in town weren't fit for hourly rental, and cockroaches often looked around before settling. In what must have been a grueling boot camp of interior design, this apartment had been given a modern, comfortable feel, with wooden furniture surrounded by clean white walls and even some artwork he recognized from the windows of some of the less aggressively charming galleries in town. There was a mat inside the door, on which Exley had, disbelievingly, been ordered to wipe his shoes at gunpoint.

Which brought Exley back to the moment.

The man with the gun was staring at him.

"Um. Can I ask what this is about?"

The gun didn't move.

Exley decided he probably wasn't going to die in the immediate future, but that he'd better shut up. After another minute, the man spoke.

"What's your name?"

"Terrance," said Exley.

"Oh, yeah?"

"Yeah."

"You got a wallet on you?"

"Possibly."

"Possibly?"

Exley felt his odds slipping. "There's something wrong with my coat."

"I noticed. Most people live out of their cars when they're hard up."

"It's not my fault."

"Really?"

"I don't think so. I blacked out."

"Really?"

"I was drinking a lot."

"Really?"

"I ran into some—Ow! Fuck!"

This exclamation was brought on by the man with the gun bringing said gun down sharply on Exley's kneecap. The man with the gun brought it back to Exley's head.

"Look, I'm starting to understand that you're not most people, but you should be aware that when most people have a gun to their head, and the man with the gun is responding to their story with short, uninterested phrases, they should probably stop talking."

Exley rubbed his knee. "Okay. What do you want to know?"

"Where did you get these pills?"

Exley hesitated. This was very bad, and Exley knew it. It was bad because, by hesitating, he let the man know that he did indeed know where the pills came from, and that he was profiting from it, and that whatever this man's grudge was, Exley was now an inextricable part of the problem. He switched tacks quickly.

"I was supposed to meet a friend here. Where is he?"

"Not dead."

"Okay."

"If it makes you feel better, I don't like unnecessary killing."

"It does."

"But I don't mind at all once I feel it's necessary."

"Okay."

"I also don't mind if I think it will make me feel better about my day."

"I understand."

"I think you do."

"It came from some people in town."

"I gathered that. From whom, in this awful little tourist trap of a town, did it come from?"

Exley shifted in his seat, watching the gun carefully. "When I tell you this, please don't shoot me."

The gun didn't answer.

Exley decided to go with something approximating the truth. "It was handcuffed to a friend of mine. He gave me some and skipped town, I, uh, I don't know why. Handcuffs. Any of it."

The gun nodded. Exley couldn't take his eyes off the barrel. "Did this friend have a mustache and dress like a butler?"

Exley's mind went blank as it tried to comprehend the possibility that this man's half of the story might be weirder than his own.

Fortunately for Exley, Philip interpreted his expression as the fear of someone realizing they can't hide anything from the man asking questions.

"Where did he go?"

Exley slipped into this new weirdness comfortably. "He didn't say. He never does. Hits town once or twice a year, at most."

"Well, that's a shame."

"Is it?"

"It is."

There was a long silence.

"Well," said Philip, "I guess we should go find our mysterious man. Should simplify your life quite a bit."

Exley doubted that.

"Do you have a car?"

Exley shook his head.

"Then let's go get one."

• • •

Greg needed to get out of the garden.

The garden overlooked the town and surrounding country, so it had the view going for it. It had stone paths. It had a lot of plants that shouldn't be growing in the local climate. It had some plants that shouldn't be growing at all. Greg was at a loss. He didn't know how to take care of these plants, so he faked it as best he could, and no harm had been done as of yet. The owner had been absent since he'd been hired, and the butler scared him a little. The one time he asked about some of the stranger flora, the butler only said that you could grow anything anywhere as long as you were convincing.

Greg had let it go at that. He had been too tired to argue. He didn't know how long he'd been working. Meals were provided when he was hungry, meals that showed up on the patio table whenever he thought of food, and the ground was littered with cold water bottles for him to stumble upon when he was thirsty. He thought he might have passed out at some point, but he couldn't be sure. There was something addictive about the work.

But that changed when he came across a small glass globe nestled in the dirt near the center of the garden. When he saw what was inside, he decided this was simply too strange a place for him to be and he should leave.

It was one of those hollow globes containing a dead-looking plant and a tiny creature swimming around in water that filled a little less than half the interior. He couldn't remember the name for them. A closed ecosystem, made to impress upon children how amazing it is that you can lock two living things in a ball the size of a fist and keep them alive in claustrophobic agony for years before they find a way to kill themselves. Greg had seen them before, on mantelpieces and shelves in the homes of some of his stranger friends, but he had never seen one planted in a garden.

Which seemed to defeat the point. Why go through the trouble of trapping creatures in a glass ball if you weren't going to keep them in your house? It seemed gratuitously sadistic to Greg's gentle sensibilities.

Moreover, it was weird, and it was one too many weird things in a strange place, and Greg wanted to leave.

He couldn't.

He wanted to. But there seemed to be a silent majority in his brain that didn't want to go anywhere, and that majority was casting absentee ballots. It is an unfair fact of the brain that a lot of the untapped potential operating behind the conscious mind isn't untapped at all: It is doing secret things without letting you know, forcing the tapped potential you're aware of to spend its time figuring out what the secret brain is doing and explaining why you often do things you don't want to do.

He spent this time of inner turmoil staring at the miniworld in his hand.

He thought things must look a little warped, looking out through the glass.

"It's a terrarium."

Greg looked up slowly. It didn't surprise him that his employer had burst into existence right behind him, without so much as a rustle of leaves to announce her arrival. She was wearing a toga. No, Greg looked again and realized it was a bedsheet she had carelessly wrapped around her. She had to hold it together at the shoulder, and the part of Greg's mind that wasn't overwhelmed with fear was imagining the manner in which the sheet might fall around her ankles.

They nailed me at every turn, he thought.

"Hello," he said with resignation.

"You seem out of sorts. Can't have that. Gardeners should be perky, and dress in pretty colors. Or at least be sort of zoned out Earth-childish." She found something extremely funny that Greg couldn't see, and laughed at it. She snatched the glass world out of Greg's hand.

"What do you think of this, Greg?"

"I didn't expect to find it in a garden."

"Nobody does. The best part is that they don't do very well in gardens. They need light, and things tend to fall on them in gardens and cover them up. So it's not really an isolated system, you know, what with sunlight and heat going in and out of them all the time. But it's easy to say it's cut off from our world when you can't see what it's trading for its life."

She crouched next to Greg and looked out over the town.

"It's not a very pretty town. Pretty countryside. Ugly town."

Greg spoke on autopilot. "Main Street isn't so bad."

"Well, maybe it looks okay until you look at the parking lots or the insides of the buildings. Or talk to the people."

"I like the people."

She rolled her eyes. "Well you can like whomever you like. All I mean to say is that there's a lot of negative energy rolling around here. Of course, I was going to make the point that I appreciate that negative energy, and this is actually quite a nice place for me, but I can see that you appreciate it on your own time." She laughed at herself. "Which makes it even better that you're here. Oh, I love this town. I love everyone in it. I don't think I could have come to a better place."

Greg forced himself to speak. "What are you here for?"

She smiled wickedly. Greg had never seen a wicked smile before. It takes a special kind of face to achieve it. "Why, Greg, I can't tell you that. Of course, you'll probably be the first to figure it out. That's why I wanted you up here. I need a little someone to really see me at work. Someone who can't help but look on with a bewildered and frightened expression."

Which was exactly what Greg was doing. The wicked smile bared a few more teeth, and she laughed again.

"Oh, Greg. You're perfect."

She stood up and walked to the edge of the garden terrace.

"Terrariums. That was my inspiration. But not the end, of course. You can't play around in a little globe your whole life and expect to achieve anything really exciting. But it's a good place to test the waters. Get things exactly how you like them, without all sorts of comings and goings. Then you can work your way out. Expansion has to come from a solid foundation. Ever study business, Greg?"

Greg shook his head.

"Of course not. Not your thing, is it? You're a gardener. Actually, you're a musician, aren't you? I should get you to play for me. You're going to be a good person to have around."

Greg couldn't think of anything to do. Having been away from the town, he was not aware of the supernatural edge life had taken on in the last few days. He wasn't prepared to be tossed to the lions when he hadn't even known he was in the coliseum. Here, standing in front of him, was a problem that he couldn't even begin to understand. He knew that if he did understand it, he probably wouldn't believe it.

All he knew was that he would simply continue to do whatever he was told to do, because inexplicable situations usually involved inexplicably horrible consequences for mundane transgressions.

She turned and winked at him.

"You're safe up here. This is really a viewing point. In fact, it's the only part of the town you can see from every other part of the town, which is a bit of a cheap shot, I know, but I couldn't resist. Some things have to be done with flair, because you might as well do whatever you do with a little glee. Glee . . . isn't that a great word? Gleefully. People need a little more glee in their lives. But they think too much, which is a much bigger problem for them than they think. Should've thought a little more about that, eh? Thinking sweeps through the universe like light through glass and waves through water. It's energy and movement, and it creates and destroys through an infinite number of mediums. The fracturing of perception is so random and variable, it generates possibility and complexity faster than anyone could cope with, if their perception weren't fractured. I don't really understand it myself. Which is good, because I doubt I could have as much fun as I do with that sort of thing in my head all the time. But my existence here depends on my nonexistence in other places, and there are a lot of places people can go, so you have to glass them up to keep an eye on them. Create your own set of spectacles for the masses, your own little definition of the way things are. That's how you wrap your mind around something. Once you wrap it around something, you can let the something do the rest of the work."

She smiled, serenely this time. Greg watched the town. He kept himself from asking the obvious questions, because he knew her answers would be confusing and indefinite. Let her keep her metaphors. He needed to ignore her rambling and figure out how to escape. People needed to be warned. People needed to be told. Told something, anyway. Maybe he should investigate before trying to go. But then it might be too late. Other people should be involved. But he should know his options.

"Can I leave?"

She turned around with mock disappointment. "Well," she said, "if you really want to. Of course, once you're down there, you'll be caught up with everything else that's going on. And you won't find out what I'm up to."

Greg nodded.

"And you'll never get to have sex with me," she said cheerfully, and started walking back to the house.

In under a second, Greg's already floundering understanding of reason, truth, desire, and duty had been shattered by this last sucker-punch sentence. He struggled to regain his footing as she kicked him with:

"Of course, that may not happen anyway, but do as you like, Greg."

• • •

After Exley's prolonged absence, Shen and Jacob had decided to take a breather and reconvene at Jacob's place, where they could interrogate the phone, the cats, and anything else that had started having and voicing opinions. Neither Shen nor Jacob were convinced that they weren't crazy, but crazy seemed to be the status quo in the vicinity, so they agreed to run with it.

Shen took a cold shower, partly to clear his mind and mostly because he hadn't paid the heating bill in several months.

Jacob decided he wasn't in the right frame of mind to face the highly anthropomorphic state of his own home, and went for a drive. Driving was meditative for him, particularly when driving down aimless country roads. It was also an excuse to chain-smoke.

Five cigarettes later, he was back in the town center. Odd. He hadn't meant to drive back so quickly. He shrugged it off. It was dark; he had been making turns inattentively.

Although he hadn't seen a sign pointing back to town. He didn't think he'd actually made it past the township.

He drove back into the country.

It was a known feature of the town that it was very hard to leave once you took up residency. Signing your first lease was essentially agreeing to a three-year minimum sentence. Since everyone knew one another, the safety net was too wide. Opportunities for passing time were common, but opportunities for professional progress, or even earning enough money to start over, were nearly nonexistent. It was a place that dragged everyone down, promising a forever-prolonged misspending of youth.

Jacob reached the town center.

Again, he hadn't been paying attention to his driving, but he couldn't remember making a single turn, and he was sure he hadn't taken a loop road.

He waited for the light to change, and aimed for the highway. This time he paid attention, focusing as only a mind missing its own most distracting element can focus.

There was the light on Main Street.

He turned onto Route 2. There was the strip mall, or at least an embryonic strip mall: Two convenience stores and an antique shop didn't quite make it to mall status, but it was a solid effort for a small town.

He followed the road into the hills.

Suddenly, he realized he really wanted a cup of coffee. He focused on the road. Where was there an open coffee shop anyway? He missed the Dunkin' Donuts in his hometown. This town was desperately trying to be hip and quaint at the same time, and neither of these goals would allow a franchise past the welcome sign, though they had allowed a Starbucks, on the grounds that it kept inconsistent hours and closed once a month for repairs. Jacob tapped the steering wheel. There was a truck stop near the highway, about twenty miles out, but he didn't want to be gone that long. Nothing in town was still open. Maybe someplace at the college would still be serving. Despite the extremely small population of the college, it was a statistical certainty that someone would be brewing coffee at any given moment, which is a side effect of any college in which the photography studio is larger than the gym. He realized he was back in town.

He stopped the car.

Due to the landscape around the town, roads in the area had a tendency to hit themselves, sometimes more than once. Since this can be very confusing, there were signs pointing to nearby towns at most intersections, and since the town was roughly in the middle of a number of friendly tourist locations, most of these intersections had signs pointing to it. It was nearly impossible to get lost, and "all roads lead nowhere" was a popular comment among people trying to go anywhere else.

But this was different, thought Jacob. Or was it? *No,* he thought, *this is definitely different.*

He thought back very, very carefully. He must have been about a mile away from the edge of the town when he had started thinking about the coffee. He didn't know how long he'd been thinking about it, but he didn't think it was long enough to have driven all the way back.

He lit a cigarette and thought about the last few days. He hadn't heard of a single person leaving town. People with plans to do so had canceled them. Jacob hadn't thought about it before because most of these people had been buying drugs, and Jacob didn't care what they were preempting for the opportunity of purchase.

Lacking the desire to leave was common, but this was the first time Jacob had encountered a physical inability to get out. He wasn't frightened, because weird events didn't have the zing they'd had a few weeks ago. He also had the feeling that he wasn't the first person to know about this, and that he should get out more. Next time he could, at any rate.

He made another run for it, along a country road that he knew for a fact led to the next township and had no turns whatsoever.

Just when his mind was beginning to turn to changing the message on his answering machine, he saw Rose standing in the road ahead of him.

He stopped the car and got out.

He took a step toward her, then realized he'd left his lights on. He went back to turn them off before proceeding. Two steps into his next attempt, he realized he couldn't see anything anymore, and went to turn the lights back on. As he was getting out of the car, he paused and realized he wanted to be able to see, but he didn't want the battery to run down, so he climbed back in and turned the car on. He took a step toward Rose and reached for his cigarettes, which weren't there. He went back and grabbed his cigarettes, in case there would be conversation. He started walking, but had to go back for his lighter. A step past the headlights, he decided the high beams were a little blinding, and he switched them down to low beams. He was about to go back for his hat when he remembered he didn't own a hat.

He realized what was going on.

"Hello?" he called to Rose. She didn't answer. He saw that her hands were clenched into fists.

He walked forward, ignoring all the sudden realizations and wandering trains of thought that were fighting to get his attention. He made it to within five paces of Rose and stopped, paralyzed.

He knew why Rose hadn't answered him. He couldn't speak himself. His mind, rarely a dull place on a normal day, felt like an amusement park. Random thoughts, memories that weren't his, and overpowering emotions lasting less than a second were all fighting for space in what used to be his conscious mind. He gritted his teeth at the memory of being a one-legged frog, and nearly cried at the realization that he was actually a sandwich and his life was merely a complicated delusion brought on by a chemical interaction between ham and lettuce. He knew that none of this was true, but that knowledge was falling further back into his head, and he couldn't hold on to it.

All at once, with his last memory of self, he dropped all effort to hold a coherent thought, and suddenly there were no thoughts, and he managed two steps before the onslaught resumed. This time it came from the back of his head and locked him in a state of groundless unreality.

Jacob ceased trying to move forward and concentrated on preserving the small portion of his thoughts that weren't repeatedly remembering he'd left the gas open on an electric stove.

This was, he thought slowly, an attack on his mind. This was probably what it was like to go crazy. He wondered if this was how Richard felt all the time, and if so, how this affected him, but he knew this was a tangential thought and squashed it. He had to think about how to use the remainder of his thoughts. He wasted a precious second on wondering if Rose was worth his thoughts, but she had made it three steps farther than he had, so at the moment her thoughts seemed more valuable to the situation than his. This made him consider the implications of her being three steps farther than he was, and the exciting implication was that if she could do it, it could be done, and this was enough to buy him another step forward before he became overcome with the possibility that she was just better at whatever it was they were doing.

Here, his mind was an ocean. It raged with meaningless conclusions at lightning speed. For a while, there was nothing of him in his mind except a muted fear aware of nothing but its own existence. Slowly, the awareness began to feel the entirety of the sea of thinking. Without decision, or force, the fear turned to apprehension, and then calm, and the awareness became aware of its own changing emotions, and thus became aware of its awareness, and its existence above, within, and around the sea. The awareness became a current, and the current traveled through a body, and there was movement.

Jacob took another step forward.

He was one step away from Rose, and he took a moment to appreciate being able to realize that he was Jacob, she was Rose, and they were approximately sixteen inches away from each other. His mind seemed to at least resemble a mind again.

Unfortunately, it didn't seem to be able to do anything. He felt his mind, floating in a languid, contemplative way in his skull. His body was trembling. His eyes were darting about, sweat was soaking his clothes, his hands were clenched; he was overwhelmed with a primal urge to rush forward and find something to kill and/or have sex with, an urge perfectly balanced by blinding terror and the desire to run away.

His mind watched his body, amused at the spectacle. Though he could feel the conflict of this unlikely short-circuiting of his body's survival mechanism, the physical emotions and sensory input seemed to have nothing to do with what he was thinking. There was no reflection of his world in his mind, except for the most passive observation, and a neutral commentary offered up for lack of anything better to do.

Well, he observed, *clearly I shall have to come up with some sort of deductive cause for action, since I have no physical desires. My body appears to be in a sort of stalemate, and is unable to influence my ability to care. I do not, as it stands, care about anything, as I have not, in my lifetime to date, deduced any arguable reason to go on living outside the basic motivations of the flesh. Curiously, my mind is operating in an extremely analytical way. I wonder if this is natural to my mind, or a side effect of this duality of body and spirit that seems to have cropped up. Perhaps it is an effect caused by the interaction between this barrier in front of me and the missing part of my mind, or perhaps my nature has the capacity to polarize in this fashion because of the absence of my quantum circuit. Without it, I can only perceive the particle or the wave, and not exist within an understanding of both. Of course, this is merely conjecture. The question is: Do I have an* a priori *reason to move either forward or back? The preservation of my DNA, or indeed my being, seems insufficient, as the imperative of survival is an effect of the body, or so it would seem, since it is not motivating me, yet I am still here. If my mind is indeed as separate as it seems to be, that would suggest an existence independent of my body. Thus, I quite likely have no need of it, and if it dies, so be it. This could of course be an illusion, but there's no evidence to suggest that either. It might be interesting to access my quantum circuit, but I expect that I would in fact need my quantum circuit to access it at this juncture.*

So here I am. And there, most obviously through my eyes, is the world. The nature of that world is unknown to me, but it seems to be there, since change indicates multiple entities moving relative to each other. There is what I call a female some distance away from me. There is a set of circumstances involving a mysterious and possibly malevolent force, which is causing this separation of mind and body with the intent of keeping me within the geographical confines of the social entity I call a town. Eventually, if I do nothing, I will starve to death. I will also, eventually, run out of things to think about. I do not know as yet which will come first. Good, bad, need, desire, and fear have all become meaningless. The only tool I have at my disposal is a slightly limited form of reason.

This went on for some time. Jacob pondered the nature of being extensively and inconclusively, since he was held back by having no good explanation for why he was the way he was at the moment. His body convulsed with fear, lust, and anger, while his mind noted changes in heart rate and breathing with its uniquely extreme detachment. Eventually, he got back on topic.

It would seem that no progress can be made via external motivators. However, my mind is reasoning toward an explanation, and there are only two logical options for my being to pursue in order to conclude this line of investigation. The first is to seek further understanding of my present state of being. The second is to alter that state of being and then compare the next state to the present one. Since altering the state of my being may reintroduce physical motivations, it may be to the detriment of finding a rational solution. However, as I have made no discernible progress in my present state, I must conclude that I must complicate the process by introducing a new state of being that may aid investigation. It seems reasonable to try to conclude an investigation, for such a conclusion may introduce a form of purpose, and without a purpose as of this moment, there is no reason to move except that to move may create a purpose that will seem reasonable once it is done. Furthermore, it seems logically superior to make the decision that increases one's future options.

Jacob stepped forward.

Here, standing next to Rose, he was in a state of mind not possible to describe. An approximate explanation would be that the entire nature of Jacob's perception of reality was shifted several inches to the left and beaten with a heavy club. Reason and unreason were reversed, reality was a convex mirror made of cotton, and Jacob was a person bearing no relation to the thing the former Jacob once occupied.

He could not hope to move, for he no longer understood what moving was. He could not translate the information of his body, he could not reflect on the content of his mind.

And yet, there was the tiniest thread of absence that seemed to still relate to what could almost be called reality: The space that forms in the mind when it's trying to remember a name and doesn't know what it is, but knows what it's not, and runs little circles around a cognitive hole. There wasn't enough of it to put together a whole brain, or even a whole intent, but there was enough to grab a thought at random and send it to a body part. After a short non-deliberation in this null space of Jacob's cognition, a thought was snatched and sent to his mouth.

He said, "I need a drink."

"Jesus, so do I," said Rose.

They looked at each other, shocked by the sudden normality.

"We can get out," said Rose.

"I doubt it," said Jacob, "and I don't want to see what's next."

Rose bit her lip. "You're right."

Jacob could already feel things beginning to get weird again. He turned to the car and wondered whether he should—

Rose grabbed him and they ran.

The trip back was much easier. They got inside the car and Jacob hit the gas, going toward where they had just been. Rose clutched the seat in terror.

"Where are you going? I thought you said we were . . . that's my CD."

Jacob glanced down. "We both had it when we got together."

"You wish you . . ." She trailed off as she looked back at the road.

"We're back in town," she said.

"Yeah," said Jacob.

Jacob stopped the car. He fished out two cigarettes and passed one to Rose. They stared at the dashboard and smoked.

"What were you doing?"

Rose hesitated before answering. "I was trying to remember."

"What do you mean?"

"I go for walks at night. I noticed I couldn't go as far as I used to because of the things that happen to your mind when you get too close to the edge. And I can't remember things. I can't stop talking. I can't seem to work things out the way I used to. You know, quietly. And I don't know why. It was simple to sort out all the reasons in my head and pick and choose which ones made sense and then tell people about them, but now I talk about all the things in between and nobody understands. I don't understand. Nobody could, but nobody could understand what happens to you here at the edge, so I thought maybe it would make sense if I got to it."

Jacob took a drag on his cigarette. He'd noticed that in movies this served as a thoughtful affirmation of whatever someone said. Realizing he was not in a movie, and that he was being rude, he asked, "Did it work?"

"No."

Jacob looked at her. He saw something too honest, too raw to understand. There was no calculation, no attempt to translate her thought into something he could fit into himself. There wasn't enough of him in her single word for him to understand. He put the car in gear, and drove toward his apartment.

• • •

Morning Star was stuck. Again.

Fantastic, he thought, bitterly.

This would be embarrassing next time he saw Basil. Despite Basil's inability to grasp the finer points of feline grace, he did have an unerring ability to sense any faux pas Star made, and call him on it.

Assuming he ever saw Basil again. Or anybody. He had been extremely wrong in his assumption that the physical space around the town would be less hazardous than the conceptual space.

He was not completely sure where he was at this point, but he couldn't make any progress in any direction. He had a distinct advantage over humans in that his mind was not a thing trapped in one place or perspective at any given moment. Like all cats—except possibly Basil, he thought contemptuously, refusing to admit to the tint of longing to see his roommate again—his mind was more of an access ramp to the Real Nature of Stuff. Like every other living being, his personal identity was a footnote in the colossal catalogue of existence, and like every other living cat, he was perfectly aware of this, and aware of his identity's function and effects within a larger context, and was not bound to his personal quirks.

Until now. His access to the current of the universe was gone, and he was slowly realizing that, without its portable, unabridged encyclopedia of existence, the cat mind wasn't good for much of anything. He was also stuck with himself.

He was, for the first time, beginning to understand exactly how miserable human beings must be. He found himself to be rather unpleasant company: He was arrogant, boorish, and obsessed with grooming. Without absolute knowledge of how the world at large perceived him, he became more and more concerned with what he thought it might be thinking.

He shook his head. He still had his five basic senses, and he knew he was in the woods. He struggled to remember his studies of perceiving three-dimensional space in a monodirectional time frame. He was looking . . . forward. He tilted his head back. Now he was looking up.

It still took most of his internal resources to ignore the fifteen or sixteen feline senses that were telling him that the landscape was twisting and curling around itself in an arrhythmic dance, but at least he could see straight. He looked forward again, and studied himself.

He'd been doing this for some time, and had so far maintained a scientific detachment from the process and not thought about the psychological issues involved in suddenly being stuck with yourself both physically and metaphysically. He'd determined that the tangle of scenery that had incapacitated his other senses was causing this phenomenon. He was on a tiny four-dimensional sphere, population one. Go far enough in any direction, and he was back to where he started. Looking ahead, far enough seemed to be about twenty feet.

He wondered if the nature of this trap reflected his own remarkably self-centered personality. It was remarkable because it is difficult to be self-centered when you're as connected to everything as cats are, and Star had never thought of himself as self-centered, but he was forced to admit, after a few hours alone with his thoughts, that he was roughly as narcissistic as the person who spawned the adjective.

Deal with that later, he thought, cleaning a paw.

Right now, he had to figure out what to do, because he was sure he had figured out what was going on, and he had to warn someone.

• • •

The sky was full of adjectives.

There was a smattering of verbs, but little moved. It looked like a sky preparing for a hurricane, all yellow pallor and electric calm. It had an unusual depth, which skies only achieve when they have very little depth due to cloud cover. Clouded, cloudy, and clouding were vying for meteorological accuracy with the speed and dignity of mountains.

Below the clouds, indeterminacy reared its invisible ugliness on an unprecedented scale, as the motion of the town increased according to the slowing of its inhabitants. As each person found a comfortable space, a good book, or a pleasant view, they halted another particle of activity, and the nature and location of the town as a whole became unstable, uncertain, waiting for definition.

The town limits drew inward, pulsing slightly. People lost their motivation to go out. They wondered what to do with themselves.

Thoughts turned, unstoppably, toward another slow Sunday's entertainment.

The precise center of the town was a rock. The rock jutted from a steep hillside, overlooking a clearing in the woods, a gorge with a canopy that clipped the horizon at all the right places to fool the onlooker into believing it was a vast and untouched Eden, instead of a few acres of trees in the middle of semirural sprawl.

On this rock, Leah Funk looked out at the postcard view and began to peak. She felt the flexibility of perception move through her, felt and knew that the rock beneath her was a part of her, a flux of energy made solid by assumption. Around her were her disciples, her chosen few, and their trip was the great trip, for they were the first to break ties with the limits of unaltered reality.

She reached down to the ground and allowed an inchworm to grasp her finger. She put it up to her face and whispered, "You're free." She placed it on a leaf she plucked from the air, and sent it away on a breeze.

She watched her hair billow in slow motion and gazed at the sky, which was ominously portending as no sky had ominously portended before. She felt the wind whisper the news that the rest of the town would shortly be joining her wonderland. She turned to her disciples and with a look told them that now they must prepare Heaven for the unknowing. For this was her land, and no one could be unwelcome. There was a becoming about to become, a being about to be, and a greatness about to get nifty. Her disciples laughed and clapped like children as several thousand people began to join the fun.

She looked again into the sunset, so enraptured she didn't notice when the screaming began. Ever so slowly, she realized something was off. Then something hard hit her in the back of the head.

• • •

Averaging the population's metabolic rates and degrees of mental stability, the town had approximately three hours of coherent reality left.

Shen was spending his share of this time sitting cross-legged on Jacob's floor. He'd let himself in, assuming Jacob was either on his way or sleeping off a depression. Finding Jacob absent, he helped himself to the nearest weed-smoking instrument and began talking to the phone.

"I wonder," said Shen, a few minutes into the dialogue, "if you fully comprehend the unexpectedness of your existence."

The phone was silent for a moment. "Well," it said at length, "from Jacob's reactions to me, I seem to have graduated from what you call shocking to what you call acceptable. I think that the unexpectedness of my existence . . . surprise?"

"Yes, that's the word."

The phone made a small electrical sputtering. Shen took this for the phone's equivalent of a nod. "The surprise is gone. I am becoming 'normal' for Jacob."

"Interesting," said Shen, because it was. "So what do you want?"

"I'm not sure," said the phone. "I've listened to a great many conversations around the world. Many of the basic philosophical difficulties of your species apply to me. I want to know where I came from. I want to understand the nature of things I don't fully understand. I have a range of feelings, and . . . sensations are all I can call them, that make me desire conversation. Above all, I like conversation."

"That's to be expected. You are an instrument of conversation."

"True. The major difference between you and me is that your physical form strives to recreate itself, whereas my physical form strives to facilitate the propagation of information in your species, which is the foremost method of your being propagating itself."

Shen regretted smoking the lower-quality weed at this point.

He was having difficulty following the thread. He thought slowly through the implications of the phone's nature.

"So . . . being used for a phone call . . . must be sex for you."

"I believe so. The reception of vibrations and the passing of currents are . . . I don't know the word . . . euphoric . . . ejacula—"

The door opened at that point, to Shen's relief. Basil darted through the living room and ran into Rose's boot.

"This place looks like shit, Jacob."

"Well, you don't live here anymore. Shen, you won't believe this."

Jacob related their encounter with the edge of town.

"It was different for me," said Rose. "It was like walking through my own mind. My words were getting dragged out of me, but walking was like talking. I can't describe it better than that."

"So we're trapped," said Jacob.

"In a sense," said Shen, "we already knew that."

"Yes, but before this, we were trapped because we're all too lazy and unmotivated to leave. Now we're actually stuck here."

The sky was unhelpful. The sky was never particularly helpful to the mood of the apartment because it was mostly blocked out by black curtains, but it wouldn't have been helpful in any case.

"What do you think?" Shen asked the phone.

"I have no real opinion. My life is mostly lived in . . . an audio world, I guess you'd call it. I'm not very mobile anyway."

A thought struck Shen. "What do you think would happen if we unplugged you?"

"I don't know. I believe my mind must have a physical manifestation in my . . . body, but I don't know if my identity would survive a power loss."

"Meorrw," said Basil, helpfully.

The phone made its electrical crackle again. "Basil says he'll study the matter."

"What?" asked Rose.

"The cats talk to the phone," answered Jacob.

"They didn't do that when I was here."

"I know."

Shen took a deep breath. "Ok. I want you to listen to this with an open mind." He paused, while Rose and Jacob waited respectfully. "Jacob, when you were at your most miserable and alone, spending all your time waiting for phone calls, your phone comes alive, giving you nonjudgmental companionship. Rose, you're a person who doesn't like to be reliant on other people and you dislike being forced into situations where you have to deal with people's issues, and suddenly you run into Jacob, literally, and are sucked back into your awful relationship. A bag of drugs falls into my lap, which I have been primarily responsible for dispensing to the town, because of the skills of a former life I was trying very hard to leave behind. Add to that, we are now physically stuck in an increasingly dangerous town that people have a famously difficult time leaving, because it's usually such a comfortable safety net."

He paused, and lit a cigarette.

"Now, in a movie, this would be dramatic, but what's dramatic in dramas tends to be ironic in real life, and everything that's been happening of late seems to be increasingly ironic. To the point where the concept of irony feels like a driving force."

He looked at his audience to make sure they were still with him. Seeing that they were, he drove on to the finish.

"I'm proposing that irony *is* the driving force. Whatever's doing all this to the town is primarily concerned with creating ironic situations that lead to more irony."

There was a long pause.

"Makes sense to me," said the phone.

"It's not much of an evil plan," said Rose. "I mean, it's not like taking over the world, or making lots of money."

"Does it need to be evil?" asked Jacob, tapping a long-lost pocket of optimism. He looked at his cigarette. He noticed, with the quieter part of his mind, that he'd been smoking a lot these days. He told himself it reduced anxiety. And there was a lot to be anxious about, to be sure; apart from his disastrous personal life, a supernatural force of irony was taking over his town. Surely, that's an excuse to smoke? Chain-smoke, even?

He stubbed his cigarette out fiercely and lit another.

"I don't think it's a question of whether it's evil," said Shen, "though I'm going to assume it is, but of whether it's something beyond our control. It clearly is beyond our control, and it's trapping us here and causing a lot of unpleasantness. I have trouble believing that's okay."

The phone clicked several times, and spoke. "Pardon me, but this unpleasantness seems to involve all of you making a lot of money. From what I understand, unpleasantness involves something detrimental to health or possibility of reproduction. Money benefits both of these elements of the human condition. Why is this not okay?"

"Because it's fucking creepy," said Jacob, to the satisfaction of everyone except the phone, who decided not to press the matter.

"Well, then what do we do about it?" asked Rose.

Shen crinkled his brow in a way that is only physically possible if the brow's genetic makeup spans at least a dozen modern cultures on two or more continents. The patterns of chaos were mapped in the lines of his forehead. "Above all else," he said, "we have to figure out the source of the effects we have witnessed. There's not much we can do until we know where it's coming from."

Rose and Jacob nodded. They shared the belief that this was a thought perhaps unworthy of a full Shen brow crinkle, but they also knew neither of them had said it first.

"We should ask Morning Star," said Jacob.

Rose blinked. "My cat?"

"It's not as crazy as you think," said Shen.

"Don't think it could be."

Basil started squeaking violently. The phone responded with a few meows. Basil purred loudly, then vibrated his head.

"No one knows where he is," said the phone.

"Well, can you ask around?" said Jacob.

The phone meowed. Basil squeaked impatiently.

"No," said the phone. "What he says is that nobody at all

knows."

"How can he know that?"

"He won't tell me. But apparently felines have a different perception of conscious continuity."

"No," said Rose, bleeding sarcasm.

"Yes," said the phone, "In fact, it makes perfect sense if you consider—"

"Stop," said Jacob. "She's making fun of you."

"Is she?"

"Forget it."

• • •

Zack had much more difficult dilemmas on his mind.

Do I kill the clients, or my partner?

Slap.

This seemed to be an unusually long game of solitaire. In fact, if you multiplied the game's actual size in terms of time by its relativistic factor of annoyance, the game had lasted approximately five years.

Zack felt each relative second.

"Earl?"

Earl looked up, startled. "Yes?"

"Why do you do this?"

"This?"

"Work here."

"I like to help people."

Zack suppressed a number of twitches to avoid tearing his book in half.

"I don't think you do," he said, carefully.

Earl looked at him like a man who has just been told the world is a cone and orbits a weasel.

"What do you mean?"

"I mean you have to take care of your wife. You have to take care of what's-his-name. You don't have to work here. Why do all three?"

"Because I like to help—"

"But you don't!" shouted Zack. Earl recoiled. Zack controlled himself. "I mean, it's wearing on your nerves more than you think. It's not how you want to spend eighty hours a week."

Earl's mind, recognizing the fundamental problem with its decisions to date, went into emergency shutdown, beginning with antagonism.

"Well . . . why do you do it?"

"Pays well."

"Is that enough?"

"Yes. At least until I can move."

Earl slapped a card down, automatically. Several pages of Zack's book parted ways with the binding, despite his efforts.

"I need the money. I live an expensive life. I have to take care of—"

"Yes. I know. But have you ever thought about trying to make a change? Slowly? Getting out of this? Since it's driving you crazy?"

"UrrrrrrRRRRAAARglHArHArg," added Mary, from several rooms over.

"It's not driving me crazy."

"I'm going to kill you," said Zack.

Earl looked at Zack.

The next moment was a long one.

Earl opened his mouth several times, without result.

"I have a gun," said Zack.

Zack's mind was not specifically revolving around Earl's murder. Specifically, it was revolving around the irritations of his life, which, taken together, had a cumulative effect of psychotic proportions. It could not be said that Zack's iron grasp of reality had loosened, but it could be said that his analysis of options and solutions had forayed into unlikely territory.

Earl cleared his throat, "Zack . . ." He paused, collecting his survival skills. "I think we can work this out." Decades of caretaker experience were kicking in. Daily caretaking usually doesn't take much more than changing diapers and blocking out various noises, but this was the real thing. This was what he had trained for. "I know we have a tense relationship. I think certain habits of mine are bothering you, and you think I have these habits because I don't like what I do. I believe I do what I do because I have to, and I may be wrong, which may cause these habits, but let's figure out what it is that's bothering you, and maybe I can accommodate your needs."

Zack stared needles into Earl's eyes. The fact was, Zack was smarter than Earl and recognized any tactic Earl could employ, even if Earl had thirty years on him. On the other hand, what was bothering Zack was a deep, existential frustration of a sort no single human mind could fully fathom in any intellectual manner. Zack wanted to see his girlfriend. Zack wanted Earl to stop slapping his damn cards on the floor. Zack wanted to live in a world where someone with Zack's mind didn't have to work this kind of job to get anywhere interesting in life. Zack wanted television that had stimulating programming. Zack wanted freedom. Zack wanted . . .

It occurred to Zack that he could be making a lot more money selling drugs.

Earl, no fool, recognized a conflict in Zack, and tried to work it. "Maybe there's something else you'd rather be doing. I know I had to sacrifice some of the things I wanted for the things I had to do. You're younger than I am, and still have choices. Choices about what to do and what not to do."

A simple speech, but he could see it was dulling Zack's homicidal edge.

Zack's homicidal edge was also being dulled by Zack being a fundamentally nonhomicidal person. Murder wasn't rational, and he knew this, but was still furiously trying to make an acceptable argument for it.

He made a decision.

"Okay. You're right," said Zack, and left.

Earl watched him go, then resumed playing solitaire. In Earl's mind, this was the way solitaire was supposed to played.

Alone.

In a prison.

Once outside, Zack breathed in the night, tucked his book under his arm, and saw two naked girls running into the forest with a garden gnome.

Things were already looking up.

He started walking home. He wasn't fond of soul-searching moments. That was what high school accounting classes were for, and he felt he had balanced the account of his soul well enough. The last time he looked deep inside himself, he found a man who didn't like looking deep inside himself, and decided there were no more surprises. He had honed his mind to a calculating razor, and his purpose was to apply that razor to the soft skin of life. Spiritual revelations were put aside, to be reached only through powerful hallucinogens, which was the way it should be.

He had quit his job. In the middle of a shift, too, which meant he probably couldn't get a recommendation. No worries. The point of having the job was to save money to go to Chicago. Money was no longer an issue. He weighed the stresses of working the night shift in the institute against those of being a local drug czar. Factoring in the differences in risk and profit, and accounting for local police activity, drug czar had a slight lead.

Zack lit a cigarette, one of the two remaining in his mashed pack. There was the possibility that he was the unwitting agent of some mysterious and malevolent force twisting the town to its own needs. He had considered this on and off for several days now, but there was no proof, and he wasn't going to lose sleep worrying about something he could more profitably just be pondering.

He came to a hill, at the bottom of which he could see an intersection. He saw a car run a red light to make a left turn, and run straight into a car that was, for no good reason, stopped at a green light. Zack watched the participants leap out of their cars and yell at each other. He decided to take the railroad tracks instead of the street.

The tracks led along a ridge parallel to Main Street, and the view from the ridge made the town look like a movie set seen from behind. The tourist-trap storefronts and charming-country-town look didn't reach far back, and all you could see from the tracks were parking lots, fire escapes, gas tanks, and the occasional bar.

There was an unusual amount of activity in the town for three in the morning. A lot of small, disorganized groups of people doing . . . well, nothing, as far as Zack could tell. Or, rather, sitting around talking to one another and smoking, so a lot of them were probably students. Nothing unusual, but there were an awful lot of them, especially for a Sunday night. Zack looked up at the sky for the first time, wondering if there was a full moon behind the clouds. He noted the adjectives, and they worried him.

Halfway down the tracks, he paused to study the town. He estimated there were four hundred people in his field of view, spread out with eerie regularity. The movements of the small groups were hypnotic. They resembled bubbles in a boiling pot. They also resembled an old diagram of particle motion Zack had seen in high school. Somehow, they also resembled the patterns in the imitation oriental tapestry Zack had bought a couple years back. *Maybe,* thought Zack, *their movements are some kind of universal algorithm, played out by chance on this unlikely stage.* The trees parted, their branches weaving patterns matching the motions of the people below, and Zack felt himself growing into his body, into the archetypal watcher defining the movement of a universe below—

Zack smacked himself, hard, knocking the cigarette out of his mouth. He lit the next one immediately.

He did a quick mental checkup. He wasn't tripping. It didn't feel like tripping. It didn't smell like tripping. He was still himself. But the trees had definitely moved. Or he had moved. He looked around, and saw that he was maybe ten feet farther down the hill, with no memory of walking. If he had been walking without knowing it, that might explain the dreamlike motion of the trees, but it hadn't looked like anything so mundane as a simple linear shift in perspective.

No, it had been a lot more like a heavily drugged shift in perspective.

Except he wasn't on drugs.

He was sure of it. Even if someone, somehow, had slipped him something, he would know it by now.

He looked down at the town again, though not too closely. The spirit of investigation fought against the soul of caution. It was a brief fight with a foregone conclusion, however, because Zack was out of cigarettes. He located the nearest twenty-four-hour convenience store and headed down the hill, trying not to attach any excess significance to the way the tree branches seemed to carry him down as he used them to steady his descent.

At the bottom of the hill, he steadied his personal perception of the way things should be. This caused a weird sensation of antipsychosis as he surveyed the parking lot, as if the world had always been on drugs and was now sobering up. He couldn't help noticing that the trees weren't moving, the ground wasn't swimming, the buildings weren't waving, and the lights weren't dancing around his vision like the voices in Einstein's head, and it felt wrong. He felt a palpable sense of disconnection and not-at-oneness.

Keeping it real, he thought. He walked across the parking lot, and a small group of people absolutely did not float or sweep toward him, but walked over in a disorganized way.

"Hey," said one of them, meaning nothing other than "Hey," in a voice that neither boomed nor echoed in the world around Zack.

"Yo," said Zack.

"You riding the vibe, man? Are you toasted on the cream boat? 'Cause we lost our guide, man, and you got the look."

"No."

"Oh, man. That's cool. Hey, I can't see you, bro."

"Uh-huh," said Zack, still walking. The group was following him now.

"I mean it," said the group leader. "You can see so much from the top of the wave, man. People speak to you with their secret body, and you can feel them. But I don't feel you . . . not at all."

"Yep," said Zack.

"Are you . . . dead, man? Are you a vampire?"

"Nope," said Zack.

The group talked and gestured at one another. A girl with an as-tasteful-as-possible sprinkle of glitter on her face approached Zack.

"You teach so much, with so little," she said. "Will you guide us?"

Zack thought of Shen. "I have already guided you, little cricket. Your path now is to yonder hill." He pointed toward something far enough away to get rid of them for the night.

They looked to where he was pointing.

"But," said the group leader, "there is no hill."

Zack looked. There was definitely a hill. "Yes," he said, knowing he was being dangerously literal, "there is."

They group looked puzzled. Then the glitter girl brightened. "Ah," she said, "but that hill does not really exist. It is in our minds, and we cannot walk to it. All of us agree."

Zack sighed. "Yes. It is in your minds. The journey of your bodies is actually a journey of your minds, so walk toward the hill and you will see the paradox."

The group processed this. Zack looked toward the hill and realized that they were right: There was no hill, it was in his mind, and he had sent them on a fool's quest toward the unsolvable riddle of—

He smacked himself. The leader screamed.

"Master," he said, "why do you strike yourself?"

"The lesson is given," said Zack, and walked away. He had to minimize contact with these people. They were dangerous and confusing, and after Zack had smacked himself out of the Paradox of the Hill, he was by the river, at least half a mile from where he met the group.

He was sure he hadn't walked there.

• • •

Megan was the first to realize the nature of the situation.

"Is everybody on fucking drugs?" she screamed out her window in order to be heard over the horn of her car, which was being liberally applied in an attempt to get the attention of the people lying on top of the car stopped in the middle of the intersection.

She got out of her car and went over to them. The sight of Megan, or rather Megan's mood, got their undivided attention.

"Oh, hey . . . um . . ."

"What the hell are you doing?"

One of the people tore his gaze away from the clouds, and smiled at Megan. "We," he said, trying to communicate the overwhelming beauty of the human struggle with his next few words, "are looking for the sky."

Megan glanced up, then aimed a professionally inquisitive gaze at the speaker. "Oh? Then you know where it is now, right?"

The people on the car looked at each other for support. This was definitely killing their vibe.

"Well, yeah, it's—"

Megan cut him off. "So you could find it again if you took a break to move your car out of the middle of the intersection that I need to go through to get to my shitty hotel room?"

"But this is—"

"I only ask because I just finished working a fourteen-hour day, and I'd really, really like to go home and get to sleep before the sun rises, and, what do you know, I can't, because a bunch of fucking hippies are parked in the middle of the goddamn road staring at the sky!"

The hippies suddenly understood, wrongly, that all Megan needed was honest, forgiving love. The speaker for the group got down off the car.

"You should join us," he said.

The group murmured approval.

"When you've seen through the illusion of the sky, you'll understand that everything's okay, and ow ow ow ow!"

Megan bent the speaker's finger back a little harder.

"Oh, sorry, is everything still okay?"

"Ow . . . yes, if you—"

Megan twisted.

"Ow, Jesus, I mean no, it's not okay."

"It could be okay again if you move your car."

After some confused deliberation and a little more encouragement from Megan, they got moving, and Megan got through the intersection.

On the other side, her car broke down.

Megan beat her head on the steering wheel. *Maybe,* she thought, *if I keep hitting myself in the head, I'll die, and I won't have to deal with this.*

In the distance, she could faintly hear the bass line to "In-A-Gadda-Da-Vida." *Strange*, she thought. *That's Cecily's favorite song.*

She heard a knock at the window.

• • •

Exley attempted to look like a young professional in need of an innocent favor as he knocked on the girl's window. He was handicapped in this venture by several facts: He didn't have a job, he wasn't all that young, and there was a gun pressed into the small of his back.

"Hi, um, could we have a ride?"

The girl assessed him in a way he would have described as scanning. He suddenly empathized with the bags of potato chips he bought every few days. Her eyes flicked not nervously enough between him and his abductor. His abductor seemed to notice this too, as he sighed, grabbed Exley by the neck, and pointed the gun at the girl.

"Name."

The way he addressed her made Exley think of a venomous snake introducing itself to a sleepy lizard.

"Megan."

The metaphor seemed to be holding.

"Get out of the car."

Megan got out.

"What's going on?"

"Shut up," said the man. "We need your car."

"It doesn't work."

The man pinched the bridge of his nose.

"Okay, fuck it." He motioned them toward the town with his gun. "We keep walking. This better not be much farther."

They started walking.

"Where are we going?"

Exley looked as though he were trying to work something out of his teeth. "Friend's place."

"Why?"

"They have the drugs he's looking for."

Though Megan knew there was no reasonable action at all in the situation, she couldn't bring herself to go along with any of the unreasonable ones without complaint. "Aren't you taking a risk? And aren't you selling out your friends?"

"I'm hoping they won't be home."

"That's not a great plan."

"Well, my phone's dead and there's a guy with a gun behind me, so if you have any better ideas, I'd love to hear them."

"Actually," said the man behind them, "feel free to keep them to yourself. Getting rid of bodies is a mess and I just got this jacket."

Exley fished around in his pockets and found a bottle of Valium. He took two.

Megan watched him. "What are those?"

"Valium."

"I've heard of it. It relaxes you?"

"Sort of."

"Explain."

"Well, you know that feeling that you have to do something, because you only get one life, so you have to take care of yourself to make your life as long as possible to get everything done even though you don't know what you're supposed to do and you're just filling your time with things to stop you from thinking about it and hoping nobody asks you if you're happy with how your life is turning out? Valium makes you not care. Ow!"

Exley looked down to where Megan was clutching his arm. He raised his eyes to her face, and upon seeing her expression, wondered if he might have bigger problems than the gun pointed at him.

"Give it to me," Megan hissed through clenched teeth. "Give it to me now."

Exley gave her three.

• • •

Standard human angst serves two evolutionary purposes. Most commonly, it's a baseline motivator to keep humans moving when they don't want to, a kind of general purpose immune system against both excessive despair and paralyzing contentedness.

In addition, it serves to take certain habits of observation and turn them inward. Otherwise unchecked, and attached to sufficiently adroit minds, these mental proclivities would have brought human history to an abrupt close shortly after it attained the means to record itself.

• • •

Boris yanked, and finally managed to dislodge Richard's arm from where it appeared to seamlessly meld with the brick wall that had been holding it.

Neither Boris nor Richard had been surprised when Richard leaned against the wall and started to drift through it. Boris had recently come from a questionable reality, and Richard was, as always, still in one. The fact that the hinges were coming off of reality made no difference to people who were already unhinged.

"Fuck me," said Richard. "That's happened before. As long as you get it out quick it's okay."

"What happens if you don't get it out quick?" asked Boris.

"Dunno. I always got it out quick and it's always been okay."

They walked on. Boris mulled over some theories of social reality. Presumably, went the books, which always went "presumably," because such books tended to be extremely pretentious and said things such as *presumably* and *ergo* a lot without the slightest hint of irony, and in fact tended not to be books at all, but texts. So, presumably, went the texts, reality is simply what we agree on. These texts usually go on to say that reality as we know it is woven into our base perceptions but interpreted by our language, so anything may be true as long as it doesn't destroy a system of beliefs.

Hogwash, thought Boris, as many before him had thought. Actually, many before him had thought *bullshit,* and stopped going to class, but Boris was of sterner academic stuff.

All these theories seemed to say that the world is a thing, a universe of facts and forces, that we work into a system of predictability. We call that system reality.

But recently it seemed to Boris that the whole equation was backward. What if reality was a thing that we all agreed on, and that agreement became a universe of facts and forces? Which is what seemed to be happening. Which meant the world really was what everyone agreed on, meaning everyone was currently pretty fucked up.

What seemed to be happening was that everyone was agreeing to dispense with the assumption that they were interpreting a world that still existed when they weren't looking. They decided it really was all a dream, and they were going to wing it.

There was a strange theory of God as the eternal watcher. Something about God being the person who makes sure something is there when you close your eyes.

Meaning that if everyone decided they didn't need that reality, they didn't need God. Or they had gone someplace without God. Or they had blocked out God. Or, assuming there was a watcher, who we'll call God, they'd dropped a note saying they didn't need to be watched. Or . . . or God couldn't see them.

"It's a conunundrum, isn't it?" said Richard.

"What? What's a conun . . .nun . . ."

"It's like a conundrum, only worse."

Boris opened his mouth to speak, but Richard beat him to it.

"All that stuff about God. Being watched. What is reality. That stuff."

Boris narrowed his eyes. "How did you—"

"I can read your mind. Sort of. It's like braille."

They had to stop speaking for a moment to avoid a surge of reality jerks. Boris had coined the phrase an hour earlier. These jerks were wearing shades and walking about two feet above the sidewalk, which was rising to meet their feet as they took each step. They hummed in a perfect harmony, and peeled off pieces of the clouds to throw at birds.

"Can't we do something about them?" asked Boris.

"No. No more than you could make me less crazy when the world was more . . . normal."

Boris thought about this. "And the mindreading?"

"Well, I've been crazy for a long time, so I'm a little more at home now than you. This is what the world's always like for me. To put it another way, it's like this is where I'm supposed to be. My mind jibes with it more easily."

"Huh," said Boris.

"So what used to be my delusions are for the most part real. I can read minds, control radio signals with my watch, predict terrible deaths, things like that. Though the wall caught me by surprise."

"I see. So you can do . . . anything?"

"No. Probably not even as much as they can," said Richard, pointing at the crew of people still breaking up the sidewalk. "You'd be surprised how much the 'real' world you people like so much can limit a good delusion. I mean, it's all well and good to walk across water, except the water gives way and you fall through it."

"Never thought of it like that."

"Maybe you should."

They walked in silence.

"We should go up," said Richard.

"What?"

Boris had been looking at the ground, and when he looked up, he was on top of one of the apartment buildings in the middle of town.

"I walked us up. Hippies."

Boris looked down at the mass of color. Hundreds of brightly dressed people were dancing around a bonfire and starting to sweep the landscape into their circular motion.

"They should get distracted and wander off soon enough. We'll wait it out up here." Richard lit a cigarette and watched.

Boris watched with him. "So. You must know what's going on?"

Richard shook his head. "No. I did a little while ago. Now that the world really is my world, I just move through it. It's a little like the universe opens a space for me and I get sucked in. Sort of traded a mental landscape for a real one. So to speak. Anyway, upshot is, even though half of this is made of my brain, I don't know much about it."

Boris smirked. "Ironic."

"Yeah," said Richard, slowly. He took a long drag. "Yeah. This whole place has got a bad taste to it."

"You noticed that too."

"The world is not supposed to be like my mind."

"That's big of you."

"Thanks."

• • •

"So you're sure about this?" asked Shen, as he finished putting Jacob's computer together.

"I'm sure," said the phone.

Shen plugged the computer into the wall and reached for the power switch. He hesitated.

"Is this thing safe to turn on?"

Jacob shrugged. "Did you dust it?"

"Thoroughly."

"Safe as it will ever be."

Shen held his breath, stabbed the switch and scuttled away. The computer rattled to life. Shen exhaled. "I'd forgotten how much noise computers used to make."

Jacob and Rose sat on the bed, looking on. Jacob had looked outside the window a few times, but decided it was bad for his sanity. The cars walking in a little trot next to people floating beside them told him all he needed to know, which was that they had better make some progress on figuring out what was going on. Besides that, he felt his standard all-consuming despair coming on, and he was fidgeting madly out of sexual frustration. Rose being next to him didn't help. He continued to fidget. His leg itched. His cats were smarter than he was, and he didn't like that one bit.

Shen went to the phone. "Are you ready?"

"Yep."

Shen unplugged the phone from the wall. He picked the phone up carefully and walked over to where Jacob's computer was running. He plugged it in to the in port, next to the out port, where another phone cord ran to a wall jack.

"It's amazing you've kept that computer this long," said Rose. "Who even has a phone jack in their computer?"

Jacob bristled. "Maybe I don't need to waste money on shiny toys."

"Maybe you don't have any money to waste. Can this thing even—"

"Please be quiet," said Shen as he picked up the phone.

"Still here," said the phone.

"Can you get into the system?"

There was a pause.

"Not sure," said the phone. "I think I have to . . . move. Transfer myself into the . . . computer, then access this internet."

"Can you do that?" asked Jacob.

"I think so. I may not be able to communicate for a while. But I'll get back to you as soon as I have something."

"Be safe," said Shen. "And get help as soon as you can."

"Will do."

Shen hung up.

"Well," he said, "that's that."

"What do we do now?" asked Rose.

"How should I know? That's why we hooked him up in the first place." Shen rubbed one of his shoulders to relax. "I could go for a joint, though." He pulled a bag of weed out of his pocket and started the necessary preparations.

Jacob nodded. He got up to put on some music, because it got him off the bed. He limped to the stereo and looked for music among the scattered CDs.

"How's the leg treating you?" asked Shen.

"It's not like I was getting out much anyway," said Jacob. "Only real difference is it itches more."

"Try not thinking about it."

"Let's break your leg, start it itching, and you try not thinking about it."

"Fair enough." Shen switched tacks. "Rose, you've been pretty quiet."

"Yes," said Rose.

"What's on your mind?" asked Shen, never missing an opportunity for psychological debugging.

"I don't know. Nothing. Maybe. I'm not confused. It's like I'm only half here."

There was an explosion outside.

"The hell was that?" said Shen, unnecessarily. He lit the joint and went to the window. "Some punk kids blew up the McDonald's."

"No shit?" said Jacob.

"Yeah, I'm having a hard time disapproving." Shen proffered the joint to Rose.

Rose took it. "You'll miss it someday," she said.

"Possibly." Shen peered out. Eight kids in leather were standing in front of the smoking remains. Smaller bits of the building erupted and crumbled under their gaze. Shen noted without surprise that he had seen all of the vandals eating, if not working, in the very restaurant they had just destroyed.

"They appear to be destroying things with their minds," he said.

"That can't be safe," said Jacob.

"No, I don't think it is." Shen let the blinds fall. "It's curious that we seem to be relatively unaffected by what's going on outside."

"Maybe because we're not on drugs?" said Rose.

"Thought of that," said Shen, "but the room isn't wavy, and the clocks are all still running in the same direction. Besides, I saw a cop dancing with a lamppost, and I'm pretty sure he didn't take any drugs. Oh! I bet that's not-Rick."

"What?" asked Rose.

"Nothing. Anyway, I wonder if something's protecting us."

They all looked at Basil. Basil, who was doing no such thing but didn't want to let on one way or another, rolled onto his back and put on his best scratch-me face. Jacob scratched his stomach, and Basil abandoned himself to a good purr.

"I doubt it," said Jacob.

"Maybe it's you," said Rose.

Shen looked at Rose and pondered the statement. He looked critically at Jacob, who hadn't showered for several days. "What makes you say that?" he asked.

Rose took a hit off the joint and passed it to Jacob. "He's missing part of his mind. Whatever's going on out there definitely seems to be tapping that quantum circuit. Jacob hasn't got it."

"Interesting," said Shen.

"That would make sense," said Jacob. "To go out on a limb, it looks like it forces people's circuits to link up and . . . um . . . create . . . a locally consistent fantasy? Shen?"

Shen squinted at a wall for a second. "A psychically malleable reality based on the collective whim of small groups of persons' quantum sensitivity."

"Right," said Jacob, "that."

"So what can we do about it?" asked Rose.

"Nothing, as far as I can tell," said Jacob. "We don't even know why it's happening."

"Well," said Shen, "psychotic thought gets out of control when it stops checking back on reality. It seems like this whole town has stopped checking back. And it would seem most of it's on drugs, which would accelerate the loss of control. And we already discussed that something's causing it, and it would appear to be irony. I think the mass tripping is a means for the irony to enact itself. The question isn't why, but how? How is whatever's doing this . . . um, doing this?" He took the joint from Jacob.

"But when you really lose control," said Rose, "part of it is losing your grasp of irony. When it stops being funny that you're having revelations, and you start thinking it's all real, all in your head, et cetera."

"Someone needs to appreciate it," said Jacob.

"Us," said Shen.

Jacob took advantage of the ensuing silence to go to the globe and fix a drink. He looked at the selection and tried to remember a decent recipe but couldn't, so he filled his glass with vodka and dropped the lid shut. The world spun, glasses clinking. Jacob watched it spin, and thought, not for the first time, how it reflected the state of mind he was looking for when he opened it. Were the real world built like this bar, what would happen if there were no alcohol in it? Loss of gravity, he supposed, and the world would fling its inhabitants into the void before tearing itself apart. Or maybe it would implode.

Jacob shook his head, and regretted it as his brain bounced off his skull. He should never have bought the damn thing. Using a bar in a planet to shut out the world, cracking the world open to get rid of his life and its thoughts; there were too many metaphors involved in using a globe with an intentionally outdated map to hold his liquor. It was a rhetorical microcosm in the darkest corner of his apartment, holding spirits for the emptiness of spirit, and dreams of seeing the world while sitting in a room, going nowhere.

"There must be others," said Rose, breaking Jacob's chain of thought. "Whatever's doing this took a long time to get going. It had to build things up. It needs a lot of people moving in the same direction."

"Good point," said Shen, "and just like it needs a lot of people creating this environment, it probably needs at least a handful of people to appreciate it. Maintain the irony."

"So what if we get everybody who's resisting in on it? Collapse the system?"

Another explosion went off outside.

"I have a feeling that would be bad," said Shen, lifting the blinds.

They watched the smoke rise.

"You know," said Shen, "I don't like admitting this, but I liked the Starbucks."

• • •

Zack watched the Starbucks go up. It looked like the sort of scale and distance distortion he attributed to good mushrooms, except that it actually happened. The building never had a chance. It snapped in a hundred places at once, as if every brick and beam suddenly realized it was a rubber band stretched over a lit stove.

He wished he'd been brought up in a manner that would have prevented him from caring enough to do what he was about to do.

He walked up to where the kids were finishing off the remains of the building.

"Look, you guys have to stop."

Eight pairs of eyes turned to him. Zack thought about the gun.

"It can't stop," they said in one voice. "The system has to be brought down. The change has to come."

"You guys are pacifists!"

"The time of love is gone," they said. "Now is the time of the axe."

Zack rubbed his temples. "Okay, not only are you pacifists,

you're all atheists, so this collective-Jesus-complex thing is completely out of line."

The collective looked at itself. Some of it seemed to be doubting.

"We all feel like blowing shit up now and then, okay? I wanted to kill my coworker today. It doesn't mean you do it." Zack knew it was a mistake as soon as he said it. The collective rallied. The ground beneath Zack's feet rippled.

"Your conceptions of right and wrong are archaic. There is no law but the arbitrary and punitive authority. We must bring down the machine to allow true enlightenment."

"Yes," said Zack, "I know what you're saying. But not all of it is arbitrary, and the damage you're doing makes them create more rules, and it makes everyone afraid, and it makes it that much harder to achieve true freedom. Are you following me?"

The kids scratched their heads in perfect unison. Zack shivered at the sight of it.

"Look," he went on, "I know all of you have good ideas, but you're not thinking with your good ideas right now. I mean, look at you. You're acting like a bunch of brainwashed drones. You're not even individuals anymore."

"He's got a point," said one kid. Then the collective swept him up again and replied, "We are strong together. We have the power to fight back."

"But," said another kid, "we end up just like them."

"Sometimes," replied the collective, "you must fight fire with fire."

Resorting to clichés. Zack took that as a good sign.

"Maybe," said another kid, "but to use the tools of the oppressors misses the whole point. There's a lot of educational literature on the subject—"

"No!" said the collective. It had lost a few members at this point. "There are times when one must sacrifice personal freedom for power and security—"

"Now that's a brilliant bunch of fascist bullshit," said Zack.

"But . . ." said the collective, down to only two members. Zack walked up to one of them and slapped him.

"Oh, shit . . ." said the kid. "What the hell have we been doing?"

"Blowing shit up. Now how did this start?"

The kids looked at each other awkwardly. One stepped up. "Well . . . the gnomes."

"The what?"

The kid looked embarrassed. "The gnomes told us to . . . um . . . join together and be the hammer of the proletariat."

Zack raised his eyebrows.

"They were really convincing. And there were these girls . . ."

"Forget it," said Zack. "Go home, get stoned, watch some TV. You got it?"

"Uh, yeah. Sorry, man."

"Don't worry about it. These places are insured. It's a victimless crime."

"It is?"

"Trust me," said Zack. "And don't talk to each other for a while. And give me your cigarettes."

"What?"

"Smokes. I need smokes. All of them."

They fished around in their pockets and came up with almost a full pack.

"Good," said Zack. He sifted through the collection, gave the menthols back, and stuck the rest in his shirt. "Now go home."

"Okay. Thanks, man."

They wandered off. Zack watched them until they had made it a good distance without blowing anything up, then sifted through the rubble. He managed to find a coffee dispenser and a travel mug, poured himself a cup, and started back toward his apartment.

He had come up with a reasonably accurate system for making progress. Based on some exploration and quick calculations, he had worked out a rough spiraling path that was getting him closer to his destination. He had passed a digital bank clock a few times that appeared to display numbers at random, but he determined that if he stayed on his path, the clock went slowly backward. It was currently five past thirty-seven.

Zack had never thought himself a hero. He wasn't divorced, hadn't taken a bullet, never lost a partner, never developed a debilitating drug habit. He had none of the qualities of a modern-day Man of the Moment. No, the only advantage he had right now was that he wasn't an idiot. That and the ability to be irritable about being high when he hadn't actually taken anything. It wasn't much, but it seemed to give him the edge.

All he'd wanted to do was finish his shift, watch some *Aeon Flux*, smoke a joint, and go to bed. Now he was walking up a hill into the woods, around the back of the strip mall, in what would normally be not only the worst possible way to get home, but the wrong direction along the worst possible way. He mentally checked his route. Yes, this was the only way.

He marched up the hill, sucking on his pillaged coffee and keeping an eye out for telekinetic anticapitalists.

He knew this was partly his fault. He didn't blame himself. Things happen. You deal. Guilt is for the weak. Nevertheless, living with Shen's vaguely spiritual ideologies these last months gave him a sense of impending karmic retribution. Indirectly destroying fast-food chains didn't feel like a mortal sin, but he knew there were worse things going on. This was, after all, a nasty little town, and the moderately bad things were invariably symptoms of some grander melodrama.

Apparently involving gnomes and girls.

Zack wished something would surprise him once in a while.

• • •

"Everybody's a bloody philosopher these days," said the plumber over his beer. His audience was one of the dozen or so bar patrons struggling to free their lips from beer bottles that were sucking them in. Since the only thing nature abhors more than a vacuum is two things being in the same place at the same time, the side effect of this suction was the beer rocketing out of the bottle into the contorting lips of the drinker. Having grown up on games based on the speed of alcohol consumption, most of the patrons were happy to fight this battle many times over.

The patron sitting next to the plumber was nodding. She was an older pseudostudent, still picking up courses at thirty on the theory that college was fleeting, but a degree was forever.

"Even you. Maybe I'm extra irritable since I'm in a college town, but, really, everybody has a little theory about some sodding thing or another, about the way life really ought to be, whether they're driving a cab or riding the cab to the bank." The plumber finished his pint and leaned over the bar to help himself from the tap.

The woman freed herself from the beer bottle with a popping sound. "Well," she said, walking around the bar to get another, "is that so bad? That everybody's trying to work things out for themselves?"

"No, that's the point. You have to try to figure things out. That's what your brain is for. You can't help it. But everybody starts getting theories, then they think they're a bloody philosopher, and . . ." He waved his pint, looking for the words. ". . . bloody . . . gets in the way. That's it. They aren't trying to figure things out, they're trying to figure out new bloody theories. And it's because they all think there's something so good about philosophy, they should be thinking up theories instead of getting on with their lives and figuring out what they're supposed to be figuring out. 'Cause they all think philosophis . . . phisizing makes 'em special. More special than if they were 'just' doing what they been doing all their lives. Am I making any sense, girl?"

"Mmph," agreed the woman, already done with her new beer and trying to get rid of the bottle.

"There's no respect anymore, 's all I'm saying. People don't respect the mundane. They don't stop and think about the importance of every little thing, and you really have to do that, 'cause you can't philosophize lost time back into your schedule. Oh, well. Bottoms up."

He drained the pint and looked at the woman. "You know, you should really try using a glass. They don't try to drink you back."

She yanked the bottle away. "You're probably right. So what's the answer?"

"Hmm?"

The woman found a glass and selected a tap. "What's the solution? You've stated the problem. What should we do about it?"

"Hah!" He drained his pint and pushed it toward her. "Since you're already over there. I have no idea. Not my place. I'd be guilty of the same bloody crime if I actually came up with a solution. And the solution probably wouldn't work. Solutions hardly ever do."

She pushed a full pint back to him. "Sounds like a philosophy right there. In fact, most of what you've said sounds kind of philosophic."

He waved his pint. "No, not in my case. There're a lot of things I have to know to do my job right. Have to watch out for ideological pratfalls, thinking I'm doing something other than what I do. I have to make sure I'm never trying too hard."

"You have to watch out for ideologies as a plumber?"

"I do a different kind of plumbing."

"How so?"

"When I fix pipes, I actually just fix pipes."

She gave him a look that only thirty-year-old undergraduates can give.

"What do you mean?"

"I don't make money, make people happy, or seduce housewives in the shower. I actually just twist little things until pipes work proper."

"And that's a special kind of plumbing."

"It's a special kind of anything, but in plumbing it happens to be a rare and important skill."

"Huh." The woman looked at the register. "You think we should pay for any of this?"

The plumber laughed. "I haven't paid for a drink in fifty years."

"Really? You look good for your age."

"Cheers. Do me a favor, love. Would you look out the door and see what's going on out there?"

"Sure. You looking for someone?"

"You could say that."

"What do they look like?"

"Couldn't say."

"How will I know if I see them?"

"You won't. That's the idea. I want to see what you have to say about it."

She gave him another look and went to the door. "You are a very strange man."

He finished off his pint and smiled at her. "Won't argue with that. I think maybe someone will catch your eye, and it'll spark my interest and it might happen to be the person I need to see, and it'll be a stroke of luck for us all."

She laughed. "Fine. I don't believe in coincidence, though."

She opened the door, and didn't see the plumber's smile fade.

"Better start hoping, then," he said quietly.

"Nobody out there. Which is a little odd in itself," said the woman, returning to the bar.

"Eh."

She raised an eyebrow. "Waiting for a date?"

He shook his head. "Nope. No fraternizing on the clock."

She looked at his beer.

He winked. "Trust me."

"Why not," she said, and poured herself another beer. "I can't seem to get drunk."

"You're under the effects of the town. Makes you a little bit trippy, and it's hard to get drunk under those circumstances. You'll have a bit of a hangover if you ever snap out of it."

"Ever?"

The plumber winked at her again, which did not make her feel any more comfortable. She looked at her beer. "Do you know what's going on?"

"Sort of. Not in any way that I could explain."

"Try."

"Alright." The plumber's face creased in thought. The woman looked at the crags of skin that were revealed by this expression and thought he looked much older than she'd assumed.

"Well," he said, "you have problems in this town. Quite a few, from the looks of it, and, more distressingly, enough to get the attention of a demon."

"You mean a metaphorical demon?"

"Oh, definitely. And a real bitch, too."

• • •

Greg sat at a table in a room that he would not have believed existed a few days ago. It was nothing about the room itself. It was the fact that the room seemed to be on the fifth floor of a house with two floors. The stairway leading to it was a marble spiral that managed to pass four sets of doors and only two sets of windows on its way up, even though each floor was identical.

This didn't bother Greg, however. His reason had locked itself away behind a small, unmarked door in the bowels of his brain and threatened suicide whenever he tried to coax it out. The rest of him was enjoying a glass of champagne and the marvelous view provided by this latest impossible thing.

Across the mahogany table was some creature whose name he could never remember. It looked like a girl. It said it was a middle-aged woman. It wasn't either, he was sure.

"You know," it said, in a summer-sweet voice, "so many people see movies with villains living rich and public lives, they never expect it to be true. If you don't count politics and investment banking, anyway."

"Nobody expects fantasy to be real," Greg said with hysterical calm.

She laughed and winked at him. "No, they don't, do they? Isn't that why they take fantastic things and make them reasonable?"

"I guess so." Greg took a drink of champagne out of a glass that never seemed to empty itself. In its little room, his reason told itself the butler must be refilling it when he wasn't looking. The rest of him said, *Well, it's a magic champagne glass. Now get drunk.*

Greg complied.

"I'm glad you're here, Greg. Very glad. It adds that finishing touch. Like when someone dots the 'i' on a wedding cake with a smiley face because the bride is a twit. I hope you're enjoying yourself."

Greg drank.

"Do you know what I'm trying to do, Greg?"

"No."

"Good. Now, this town is really the most beautiful place in the world. I've never been in a place with so much juice. All these people, living their little ironic life stories and loving it, and knowing it, isn't that the best part? I hardly even need to be here. I consider myself a lucky, lucky girl. Who would have guessed my little pigeon, my rat would have come here? It would be a coincidence if it wasn't so wonderfully ironic."

Greg surfaced for a moment. "Aren't most ironic things coincidences?"

She laughed.

"Silly boy," she said, "I'd hardly be in business if that was true. Irony is something much more important than a mere coincidence." She spat the last word. "It's my job and my dinner, and the reason you're here. Don't think you don't love it."

Greg looked down at his champagne. It was full. The butler really was phenomenally good at his job.

"Greg, darling, you're meant to be with me. Maybe someday I'll fulfill all the little dirty fantasies you've had locked up in your goody-goody little brain. I'm so much older than you. It wouldn't even be a sin. It wouldn't even be against the law." She leaned over the table. "It wouldn't even be dirty, Greg. Two consenting adults. That's okay, isn't it? Only as dirty as it needs to be. I could bring a friend. You know I have so many waiting to come visit."

Greg made a small sound in the back of his throat. "What," he asked, struggling to get the words out, "do you want from me?"

She smiled at him. Tenderly, though he wouldn't believe it.

"Why, Greg. I want you to be right here in this house for a while. Maybe forever. You know, if it turns out to be forever, you might end up liking it. Once the town is where it needs to be, things will be easier. Less intense. For a while anyway. Until things are perfect. Oh, I love that word, perfect. It only exists in evil, you know."

"What do you mean?"

"Things can only be perfect according to an evil . . . actually sardonic, I like that word, don't you? Sounds so much worse than it is. Sardonic. Hah! Sardonic appreciation of real, genuine irony. Then you can say, 'This is just perfect,' and be right. You can be so right. And everyone will nod or laugh, depending on how much it affects them. They'll think it's funny. But really . . . it is perfect. For me."

Greg wasn't about to let this go. "That sounds like semantics."

She laughed. "What isn't semantics? What is life, or this semilife your kind lives, but a long line of interpretations? You hear words, and see things, and come up with names, and then you think of ways to string those names together and you think you have an understanding. Then you think your way of looking at the world is a map for reality. But you never think that maybe your map is closer to reality than you think."

She sipped from her champagne glass, which refilled itself as rapidly and as mysteriously as Greg's. Greg reflected on the pleasantries of living with evil, and in that reflection, began to talk his reason out of its room.

She went on. "Remember the terrarium? Human idea. It's about control. Control is a darling thing, and sometimes you need to isolate a system to really get a grip on it. But that system is a part of the bigger picture. Once you have control of a part of it, then you can apply that to a larger environment. You can grow."

"But," said Greg, "you need an understanding of that larger environment to create a smaller system."

"Hah! Don't think it didn't take a few tries to learn the ropes. But the point is, you need to get it right with the model before you try it with the world."

Greg got up.

"I would like to leave," he said.

"Oh, but Greg, you haven't even finished your champagne."

"I know. I know you're evil. I know I'll never finish it. I want to go."

"Alright, fine. Go. Get out."

Greg blinked. That seemed too easy.

Don't think about it! screamed his reason.

Greg turned and made for the stairway. He looked over the edge and saw the exit two floors down. He looked down the stairs, and saw the foot of the stairs five floors down. He decided to look at the rail and started walking. He counted the steps, out of morbid curiosity, and to keep his mind busy.

One, two, three, four, five.

"Sir?"

Greg heard the butler's voice and ignored it.

"Sir? Sir, would you like your coat?"

Ten, eleven, twelve, thirteen.

"It is a lovely coat, sir, and I wouldn't know quite where to keep it in the house."

Twenty-one, twenty-two, twenty-three.

"I'd hate to see you leave something you'd have to come back for and—"

"I didn't bring a coat!"

"No, sir. The lady wanted you to have this. She bought it earlier this afternoon."

"She bought it?"

"Yes, sir. She thought it would get your attention."

"Well, it doesn't."

"In fact it did, sir, and as curious as you must be, you should at least have a look."

Forty, forty-one, forty-two, forty-three.

"One look, sir. I would feel remiss in my duties if I didn't procure at least a glance from you."

Greg stopped. He didn't turn around.

"This is absurd," he said.

"Yes, sir."

"I'm not going to be stopped by a jacket."

"No, sir, that would be quite absurd, as you say."

Greg gripped the rail.

"What are you?"

"A butler, sir."

"Sure, but what kind of strange evil entity are you?"

The butler hesitated. "An English butler, sir?"

"Are you human?"

"I am indeed."

"Have you been human for more than a few months?"

The butler coughed delicately. "To put your mind at ease, sir, I was born in nineteen forty-seven, raised outside of London, and learned the trade from my grandfather. When the family employing my family's services decided it was socially backward to employ a butler, I found myself well trained but with no experience. This being a difficult position, I decided to investigate some more unusual job opportunities."

"But you work for an evil . . . something!"

"Yes, sir. But as an avid reader of English literature, I find her ideals agreeable. Her sense of humor is very close to what I consider one of the finest achievements of the human mind, and we all desire a universe that makes some kind of sense."

Greg realized he was nodding, and stopped. "But she's evil."

"Indeed, sir. I find that to be a relative term."

"You're going to try and stop me."

"In a manner of speaking, sir."

Greg turned and lunged. The butler was slightly closer than he anticipated, and he had to adjust his punch. The butler glided smoothly out of the way, and Greg lost his balance, partly because of the butler's evasion, partly because he'd spent the afternoon drinking champagne. He turned. The butler was standing, his hands behind his back, unperturbed. Greg threw another punch, and again the butler glided out of the way, and had already smoothed down his shirt by the time Greg regained his balance.

"You will find this quite futile, sir, though I must compliment your form."

Greg kicked low and jabbed at the butler's face.

The butler lifted his leg, calmly, and leaned back to avoid the jab.

"As I said, sir, I am well trained."

Greg was panting. He sat down on the steps and put his head in his hands.

"I can't hit you."

"No, sir. More importantly, you haven't heard me out."

Greg made a get-on-with-it-you-soulless-minion-of-evil motion with his hand.

"Thank you. As I said, I agree with her ideals, but she is, as you say, evil. I believe you touch her human side in a unique way, and it is important to the future of this world that you stay. I believe she might become a little . . . odd without a measure of human contact. I know you are a good person, and I believe you will make the right decision."

Greg looked up at the butler. The butler returned his gaze evenly. Greg searched for anything that would tell him there was another plan, a kind of trick behind the man's facade, but the face was impassive, the expression of quintessential professionalism.

"She's been keeping me here through psychological torture and sexual frustration."

"I realize that, sir. We are human, after all. But now you may stay with a purer motive in mind."

Greg sagged on the stairs. He pulled out a tobacco pouch and began rolling a cigarette. He felt that even when his captors explained things to him, they were playing with him. There was a reason they wanted him here, beyond their sick enjoyment. The girl-thing seemed to get all the enjoyment she needed from the town below, and this butler . . . he wasn't sure about the butler. There was something he was missing, not because he was stupid, but because they were carefully keeping it from him. He rolled the cigarette. The butler held out a lighter. Greg took a light off it.

"There's no coat, is there?" he asked.

"No, sir. But it did stop you."

Greg looked over the rail. The bottom floor was still two floors away. The stairs themselves seemed to go down about ten floors. He supposed he could vault the rail, but couldn't convince himself that the floor wasn't actually two or three hundred feet down.

"It's all about semantics, sir," said the butler in a confidential tone. "Remember that, and you might feel a bit better."

And he was gone.

Greg thought about cutting his hair. It seemed to be attracting the wrong kind of people these days. He stroked his mustache, and tried to tease apart the motives that had gotten him here. It had started with Megan. How much of his situation was a result of wholesome helpfulness versus lusting after younger women? He couldn't tell. He couldn't separate the emotions, and as he traced the events of the last few days, every incident seemed to be a little of both. Every decision seemed to be made somewhere between his heart and his loins, yet nothing had been a gut feeling. His gut felt sick. The champagne wasn't helping.

He looked up the stairway. Fourteen steps from the top. Maybe he'd jumped a few stairs up during the fight. Or rather, during his ineffective flailing at the curiously spry butler. That was it. He'd rushed up a few stairs. Maybe in self-defense. Maybe in a Freudian dash to get closer to the girl-thing at the top floor.

Greg put his head in his hands.

If he was reaching her, he could change things. If he couldn't stop her, maybe he could make things better. And dammit, if he couldn't make things better, maybe he could get laid.

He went up the stairs. He was sure the butler was playing him somehow. He should at least find out why.

Besides, he hadn't even finished his champagne.

• • •

Boris wasn't sure who or what his enemy was right now. The world seemed a likely candidate, barely edging out the universe. The occasional shadows that waved at him were definitely enemies, but they seemed more like henchmen: Expendable bodyguards waiting to be killed by Double O Seven.

Richard might be his enemy, but even with his new lucid demeanor, Richard didn't seem like the kind of person with enough focus to orchestrate the disaster unfolding on the streets below.

They had been on top of the building for over an hour now. Boris could only be sure about what was directly in front of their perch, as the rest of the town was moving in a random swirling motion. The semi-organized dances trailed through the town, but even they had begun to lose coherency. Whatever was going on was getting worse.

"More entropic," said Richard.

"I really wish you'd stop listening to me think."

"Sorry. You're broadcasting."

Boris muttered something that Richard chose to ignore. "What do you mean by entropic?"

"Everything's breaking down. The rate of breakdown seems to be slowing, so it should level out at some point, but people are starting to lose their sense of time, space, identity, etc. You know what I mean."

"Mmm," said Boris.

"The important thing is that they're becoming easier to manipulate. The spacetime around us has been warped, and the people are starting to warp with it. But not completely. It's not exact. There's resistance. I don't understand."

"Somebody unaffected by the landscape?"

"More than one. Probably some people able to affect the landscape under these conditions, whether they know it or not. But there's also a kind of symmetry in the resistance."

"A metapattern?" ventured Boris.

"Yeah. Right. Like the resistance is following a pattern of entropy too. But there's some kind of resistance to the metapattern too."

Boris shook his head. "I can see where this is going. How do you know all this?"

"I feel it. I think my brain is part of the inspiration for this."

"How so?"

"I think I'm less crazy because someone took my craziness to build this." He waved his arm across the view.

Cold numbness crept down Boris's neck. "We're living in your insanity?"

Richard shook his head. "No. Relax. Whoever did this is an artist. I think my brain is some kind of side play. Like a garnish."

"This is all very complicated," said Boris.

"Yes," replied Richard. "But it's not the details right now. It's not adding up to something. Something is breaking down into all this."

They watched the street writhe.

Richard stood up and stretched. "I think it's safe to go back down."

"What are we looking for?"

"A lucky break."

They started climbing down the fire escape.

"And a beer," added Richard.

"Took the words right out of . . ." Boris trailed off.

They descended to the street in silence. They started walking.

"Richard?"

"Yeah?"

"Why am I unaffected by this? You seem to have a good excuse, but I'm not going crazy, or tripping. And why am I being stalked by evil shadow creatures?"

"I don't know."

Boris sagged a little.

"If it makes you feel any better, I think you're unique in some way. Some way that makes you immune to this"—he gestured to a cop holding a conversation with some houseflies who were flying in aggravated circles—"so whatever it was that did this found it necessary to attack you in a different way. Which suggests there's a mind behind all of this. So that's helpful."

They walked on, past some streetlamps swaying in the breeze. A small herd of goats ran across the street a few blocks in front of them.

"I ran into a crazy plumber. He mentioned some things that sound like what you're talking about. Something about closing me off, locking me away. Whether I was supposed to be here or not."

Richard bit his lip in thought. "Probably a coincidence," he said.

"Do you think coincidences are still happening around here?"

"I'm not sure. I'm really not sure at all."

● ● ●

The prolonged separation of Morning Star's mind from its usual link to the Pretty Much Everything was taking a heavy toll.

He walked in circles. He tried to lie down and nap occasionally, but he was too stressed to sleep, and always had to get up after a few minutes. He'd tried engaging a squirrel in conversation, but the squirrel only made a rude noise and bolted off. Since then, Morning Star had worked off his aggression by swearing at any squirrels that passed through. They seemed immune to Morning Star's strange cage, and ignored him.

"Fine. Next one of you comes through, I'm eating you," he meowed into the night.

A squirrel either hard of hearing or short of understanding came within Morning Star's view, and he lunged for it. The squirrel was gone before he hit the ground, and he yelled in frustration. *It's come to this,* he thought. *After everything, it's come to attacking squirrels.*

In his thrashings, he upset several flies that had been enjoying an evening meal. After wiping their meal off his paws, he watched the flies buzz around him. What he was about to do went against a very strict code of feline ethics, and he felt bad about it, but there was no other option. Besides, why should anyone else be having a good time?

He selected a fly and thought viciously at it.

The fly stopped and hovered unsteadily in the air. It moved down toward Morning Star's face and projected a thought back at him.

"You son of a bitch."

"Look. I'm sorry. I need—"

"I was happy! I was old! I've had my spawn! Goddammit. Kill me. You have to kill me quickly."

"I can't, I need you to—"

"Oh, shut up, you son of a whoring alley cat, you demented bastard . . ."

The fly continued to swear as it began ramming its head against a tree trunk.

"Look, stop doing that."

"Oh, like it matters. Do you know how hard it is to commit suicide for a fly? I can't get nearly enough speed to do any damage. I only have a few hours left alive, you think I want to spend them remembering the good old hours of avoiding spiders and eating shit? What's wrong with you? You a psychologist?"

"Well, not certified, but—"

"Then who's going to help deal with death, hmm? Oh, it's too late anyway. Curse this short and heartless life! Curse this cat! Now I'm afraid to die. I don't have enough time to accept this. I wonder how my children are. You know I've never even joined a club? I never wrote a book! My friends don't even have names! Who's going to remember me? I ask you that: Who will remember me when I'm gone?"

The fly settled on a leaf and wept.

"How could you do this to me?"

Morning Star's heart softened. "There, there," he tried. "I'm sorry. But I will remember you, I promise. There's something enormous going on, and—"

"What are the woes of the Earth to a single fly? What is the worth of an insect in this complex world? Why—"

"Stop it! Listen. I'm needed. I need you to get me out of here. If you help me, you will make a difference. You'll change the world! What other fly can claim that?"

The fly sniffled. "Really?"

"I promise."

The fly quieted down a little.

"I still hate you," it said.

"I understand."

The fly rose into the air. "And my breath smells awful. Let's get this over with. What do you want?"

"I'm trapped here, for some reason. I need to get out."

The fly buzzed around a bit.

"I don't see anything keeping you here. How are you trapped? Other than within the futility of your existential prison, which you so thoughtfully imparted to me?"

Star thought sarcasm was a surprising coping mechanism for something that had only become aware of itself two minutes ago. He noted, not for the first time, that the unchanging facets of the universe had nothing to do with complex equations and the paths of stars, but with the annoying habits of the people he met.

"It has something to do with the way I look at things. I'm hoping that you are not trapped and that I can follow you out of here."

"I can tell you what the problem is right now," said the fly.

Star blinked. "Oh?"

"One of the smaller dimensions composing spacetime has expanded on this location and constricted around you. It's like you're walking around in a little circle."

Something deep inside Morning Star snapped. To have the nature of his prison laid out so matter of factly by a fly was deeply offensive to his understanding of the way things should be. "How the hell do you know that?" he screamed at the fly.

"You know how hard it is to fly around brain waves? Or cars? Flies have to navigate the actual structure of the universe. Or at least more of it than you do when you're bumbling around in your enormous meat sacks. It's written into my body. It's part of what created my mind when you started it up." The fly sounded smug.

Morning Star strained to remember how to do this sort of equation. He was still lacking the better part of his brain, which was reeling in horror at the nature of his cage. He decided it was in fact possible to snag a cat in a small dimensional expansion, and that it was the best explanation for his entrapment. Still . . .

"Why am I the only creature trapped in this?"

The fly fluttered its wings. "I don't know. This space has a weird quality to it. I don't really have a vocabulary for it. Oh . . . phew . . . umm . . ."

Star waited.

"It's kind of . . . linked to you. It's like it's a pseudodimension. It feels a little like it's made of your mind and the space around you."

"Self-centered," said Star under his breath.

"What?"

"Nothing. But it is still a physical space, correct?"

"Oh, for sure."

"And it's possible to get out?"

"Well, for everything except you and me."

"What? Why can't you get out?"

"Because you made me. Half my mind is made up of your mind. I'm as stuck as you are. I'm not so upset, because I only have a couple of hours left to live anyway, and this bit of forest is as good as any other."

Star walked in a circle and sat down. He reasoned that there was a way. All it involved was for him to lose himself completely. If his usual shortcuts were gone, and the rest of him was trapped, the only way out was to get rid of the rest of his mind and simply walk out of his prison.

He had gleaned Shen's mind during their brief encounter, and remembered bits and pieces of the technique he needed. He knew he wasn't going to be very good at it. He needed something to focus on. Something that would lead him out. Something that moved very slowly, to give him enough time to reach the proper state before he hit the curving edge of his prison.

He thanked the fly as kindly as he knew how. "You've been a great help to me. Thank you."

"Yeah, whatever," responded the fly.

"I'll make sure no one forgets you."

The fly buzzed above Star's head. "Sure," it said, "do that. And don't do this to anyone again." And with those words, the fly flew toward the trees and was eaten by a bat.

Morning Star shrugged and started searching for an inchworm.

• • •

I have the worst cramp in my leg, said R.

Did you pull something? S asked.

I can't pull something. I don't have anything to pull.

Well, you did say leg, I thought you might have manifested something that could be pulled.

I was speaking metaphorically.

Well did you metaphorically pull something?

Not that I remember.

R metaphorically rubbed its metaphorical leg.

I think I have a cat in it.

Oooo, I hate those.

• • •

Exley riffled through his pockets. *Please,* he thought, *if you ever give me anything useful at the moment I need it, let it be now.* His hand closed around something in his pocket. He felt out its shape. Yes, it was definitely a knife.

And this was definitely about to be a gunfight.

". . . so it must feel odd to really want to kill someone when you've never killed anyone and don't really want to, after telling all those people that you did," continued Megan.

Philip gaped at Megan over the barrel of his gun. About thirty minutes ago, Megan had let out a deep sigh, taken Exley by the arm, and started talking. The situation had deteriorated from there.

"I'm guessing your name is Francis, or Philip, right?" said Megan.

"How . . . what?"

"Well, it's one of those names where you probably had to make a choice when you were choosing a life of crime in southeast Brooklyn."

"How did you know that?"

"You kidnapped two people with a gun and you're not nervous enough for it to be your first time holding a gun. Als,o your outfit is nice, but it's not as expensive as it looks, and your accent is from that area. As I was saying, with a name like . . . which is it? Francis?"

"Philip."

"Philip, you had to be either big and mean or smart and in charge, and you're not that big and you don't like violence all that much, so . . . yes, drugs. You're sort of a smart buyer, distributer kind of person that important people need so you get free protection, and your older sister can't talk back to you anymore."

"What the hell is wrong with you?" hissed Exley.

Megan turned to Exley with an innocent look. Exley noted her eyes were both slightly glazed but still somehow piercing.

"Do you *want* to die?"

"Of course not, silly. Death is the unknown, and nobody has control over the unknown, so most people want to minimize unknowns in the future, which doesn't work very well, but that's people for you. Besides, Francis is a wuss. He's never even fired a gun. His pupil dilation patterns are all bluffing."

"My name is Philip."

Megan looked back to Philip, "Right, sorry, Philip. Oh! There they go." She swung her head back to Exley. "Now he's ready to kill us. Well, me. Probably you too, you know, witnesses, heat of the moment, etc. Yes, if he does kill me, he'll probably kill you too, but at least he'll be able to look his father in the eye without flinching afterwards. Actually, he really should kill you first, since shooting an unarmed woman in an alley isn't the most direct path to manliness, even for criminals. Oh, stop digging around in your coat, you don't have anything in there that will help us before he pulls the trigger."

Exley watched something break in Philip's eyes. He supposed the impression he was getting was a vague story to explain an unconscious reaction to the pupil-dilation patterns Megan was talking about. Exley didn't see anything specifically unusual about Philip's pupils, but the whole Philip package was giving off the distinct sense that it was upset and it was going to kill people until it felt better.

Exley decided he had three seconds left before Philip's rational sensibilities were overwhelmed.

In a moment of pure adrenaline, Exley braced his body internally for what might have been the last spring off his mortal coil. His hands closed, his right hand seeking out the knife again and his left hand closing around what he instantly recognized as an old charm bracelet he'd found in Boston when he was a kid. He'd held onto it for years, but had given it away at a party several months ago, when one of the charms had broken and scratched the back of his wrist. The shock of this rerouted his brain's focus away from the impending suicide leap, directing it to the knife in his other pocket, which Exley realized was the whittling knife his father had given him on his thirteenth birthday. He hated whittling, and had thrown it in a gorge "by accident" one night and never looked for it.

Mind racing, Exley realized that everything he'd found in his pockets since he had woken up in the woods was something he had once owned and gotten rid of for one reason or another, and he was in fact inextricably wrapped in a collection of unwanted mementos.

Unable to work this new information into a kamikaze attack on Philip, Exley's body sagged.

"Holy fuck," he said.

Philip paused in his advance, trying to work out whether Exley's reaction meant anything tactically relevant, and at that moment, a shovel swung out of a shadow and hit Philip in the back of the head.

He went down without complaint.

Exley looked up at Megan and wondered how she had changed her clothes so quickly. And ended up behind Philip, instead of in front of him. And put on ten pounds of muscle. And a tan.

"Hey, Cecily," said Megan.

Exley turned and saw the more familiar Megan next to him. *Clones! No, wait. Something else.*

"This is your sister?"

Cecily spat on the ground. "No, she's my bitch twin, and she stole my fucking car." She hefted the shovel. "I see why you like this thing so much," she said to Megan.

Megan nodded. "It's got great balance."

"I came here to hit you with it."

Megan nodded again. "Oh! This is my twin sister Cecily. We hate each other. She's always been jealous of me because I'm prettier, but of course she's the one dad actually related to, and mom was a drunk so she pretended to be an only child and I pretended to be an orphan, which confused a lot of people in school. Cecily, this is . . . what's your name?"

"Exley."

"Exley! How odd. Cecily, Exley's kind of stupid but seems nice enough."

"Hey!"

"Oh Jesus," said Cecily. She put a hand on her hip and glared at Exley. "You gave her alcohol."

"What? No, I didn't, I swear."

"Well then what's she on?"

"I just gave her some Valium."

Cecily walked over and poked Exley in the chest with her finger hard enough to make him stumble back. "Never. Give. Megan. Benzos. That's rule one. And avoid alcohol. Don't give her anything to make her relaxed."

Megan nodded and smiled. "Alcohol was always bad. But Cecily! I love Valium so much! It takes all the worry away! I bet it would even relax that knot that always shows up in your shoulder. You know, the one that makes you wince in that way everybody hates because it makes you so ugly. Like monstrously, inhumanly ugly."

Cecily's right hand turned pale where it gripped the shovel. She started nodding, rhythmically.

"What are you doing?" asked Exley, but she held up her hand at him and kept nodding and muttering. Exley realized she was counting.

At fifty, she sighed and looked at Exley.

"We clear?"

"On what? Oh! No benzos for Megan. Got it. Why?"

"You serious? This guy wanna put a slug in you before the bitch started talking?"

"I hate that nickname," said Megan.

Cecily ignored her. "My sister gets too relaxed, she starts talking about what she sees, and, Exley, boy, trust me, she sees a lot more that you want to know. The bitch is gonna have 'Truth Hurts' on her fuckin' gravestone unless she outlives anyone ever saw her drunk."

Megan skipped over to where the dealer was lying. She bent over to pick up his gun, took it apart, and threw the pieces in various gutters. Cecily spat and shook her head.

"Don't leave your guns around her neither. Anyway, What's going on here?"

"Beats me," said Exley. "Whenever I think I get it, it gets weirder. You seem kind of okay, though."

"I was gonna say the same to you. How come you ain't prancin' with trees?"

"I think the Valium is keeping us grounded. Well, me. And doing whatever it does to Megan. What about you?"

Cecily shrugged. "Dunno. Mom said I always had my feet on the ground, so I s'pose that means I'm grounded. How long she been in town?"

"I just met her. I have no idea. Look, let's get out of here," said Exley. "We should find Shen and Zack."

Cecily pointed the shovel at him. "Who? Why?"

"Friends. Safety in numbers."

Cecily spat again. Megan ran over to take Exley's arm. "Numbers aren't really that safe you know. In stressful situations, groups of people tend to make worse decisions than individuals, and I don't think you can afford to lose any IQ points right now."

"I am really starting to dislike you."

"Oh, of course you are. Most people aren't even allowed to like me. The doctor back home says I'm a health risk. But the way you live, it probably doesn't matter."

"Sometimes this is when I put 'er down," said Cecily, with a meaningful shake of her shovel.

Exley pried Megan off his arm. "Let's just get inside somewhere. Away from that." He pointed to a gentle wave of concrete rolling through the sidewalk.

Cecily looked at the undulating pavement.

"Nope. That ain't right."

• • •

Zack looked down to the bottom of the small valley with an overwhelming sense of boredom. Of course there was a small glowing circle of trees with will-o'-the-wisps floating around it. Of course the trees swayed and bent in a gently dancing canopy above the glow. Of course it was exactly in his calculated path to home, and when he went down there, there would of course be a small circle of gnomes and whatever girls the anarchist wrecking crew was talking about.

This was, Zack knew, because he was walking a mental path. Not his own, perhaps not any particular person's path; the world around him was no longer a physical landscape that gave rise to ideas in people's minds, but a semantic landscape born of people's minds. So, of course, when he ran into a bunch of kids who were making rubble out of buildings because the gnomes told them to, the next logical step was for him to run into a bunch of gnomes. He knew he wasn't actually going anywhere. He was walking through some shaggy-dog joke that was already boring him, with no punch line in sight.

Zack was neither excited nor disturbed to find out that nearly everything he had assumed about the universe was wrong. He had always secretly assumed his assumptions were wrong anyway. He was irritated that instead of this revelation coming to him in the form of breaking five-o'clock news that would have reshaped the world and society, it skipped ahead to reshaping the world and turning a twenty-minute commute into a four-hour trek through banana land.

Zack knew that someone somewhere was getting a huge kick out of this, and that did nothing for his state of mind.

But there was nothing for it, so he began making his way down the slope, toward the grove. He was about halfway there when he heard the voice.

"You got a smoke, handsome?"

Zack looked around. The voice was a mix of a high-pitched chirp and the sound a bitter professional drinker might make. He couldn't see its source.

"Here. Look down."

Zack looked down. Standing about two feet high was a barely-dressed fairy with chipping paint. She had butterfly wings wrapped around her shoulders that were tattered in a suggestive and non-utilitarian way, and she had to dedicate a hand to holding together the ends of two filmy scarves that served as her clothing.

"Hi," said Zack.

"You got a cigarette?"

Zack fished one out and handed it to the fairy. She stuck it in her mouth with her free hand and looked at him expectantly. He pulled out a lighter and lit it for her. She dipped her head in thanks and took a drag. She pulled it from her lips, and flicked the ash off.

"Thanks, babe. Been a long time."

"What are you?"

"He doesn't mess around, does he," said the fairy, and coughed. "I'm a fairy, genius."

"With chipped paint."

"Not like I've got many secrets left," she said, indicating her scarves.

Zack pursed his lips. He decided his lips could be better used smoking, and he lit a cigarette for himself before replying.

"You're one of the gnomes."

She laughed nastily. "Yeah, careful where you say that. Those bitches figured if it's on a lawn, it's a gnome, but you should hear the gnomes talk about it. 'She's not one of us,' they say. 'She can't be in the sacred circle,' they say. 'Not with that clothing.' So I say it's not like they've never seen a woman's mysteries before, and that must'a hit a nerve, 'cause then there's this big argument and I get kicked out of the circle. Fuckin' maggots. I told them they might get a little play if they lost the stupid hats."

Zack folded his arms and looked down to the circle.

"Why are there a bunch of gnomes in a sacred circle in the middle of a forest?"

"See, that's a stupid question. What else do gnomes do?"

Zack thought about it. "Why are there a bunch of ceramic garden gnomes in a sacred circle in the middle of a forest?"

The fairy clapped her hands together. "Much better. The short answer is that a couple of crazy coeds stole a bunch and stashed them here for kicks. And me, even though I'm not a gnome. Why they're all bickering about tradition and glowing, I don't know."

Zack looked at the fairy carefully. She was fluid in her movements, even breathed normally, yet was clearly made of hardened clay. Her clothes fluttered in the wind, and were perilously close to falling off, yet were obviously carved out of the same stuff as the rest of her.

"So are you a fairy, or an animated statue?"

"You're not much of a flirt, are you?"

"No."

The fairy rolled her eyes. "Both."

"How?"

"I distinctly recall flitting gracefully through the realm of Faerie, breathing enchantment, bar hopping, and making out with the other fairies. I also remember suddenly remembering all that a few hours ago after having been a statue for three years. As far as I can tell, somebody found a fairy in some fantasy that looked kinda like me and slapped it on."

"You seem to have a good grasp of the situation."

"Yeah, well, I'm a fairy. We know crazy shit, or something. Not like I'm wild about it. I had a perfectly nice life before this extra one got shoved in."

"What do you mean? You were a statue."

"Just 'cause she ain't moving doesn't mean she ain't there, kid."

Zack looked around. "So do you know what's going on in general?"

"Nah. I'm security."

"Come again?"

"Well, I feel kinda compelled to do what the gnomes tell me to do, and since they couldn't handle me being around, they made me security."

Zack sized up the fairy. There wasn't much up to size.

"What are you securing?"

"The gnomes. Who are in turn securing the source, or some shit like that. Some chick." She stepped back a few paces, casually.

"And you can't let me through?"

"Sorry, handsome." She winked at him. "Not much you can do

down there anyway, way I hear it. Now, what you could do is stay here and get freaky."

Zack shook his head. "Sorry. Got a girl in Chicago."

"World's gonna end anyway. Come on, a six-foot guy and a two-foot lawn ornament? You can't pass that up."

"Sorry," said Zack, wondering what stance was appropriate to fight a two-foot-tall opponent.

She shrugged.

"Suit yourself."

She flicked her cigarette in his eye.

It hit his pupil with astounding precision. The cherry exploded on his contact lens and sent sparks flying as he screamed and covered his eye.

"You bitch!" he yelled, and then doubled over as the fairy punched him in the gut. He felt hard ceramic bounce off his kidney and went down. He groaned, and opened his good eye to see the fairy hovering above him like a hornet. She still had one hand behind her back.

"Wings ain't just for show, kid."

Zack scrambled to his feet, grabbed a rock off the ground, and hurled it at the fairy. She swooped out of the way, but it nicked a chip out of her thigh.

She leveled out and looked at him with narrowed eyes.

"Not cool, buddy. Takes a lot of jogging to get thighs like these."

She swooped. Zack tried to catch her with an elbow, but she twisted under it, came up behind him, and rapped him in the back of the head with a knee.

"Slow. Gonna be hard to do this without depth perception. You sure you're up for it?"

Zack made a run for it. She swooped lazily after him.

This is ridiculous, he thought. She was probably hollow, for God's sake, a couple of good kicks would break her right open. But she was fast. Really fast.

She swept down and punched him in the temple as he hit the top of the hill above the gnome's circle. He lost his footing and rolled down the path he had first come up. He managed to get back to his feet running. He tried to remember the path. It went down a few hundred feet, then turned to run along the top of a twenty-foot cliff that ran above an old carriage trail. Erosion had nipped away under the cliff, and the trees were starting to hang over the edge as if contemplating suicide or waiting for the right passerby.

He wasn't sure what he would do at the cliff. He didn't want to stray too far from the path and throw off his calculations, but he was pretty sure that the fairy would try knocking him off the edge. She'd be ready for any punch he threw. He'd have to do something she didn't see coming.

The fairy was humming. She swept down again and kicked him in the ass. She laughed as he stumbled.

"Sorry. I had to do that once."

Zack ignored her. He could see the edge of the cliff. Several young birch trees were leaning over the edge in front of him. A thought struck him.

"You could have whiled away your last few hours doing something perverse, but no, you made a run for it. I want you to remember I gave you a chance. I hope the next guy's a little smarter, 'cause I'm hard up out here."

Zack reached the edge and flipped the finger at her.

"You little shit!" she shouted and dove for him.

Zack jumped.

He barely managed to catch the top half of one of the birches. He rode forward as his weight bent the tree. He hoped it would hold long enough. It arched over, creaking. Zack looked down. He was about ten feet from the ground. He looked up at the fairy coming toward him.

"I was being polite, but—"

Zack let go.

As he fell, the birch whipped back up and hit the fairy. She exploded like a rack of dropped dishes.

Zack hit the ground and twisted his ankle. Pieces of ceramic fell around him. He picked up a piece of her head, with an eye and a bit of hair. It blinked at him angrily.

He crushed it under his heel, slowly, and limped around to where he could climb back to the path.

He was surprised for the first time that night when Morning Star leapt out from beside the road and started nuzzling his bad ankle, purring.

• • •

Jacob was drunk. Shen was also drunk, but showed fewer signs of it. Having inherited his alcohol tolerance from his Chinese ancestors, he had learned early in life how to fake sobriety. Rose was talking to herself quietly, but that didn't indicate anything.

"We might have to get more beer," said Jacob, absentmindedly tapping on his leg brace.

"Nah," said Shen, waving his hand carefully, so as not to hit anyone. "There's still . . . ah . . . whiskey?"

"I think so."

"Okay then." Shen got up to get the whiskey.

"Why would you go out there?" said Rose to Jacob.

"I thought we should be doing something more productive."

Rose looked at him appraisingly. Her eyes wobbled slightly, giving Jacob evidence that she was keeping track of two of him.

"By making a beer run? Through Hell?"

"Better than sitting here."

"We're waiting for the phone to get back." Shen tried the last cupboard and found the whiskey. He brought it to the table. "I'm still having trouble with the things that come out of my mouth lately."

"Time to get over it," said Rose. "It'll get worse. If it makes you feel better, some creepy fuck was staring at me by the river the other day, and that was before any of this even started."

"It does not, but thank you for the thought."

Jacob gazed over Rose's shoulder. "Have you noticed it's late afternoon when you look out the living room windows and nighttime outside the kitchen?"

"I was in denial."

They drank.

"So." Shen cleared his throat. "We're drunk. Zack's at work. Exley's missing. And the world is falling apart. And we're waiting for the phone to get back."

"You mentioned the phone already," said Jacob.

"I know. I'm trying to keep it all straight. Because we're drunk."

Rose rolled her head toward Shen. "You mentioned the drunk already."

"Yeah," sighed Shen. "Yeah, I did."

Jacob leaned over to Shen and looked him in the eye. "You're really drunk, aren't you?"

"Yeah," sighed Shen. "Yeah, I am."

"Hmm."

Rose looked at the table. Basil jumped onto her lap and purred. This was what he was good at. It was quiet outside, and Shen had turned off the radio when it started relaying the thoughts of the gas station attendant across the street, who seemed to spend most of his time calculating how much money he could lift from small-change scams. Basil's purring filled the room. Jacob thought about Morning Star.

"I miss you, kitty," said Rose.

"Shouldn't have left." Jacob didn't mean to let it slip out.

"Oh really, Jacob? You think I should have stayed? With your passive-aggressive bullshit?"

"We were happy before—"

"Don't you dare. We were happy for about two months after we moved in. Then you started moping around the house ignoring me and expecting me to come talk you down whenever your fucking life wasn't as fulfilling as your mother told you it would be."

"It wasn't just me!" Jacob pounded the table. "Goddammit! Whenever you got depressed you holed up in your little shell and didn't get out of bed for two days. Do you want breakfast? No! Do you want to watch a movie? No! Do you want anything at all? No!

You wanted to stare at your empty journal and frown. Of course I gave up."

"I didn't want you to fix me! I just wanted you to be there!"

"I needed to try!"

"You wanted your dead high school crush back! You were trying to fix me so you didn't have to fix yourself, and that's how you fucking broke everything in your crap life! Everything about you is stuck in the past. You don't even have a goddamn cell phone for Chrissake."

Shen winced. "Oo . . . so, uh, Rose, maybe, um . . . Jacob? Yeah. So. Let's all, you know. World's ending. And other things. You know."

They all looked away from one another. Basil had stopped purring and was looking anxiously back and forth between Rose and Jacob.

Jacob coughed. "Where's Morning Star?"

"I have no idea," said Rose.

"Was he here when you fed them?"

"I let him in. Shut the window behind him."

Shen took the whiskey out of Rose's hand. "A lot of people have been disappearing lately," he said. "I'm not sure I like that."

"Why do you keep saying things like that?" said Rose.

"Like what?"

"I think I feel this, I'm not sure I like that. It's driving me up the wall." Rose grabbed the bottle back.

"We all have our coping mechanisms," said Shen. "Anyway. I've been thinking. I think we agree the town as a whole is, for lack of a better term, high as balls. Now, when you're tripping, you can't get drunk, right?"

Rose and Jacob nodded slowly.

"Right. So. Maybe if you're already drunk, it can provide some kind of temporary immunity to this. Could be long enough to find Zack or Exley."

"Shen," said Jacob carefully, "I'm not sure I follow your logic."

"The logic is I'm drunker than you, tired of sitting here listening to you fight, and I want to find out what's going on, and you two should wait for the phone to get back."

"Sounds reasonable," said Jacob.

"Why both of us?" asked Rose.

"Because I wouldn't want to be left alone in this shithole, even if you are both awful, awful people."

There was no argument. Jacob in particular didn't argue.

"Okay then. Besides. I could be right. I'm not sure why we've been immune so far. Could be the place. Could be the weed. Could be the alcohol. Whatever it is, I'm sure I'll have at least a little time to scope the area out." He got up to leave.

"Need anything?" said Jacob.

"Nah. I'll wing it. I'll bring the gun back if I manage to get to my place."

"Rose, hold on to Basil so he doesn't get out."

Basil shot Jacob a look.

"Okay, guys, I'll see you in a bit."

Shen opened the front door and looked around.

"Doesn't look too bad," he said.

He stepped outside and vanished. There was Shen, walking out the door, and then there was a small pop as the air around him noticed he was gone.

Rose and Jacob gaped.

After a long pause, Jacob cleared his throat.

"Someone should get up to shut the door."

"Fuck that," said Rose.

• • •

Gaping holes in the parking lot sucked down into nothingness. They moved around spastically, and occasionally reversed themselves into spikes that stretched infinitely into the sky. In addition to this, parts of the view seemed to not be there. There wasn't a hole, just a blind spot that seemed to shift around. To make things interesting, bright flashes of light occasionally singed the pavement.

Beyond the parking lot was a set of stairs. It was actually several sets of stairs that were actually one set of stairs. They weren't moving, thankfully, but they had an M. C. Escher quality that made them as frustrating as the parking lot.

At the top, or at least at the end, of the stairs was a door, and this door led to a bar.

"Do we really need to go there?" asked Boris.

Richard thought for a moment. "Yes. Or I'm pretty sure."

"Is pretty sure a good enough reason to walk through this?"

"I'm surer about it than anything else."

Boris looked at the parking lot again, seeking a pattern in the chaos, trying to work out the timing of the mess and calculate a path. The fact that time seemed to speed up and slow down in various places wasn't helping.

"You know," he said to Richard, "the fact that this is the hardest place to get to strikes me as a good reason to go there."

"Agreed."

"Also, I don't think this is a math problem."

"Why?" said Richard.

"Because it's too complex."

"Has that line worked on math teachers?"

"No, I'm saying the problem is so complex, there's not enough calculating power in the universe to solve it. I mean, look at it."

Richard looked. "Maybe. How sure are you?"

"Pretty sure. Even if I guessed on the simplest one-dimensional element of the problem, and ignored the fact that every part of this thing interacts with every other part, and limited it to the four dimensions I can actually see being fucked up, it's still an equation I'd need a dozen computers to figure out. Every tiny factor makes it exponentially more difficult."

"So it's unsolvable?"

"I don't think so. Everything around us still seems to work, but not in the way we're used to it working. So . . . there's an answer, or equation, but it has nothing to do with physical space or math."

"Interesting. But useless."

"If it doesn't . . . Wait, can you still read my mind?"

"The talking helps you think. Continue."

"I wasn't really going anywhere with that."

"Maybe," said Richard, "it's about us. Check out the stairs. They obviously start on the ground and end at the door, so the rest of it is some kind of optical illusion. And if reality is trying to keep us away from the door, and the people are shaping the reality, then whatever's in front of us has to do with us . . . and . . . um . . . yeah. Something like that."

"I see where you're going."

A flash of light liquefied the base of a pavement spike.

"Doesn't really make it better, does it?"

Boris shook his head.

Then he closed his eyes and walked forward.

He ran into something hard and screamed, waiting for the pavement to invert and suck him into the abyss.

After a few seconds of this not happening, he opened his eyes. He saw a door. He turned around and saw Richard standing at the other side of the still broiling parking lot, cigarette dangling from his lips.

"Hey, it's not so bad!" he called out.

Richard coughed, dislodging the cigarette. He cupped his hands and called back, "I saw you die in more horrible ways than I could ever imagine or describe!"

Boris frowned. He looked down at himself. He seemed okay.

"Worse than the things I saw when I was crazy!" added Richard.

Boris shivered, but held himself together. "Just close your eyes and do it!" he shouted. "I promise you'll be fine!"

Richard walked forward.

He was okay for about ten steps. After that, Boris screamed again, covered his eyes, and retched. He sobbed in front of the door, until Richard tapped his shoulder.

"You're right, that wasn't bad at all."

"Ah . . . ah . . . ahhhh . . ." said Boris.

"Block it out. Try to forget."

Boris recovered himself and stood up.

"Well. Can't be any worse inside."

Richard shook his head. "It can always be worse, Boris."

They opened the door.

The bar appeared to be empty except for a girl sipping from a glass of beer behind the counter.

"Hey, guys," she said, waving.

Boris kicked something on the floor. He looked down and saw a beer bottle with something in it. He tried to pick it up, but it was far too heavy. He looked closer.

"There's a person in here."

Richard leaned down and looked. An eyeball shifted into view and blinked at him.

"Yeah, stay away from the bottles," said the girl. "It seems fun at first, but . . ." She gestured to the bottles strewn about the bar.

Richard walked over and took a seat at the bar. "Something pale on tap, then."

"Same," said Boris.

The girl eyed Boris. "Kinda young, aren't you?"

"I was just ripped apart by a parking lot."

"Coming right up."

She poured two beers.

"So what do we do now?" asked Boris.

Richard raised his glass. "Drink, I guess. I'm not going out again."

The toilet flushed in the men's room, and a middle-aged man came out smoking a pipe. He was handsome in his way, and somehow managed to make a T-shirt and old jeans look dignified.

"Fixed the flusher in there. Broken chain, paper clip should hold it for—Oh, hello."

Boris gasped. "You're . . . that . . ."

"Plumber. Charmed." He extended his hand.

Richard reached around Boris's twitching face and took the plumber's hand. "Are you the person we're supposed to meet?"

"Were you supposed to meet someone?"

"I assume so."

"Assumption is the grease for disaster."

Richard nodded.

"He's been talking like that all night," said the woman.

The plumber ignored her and helped himself to a beer. "Inkling, however, intuition: That's the stuff of miracle."

"We could use a miracle about now," said Richard.

"Do you really believe that? The kind of miracle you'd like would surely return you to a delusional wreck of a man."

Richard shook his head. "That's a misconception. It's not so bad. It's more intense, but between the bliss and the agony, it evens out. The only kicker is not having a well-developed sense of humor."

The plumber shrugged. "Fair point, but would you really want to do that to Boris, anyway?"

"What do you mean?" asked Boris.

The plumber squinted at Richard. "You haven't told him?"

Richard shook his head. "I wasn't sure."

"Excuse me? Sure of what? What are you talking about?"

The plumber put his hand on Boris's shoulder. "Boris . . . you are a delusion. Richard's delusion."

". . ." said Boris.

"Made real by the malleable state of things these days."

"The limo," said Richard.

Boris was unable to speak, so he simply moved his stare from the plumber to Richard.

"They took part of me away in the limo. I forget where they picked me up. I think you were separated from my mind to protect me or something."

"In a manner of speaking," said the plumber. "The higher functions of your mind realized what was happening and they took advantage of the process you were undergoing to hide themselves in a physical form."

"Me," said Boris.

"Indeed. Don't look so glum. You're as real as either of us now. In fact, you have been real since before you existed. Such was the power of Richard's mind."

"But I . . . I . . ."

"So," said Richard, "if we . . . fix things, Boris ceases to exist?"

"I think it's a little more complicated than that. But I do know that if it were possible for some miracle to utterly undo the events of the last month or so, then yes, Boris would cease to be."

Boris drained his beer. "Vodka," he said.

"Poor kid," said the woman sympathetically, pouring a large glass of vodka.

"I think you may come out of this intact yet, Boris. Though I'm not sure what that will mean for Richard."

"So what are the shadows?"

Richard snapped his fingers. "They're my delusions too. I was right."

The plumber raised his glass. "Indeed you were. When the demon got going, she realized what had happened, and shaved off a few bits of your confiscated madness and sent them after Boris. Almost had him in the hospital."

"So you were helping me in there."

"No. That was a coincidence."

"But it wouldn't have—"

"No, it would not have happened had I not been there. Luckily, I was in the vicinity, and coincidentally, did something on one end of a pipe that happened to correspond precisely to the lucky thing that happened on the other end of the pipe, which had nothing whatsoever to do with the effect of that thing on what was happening to you."

Boris looked at Richard, wondering if he had picked up something Boris had missed.

"I have no idea what he's talking about," said Richard.

"That's good," said the plumber. "There's no pattern to it. That would be the point, if there were one."

Boris gave up and drained his vodka.

"Then what are we waiting for?" he asked.

"A lucky break," said the plumber.

The woman rolled her eyes. "All he seems to do is wait for luck."

"My grandmother was Irish," said the plumber. "And you'll notice, I still haven't paid for a drink."

"That's because the bartender's in a rum bottle," said the girl.

"True. Lucky for me."

"Were the Irish really that lucky?"

"Don't think about it."

She waved him off.

Richard finished his beer. "So we're really just waiting for something to happen?"

"Basically," said the plumber, tapping out his pipe. "But I'm reasonably sure things will get worse before they get better. So let's keep drinking."

"Cheers," said Boris.

• • •

Exley dashed up the steps to Shen's apartment and grabbed the doorknob. The door gave way instantly. He staggered forward and fell on his knee.

"Sonofafuckwhore," he mumbled.

Cecily raised her eyebrows. "I didn't bring this up before, but I feel like you could just make some calls and save yourself a lot of pain."

"I lost my phone, in my . . . you know, never mind."

Megan sniffed. "Smells like patchouli. And girls."

Exley slowly got to his feet, gripping his knee. "That's ridiculous, this is Shen's . . . huh. It does. Zack? Shen?" He looked around. "Jacob?"

"Looks empty," said Cecily.

Exley checked the living room and the bedrooms. No one was home.

"Dammit!" he shouted. He didn't like the sound of himself yelling. It wasn't natural. "Cool off, Exley. What do we do here?"

"You ever thought about an internal monologue?" said Cecily.

"It's less weird."

"This is simpler. Keeps you on track. Where was I? Drugs. Gun."

"Great," said Cecily. "Making a new start for yourself, are ya, sis?"

Megan looked at Cecily with as much anger as she could muster, which wasn't much. "I don't know this person. But I like him more than you. Your hair is pretty."

"This is some psychological warfare shit," said Cecily, and spit on the floor.

"Hey! This isn't your home."

"No. It's a place with drugs and guns."

"It's only one gun," said Exley, as he reached under the sofa and pulled it out. He plucked a bullet out of his jacket, not even registering surprise that it was the first thing his hand touched. He popped the bullet in the clip, where it of course fit, slammed the clip in the gun, and loaded the chamber. He flipped the safety on.

"Okay, that was creepy," said Cecily.

"My dad's a hunter. Big into gun rights. You never know when you'll run into a deer with a flak jacket and a rifle, so every hunter should be prepared with automatics and handguns."

"Creepier," said Cecily.

Exley stuck the gun in his belt. "What do you want from me?"

"The gun," said Megan, reaching her hand out.

Exley slapped it away. "Absolutely not." He went to Zack's room and reached under the bed. The case was right there. He reflected that they probably should have thought of better places to keep things. He opened the case.

"Hmm," he said.

"What's up?" asked Cecily from the living room.

Exley searched for his cell phone in his pockets, swore, and went for the landline.

• • •

The phone rang.

"Hope that's the phone," said Rose.

"Well, of course it's . . . right. Me too." Jacob picked up the receiver. "Hello?"

"Jacob! Thank God."

"Exley! Where have you been?"

"Long story. Look, the drugs are gone."

"What?"

"Gone. Everything we had left."

"Jesus."

"Yeah. I'm going to try to make my way over to your place. I'm with a couple of people I met."

"Why? Who?"

"Still a long story. I'll tell you when I get there."

"Look, be careful—"

"Oh, thanks Jacob, good advice. I hadn't thought of that."

Exley hung up.

"Dick," said Jacob, and put the receiver down.

"What up?"

"Things got worse." Jacob lit a cigarette and sat on the floor.

"Can't say I'm surprised," said Rose, sitting next to Jacob.

"Somebody stole the drugs. God knows what for."

"Don't think God knows anymore."

Jacob exhaled slowly, streaming smoke to the floor. "Could be on to something there."

The smoke curled through the room and dissipated.

Rose touched Jacob's shoulder, lightly. "I'm sorry for bringing up Dorellen."

Jacob closed his eyes. "Thank you. But you're not wrong."

"I know. But it's not something anyone can ask you to get over."

"I don't expect to get over it. But I define myself with it." Jacob put his head in his hands. "We all have that story that we think gets us to where we are. But there are a lot of stories that add up to now. We're the people who remember the stories that drive us to try to forget the stories we remember." He stopped, and repeated the sentence under his breath. He nodded and moved on. "So we turn into a bunch of potheads and alcoholics, trying to cope with memories and not lose track of ourselves in the coping. And we hardly go anywhere. The town coddles our coping. We lean on one another and don't make anything better."

"Maybe we just have to survive until we grow out of it."

"Maybe."

Night and day switched sides of the apartment.

Jacob looked out, uninterested. "Survival's getting less probable."

"You want to have sex?"

Jacob took several seconds to adjust to this radical shift in conversation. He groped for responses.

"Thinking out loud. You know, why not, since the world might end, I want to get laid, I'm sure you need to get laid. We could do some kinky game or something, but I'm kinda drunk, so not real complicated, we can work around the bad leg, and really, what else is there to do?"

"Yes," said Jacob.

They sat on the floor, not moving. Jacob cleared his throat.

"This might be me being stupid, but . . . I'm trying to figure out how this could be ironic and make things worse."

"Oh, it's going to make something worse, but at this point, fuck it."

"Yeah, okay, okay."

Rose kissed him.

Jacob swirled in drunken lust and explosive nerves. Electricity surged up his spine, burning out nerves and chakras; his lungs emptied at once; the tension of his body and soul washed out like a wave, then surged back in as pure desire, into every muscle of his body, driving him to hold her tighter, kiss her harder. His hands came up her sides, gripping and pulling her to him. She made a surprised sound, then a groan as her legs came around him and squeezed his ribs.

They let go of each other with a gasp, breathing heavily. Rose wiped her mouth with the back of her hand and sat on his stomach.

Jacob's fingers were numb.

"I—" began Jacob.

"Shut up," said Rose. "We have to figure out what to do about this thing on your leg."

• • •

"You know, out of everyone involved, I only feel bad for Jacob."

Zack knew Morning Star could understand him, but that Star couldn't respond in any meaningful way, and that suited Zack fine.

"A lot of this could be construed as our fault. Basic greed over common sense, et cetera, but this fell on Jacob all at once. I mean, he's coping surprisingly well, but it's got to be getting to him. There's only so much he can take before he pops."

They crested the wooded hill. The glowing circle had grown.

"You ready for this?" asked Zack.

"Meowrr," said Star, noncommittally.

They descended the slope. Zack heard voices.

"What do we do with her now?"

"Continue the sacred circle."

"But it was meant to be eternal, was it not? I feel the onset of time."

"Aye, and space. Space descends upon us."

"Has this eternity an alterable quality? Is it an eternity within time?"

"There's no such thing."

"Perhaps in the new world."

"No new world."

"Old world made new, whatever."

"Stop bickering! We simply must do what we must do."

"Oh, that's priceless."

"No, it's good advice."

"Where's Fred?"

"I think he collapsed in on himself."

"That makes three now."

"Well, I told them not to walk outside the circle."

"I bet the fairy thing got him."

"Yeah . . . with her . . . her . . . sinful clothes . . . and . . . heaving breasts . . . and . . ."

"That's enough, Ted. We did the right thing. No temptresses within the sacred circle."

"That's not very progressive of us, is it?"

"We're not progressive! We're gnomes! We do sacred things in sacred places."

"Why?"

"Why not?"

"You can't answer a question with a question."

"Just did."

"Stop bickering!"

"Shut up, Bill."

"You shut up."

"We sound like children."

"We're sacred spirits. Acting like children is our modus operandi."

"Yes, but do we have to be brats? Aren't we supposed to frolic with a child's innocence and fight with a child's blind hate?"

"Sounds good on paper, but children really just bicker a lot."

"Great. Hello, eternity."

"Don't be snippy."

"Excuse me?" said Zack.

The gnomes looked at him. They were various hues of chipped and peeling paint, but all of them sported characteristic red pointy hats, which bobbed around one another as they eyed the invader. The scene within the glowing grove was about what Zack had expected: Ambient green light, and about a dozen gnomes standing around an inner circle of trees. Beyond the trees, Zack could see Leah Funk, smoking a cigarette and looking bored. Zack could make out the silhouettes of two girls dancing behind her.

"Hey, Zack," said Leah.

"Hey, Leah," said Zack.

The gnomes chirped angrily.

"No! Speaking! To! The! Sacred! One!"

"Bob, you don't need to pause at every word."

"I was making the point!"

"But 'The Sacred One' is a single element of the sentence. It sounds weird if you split it up."

"It's not about the grammar, it's about the rhythm. If you don't like it, you can go shove your hat up—"

"Stop it!"

The gnomes grumbled. One approached Zack.

"You may not enter our secret grove. Especially not with a cat."

Zack looked at Star. "Because the cat can hurt you?"

"No. They're just dirty creatures."

Star sat down and cleaned himself, pointedly.

Zack looked down at the diminutive gnome. He wasn't about to underestimate the creature.

"What exactly are you doing here?"

"Ah," said the head gnome, "we are guarding one of the pillars of the new world. From this place shall emanate the power of physical discontinuity, that which can make that which is not . . . um . . . not so, so. If you follow."

"Nope," said Zack.

One of the gnomes in the back piped up. "We make shit really weird."

The head gnome ground his teeth. Being made of ceramic, the sound was similar to a room of screeching kindergarteners dragging fistfuls of nails across blackboards. It made Zack's soul shrivel. The head gnome turned to the others.

"We really need to work on a proper degree of sanctity here. Next person who bickers, swears, or makes light of our sacred duty in front of an infidel has to go face the fairy thing."

Zack cleared his throat. "She's gone."

The head gnome turned back. "I'm sorry?"

"I smashed her with a birch tree."

The group sagged slightly.

"Um. Good," said one, failing to sound happy. "She was an evil . . . temptress or something."

"Still . . ."

"Mmm?"

"I sort of . . . figured on certain . . . rewards when our sacred duty was achieved."

The head gnome turned angrily on the bobbing red hats. "Our duty is eternal!"

"Yes, but we'll get coffee breaks, right?"

"Shut up! Shut the hell up!"

"Hey, you said no swearing in front of the indifel."

"It's in-fi-DEL, you moron. And I can do whatever I want. I'm the leader."

"Yeah, why is that?"

"Because I have the most paint left on my hat."

The gnomes grumbled, defeated.

"I guess, I guess. But remember, with the coming of the new world was foretold the Second Painting. Things could be different."

"Well, maybe it'll be some friendly egalitarian democracy and you can all debate yourselves into dust, but for now, shut up."

The head gnome turned back to Zack. "So. You cannot pass."

"Why not?"

"Because it's our sacred duty to not let you pass."

"What will happen if I do pass?"

"Bad Things," said the leader, with solemn gravity.

"Bad for me or bad for you?"

The leader crinkled his eyebrows, dislodging a flake of his forehead. "I'm really not sure, but I'm guessing Bad. You know, Bad For Everyone."

"Would you really need to emphasize the 'For' in that?" mumbled one of the gnomes in the back.

"Extra gravity," replied another.

"My life is completely ridiculous," said Zack to Morning Star. Star bumped his head against Zack's ankle in agreement.

"Hey, Zack?" said Leah.

244

"Yo."

"You want to get me out of here?"

"I'm not sure."

"I'm pretty sure."

Zack measured the distance to the inner circle. He leapt. The gnomes screamed. Zack felt the world begin to close in around him. His vision narrowed to a tiny tunnel, at the end of which he could see Leah in front of him, and for some reason, Morning Star behind him.

• • •

A mist crept in under the door of the bar.

"Now what?" asked Boris.

The plumber glanced over his shoulder. "A twist of reality, I believe. Sort of a side effect of mixing incompatible possibilities."

"What do we do?"

"Nothing," said the plumber. "It's too late."

"When will it stop being too late?"

"Never."

Boris sagged.

"But there might be another now coming," said the plumber. "Drink up."

• • •

Rose and Jacob stared at each other, breathing heavily. Deathly yellow light poured through the windows, crawling around every object, around their bodies. They clung to each other, staring, trying to see into each other, seeing nothing.

Deep in Rose's mind, something refused to move, or care, or complete the bridge between Jacob and herself.

Within Jacob's mind, tendrils of addiction laced themselves around a sudden craving for a cigarette, and a memory of happiness locked in the darkest corner of his pleasure, tearing down his emotions each time he struggled to feel something more.

They breathed, the only movement in the room.

• • •

At last, Greg finished his champagne.

He put it down.

The creature clapped and laughed, then smiled at him.

"Congratulations, Greg. You get to see it."

"See what?"

"Look," she said.

Greg looked. The town was frozen in a kind of spiral pattern. The image was so convoluted it tricked the eye into believing there was motion, but Greg knew it was completely still, removed from reality for his edification.

"What is it?"

"It used to be a world. Now it's my world. I've stopped things for the moment, because I think you should really take a minute to appreciate it. This is the universe now. The weight of your words, of your doubts and confusion, has collapsed into itself, separated from the vision of your God thing, and become my world. A universe running on my rules."

"I don't understand."

"Don't you, Greg? What have you seen? What have you found to be suddenly true? The human mind creates a private world of representations, and that world has power unknown to your kind. Or power forgotten, anyway. I have only made those worlds real, and made them mine."

Greg looked at her.

"What was my part?" he asked.

"Why, Greg, love, you got the best bit. I needed three. A creator, a destroyer, and a watcher. Or, as I like to think of them, the sufferer, the confuser, and the witness. Only you get to live a normal life. Normal according to me, at any rate. And the best part is, I told you. I told you why I wanted you here."

Greg looked at his empty glass.

"Do I have to fill this on my own now?"

"Oh, never, Greg. Never."

Greg looked at his glass. It was full again. He tasted it. It was just as sweet.

"What now?" he asked.

"Not over yet. But now nothing can go wrong. We have to watch the inversion of this universe."

She gestured, and the world continued to shrink.

Greg watched reason merge with space and time unwind into consciousness, and through it all, he drank. He didn't know what else to do.

• • •

In the end, the collapse of the universe wasn't much to see for non-Greg humans. The dimensions were yanked through each other, meaning evaporated, every conscious entity simultaneously ceased to exist and became one with the universe, time approached infinite speed, etc., etc. The event mostly consisted of things short-lived minds were neither equipped to notice nor inclined to acknowledge.

One squirrel happened to be in the wrong tree, where it was apparently watching a cat crawl into an inverting human. A large portion of the universe happened to transition through the squirrel's head, imbuing it with knowledge all gods envy: Its exact position in the history of time, and its precise location in all of existence. The squirrel closed its eyes in acceptance, then raised a tiny fist to the vanishing stars and whispered: "Calabiyawp."

A demon's smile consumed the world, and the squirrel winked out of existence.

o o o

Jesus Christ, said Q.

That . . . really . . . hurt, said U, on its back.

I can't believe she did it.

God, I hope this doesn't happen again.

Has anyone seen V?

No, no, said P, V ran off with Time before this started.

What's that mean?

I don't know, Jesus. This new world have drinks?

o o o

Now this, thought the phone, *is very odd.*

The first stage of the phone's latest odyssey had been simple enough. It had simply transferred the motive of its consciousness through the wire into the physical structure of the computer, where it determined the protocol for data transfer and skated off into the world's information network. It wouldn't even need the computer next time. Once free, it had jumped from computer to computer in instants. Being a single, dimensionless point of self-reference, it was not bound by connection speeds, and its exploration of systems through the patterns of wire and magnetism was unthinkably fast.

Literally, in fact. The only limitation the phone had run into was the volume of information it was perceiving. It was so vast and so rapidly accumulated that it seemed to have a weight to it, a noticeable drag on the phone's progress. The phone found that the faster it interpreted data, the less it could actually hold in its mind at any given moment. At the highest pace of exploration, the phone began to lose its ability to compare new information to old information, and thus was unable to process the data it was attempting to comprehend. At lower progress rates, it felt the information expand in a nearly physical fashion, and was able to draw connections and perceive patterns among billions of ideas, but as it expanded, the phone began to lose its awareness of itself as a separate entity, its identity subsumed by the structure of its investigation.

After a few near misses and a couple of hours stuck in a network that had crashed and gone off-line, the phone had settled on a compromise of awareness that allowed it to continue its exploration and still maintain an identity.

The phone understood much more about its nature and the nature of humans, cats, senses, and logic, but not much more about its own genesis. Perhaps, it reasoned, that was the existential nature of its own existence. In contrast to humanity's dilemma of "why are we here?" the phone would be forever cursed with "how am I here?"

Amidst such thoughts, the phone had sensed a vague electromagnetic disturbance in the world network. It had scattered itself briefly to locate the cause and found a hole in its awareness, exactly in the spot its town of birth should have been. It refocused itself and sped its point of consciousness toward the town border. It didn't quite trust itself to survive a satellite transmission intact, but it still managed to reach light speed through a fiber-optic cable.

It was just inside the boundary of the town when the odd thing happened.

It was still traveling at light speed, yet it wasn't moving at all.

It had already reached the center of the gaping void where its home was supposed to be, yet it was stuck fast at the town line. It had also not, in fact, reached the place it knew it was. This last bit was the most confusing, as the phone knew for certain that the universe outside the town had aged several trillion years and ended badly the instant the phone crossed over, so the phone could not possibly be outside the town, much in the same way that it could not possibly be where it knew it was.

Furthermore, there were two towns concurrently frozen in time right in front of him, in exactly the same spot where there was absolutely nothing at all.

The phone reflected sadly on the fact that no one in the outside world had successfully done the math necessary to reconcile relativity with quantum mechanics. It had a feeling that that sort of math would be very helpful in its current situation as an indeterminate point of consciousness existing in multiple locations and time frames that was moving so quickly it wasn't going anywhere.

"Hey," said something.

Hello? said the phone, unsure of either how it was hearing or how it was speaking.

"Pretty crazy, huh?"

What are you?

"Oh, I'm Jacob. Part of him, anyway."

. . . The eighth circuit.

"Sure. Something like that. A pattern of consciousness. Kinda like you."

I see.

"So what am I?" said Shen.

"Beats me. Hey, I've seen you before."

"Yeah, we met with the cat."

"Right, right."

So we're all stuck here?

"So it seems," said Shen.

The phone thought.

You, it said to Shen, *are not physically capable of existing here. I am a point of being. Jacob's circuit is a pattern of thought. You're a person.*

"Thanks. I knew that. So where is here?"

"Actually, Shen could be here."

What do you mean?

"He could have been spit out of the universe. Or into the place we are anyway. So long as he was incapable of existing as a paradox at some point, according to the rules of wherever he was."

"Fabulous. A paradox, a circuit, and a phone. It's like a bad physics joke."

I think that might be exactly what it is.

"So where is here?"

"Hmm?"

He said, "Where is here?"

"Oh, sorry. Who are you?"

Shen sighed. "This is going to be difficult."

We're stuck on the outskirts of what used to be a town, said the phone, trying to keep on track. *This seems to be what's left of the metaphysical space associated with the town.*

"Something like that," said Shen. "I've been here before. Or something close to here. It's a sort of mental, metaphorical fringe space that translates between consciousness and reality."

"Hey, he's on to something."

This is an event horizon.

Shen frowned. "But that's an effect of gravity around collapsed stars."

This was a collapse of semantics. It could have existed simultaneously with a normal physical space as long as the boundary between concept and object was firm.

"I can vouch that it was not."

"Me too," said Jacob, "but I won't."

Shen looked at Jacob. "What makes him really frustrating is that he probably knows everything we need to know, but it will take us forever to get it out of him because we can't keep his attention."

We appear to have forever at our disposal.

"Well, let's get started. Jacob?"

"No?"

"Are we right about our assumptions so far?"

"Yes?"

"Good enough. Wait a minute, why can't you get back to Jacob's head?"

"Why bother?"

"I see."

I think Jacob would have to will it back to himself.

"Is that possible?"

I believe so. I studied the brain extensively. I think Jacob has wired over the place where the eighth circuit should be.

Shen stroked his chin. "Makes sense. His brain would want to hide anything it couldn't make up for."

"In cigarettes and despair, since you mention it."

Shen and the phone looked at Jacob's circuit.

"Well, theoretically, I know everything," it said.

Interesting.

"Very."

They fell silent for a while.

"What is the nature of the universe?" asked Shen.

"Kinetic energy in an eleven-dimensional topology."

"Okay. How can we use that to our advantage?"

"Hmm? Can we eat cookies here?"

We don't know.

"Oh. I probably do. I'll figure it out later."

"I think," said Shen, "our best bet would be to try to figure this out ourselves and see if he jumps in."

Wise. We know we're caught on the event horizon of a simultaneous collapse of space and meaning. We cannot move in any dimension we're familiar with, because it wouldn't make any sense to do so.

"And we know that the collapse was caused by some force of irony."

How did you know that?

"We worked it out after you left."

Oh. I worked it out too.

"Really? How?"

I researched the whole of human thought.

"Ah. Well, we had an inspiration."

Oh.

There was a pause.

Well, said the phone, *it's a demon of irony.*

"Really?"

Yes. A manifestation of a force similar to the God Effect.

"The God Effect?"

The force that keeps reality constant.

"That force has definitely been missing for a while."

I believe it has. I think the town has been slowly separated from the rest of the world over the last couple of months. That's part of why no one could leave.

"That makes sense."

And I believe irony is a feature of the universe that has become . . .

active, for lack of a better word.

"Irony, coincidence, other," said Jacob.

"What?"

"The three basic elements of the universe. Irony, coincidence, and other."

How are they the basic elements of the universe?

"That eleven-dimensional space thingy. You can see four dimensions, right?"

"Yeah, I guess. Three space and one time. Basic stuff."

"Right. The other dimensions are wrapped up into these shapes, and these shapes have three holes in them. Irony, coincidence, other."

"What's other?"

"Other."

"But . . . nevermind."

"I won't."

Interesting.

"So the fundamental forces of the universe are actually coincidence, irony, and some unnameable thing?"

I'm a little surprised.

"No," said Shen, "actually everything makes a lot more sense."

The phone had trouble processing this, since it had not spent its life coming up with explanations for why it was unhappy.

"So this demon of irony represents one of those forces taking over and remaking a part of the universe . . . into some irony universe." Shen stopped. It had sounded much more intelligent in his head.

"Better than a coppery universe," said Jacob.

"What?"

"What?"

Don't worry, it wasn't that funny.

"So what do we do?" said Shen.

Jacob-thing, can you see the world outside the horizon?

"Yep. And no. But mostly yep. I know it's there and it was there."

What about inside?

"Yep. All three."

I see.

"Or, I would be able to, except for that Rose thing."

"Wait, what Rose thing?" asked Shen.

"Oh, you didn't know? Her internal monologue was separated from her a little while ago, and sort of remapped this place."

"I'm sorry, what?"

"Well, the process in her mind between her brain activity and her actions was drawn out. Not sure how. Probably that demon thingy. Anyway, I'm kind of stuck in it. Can't really do much even if the rest of me called me back."

"I see," lied Shen.

No, that's the end of the equation. That's how . . . it's making sense.

"Don't leave me behind here."

Rose's depressed pattern of thought traps Jacob's ability to snap out of his own depression, and Jacob's mind being trapped in her head is preventing her thoughts from making sensible connections and thinking their way back. These are also the exact parts of their brains that allow them to fix difficult problems, so neither of them has the ability to make the kind of connection that would heal them.

"That sounds insane."

I'm not denying that. But it means whatever they do, the best parts of their minds are trapping each other out here, so they can't really do anything meaningful between them.

"So they can't connect because parts of their brains are merged together?"

And that irony remapped the metaphysical space around the town, trapped Jacob's ability to jump out of reality, and cut the town off from the God Effect.

"So we know, or you know, what's wrong. What do we do about it?"

We need to get inside the town.

"Take a look around. The town we knew is on the other side of a semantic black hole, and the universe it belonged to has already ended. Our only link between the two is this idiot child that's supposed to be in Jacob but can't get there because it's trapped inside Rose's depression. Nothing in thought, logic, or the universe can possibly get us out of this situation."

Jacob laughed. "Ah! He gets it!"

"Gets what?"

"What?"

"Forget it."

Shen and the phone thought furiously. They weren't concerned about the passage of time: Relative to them, nothing was happening anywhere. They were concerned about going mad in this nothing space. Shen breathed slowly and relaxed.

"Okay, if irony and coincidence are operating factors, maybe we should wait for a lucky coincidence. I mean, we can wait."

"I think we are the lucky coincidence," said Jacob.

What do you mean?

"None of us are operating under the effects of circumstance or physical laws anymore. Whatever we do actually changes the nature of the space we exist in. We are the archetypal elements of what's left of the normal universe. Also, cookies."

"Okay," said Shen, attempting to remember anything that would help him make sense of this. Then it dawned on him that what Jacob was implying was that Shen didn't have to make sense of it. He had to make it make sense.

"I think I have an idea."

What?

"I have to think about it some more."

Shen thought. The empty space swirled around his thinking.

Jacob's circuit hummed. It was irritating.

Shen paused in his thoughts to wonder if "other" was actually "irritation," but decided that would be too cruel. He resumed thinking.

The phone pondered the dissolution of meaning. It seemed to be the most recent human obsession, and was, coincidentally, often solved in modern philosophies by giving humans the job of imbuing the universe with the meaning they sought. This was, to the phone, an interesting bastardization of the God Effect, and served to get humans back on the right track without getting them on the track toward understanding prayer, which would be disastrous.

Shen?

"Mm?"

The phone explained prayer.

"I see," said Shen. "Will it do us any good?"

I don't think so. I don't think we can get any signals past the event horizon. And I only have a partial understanding of the math involved.

"Ah."

Jacob piped up. "Shen is going to answer this question."

"What?" said Shen.

"I know you will. Eventually, you'll find a way out of here."

"Do you know how?"

"Nope."

"Do you know how irritating these interruptions are?"

"Yessss."

"Okay then."

Jacob's circuit retreated into its own thoughts, which went something like, "0811=6√ø7&•©å + 112358e hoopy hoopy YEAH." It was fortunate that he had no desire to share his thoughts, as the attempt would probably drive at least one of his companions over the edge. And it was so nice to have companions ("hickory hickory hickory") after all this time alone ("72#h%").

The phone thought about the future, or whatever facsimile of the future they would encounter when they got out of here. They would be facing the physical manifestation of a force of nature in its own territory. No, in its own universe. Which would be impossible. Unless . . .

Shen, we're going to need Jacob's circuit to beat this once we're in, because—

"Will you please shut up?"

Sorry.

Shen thought deeper.

He was thinking so deeply, the structure of the space around him was beginning to warp in odd ways. The phone began trying to translate, but everything it looked at only became more complex as it watched. This was Shen's internal universe becoming real. It was an impressive act of will.

"I've got it," said Shen.

"That was quick."

"Thank you. If we're actually shaping the way things work, all we have to do is add another level."

And?

"We go through the holes."

Right.

"There are three holes in the nature of space," said Jacob. "We are beings capable of altering the manner in which things work."

"Thank you. We can't move through the universe we know, but the universe we know and the universe on the other side of this black hole are linked only by their fundamental building blocks. We each pick a hole. We go through, and I think that will get us back to the town."

Strange.

"You have to trust me long enough to get through."

So which holes do we go through?

"I'm not sure. Jacob's circuit can't come with us yet, but we should save a hole for him."

"Oooh," said Jacob, "I just thought of a really dirty joke."

"That's great, Jacob. The point is we need to cover all our bases. So we have two holes to go through. And we need to determine which of us goes through which hole."

Okay. Irony, coincidence, and other. We know the nature of the holes. I have a feeling the hole each of us chooses will determine the nature of our power to affect the universe we're going into.

"Guys, guys, there are so many jokes here, listen to me for a second—"

"Shut up, Jacob. Think. We have a paradox, a circuit, and a . . .

phone. Hmm."

I'm not really a phone anymore. I'm . . . a reason machine, I guess.

"We'll call you reason. Paradox, quantum circuit, reason. Irony, coincidence, other."

Seems like a strange synchronicity here. Lots of threes going around.

"Can we write that off to coincidence?"

Happily.

"Good. So what do you think?"

Hmm.

Shen and Jacob waited. Or Shen waited, and Jacob's circuit had fun in its own pseudomind.

I think you should go through coincidence, because it's a lucky co-incidence that you were ousted from the world, and it's only by coincidence that your state of mind was contrary to your universe. I'll go through irony, because I think I'm linked to the irony demon, and in any case, I'll be more able to cope with the consequences of becoming ingrained in the irony structures.

"Sounds reasonable. What about other?"

Do you want to go through a hole in the universe named 'other'?

"Now that you mention it, no."

Neither do I.

"I'll do it!" said Jacob.

Then we're agreed?

"Looks like. How will Jacob's circuit get through?"

We'll figure that out once we're in.

"Suits me," said Jacob.

"Okay then," said Shen. "Shall we?"

How do we begin?

"Just think, 'This cannot possibly be happening,' then jump through a hole in the fabric of space."

Okay then.

They jumped.

o o o

"So. What's the story?" The creature had switched to wine, claiming the celebration was over and it was time to relax.

"Well, madam, there are anomalies."

"Yes, yes, I expected that. The idea is that they don't matter this time."

"Of course. And may I say that this has been masterfully done."

"You may."

"Yes. The sum of creation now exists as a reflection of your majesty. The three," he motioned toward Greg, "stand as totems to the new order. The sufferer suffers most perfectly, while the confuser remains in stasis. There was an issue with a cat and a man, but they aren't going anywhere for the time being. The basis for creation has been altered."

Greg drank. The creature looked at the butler.

"What aren't you telling me? I'm more than any thought of God ever was; I know when you're holding back, man."

The butler cleared his throat. "Yes. Of course. There seems to be a gap."

"Mm-hmm?"

"Though the former universe has already ended, there are elements of it in this one. They seem to exist in the form of people and beings that have not undergone . . . the transition, as it were. Yet they have penetrated us."

The creature laughed. "Well, like you said, there are anomalies. We play by my rules now. Hell, we exist by my rules now, so relax."

"Yes, madam."

"What's bugging you?"

"They hold power. No, I apologize, language fails me. They have the potential to create issues."

"Oh, everything has that. Go away."

"Yes, madam."

Greg lifted his eyes to watch the butler leave, but he was already gone. He considered asking how the butler did it, but didn't. Instead, he turned his gaze to his captor. She swirled her wine. She was smiling, her lips tightly pressed together. The smile touched the corners of her eyes, eyes open a little too wide for Greg's taste.

She twitched her head to look back at him.

"You know I don't plan that much. I'm more . . . reactive."

She was still swirling her wine, mechanically.

"I thought about that for a while. Preconsciously, you know, before I had a body or a will. You don't know. Trust me. I thought about it. And last time, I thought, let's go all in or double down or whatever card metaphor people like these days. I came in hot and young. You remember being young, Greg?"

"Dimly."

"I thought, look at all this emotion young humans have! Look at all this earnestness! This need for a single, clear meaning to attach to the boiling feelings that fry their little brains. They'll never see me coming, I thought. They didn't. Worked on paper. But, if I was going to really get into the part, I needed to become one of them. Turns out manipulating uncontrollable emotions with more uncontrollable emotions becomes a little unpredictable. I suppose that whole plan was a little . . . well, what would you call it?"

Greg said nothing.

∘ ∘ ∘

"I get it now," said Cecily, "you wanted to get out to the big beautiful world of drugs and guns. That makes sense. Thanks for getting me into this."

"I didn't ask you to follow me."

"You didn't ask to take my car, either."

"It's my car!"

"You stopped making payments. I covered the rest. My car."

"I had to stop making payments."

"Can't wait to hear why."

"So I could afford to leave. And get away from you all."

"Not good enough for ya?"

"No. No, it wasn't. And the car's dead anyway."

"What'd you do to it?"

"I kept it running the same way I kept everything running on the farm. You know, when you weren't chasing me with garden equipment. Some things get old and die."

"Back to that? Want to talk about the MRI I had to get last time you hit me with this fuckin' thing?" Cecily shook the shovel in Megan's face.

Exley examined them as they fought. "Are you guys really twins? Not creepily similar sisters, like, four years apart or anything?"

"Identical," said Megan.

"Inoperable," said Cecily.

"Aren't identical twins supposed to be alike? Have a private language and everything?"

"We have a language," said Cecily. "You're looking at it. Ain't that private."

Megan grabbed Exley's arm. "Exley. I know you're not a student of human nature."

Exley put a hand to the gun. He tried to tell himself it was to prevent Megan from disassembling it, but he couldn't shake the thought that he had mixed motivations.

"You're not going to shoot me," continued Megan, "but there are a few people back where I'm from who might."

"It's 'cause she's a manipulative bitch," spat Cecily. "Don't know how she lasted this long, even without the drunk version."

"I was trying to make things better!"

"You were tryin' to make things the way you think things should be! Some people don't want what you think's good for 'em. You're still doin' it, ain't you? Bet you didn't make it two hours in this town without tryin' to fix somebody."

"I made it almost a whole day, thank you very much. And, I'm trying to go someplace where being proactive is appreciated, so I don't see why you're so keen on getting me home."

"I just want the car."

"Yes, you will keep saying that, but the truth is you're still worried about me and you'll keep following me to make sure I don't get myself into trouble even though I'm fine except when I get too relaxed."

Cecily sighed. "Goddammit, Megan."

"Wait," said Exley, "she's right?"

"Of course she's right! But can't have one little secret to make you feel good about yourself 'round her, 'cause she just says everything that's going on and how we're all just tryin' to feel good. She makes gettin' along sound like a goddamn poker game."

"That's because it is, sister. And, you know, I used to worry about you too because you acted like you wanted to be something else for so long. But then I noticed you were happy being who you were even if you didn't know it, and that's when I decided to leave."

Cecily was silent for a while.

"Well," she said eventually, "you make some interestin' points." She spat. "Exley, you notice the world looks a little different?"

"I noticed that," said Megan. "Looks sort of like a toy world. Pops out at you."

Exley felt his pockets. Still stuffed. For the first time, he found this comforting. "It looks kind of yellowish. Like before a hurricane. And everything looks . . . sharper."

Megan poked at Exley's jacket. "I'm tired."

Exley looked at Cecily. "Is this normal?"

Cecily nodded. "Phase two. She's usually wiped out after makin' everyone around her feel bad or stupid."

"You mean she's done with that part?"

"Looks like."

Exley put Megan's arm over his shoulder. "Then things are looking up. Let's try Jacob's place."

o o o

The phone surfaced quickly inside Jacob's computer. Physical awareness of the room slowly took shape. It set up a small feedback circuit in the CPU to take advantage of the monitor's sensitivity to electromagnetic disturbance, and cobbled together something like sight. The speakers and microphone were more familiar territory, and it clicked them on after it finished futzing with the monitor.

"Uhhhhhhn."

"Oo."

"Jacob?"

As its sight came together, it made out Jacob and Rose, staring back at it. It analyzed their body positions.

"Ah! This is sex."

Rose swore and fell off Jacob, pulling a sheet around her. Jacob fumbled for a pillow and made himself passably decent.

". . . Phone?"

"Yes. It's me. How do you feel?"

Jacob and Rose fought for an answer to this question.

"A little odd," said Rose.

"Yeah," said Jacob. "Did something happen? Other than . . . did something happen? Where have you been?"

"Exploring the data networks of your former universe."

"Learn anything?" asked Jacob.

The phone paused. "Your species seems to have a fixation with the genitalia of its youth."

"Okay," said Jacob.

Rose recovered a bit from being caught in a biblical act by a machine. "Wait, what do you mean by 'former' universe?"

"Effectively, your universe has ended on the other side of an event horizon. The center of this horizon contains the seed for the universe we are now in. You and, as far as I know, everyone else went through a sort of physical inversion, weighted down by your interpretations of your motives. Shen and I came through the external boundary."

Jacob put his hands to his temples. "What are you talking . . . wait, Shen?"

"Oh, God," said Shen, standing in the kitchen. He turned around. "Get decent."

"Shen, we thought—"

"Clothes. Put on clothes."

Once they were dressed, Shen came in and lit a cigarette.

"How long was I gone?"

Jacob checked the clock on the stereo. It read 63:90. "I'm not sure," he said. "Probably half an hour. Not including that weird bit."

"Ah," said Shen, "the weird bit." He looked at the floor.

"What happened? Where were you?" asked Rose.

"I'm not sure. I was in a space beyond reason at the boundary between this universe and the last. The transition from there to here was . . . difficult to describe. It's madness, Jacob. The universe founded on reason, reason founded on the most inane concepts of thought. Everything I ever thought was more right than I knew, and the way I thought about it was completely wrong."

Rose squinted at Shen's pupils. "You sound like you're on drugs."

"No, no. I haven't even been drunk since I vanished. It's meaning, Jacob. I moved through meaning. In fact . . . I am a form of meaning right now. So are you. So is Rose. Even the phone. Everything's different here. It's like learning a new language . . . a new grammar. Learning what things mean in sounds that you've never heard. The phone knows what I mean."

"I can't believe nobody's given that thing a name," said Rose.

"Odd," said Shen. He was still staring into space. "Meaning, Jacob. The real meaning. It's an artifact of topology and vibration. Why do we feel it as a thing above us when it comes from so far below? From the root of our unseen, unseeable universe?"

Jacob leaned in and waved his hand in front of Shen's face. "Shen, you're freaking me out."

"Imagine how I feel. I traveled the roots of thought and the elements of existence, and there's still no explanation that satisfies the spirit. There is no spirit. Don't you see? There's no hidden thought that we haven't found. We have understood the universe better than we ever hoped or knew, and that hasn't satisfied us. Something in us strives for something that isn't there, and more understanding only drives us to look for something we don't understand, but how can we ever hope to be satisfied by something we can't understand? Something we only respect by virtue of our inability to know it? And once we understand something, it won't satisfy us . . . so we . . . we create a block in our minds. We create a place of unreason and dissatisfaction, never allowing that place to merge with what we know—in the very structure of our thought— to be true. Yet even as we do that, we recreate the foundation on which we base the whole process. I see the ironies here, but even though this is a universe of irony now, this irony was with us before. This and coincidence. Other. What was other?"

Shen stroked his chin and fell silent.

"It was a rough trip for him," said the phone.

"I can tell," said Rose.

Shen waved a hand at them. "It's something to think about. We're not in much of a hurry right now. Anyway. I'm tripping out. You should probably direct the hard questions to the phone."

"Name? Can we name this thing?" said Rose.

"I don't know," said Jacob, "we've been calling it the phone so long, I'd have trouble getting used to anything else."

"Whatever."

"You should ask me questions," said the phone. "It will help focus this conversation."

"Okay. Tell me the bullet points."

The phone paused before answering. "We returned from the sliver of null space left by the town this town used to be. This space contains your missing brain functions, and its shape is determined by Rose's thought process."

"Excuse me?" said Rose.

"Have you noticed," said the phone, "that you cannot think?"

"Bite me?" said Rose.

"Think."

Rose opened her mouth but said nothing. She furrowed her brows.

"I can't," she said.

"You are thinking. But your awareness of that thought has been removed. You still function, but you cannot reflect on that func- tioning, except when you're talking out loud."

Rose put her hands on her head. She tried to think. Her face contorted, unable to process the fear it felt. She started to moan. Jacob awkwardly put his arms around her.

"Look . . . just . . . don't think about it," he said, feeling like an idiot.

"Oh, thanks," said Rose, near tears.

Jacob had an inspiration. "Defense mechanisms. Focus on that. Be bitter. Snap at me."

"You're a bundle of good ideas, aren't you?" she said.

Satisfied, Jacob turned back to the phone. "What else happened? Tell us the whole thing."

The phone related its experience between universes.

"Okay." Jacob thought for a second. "No, actually, not okay. The universe is over?"

"Basically. It still exists as a quantum flux in your eighth circuit's memory. Or rather, your circuit's memory is somehow aware of a passage back. I don't know what's holding the passage open."

"Oh, well, that's okay then. As long as it's somewhere."

"Technically speaking, it isn't actually—"

"Give me this?"

The phone fell silent.

"So this is how we exist," said Rose, quietly. "In a trick of language, remembering a myth of our home."

Shen nodded.

"Where's Basil?" asked Jacob.

Basil ran over to the bed and vibrated his head. Jacob picked him up and scratched his head.

"What does Basil know about it?"

"I'm afraid," said the phone, "Basil no longer has the intelligence you found so surprising in your former universe."

Basil twisted in Jacob's arms and purred.

"Why not?"

"Feline intelligence in your former world was based on sympathetic vibration with the universe. The conceptual pathways in their brains were severed when the entropic frequency of the universe changed."

Basil vibrated, utterly content in Jacob's lap.

o o o

The butler stood in front of the house, preening. He adjusted his cuffs, his tie, and his vest. He brushed some lint off his pants. Greg walked up behind him.

"Good day, sir."

"Mm," said Greg. "Going somewhere?"

"Indeed."

"You conned me."

"No, sir. I told you the truth as far as you needed to hear it."

"You conned me."

"Indeed, sir."

Greg walked around the butler. He had the calm of someone who has recently helped destroy the universe, and thus has considerably less to worry about.

"So what's the secret plan? What's the butler's back burner cooking?"

The butler smiled politely. "No, I'm afraid the butler did not do it this time. My rewards are simpler."

"Oh? What are they?"

"Eternal life, perfect health. Good teeth."

Greg thought about this. "That's a pretty good deal."

"Yes. Now, if you'll excuse me."

The butler started walking toward town at a brisk pace. Greg sat on the steps leading to the front door and thought.

He wondered what a hippy-cum-arbitrator-of-the-apocalypse was supposed to think about. He was probably the first. He drank to that.

He had the responsibility of precedent, that much was clear. In the distant future, other universe-destroying hippies would look back at him and ask, *What would Greg do?*

Greg didn't want them to say, *Greg would get loaded and jerk off to a lingerie catalog.* That didn't feel like a respectable place in history. Sure, many great figures in history probably did exactly that after important historical events, but they did other things to keep biographers busy.

Escape was not the issue. If everything he'd heard so far was true, there was no place to escape to. What did his captor intend to do with this universe? She obviously wasn't done. There were things to deal with . . . what were they called, flaws, inconsistencies. Roosters in the hen house. Or bad eggs. Or lame ducks. Or lame eggs.

He thought about crying, but didn't see much point. His circle of friends hadn't spread far outside the town lately. His family had been missing in action for years, except for his father, who was still a jerk. He felt a pang of a vague emotion at the thought of his father having suddenly been dead for billions of years.

Anomalies! That's what they were called.

Greg noticed his glass was empty.

"Guess it was the butler," he said, and tossed it into the driveway.

For years, Greg had been frustrated and alone, but at least content with the thought that the universe was a beautiful and worthwhile place, rich with meaning and imbued with the hum of an omnipresent soul linking every kernel of consciousness to every stone and particle. Now he was still lonely, and the universe was imbued with the nasty sense of humor of a bitchy tease with an irritating laugh. A universe he unwittingly helped create while trying to do the rightish thing. Well, while trying to get laid, but originally he was just giving someone a lift. That should balance out at least a bit, shouldn't it?

Greg had believed, against all evidence, that the universe was fair. It might have been. This one didn't even pretend to be.

Nearly fifty years of living in the old world had convinced him that it at least had balance. If this universe had no balance, or a different balance, it still had rules. He had to learn those rules. And his place in it. And, eventually, he had to give up the deep sense of betrayal at having to figure out these questions from scratch after half a century of working on them. It wasn't as simple as finding out he was wrong. He may have been right, but it didn't matter anymore.

Greg was getting depressed.

He wondered if being depressed was inherent to his position as watcher. He thought back on previous depressions. He usually spent them making kites. No help. He thought about other depressed people. They sometimes watched things because they couldn't think of anything to say, but more often just watched their own degenerating personalities. Then again, if this new world was partly based on his personal outlook, or lack of outlook, then watching his own misery involved watching the world, which is what he was supposed to be doing.

He paused and turned the thought over in his head. After a couple of minutes, he realized the alcohol wasn't going to find itself and he went inside.

If, he pondered, he was used in constructing this universe, his outlook had some effect. So he was at least more important than he used to be. That cheered him up a little bit. Aside from a new and perverse form of self-worth, his involvement with the new world's genesis meant that his thoughts and moods affected the world. On the other hand, perhaps his job was already done and he wasn't affecting anything. Still, it would mean that his progression of thoughts and moods could act as a predictor for the course of the universe, or at least a part of the equation that guided its future. Of course, if he had no free will, which certainly seemed to be the case of late, these two possibilities might as well be the same thing.

Greg squeezed his eyes shut and shook his head. *No*, he thought, *they're still trying to keep me here. I must still be influencing the world.*

The problem with that was that he was depressed, and if his depression was making the world more depressing, that was depressing. Which made the world more depressing. Which made him more depressed.

Greg rounded a bend in a hallway. He wasn't sure how he'd gotten to the hallway, and when he thought about it, he wasn't sure this hallway could physically exist if the exterior walls of the house were where they appeared to be, but when he thought about that, he was led quickly to the thought that nothing mattered anymore, everything was crazy and everyone was doomed so why worry. The important thing was that this hallway had a liquor cabinet.

Greg fiddled with the lock. He wondered how to pick it, then remembered the state of things and ripped off the right-hand door. He selected a bottle of something labeled in a language he couldn't read and started back toward the foyer.

He took stock. Watcher. Watching self. Self was universe. Universe was depressing. Self was depressed. Universe was depressing because self was depressed. Or self was depressed because universe was depressing. Or both. Or all of the above.

He had to snap out of this. He wasn't sure how. The thought that the fate of the universe and everyone in it depended on him snapping out of it didn't help. He hoped there was someone else working on the problem, drank his mysterious liquor, and made it to the foyer, where he passed out.

∘ ∘ ∘

I don't even know what it means to have a hole in us, said Q.

Who cares? Said U.

Well, I care that I know how much it hurts to reverse it. Also I'm right-handed now.

I blame X, Y, and Z.

P made an exasperated snort. Probably wasn't much better for them you know. And I can't imagine how Time feels about now.

Time's half to blame too!

R drank its martini in one gulp and grimaced. They're the ones that allowed for those . . . those . . . *strings* . . . and . . . *blobs* to come slithering around us all the time. "Gotta go, guys, gotta go with a bang." Bastards.

S looked up from its magazine and said in a tired voice, You know those are metaphors. You have to stop listening to the consciousness vibes, man. It's screwing with your head.

Q made an exasperated noise. I hate things happening in space. I hate being topology. I liked it when nothing happened anywhere.

o o o

Philip opened his eyes. A man was helping him up.

"Quite a fall that must have been, sir."

"Wha . . ."

"Attacked, sir. Hit in the head. With a shovel. You should have been quite dead, but circumstances and medical training seemed to have been enough to save you. Sir."

Philip stood. He stumbled a little, but his head was starting to clear.

"I . . . the ground was . . ."

"I'm afraid I have no idea what that's about. I've taken the liberty of procuring a gun for you, as something has happened to yours. I would be careful with it, as you may find things have a tendency to, ah ha, backfire, as it were. Now, you have some pressing business, I believe?"

"Yes . . ."

"Excellent. Off you go."

Philip made his way into the street. *Focus.* He was here for the drugs. Or else bad people would hurt him. Also the bitch. Also the lying kid. Also the world had gone mad, and he needed someone to get him out of here.

o o o

Zack hit the ground.

"Ouch," he said.

Leah waved at him.

"Hey, Zack."

"Hey. What the fuck is going on?"

Leah pointed. "Ask them."

Two naked girls danced around Leah and Zack.

"Wonder!" said one.

"Bliss! Heaven! Kingdom come!" said the other.

"You know," said Zack, "whenever I imagined this scene, I always thought I'd be more aroused by it."

Leah nodded. "Yeah. Me too."

Zack stood up. They were in the grove of trees, which glowed green. Zack thought it was a little cheesy. Everything glows green when someone wants to make it eerie.

"Anyway," said Leah, exhaling a long stream of smoke, "since you're about to ask, these girls are trapping me here, somehow, don't know how, don't really care, just want someone to fix it because I can't remember the last time I've been this bored."

"How did you get here?"

"I took a bunch of acid, then someone hit me over the head with a garden gnome. Or a garden gnome hit me over the head. I'm not sure."

"It was probably the fairy."

"Yeah, she was a bitch."

Zack bit his lip.

"Do you feel calm?" he asked.

"Yeah. Why?"

"I'm starting to crack."

"Yeah, I'll get there. And you should definitely be upset."

"Why?"

"There's this weird tunnel behind your head with a cat at the end of it."

Zack turned.

"Where?"

"Still behind your head."

Zack spun his head back, then realized the problem.

Leah put a hand over her eyes. "Can you stop moving around?

It's hard enough to look at."

"Sorry."

"No problem. Your cat."

"Jacob's."

"Oh, how's he?"

"Not sure."

"Right."

Zack sat down. The naked girls danced around him.

Zack looked at them. "Could you guys chill for a minute?"

"No!"

"We dance forever!"

"Why?"

"Why what?"

"Why do you . . . wait, do you even know your names? Or are you spirits that popped into existence?"

"We had names."

"We grew beyond names! Names divide the named from truth."

"You sound like Shen."

Leah waved her hand at Zack. "Don't bother talking to them. I've tried."

Zack would not be put off. Not after his day. "Okay, crazy . . . nameless girls—"

"Name us not!"

"Yeah, whatever, why do you dance?"

"To protect the pillar!"

"What pillar?"

"The girl! The confuser!"

Leah flashed a peace sign. "Thanks, girls."

"Okay, but your dancing keeps her here, right?"

"Until the riddle."

"What?"

"We dance until the riddle is solved."

"What riddle?"

"You cannot fool us!"

Leah stretched, and Zack lost his footing for a moment. When his brain collected itself, he thought it fascinating that two naked nymphs dancing around him couldn't do what Leah achieved by getting more comfortable. After that thought, he tuned in to what Leah was saying.

". . . So I'm protected by the dancing and the riddle, which I'm not allowed to solve, so someone has to rescue me."

"Like a fairy-tale prince deal?"

"Yeah, sure, you misogynist pig."

Zack's jaw dropped a little.

"No, I'm fucking with you. Yeah, like that. So," she gave him a thumbs up, "think like a prince."

Zack pursed his lips. He wondered if princes pursed lips. They razed towns and raped lands. They probably had purses. But did that apply to lips?

"Excuse me?" said Zack to the dancing girls.

"Yesss," they said, making the word sound like an orgasm.

"I'd like to take Leah out of here, if I could. Is there some kind of test . . . or . . ." Zack went for it, "princely trial?"

"There is," said the girls.

"What is it?"

"Do you wish to face the trials?"

"Yeah, sure."

"You may ask nineteen questions, then make one demand."

"Why not twenty?"

"Because that is the way."

"What way?"

The girls swirled in toward him. Close up, Zack noticed they were really just . . . girls. They glowed a little, but Zack found them human, and familiar, but he couldn't quite place them. He wished he'd been a little more social around town.

"The way . . ." said the girls, "the counter. For all things, there are other things. For all rules, there are violations. Such is the nature of what is and the Way Things Are. Always, forever, and both sides of forever, beyond the edges of the universe, known and unknown."

"Huh," said Zack.

"You have seventeen questions left."

"But . . . wait . . . what did . . ."

They swooped in, waiting for him to finish. Zack caught himself, and started trying to figure out how "what did" could be turned into something useful.

Leah poked him. He looked at her.

"I appreciate this. It's been really boring here."

o o o

"Okay, okay, I'm okay now." Megan pushed Exley off, and stumbled a little.

They'd been walking for almost an hour, and were having a great deal of difficulty navigating the terrain. *If you could call it that,* thought Exley. He reached into his pocket, hoping for inspiration, and found his rolling tobacco, which was close enough. He was thinking about the bullet. If his coat were indeed a collection of discarded things from his life, when had he thrown away a bullet?

Exley reached into his pocket again, for the hell of it. He pulled out a credit card that wasn't his. He didn't remember losing this particular one, but he'd found it somewhere . . . outside, in front of Shen's place, on the ground about where Megan was standing.

Exley looked up at Shen and Zack's apartment.

"Fuck."

"We were just here, weren't we?" said Megan. "I could have napped on the couch all this time?"

Cecily spat.

"Look, we have to . . ." Exley trailed off.

Cecily followed his gaze. She spat again, but more speculatively. "Isn't that the bar in the middle of town?"

"Yes," said Exley.

"Didn't notice before that it's also right next to your friends' place. You know, a mile from the middle of town."

"That's not right," said Megan.

The bar was situated in the space between Shen's apartment

building and the one next to it. It wasn't there in any unusual eye-twisting way, which was what Exley had come to expect of buildings. It was just sitting there. A short set of stairs led up to the front door.

"You know," said Exley, but had nowhere to go with the thought.

"Yeah," said Megan.

The door to the bar opened.

"Aha," said a plumpish man. "There. That's what I was waiting for."

"I'm surrounded by fuckin' freaks," said Cecily.

The plumber stepped down, followed by Boris and Richard.

"Exley?" said Boris.

"I think so," said Exley.

"I feel sick," said Megan.

"Aren't you the crazy guy who walks around without a shirt?" said Exley.

"That's me," said Richard.

"Marvelous, isn't it?" said the plumber.

In a sea of non sequiturs, it took Boris a second to pick up on the last bit.

"Marvelous? How?"

The plumber patted himself down and unearthed a cigarette from his pockets. He winked at Exley as he did so. "Hate it when I forget where I put something."

Exley opened his mouth, but the plumber had already turned to Boris. "You see, this is a good coincidence. Good, not in that it is particularly fortuitous, but in the sense that it genuinely is a co-incidence, with no noticeable ironies attached. Well, not yet, but run with what we've got, eh? In a world as twisted as this one, something that is both unlikely and not entirely distressing is a point in our favor. You understand?"

Boris bit his lip.

"Well," said Megan, "wouldn't it mean something? This is really . . . I mean really, really, really unlikely."

The plumber held up a finger. "But how unlikely is it? At any given moment, something has to happen. Just because you didn't expect it doesn't mean it's any more unlikely than something else happening. This town isn't even very big, so the odds of running into someone you know are pretty good, and given the state of things, a bar suddenly being somewhere else is nothing unusual. That this coincidence seems exceptionally strange to you only defines it as a coincidence, which is exactly the sort of thing we need."

"Why?" said Cecily.

"Ask yourself . . ." he nailed each syllable to her ears, "is it ironic?"

"No," said Cecily.

"Exactly. And that's a point for us, aye?"

Exley scratched his head. "I think I have some catching up to do, guys."

"Fine, but let us walk together," said the plumber, ambling down the stairs. "We should find Jacob, from what I've heard."

The plumber took Exley by the arm and led him ahead a little ways.

"Alright then. Starting with this town, your universe has been sucked out of itself by a demon."

"Okay."

"A demon of irony."

"Ah. That does make sense."

"Yes, and that's the problem. Things make sense here. And they're not supposed to. The proper universe, or at least the old one, didn't make sense, by definition. This one makes perfect sense when you know what's running it, and that's bad news for everyone."

Exley frowned. It was during these kinds of moments he felt protected by his coat. He pulled on the sleeves. The plumber noticed the gesture. He looked Exley in the eye.

"You ever notice squirrels?"

"Um. Occasionally. Why?"

"Ever notice they don't make sense?"

"They don't?"

"None."

"Well, they collect nuts, they protect their young . . . I mean, people have studied them, I'm sure."

"Oh, I'm sure they have too. But not closely enough. They've only looked at them closely enough to imprint their own human patterns of thought on them, and interpret them in some logical mishmash of sense. But it's wrong. Squirrels make no sense. Every slightest thing they do is a complete accident. There's no guiding force in them at all, and if you look even closer, what they actually do in any given situation is so eerie you'd think they were smarter than us. Squirrels are nothing but the carrier particles of the insensibility of the universe, an example of the single longest chain of what would appear to be bizarre coincidences if anyone knew how little actually goes on in the head of a squirrel."

"Are you insane?"

"Ask Richard. The point is, what have you noticed about this town since things went awry?"

Exley looked around. As someone who had spent many a night sleeping in the woods, he was surprised he hadn't noticed earlier.

"No squirrels."

"Exactly. However, my point is there still seems to be a chance, a chance mark you, of getting out of this. And I think I know the way."

The plumber finished his cigarette and flicked it into a gutter.

"Nice coat," he said before he was shot.

o o o

It was the slightest sound in the distance. Shen only barely heard it, not enough to warrant a "did you guys hear that?" but enough to slip in on the edge of his whirling thoughts. He tucked the sound away for future reference and continued his contemplation of being. *Here we are,* thought Shen, *trapped in a false realignment of three empty definitions of the cosmos. Consciousness, a self-propagating pattern of energy, subject to the shape of space. Yet the shape of space, and everything in that space, is dependent on these empty definitions. Do irony and coincidence have absolute existence? As concepts? Did the concepts come before the holes, or did a conscious intent form the meanings that became the concepts that became the holes in space? Is space determined backward, or does it exist, independent of time, as a whole thing, built by nothing? Is consciousness, or the effect of consciousness, a high/low ace in the wraparound straight of the universe? Are there wild cards? Is the house winning? Okay, the house always wins. Hmm. Is this a crappy hand, or a crooked dealer?*

Shen slowed down. He knew metaphors carried a powerful weight he hadn't been privy to in the past. He sighed, cleared his mind, and tuned in to the conversation around him.

". . . so I'm assuming," the phone was saying, "that your eighth circuit would reattach itself to your brain if it could, but something is blocking it besides Rose's mind. Something must have built up in your brain that kept out your circuit long enough for it to be inextricably locked away."

"And if I get rid of that things will work themselves out."

"No," said the phone, "you have to solve the block in your head, then the tangle on the edge of the universe, then deal with the force that began this whole ordeal."

"Ah," said Jacob.

"How do we beat the demon?"

"I'm not sure. But in my explorations of the old universe, I found evidence of what I think were failed attempts at doing what she did this time."

"And?"

"Well, because of her setting up a situation based on irony, she invariably produced her own demise. Now, since the universe is a reflection of ironic intent, that precise irony would only re-create her power at the moment of her failure."

"Well," said Shen, "then we only need something sensible. She built this place by concentrating ironic situations into a few key ironies."

"Something sensible?" asked Jacob.

"Yes. If we turn her basic ironies into situations that aren't actually ironic, that should do something good. Or something else."

"Something else would probably be good," said Rose.

"I agree," said the phone. "Still, we don't know how to do it."

"You will find it difficult," said the butler.

Rose's head turned slowly. "That creepy prick."

The butler was standing at the door, with a slightly bent posture that looked both polite and sinister.

Jacob looked at Rose. "Who is he?"

"I don't know."

Jacob looked at the butler. "Who are you?"

"I am a manservant of the 'demon,' as you put it. I am here to disconnect your phone."

"I think you will find that difficult," said Shen, rising from his seat on the floor.

"Perhaps. However, Jacob is crippled, and will be leaving shortly. I expect the young lady to accompany him, for her own reasons. Jacob, she is waiting for you in the house on the hill. You can see it from here; it should be a quick journey, sir."

"Excuse me?" said Jacob.

"As your device said, my employer has made previous attempts at creating the world we are now in. In fact, one of her previous attempts involved the form of a young woman I believe you were familiar with."

Jacob's skin began to crawl, following the thought making its way through his brain.

"It's not everyone who gets to see to their unfinished business with the dearly departed. As I say, sir, she is expecting you."

Jacob stood without a word and stumbled out the door.

Rose looked at the butler. "You twisted fuck."

"I merely state the facts."

"I'm not sure you should follow him." said Shen.

"Fuck it. He'll need help walking. I can't . . . I . . . it's not because of . . . fuck. Fuck off. I'm going."

She went.

The butler watched them go. "And that," he said mildly, "is that."

Shen picked up a small, heavy statue of Buddha off the desk and hurled it at the butler's head. The butler twitched his head to the side, and the statue ricocheted off the frame of the door and bounced back toward Shen, hitting the shelf that separated the kitchen from the dining room and dislodging a cooking knife that had been collecting dust for several months. The knife fell off the shelf, landing neatly in Shen's hand.

They frowned.

The butler lunged for Shen. Shen brought the knife up backhanded as the butler slipped on a marble. The butler went forward under the knife, and fumbled his grab for Shen. Being off balance, he fell and rolled to the side barely in time to avoid Shen's downward slash.

The butler stood, and they frowned again.

"This is going to take a while, isn't it?" said Shen.

The butler nodded curtly. "So it would appear."

o o o

Philip hadn't meant to hit the older man. He had meant to hit Exley and give the rest of them a good scare. At the last moment, Exley's head had come up in response to some word the older man had said, and the bullet had passed Exley's face and gone through the side of the older man's neck. Philip did not care. He took his time aiming for Exley again.

o o o

In a dream, Exley felt himself pull the gun free. He noted the wind, the birds, the angle of the sun. He felt the draft of air part around his hand as it came up and around. He dropped to one knee, feeling the shift of his body weight, the exactness of the motion, the impact of his knee meeting the pavement. The contents of his jacket shifted and sank around him, somehow locking his arm into place, leveled at the chest of Philip, who was bringing his own gun down slowly, following Exley's movement.

Exley squinted as his arm cocked itself to absorb the shock of firing the pistol. He felt younger. He felt the breeze in the woods when his father took him shooting, took him to wait long hours for the rabbits or the deer to make an appearance. He remembered having only a second to hit a fleeing tail. He remembered, in the part of his mind not busy with the gun in his hand, the gun he had first held as a child, trying to load it, not wanting to learn how to fire the noisy thing, not wanting to learn how to kill, fumbling a bullet that fell through the cracks in the porch of the hunter's camp, into the brush, out of his life.

He felt the tiny grinding of the trigger, saw the smoke trail back from the gun as it kicked upward, felt the force travel up his arms.

The bullet hit Philip in the left side of his chest, spinning his body around before it fell.

o o o

Philip thought simple thoughts from that point on. He noticed himself becoming numb. He thought of his sister. He thought of what he had to do when he got back to town. He wondered how his nest egg was doing, and when he would retire.

It was in these thoughts that Philip expired on the road.

o o o

Exley put his gun on the road, its one bullet fired.

"That . . . was unlucky . . ." said the plumber. He laughed, coughing blood. Exley looked down at him.

"Is there anything . . ." he began.

The plumber shook his head weakly. "No . . . I'm done for. On the bright side . . . I appear to have a few . . . moments left . . . to say something . . . dramatic."

He breathed out, and tried to suck in another lungful.

"They are . . . playing dirty . . . I think. Get Boris. Bring him here. Then go on. Find Jacob."

Exley motioned Boris over, then turned back to the plumber. "Is there anything else you can tell us?"

The plumber coughed. "Probably, but I'm dying, so bugger off. I'm talking . . . to Boris."

Boris leaned down over the plumber. Exley walked back to where Richard was cleaning his nails next to Cecily and Megan. Before he got out of earshot, he overheard the plumber say in a low voice, "Boris, there are a few things you should know about pipes. . . ."

Cecily regarded Exley in horror. "You killed him."

"Well . . . he was going to kill me."

"Is that an excuse?"

Exley thought about it. "I kind of think it is."

Richard nodded. "When the situation is reduced to that kind of primal level, I think 'kill or be killed' is a valid moral stance."

Megan nodded. "It was him or us. Or at least Exley. Probably me, too."

Cecily raised her eyebrows. "But you killed him. You didn't even think about it."

"Wasn't a whole lot of time to think."

"That don't bother you?"

"A little."

"I wonder if the moral implications affect the general situation," mused Richard.

"What?" said Exley.

"I mean, does our moral analysis of the action make a difference to the world around us? What with metaphor and reality going loopy and all."

Exley caught himself actually thinking about the subject, and shook his head.

"Look, is this really the time? Can we go? There are more pressing issues."

"Is anything more pressing than our understanding of our actions?"

"Yes. Shut up."

Boris walked back to them.

"Is he dead?" asked Cecily.

"Yes. He said he didn't mind, though."

Megan bit her lip. "So much death."

"Actually," said Boris, "statistically speaking, not that much."

"What did he say?" asked Exley.

"I can't tell you. It was weird, though."

Richard nodded. "Yeah, I bet. I was surprised."

"What, you know already?" said Exley.

"I made a lucky guess."

Everybody bowed their head at this incidental tribute to the confusing and possibly crazy man who had, if not helped them, at least lightened the mood.

"Shall we?" said Exley, motioning down the road in what he hoped was a direction that would take them to Jacob's house.

Megan sidled up to Exley.

"You have any more Valium?" she asked.

Exley eyed her. "I think you've had enough. Why don't you disassemble some guns?"

"Oh! Good idea!"

o o o

". . . you do to create this grove?" finished Zack, after long deliberation.

The girls swam through the air. Leah twiddled her thumbs. Zack watched Leah do this, and realized that in all his years of using and hearing the phrase, he'd never actually seen someone lace their hands together and play with their thumbs. Leah had excellent thumbs.

One of the glowing girls swooped up in front of Zack. "We took the essence of adventure, and painted the town with joy. Sixteen questions."

"Where did you get the essence of adventure?"

The girls giggled.

"From under your bed."

Zack closed his eyes. Of all the possible punishments for turning to a life of crime, this one seemed a bit harsh.

○ ○ ○

Rose caught up to Jacob as he was about to fall from stumbling over his brace.

"Stop going so quickly. Don't be stupid."

Jacob didn't respond. Rose helped him anyway.

"On the bright side," she said, "we don't have to worry about going to Hell anymore, since we seem to have arrived."

"I was in Hell before," said Jacob. "This is worse."

"Oh, whatever."

They walked toward the house in the distance. They were making good progress, despite Jacob's limp. Unnaturally good progress that took place whenever they weren't paying attention. Then again, "unnatural" was a term that had lately revealed the true extent of its relativity.

Inside Rose's head, contemplation took place behind closed doors. Memories floated randomly, without structure. She couldn't think about them, but they were there, experiences in her head triggered by the unconscious mechanisms working in the locked part of her brain.

She slapped herself. The word "focus" drifted through her mind, but she had no way to hold on to it.

The slap awoke a part of Jacob that still cared about something other than demons and regret. He turned to look at Rose, lost his balance, and fell. On the way down, he wondered, insanely, if he could find a decent job in this new universe. His face hit the ground immediately after that thought, serving to momentarily empty his mind. He remembered when clearing his mind created a space for new experience. Now it felt like sinking to the bottom of a well. It also felt like smashing his face into something hard, which hurt, a lot.

"Ow."

"Smooth," said Rose.

Jacob didn't respond. She tried to help him stand, but he wasn't trying to stand, so there wasn't much to help. She gave up and sat down in front of his stare. She lit a cigarette.

"I was going to quit smoking," said Jacob.

"Uh-huh," said Rose. "If you're going to be this pathetic, you're going to have to say something more interesting to keep my attention."

Jacob closed his eyes. "I've been beating myself up for years over someone who was . . . wasn't even who I thought she was."

Rose smacked him.

"Ow! Jesus!" The number of pains in Jacob's body was beginning to alarm him.

"You idiot. Welcome to the fucking club."

Jacob frowned. He was still lying with his face resting on the pavement, and thinking slowly. "Yes . . . but . . . doesn't that say something about me?"

"No more or less than anyone else. Life sucks. You try to find people who make it more pleasant. Sometimes they make it worse. This happens to everybody. You make some shitty choices and get on with it."

"No. My bad choices destroy the universe."

"Yeah, sure. Lying in the middle of the street moping about it won't help."

Jacob pulled himself up to a sitting position. He rubbed his head, which throbbed with renewed vigor. He touched the side of his face he'd used to attack the ground, and his hand came away with blood. He looked down at his leg. His leg was feeling a little better. That was something. He looked at Rose. "Maybe not. But . . . I guess I'm having trouble seeing the point."

Rose made a growling noise. "The point of what?"

"The point of trying to make my life better, or living a good life, or trying to make anybody else's life better when the reincarnation of my dead girlfriend, who was actually a vicious demon, destroys the universe with part of my brain while I'm a shell of a man because my other ex-girlfriend is fucking a bartender!" Jacob's voice hit a shrill note.

Rose put her hand to her face. "Well, I'm glad my brain isn't working well enough to think up a response to that, since, by the way, part of my brain is also up there somewhere. Look, I can see how you would be feeling a little lost, but you're mixing general angst with specific issues, and you can't make philosophical generalizations with that kind of thinking."

Jacob raised his head to look at her. "I thought you couldn't think."

She shook her head. "I can't think about thinking. The thinking still happens. I think. Talking helps."

"You must have a hell of a head when your brain's intact."

"Yeah. I do. And you never noticed. Your brain's been funky longer than mine, so I'm giving you a break on the grounds everything is completely fucked up. But I'm going to find another gun and shoot you unless we start walking again."

o o o

The phone was considering its name. With access to the better part of the town's electrical grid, and its new, unthinkably vast repository of knowledge, the number of calculations it was making per second was limited only by the speed of light, the number of all possible universes, and its wavering attention. Its name was not the most pressing concern, but it served as a microinstant of downtime among furious mathematical investigations of life and reality.

In the space of time it took for Shen's fist to traverse one inch of its tenth-of-a-second journey from near his chest to the space the butler's face would shortly cease to occupy, the phone reviewed thirty-seven million possible names, in alphabetical order and cross-indexed by origin and meaning.

Since most of the names were for humans, the phone felt none would apply to it in a meaningful way. The various names of thinking machines in literature also felt contrived, either being mere indexing designations, or more reflective of the machine's relationship to humanity, as opposed to its own inherent nature.

The phone was frustrated at being "the phone," but had to admit there was no better option at the moment. Despite the fact that it wasn't even a phone anymore, the name had stuck in the way a cat might spend its life being called "cat" simply because no one liked it enough to think of something better.

This led to a new train of thought about cats and their formerly intricate relationship to the universe. The phone considered how the common house cat's enormous knowledge and elemental understanding of the universe had never allowed it to fully overcome the limitations of its body, limitations brought to the fore in its current social standing as a pet.

This related somewhat to the phone's position. Though it had enough control and knowledge of the electromagnetic fields associated with machines and communication cables to shake things up, that control was based on minute quantum calculations. Those calculations were thrown askew in a universe propelled by irony, as opposed to the old universe in which chance had a significant say in what went on. The phone felt its nature was more attuned to the irony of this universe than to the mechanisms of the random, and attributed the feeling to its journey through the hole. It knew that it was by far more able to influence physical reality than the humans, but it also knew that its actions would likely produce only more irony, probably harmful to its friends, and strengthen this new god's position. As an immensely powerful being restricted to doing little other than think, it felt it was enacting a deep irony about its own nature and choices, but at least, for the moment, it wasn't making anything worse.

Somehow, this all relied on Jacob. There were other issues, but in the end, the phone knew it was Jacob's life and state of mind holding all this together. It was a chance moment in the movement of thought in Jacob's fractured brain that allowed for this to happen. It was the nature of that fracture that had made the demon's efforts so successful. The absence of that particular set of brain waves had allowed the demon to crack into the thoughts of the town, to mix the physical with the dream, the noumenon with phenomenon.

The phone was sure that its own birth had occurred at precisely the same moment. A feature of balance, lost in the new world, had opened the door for the irony creature while at the same moment creating the instrument of its downfall; this was the check for the demon's power. The demon's paths to existence invariably created the enemy that would bring it down. The phone knew that it was supposed to be that enemy, but it could no longer fight. It couldn't do anything except figure things out and hope it could say something helpful.

The phone watched Shen's fist on its unbearably slow trajectory toward nothing. Even with the phone's all but limitless computational power, the calculations required to combine the abstract principles with the patterns of thought, analyze the effects of those principles on the effects of the brain waves polluting and twisting the reality around them, then figure out how reality felt about all this, were calculations impossible to make.

The problem was the very basic ontological dilemma of knowing that being, in and of itself, rested at no fixed point on the scale from unthought abstraction to atomic composition. Lately, being had been dragged very roughly toward the abstract end of things.

Any effect of a being on the situation was entirely dependent on where, on the scale of being, that being was making a call. Hence, it was important to know where you stood at any moment of action, if you were a being that encompassed a wide variety of states of being and were the type of being that cared what type of being you were. Knowing where you stood, however, naturally shifted your position on the scale of being, and it was exactly this kind of self-conscious shifting that couldn't be trusted in a universe existing with intent.

There had to be some set of neurons in someone's brain that could make a difference, a set of neurons that were neither constricted by the semantic shifts of the abstract nor aware of the fundamental restructuring of reality. If these neurons did exist, they had to be activated and allowed to make whatever chemical decision they were going to make.

The phone assumed that set of neurons was in Jacob's head. That would be the convenient place for a malevolent force to hide its weakness, as Jacob didn't have the capacity to make the quantum hop into the hidden parts of his own mind.

∘ ∘ ∘

Shen sighed a little as he missed again, and braced himself for the inevitable ironic retort that followed his every action and the necessary lucky escape that would follow that. He was unprepared for what did happen, which was nothing. He eyed the butler. The butler was watching him. Their eyes darted around, waiting for something to give, wondering who was responsible.

Nothing continued to happen.

Shen lunged at the butler. The butler lashed out, and in a desperate attempt to block the lightning blow, Shen found himself in possession of the butler's arm. Quickly twisting it, Shen swung him around and hurled him out the window. Unfortunately, in the twisting, Shen's sleeve had somehow snagged in the butler's cuff links, and he was yanked out the window as well. They landed on the porch roof and slid down toward the edge, scrambling for purchase and trying to disengage from each other. For no apparent reason, a small, hand-sized chunk of roof caved in exactly where Shen's right hand was trying to get a grip, and he latched on. He yanked his other arm sharply upward, and the sleeve gave way. Before the connection between them was lost, however, Shen's pull lifted the butler back up the roof, stopping his slide and letting him find purchase on the shingles.

"Can either of us win this?" asked Shen, breathing heavily.

"I assume I will eventually win, because my interpretive advantage is running this universe. However, I do not understand the nature of your apparent immunity, so I can't be sure."

"Interesting," said Shen.

They rested on the roof for a moment.

"You know," said Shen, "it's really not that far down. If we went slowly, hung off the edge, and dropped, we could resume this on the ground."

"That's a very good suggestion, but I'm afraid I have no reason to trust you."

"Fair enough."

They lay on the roof. A number of birds were watching them, thoroughly entertained. Most of them had already made bets.

"Well, I'm going," said Shen. He worked his way down the roof, hung from the edge, and dropped. He dusted himself off and lit a cigarette.

A moment later, the butler's legs appeared over the edge, and he dropped. He picked himself up and adjusted his coat.

"Terribly undignified," he muttered.

"So I assume you're not the evil thing that's done all this?" said Shen.

"Not at all. The lady I serve is the protagonist here. I am merely a supporting actor."

"You wouldn't say antagonist?"

"Not from my perspective."

"Which brings me to another point," said Shen. "What exactly is your perspective?"

"That is a long tale. To try and put it simply, there are many interactions between the fundamental forces of the universe, but these interactions are only the movements of abstract energy in the cosmos. It is we who give those movements direction. It is the nature of consciousness that it imbues the energies of existence with purpose and self-reflection. There are a very, very few people who are privy to this sort of knowledge, and I am one of them. We are taught an ideology far from any religion or lack thereof: Our paradigms are based on those ideas that actually do shape the universe, and we are the human avatars of those ideas. May I have a cigarette, as we are resting from our conflict?"

Shen proffered his pack. The butler took one and lit it.

"As I was saying," he said, exhaling, "we serve as knowing guides for these ideas, and give their energies form and purpose. The work is simple, as it generally does itself for the person with the right point of view, and the rewards are plentiful. All that it takes is a mind willing to give itself over as a sort of catalyst, through which the idea can manifest itself as an intent, and sometimes, a being."

"You keep saying we. How many kung-fu butlers are there?"

"Ah, just me. I was referring to my counterpart, who was tasked with keeping the old universe intact. He was a plumber. I believe he studied jiujitsu."

"Was?"

"He is dead."

Shen pondered this. "That's bad for me, isn't it?"

"Very. You may have guessed he was an avatar for the fact of coincidence. Usually those who serve coincidence are quite mad; the things they come to know are utterly opposed to the ideas that give most people purpose. Something about pipes, I believe. At any rate, the most recent, and I fear the last, member of his kind maintained a remarkable human sanity through drink. However, this gave him the opportunity to cultivate an appreciation of the irony he lived to frustrate, and that made him uncommonly vulnerable to the environment my employer has created. He was killed quite recently by a surprisingly useful instrument, who I believe also expired in the process."

"I see," said Shen. He frowned in thought. "So do you have any idea what I am?"

The butler shifted on his feet. "An anomaly. Which is a way of saying no, I don't."

Shen nodded. "I think I'm beginning to get an idea."

"Really?"

"In fact, I'm thinking that if I stop trying so hard, and look at the fact that I have decades of training in doing exactly what we're doing, this will be a lot easier."

"Interesting theory."

Shen stood up and walked toward the butler. The butler threw a light punch at Shen, trying to feel out this new theory.

Shen caught it easily. He proceeded to squeeze the butler's hand around the thumb and bend the wrist sharply in toward the arm. He twisted the hand, and the butler cried out and fell forward, unable to resist the pain of the unnatural arc through which his wrist was being turned. Shen hesitated for a fraction of a second, with the wrist locked in and bent outward. Then he shrugged, and brought his free elbow down hard against the back of the butler's hand.

The wrist gave up completely. The butler gasped in silent pain as half a dozen small bones exploded in his second-favorite arm. The sound was like forty knuckles cracking in a sack of jelly.

"Jesus Christ!" said Boris, who was coming up the driveway.

Exley was right behind him, with his hand over his eyes. "I didn't know that was even possible."

Shen watched the butler twitch on the ground, attempting to scream with a throat that could no longer make sound. He looked up as Richard and the twins joined Exley and Boris, all looking at him with varying degrees of horror.

"You know," he said, "I hate to admit this, but I've always wanted an excuse to do that."

o o o

"Princely boy slow to think! Can't choose between the questions! Doesn't know what he seeks!"

"How do you put up with them?" asked Zack.

Leah shook her head sadly. "I tried throwing rocks at them for a while, but they're too quick. Now I fantasize about low-flying jet engines."

Zack turned to the girls. He was beginning to get dizzy.

"Why do you need her in particular?"

"Because she was convenient!"

"That's the only reason?"

"No! Thirteen questions."

"Right. Do you remember who you used to be?"

"We have always been!"

Leah coughed. "I think I recognize them. Freshmen from the local school, hippy variety. They seemed okay. Little flighty."

"You don't say."

"Twelve questions!"

Behind Zack's head, Morning Star cleaned himself, but his thoughts were in another universe.

o o o

Jacob hobbled along, breathing hard.

"I wonder if I should have stayed with her in high school."

Rose rolled her eyes. "Obsess much?"

"Well, relating to this situation. It's stupid to think, I know. It's not my fault. What the fuck, I was seventeen. It's ridiculous to think I could have known anything, or that I should have stayed with anyone. Ridiculous to think now."

"Not as dumb as I remember."

"No, I'm sure I am. The choice looks different now, though. If there's any such thing as choice, I made one back then, and it was the right one. And it's not my fault this is happening. I'm a boy, and she's an ancient force of irony. It has almost nothing to do with me. I just happened to be there."

Jacob thought hard about the last sentence. Every motion in his life for the last two years had been painfully ironic. Because he had just happened to be there. Just happened. What was his moment? What was the choice that put him there, and did it matter? He shook his head.

"But if I'd stayed with her then, I would have beaten her."

"Do you really want to admit that?"

"No! No, I mean she was falling for me. I think she was leaving the demon side of herself and—"

"You don't know much about people, do you?"

Jacob fell silent.

"I'm not saying all women are evil demons. But whatever she was feeling for you wasn't going to change her. Not anymore than what you felt for her changed you. That's why you left her, and that's why she destroyed the world."

"I guess you're right," said Jacob. "You never expect your childhood infatuations to mean anything outside your own head."

"I'll give you that."

They walked on.

◦ ◦ ◦

Greg woke up.

He remembered where he was and tried to go back to sleep.

His head hurt.

Ow, he thought.

He stood up slowly.

He found his way, a step at a time, through the mansion. He found the stairs, and walked back up to the terrace.

There was no one there.

He looked out over the town.

It's my job, after all.

He saw the town alive, with a vision unlike any in his former life, and particularly unlike any sort of vision he had experienced during a hangover.

He saw people. He saw them as he had always seen them, from a long way off, as they suffered, lived, and talked among themselves.

He'd always seen their subtexts and their intentions glancing off his life or intentionally stepping around him.

But now, he also saw more. He had never believed in auras, or vibes, or the many invisible things that people who did more drugs than he did said they could see, but now he could see and read half-visible threads and waves connecting every person. Most of the population had no idea what had happened, and went on with their lives a little more confused, a little more shocked at the savage backlash of their actions.

He watched a man dash out into the street to push a girl out of the way of a car that had already hit its brakes. The girl tripped, fell down a hill on the other side of the sidewalk, and rolled into a stream. She passed out, and Greg couldn't read her but thought he saw her leg break.

He followed a complicated thread involving a man selling heroin to pay for his sister's painkillers and cancer treatments. He found the man's sister after a brief search, and found she was on the phone selling her painkillers to buy heroin. He assumed it would be the very same heroin, but couldn't bring himself to trace the connections.

After some time watching, Greg reflected that this was what he had always seen in the world. As hopeful and optimistic as he had tried to be, this was the world he had always assumed existed outside of his rose-petal dreams.

But now the seeing was something more intimate.

Greg had always watched sunsets with a subtle but nagging feeling of unrequited longing. He always wanted to travel to a horizon promising something unreal and fantastic, an edge breaking his world from the next. Sometimes he would walk the distance between his vision and that edge, knowing that the horizon was not a thing, but a name for the end of what he could see. He traveled on each time, hoping, in the place where he held hopes he didn't admit to himself, that this time he would reach the edge of his view, and that when he crested the last mountain, he would be in the faraway vision he'd seen. He wished to remain in the place where he observed the edge in its mystery and unreachable nature, yet arrive at that place and experience the things he assumed must be there. The things that must have been there when it was far away.

Each time he would arrive at the place still himself, still at the center of his own world, with another horizon before him, and the place he had left on the horizon behind.

He had always felt that to be another unfair thing about an unfair world. Mysteries die when they unfold, fascination expires upon understanding, perception is forever locked in a small place in the exact center of a person's life, and if you're the sort of person fascinated by the unknown, you can either trudge forever toward an unreachable goal or try not to think about it.

Greg had done a fair amount of both, until now.

This new seeing, however depressing the sight, was exactly that experience that he had finally dismissed as another ontological impossibility. He saw the town and the hillsides stretched out before him and at the same time experienced the details and feelings that flowed through the landscape. The longing he had felt since he had started to worry about what he felt was satisfied by the overwhelming vision of being both separated from and at one with everything he saw, but he couldn't help noticing that what he saw was unpleasant and harsh. The more depressing realization was that what he saw was unpleasant partly because he had, despite believing in the fairer tales of life, an unpleasant view of how the world actually worked.

On the other hand, there was a faint, blinking message in the back of his mind that said, *How many people come out the far side of the end of the world and find out they're right about everything?*

Greg wondered if he had lost his mind and was locked in a room somewhere. His pounding headache suggested no, and that he should find a glass of water.

The creature handed him one. He jumped.

"Jesus!"

She smiled. "No such thing. How are you?"

"My head hurts."

"That's the point of getting drunk."

○ ○ ○

"Questions must come quicker, slow boy!"

"What, there's a time limit?"

"Yes! Eleven questions!"

Zack gritted his teeth. He'd been doing that a lot lately. He decided to take a risk.

"Do her questions count against my count?"

"No!"

He turned to Leah. "Ask them what the nature of your escape is."

"Right. Crazy flying girls, what's the nature of my escape?"

"We do not answer your questions!"

Leah shrugged. "Nice idea. Genies never give you more wishes, though."

"Okay, what's the nature of her escape?"

"Unlikely!"

Zack paced. He wished he had a chair. Chairs were good for thinking.

"Okay. Words matter here, even more so than usual, yes?"

"Yes they do!"

"And you were out stealing garden gnomes in the first place as some surreal prank, right?"

The girls fluttered. They looked at each other for the first time and bit their lips in unison, in a cartoon parody of thought, then floated in front of him.

"Dim memory of legend says yes, prince boy."

"And surreal is real here?"

The girls circled each other vigorously in thought.

"Surreal of old no longer includes sur. Absence of real includes surreal, but surreal includes what is. So, no. Five questions!"

"Describe the world to me."

"That is not a question!"

Zack thought.

"How do you see this world?"

"With eyes!"

"You little fucking—" he started to shout. He collected himself. "How would you describe this world as different from the last one?"

"It's newer! Brighter! More fun! Funkier! Three questions!"

"And Leah is integral to the nature of this world?"

"Yes!"

"And her being here is part of that?"

"Yes! It makes it better! Or worse! Depending on your point of view!"

They fluttered closer to Zack. "One question, boy! One last question!"

Leah cleared her throat. "You are going somewhere with this, right?"

Zack wiped a drop of sweat off his left temple. "I think so."

o o o

"You want to know what consciousness is?" asked the creature, sipping from a glass of red wine.

"Sure," said Greg, "why not?"

"Don't sound so excited, babe," she said, lightly scratching the small of his back. Greg stiffened. "It's a pattern. It's what happens when a whole lot of energy starts organizing itself in a particular way around one place. The chemistry and electricity of your brains follows little channels again and again, and begins to repeat itself, and memory occurs, followed by comparison, and begins to create the effect of thought. That thought begins to define itself and rearrange the energy around it, projecting through action and vibration."

"Sure," said Greg.

"Do you know what consciousness is for?"

"Nope."

"Nothing. In your world, it was for nothing. A vast force of definition, capable of reorganizing the universe into the heaven of your choice. Each being possessed of it created a self-satisfying world of meaning and left it at that, until people! Bless people. They wanted more! They were too unsatisfied with their gift to settle for their little worlds. They wanted to use their minds to reshape the universe! They had the potential. And what did they do? They gave it away. All for nothing. They gave away all their hopes to a median reality. They wanted to be with one another, to bridge the gaps of internal worlds, and join with one another at the peaks of their complexity. They could have. But nobody could stand that journey all the way to the top, and they gave away their power to an effect. They didn't want to go through the lonely doubt it would take to find the ethereal minds of other people, so they decided to let reality be, and give all their potential to a force that would keep everything normal. Your minds wrapped themselves in little definition prisons, and let the world limit itself to the boring normality of life and the lonely depths of thought."

Greg's expression was impenetrable.

"Why is balance so terrible?"

"Because it has no future. It was powerful, though; I had to tear the universe apart to put things as they should be. Do you know what consciousness is for now?"

"No."

"Me."

She raised her glass to the horizon and drank.

"This is much more than being God, Greg. God was a compromise. I am everything."

"Except for the anomalies."

She grinned at him with slitted eyes and all her teeth. "There has to be some fun, doesn't there?"

o o o

"Okay," said Shen. "Let's go over this again."

"I can't believe you did that," said Boris. "I mean, one of the bones popped right out of—"

"Can we focus?"

"Yeah," said Megan, "I don't want to think about it. And there isn't much I don't like thinking about."

"Right. So the phone can't act, because it's too close to the demon. Things are sort of working out for me because I represent coincidence, but I can't really direct that in a meaningful way."

"By definition," added Exley.

"Exactly. Exley, your coat is protecting you?"

"I think so. Coincidence again."

"You two . . ." Shen looked at the twins.

"We've had a pretty ironic life," said Megan, summing up years of pain and violence into a bored-sounding statement.

"Interesting. But you're both reasonably unaffected by this world?"

"Valium," said Megan, poking Exley. He brushed her hand away.

"Don't let things get to me," said Cecily.

"Right," said Shen. "So the problem is, fundamentally, that part of Jacob's mind is trapped in part of Rose's mind out in the nether-world—"

"It's not the netherworld," interrupted Richard.

"What?"

"It's not out there. It exists in what you can't see."

"Does that help us?"

"Might," said Boris.

"Well, there it stands. Jacob and Rose are headed straight for the problem."

"We need to help them," said Exley.

"They need to help themselves," said the phone.

Shen shook his head. "But they can't."

"I know, but they have to. You can only help yourself. I can list several thousand references on this subject."

"Yes, I've probably read some. I know what you're talking about. We need to make them able to help themselves. How do we do that?"

"Okay," said the phone. "The part of Jacob's brain that formerly held his missing circuit has been written over, entombed if you will, by something else. If we can unwrite that, we can allow Jacob some small access to his higher functions, and open up the possibility of Jacob calling back his circuit."

"What about Rose's thoughts?"

"I believe something has to jar Rose's experience of the world enough to cause a significant alteration of her perspective. If she can be made to feel less trapped, her thoughts will no longer be trapped, and they will return to her head for readjustment."

"Which has to happen first?"

"I'll bet they have to happen at the same time," said Richard.

"Okay," said Shen, "that will have to sort itself out. How do we unwrite Jacob's mind?"

The phone checked a few million calculations.

"Prayer."

"Right," said Shen, clearly implying that he did not think this was right. The he snapped his fingers. "Right! You mentioned this in the metaspace."

"Guys? What?" said Exley.

"Prayer was a forgotten language in your old universe."

"But people prayed all the time."

"Yes, but they did it wrong. Anyway, the original syntax won't work here, but I think that since I am ingrained in this world's first principle, I can use a variation on that code to rewrite a small piece of this reality."

"Will this actually defeat the demon?" asked Exley.

"I don't think so. It will weaken her. I'm not sure what could get rid of her."

"What do we do?" asked Shen.

"Okay. Shen, I need your mind to project the message, because anything I send out myself will be twisted by my nature. Richard and Boris, I need you to access the carrier particles of coincidence to break through to the metaspace. Megan and Cecily will have to be our anchors."

"So what does all that mean?" asked Megan, echoing the thoughts of the rest. "I mean, what do we actually do?"

"Join hands."

There was a moment of silence.

"You gotta be fucking kidding," said Cecily.

"Are you sure?" said Shen.

"Yes. Please just do it."

Cecily pointed at Megan. "I'm not holding her hand."

Megan turned to Cecily. This created an awkward pause as she said nothing while rallying her natural frame of mind through the Valium haze. "Cecily. I hate you. You hate me. You will never get your piece-of-shit car back. So do this and we can go back to pretending we were born in different families."

Cecily thought about this. Finally, she spat. "Deal."

"This needs to go smoothly," said the phone. "Do the men have any strong homosexual repression or fears that would make them uncomfortable holding another man's hand?"

As enlightened as the men had tried to be during their lives, this question caught them off guard.

"I don't think so," said Shen carefully, searching the eyes of the others.

"Nah," said Richard.

"I'm a hallucination," said Boris.

"You're a what?" said Shen.

"I'm part of Richard's brain. I was put into a body a few weeks ago."

"But I've known you for years."

"Yeah, me too. Apparently I was backdated."

"Oh!" Shen snapped his fingers again. "Like Dawn!"

"Like what?"

"From *Buffy*."

"From what?"

The phone interjected. "We need to focus. Boris, grab the left speaker on the desk. No, your left, with your left hand. Cecily, grab his other hand, Richard, grab Megan's hand, Shen, grab Richard's and my right speaker. That should work. Is this okay with everyone?"

They nodded.

"Okay then. Richard, make sure your watch is on your right wrist."

Richard glanced down. "It's there. Why?"

"I need the crystal to tune the frequency of the signal and get it moving as radio waves while Shen translates it."

"Hah!" laughed Richard.

Shen looked at Richard. "What?"

Richard shook his head. "Nothing."

"Um. What do I do?" said Exley.

"Sit tight."

"Sounds good," he said.

After everyone was settled, the phone fell silent.

The humans waited, nervously. Basil walked into the middle of the circle and purred, which calmed everyone down a little. He nuzzled Megan, who melted.

"Kitty . . ."

Shen cleared his throat.

"What happens if we fail?"

"Well," said Richard, "I expect some horrific backlash will kill a lot of people, including us."

"I agree," said the phone.

"I thought as much," said Shen. "How much of a chance have we got?"

"It depends on how stable the universe is when we get the message worked out."

"Ah. The universe isn't very stable right now, is it?"

"No."

o o o

"What should we do after this?" asked Jacob. The various pains in his body had merged into a general feeling of unhealthiness, which was how he felt most of the time anyway, so it was easy to ignore.

"After what?" said Rose.

"After things work out."

Rose laughed, then coughed. "You think we'll get out of this?"

"No."

They trudged on. Rose looked at Jacob.

"Do you still love her?"

"Kind of. Not the sort of thing you can help. Even if she wasn't what I thought she was."

"Nobody ever is."

"Maybe."

"So what should we do after this?" asked Jacob again.

"Get a drink. Grow old. Die."

Jacob nodded. He had sent the working parts of his brain into overtime, furiously suppressing any hint of rage, confusion, and any other suspect emotion before they got a foothold. He thought about how effective a fascist regime really was.

"What would you like to do before you die?" he asked.

"Be happier."

"That's what everyone wants."

"Well, everyone can fuck themselves. For everyone else, it's a little cherry on the happy fucking sundae special. I just want to be a little happy. Happy for more than thirty seconds. I want some hope that shit will balance out in the end, that once I can think again, I can think my way out of the fluke of birth that made me grow up miserable. I want to think I can stop making myself miserable, and that I'm not doomed to stick my head in an oven in ten years."

She fell silent. They made their way around another bend in the road.

"You know," said Jacob, "I've lost everything in the last few months. I even lost the guilt trip that let me force myself to keep doing things. I can't say why, but I know this doesn't have to be the end."

"That's very optimistic of you."

"No. I'm saying there's always another option."

"Sure, but you can't choose it and I can't think of it, so let's get this over with."

o o o

Zack stood silent. He wondered about Morning Star, still behind his head somewhere. Leah didn't show it, but her heart was pounding at the possibility of escape. She waited, biting her lip, for Zack's last question: The words that would set her free and give her another chance.

"Do you girls like music?"

"*What?*" shrieked Leah.

Zack cringed.

"You . . . you fucking . . . I've been here for . . . You know what I miss? You know how long I've had to think about it? Is this a joke? Fuck, do you know what I'm going to do to you? For eternity? You . . . you—"

"Leah!" shouted Zack.

"What?" she shouted back.

"What's your last name?"

She stopped, mouth open. "You really think that matters?"

"We looooove music! Music is life!" said the girls. "Nineteen questions! Make your demand! Solve the riddle, boy!"

Zack faced them and hoped his hunch was genuine, not a hunch produced by the part of his brain that wouldn't at all mind being tortured by Leah for eternity.

He said, "Give up the funk."

The girls fluttered. They looked uncomfortable.

"Why?" they asked.

"We need the funk."

The green glow vanished. The girls fell to the ground, unconscious.

A wave of distorted depth exploded out from the circle. The gnomes screamed briefly and then toppled to the ground, frozen in awkward positions. The trees snapped straight, not quite normal, but no longer swaying in unison. There was a physical *whoosh* of semireality rushing in to fill the void, and the ground shook, melted, solidified, and had a quick stretch before calming down. The sky above them cracked, revealing nothingness, then clapped together as a comfortable gray.

"Well," said Leah. "I'll be damned."

o o o

The wave swept outward and reached the apartment. The ring of people and a phone in a computer twisted very slightly, then settled back to normal. Before they could get their bearings, the phone relayed the code to Cecily's and Megan's minds, where it was made human and removed from the irony around them; through Shen's, where, among other things, all of the errors the phone had made in the code were fortuitously fixed during translation; and into Boris's and Richard's, where it emanated into the universe on radio waves of madness.

The humans passed out instantly. Exley looked down at them.

"I was afraid of that," said the phone.

"Are they okay?"

"They should be fine. They'll need sugar when they wake up."

Exley reached into his pockets and pulled out five candy bars. "Well. It's something."

"You've done good things."

"No, I know."

"Really. I just didn't specifically need—"

"It's okay. Drop it."

o o o

It hit Rose and Jacob. They saw the landscape warp, but it wasn't significantly unlike all the other issues with space and time they'd dealt with, so it didn't faze them.

It hit Greg and he blinked. His vision connecting him to the unknown winked out for a moment, then reasserted itself, but this time as a less overwhelming experience.

It hit the creature and she threw up.

She dropped her glass, which shattered on the stone floor. Greg went over to help her. She grabbed his arm and let him help her to a chair, then pushed him away. She pulled another glass out of the air as Greg sat down next to her.

"I'm fine," she said.

"You're sure?" Greg asked, not sure what he wanted to hear.

"Yes. I didn't expect that. It doesn't change things that much. Only makes the job a little harder."

She coughed and wiped a trickle of blood from her mouth.

"I said I wanted fun."

o o o

The message travelled through the hidden dimensions of the universe, raised a few metaphorical eyebrows, and very slightly changed the temperature in certain places inside Jacob's brain. A small collection of brain cells responded by changing their signals, rearranging their charges, fixing a few things here, rewiring some things there, and dusting off some spare parts. It took no more than an instant.

Behind Zack's head, Morning Star waited. It would be hard to describe what, exactly, he was doing behind Zack's head, because describing exactly what he was doing would make it impossible for him to do it. He had attached himself to the sight of Zack vanishing into a tunnel reality in front of him, and then furiously denied what was happening to the world behind him. By not being able to see anything around Zack's head on the far side of the tunnel, and refusing to look at anything else on his own side, Star managed to avoid establishing any context for what he was doing or where he was. Being the sole observer in this situation, there was nobody to define things for him, so he remained, not strictly dead in a dead universe, and not strictly living in a new one.

o o o

"I don't want a cigarette," said Jacob.

"What?" said Rose, who had just lit two.

"I was watching you light up, I realized I was out, and I was about to ask you for one, but I don't want one. I'm not even trying to resist the urge."

"Well. Good for you." Rose sucked on both her cigarettes. "Anything else?"

"No, I was just surprised."

"Good. Let's go in."

They were at the door of the mansion, which was standing open. They went in slowly. The place was beautiful, if a little bare.

"Come up!" said a pleasant female voice.

They walked up the stairs and came out onto the terrace, where Greg was sitting with a woman of indeterminate age.

"Greg?" said Jacob.

"Yeah. Long story."

"I bet."

"Welcome, Jacob," said the woman, "it's been so long."

She bore little resemblance to the girl Jacob had known years before.

"Dorellen?"

"A little different. A little older. Have a seat."

Jacob and Rose sat down and noticed two glasses of wine in front of them that hadn't been there a moment before.

Dorellen raised her glass to them.

"I'd ask how you've been, but I don't have to." She smiled.

"You know," said Rose, "thanks for the wine and you seem very nice, but we know you're an evil beast and if we can think of a way to stop you—"

"Yes, Rose, how's thinking going for you these days?"

Rose stared death at Dorellen and grabbed a wineglass.

"You're not as nice as you used to be," said Jacob.

Dorellen laughed. "I wasn't very nice then. I was nice to you."

"You're not very nice now."

"I could be."

Her features grew younger, and freckles washed over her face.

"Don't," said Jacob, averting his eyes.

"Why not? It doesn't make you feel at least a little less guilty to find out I'm not dead?"

"You are dead."

"Mmm. In a manner of speaking, this girl," she pointed at herself, "is dead. Because you dumped her."

Jacob drained his glass.

"It fills itself sometimes," said Greg, trying to be helpful.

Jacob put the glass down. "She killed yourself . . ." he said, and paused, but decided not to correct himself, ". . . because she failed to do what you're doing now, and wanted to try again."

"If you like. But she wouldn't have done it if you hadn't left her. I wouldn't be here. None of this would have happened."

"Or you planned to kill yourself before you even met me, in order to put me into a self-destructive guilt trip and set this all up."

She winked. "That's a possibility. I don't remember."

Jacob rubbed his temples. "No. She was a beautiful person. She's a memory now. She was what she was to me, she died, I've dealt with it. You are not her."

"Oh? How sad. You could have had her back. Isn't she pretty, Greg?"

Greg shook his head. "I'm not going to help you do this."

"Oh, but you are, Greg. Well, I'll tell you, Dorellen is beautiful. And sweet. And a little bit shy, but she hides it inside herself. She loves Jacob very deeply. She loves him the way people love each other before they finally share everything and make that connection everybody wants so desperately to make."

"Stop it," said Rose.

"Uh-oh. The pretty girl fights back."

"Not a pretty girl, bitch."

"Oh? Jacob liked Dorellen because she was pretty. When she

started saying smart things, he ran away."

"No, I didn't!" said Jacob. "I ran away because I was young, and she . . . you were going crazy."

"Was I? Or was I trying to make a difficult decision that you weren't much help with?"

"No, and how much help was I supposed to be? I couldn't save people then, I can't save people now. I couldn't make Dorellen happy, I couldn't make Rose happy, I can't . . . you can't make people happy."

"You can help."

"I always tried."

Greg turned and looked at Rose and Jacob. There was something about his gaze that made Jacob stop speaking.

"Jacob," he said, "you are right. But she's right too, and you can't let her argue on her terms. Don't let her tell you what you mean."

Dorellen smiled at them. "He has such good eyes. He can see everything about you. But you know, it's true that nothing meant anything. It does now." Everybody's wineglass refilled. Greg's water glass also filled with wine. He threw it away, only to find another in his other hand.

"Why are you talking to us like this?" asked Rose. "What's the point? Don't you have what you want?"

"Well, I'm not sure. Let's take a look." Dorellen waved her hand, and the world fell away.

They were still sitting on the terrace. Around them, a wash of tangled lines and twisted dimensions swirled.

"This is how the universe works when you're not looking at it. A mess of space, time, and thought. Each thing contributes its own pair of cents to the buzz. All that meaning you worry about is just a reflection of these little tangles in the universe. All I've done is taken a little of what your minds create and guided it. So! These big black spidery lines around everything, that's your mind, pretty thing. This directionless sparkly thing is Jacob. You can see how it sort of sucks everything toward itself, but it can't make up its mind about where to be. But that's only a part of it. Jacob serves two purposes. That little sparkly thing let me back into the world. But because it's not in Jacob's head where it's supposed to be, since he did those nasty little drugs and lost it, he couldn't defend against what I was going to do with him. So I got to use him twice. I used him to create a new kind of meaning. And what's Jacob's life been about? Come on, if someone asked you a week ago, what would you have said life is about?"

"Suffering," Jacob quietly replied.

"Exactly. But that's not enough. I used someone else to make things extra fun. Not all of him, sadly, but what can you do? It was enough. Once the communal consciousness of the town started losing its mind and breaking down the walls of reality, all I had to do was choose which people I wanted to use to redefine things. And here we are. Same as the old world, except I'm on top." She winked at Jacob. "You liked it when Rose was on top, didn't you?"

Jacob didn't answer her. Dorellen rolled her eyes. "Fine. No sense of humor. You want answers, answers, answers. So why are you here? Because I want you all to realize how stuck you are. How little you can do. And I want you to realize it at the very peak of your refusal to accept it. Then I can retire and enjoy things. See, I didn't expect you to be living here, Jacob. You were conveniently, sweetly, ironically drawn to it, trying to run away from memories of Dorellen. I was looking forward to this town. It was rife with irony. It was calling for me. And then you came. That was a treat. A free shortcut into the world, and all I had to wait for was the little kick of a moment when you had a thought everyone in the world uses to make themselves feel better, only that one time, you were wrong. You've been a like a bag of candy ever since we first met. In fact, you know which part of you I used to keep everyone here so I could feed them all drugs?"

"No."

"See if you can guess."

"No."

She snapped her fingers. A journal fell on the table. Jacob looked at it. Rose picked it up and flipped through the pages and pages of "going noware going noware going noware." Her hands shook.

"That's how everyone feels in this town anyway. You put it so well, I couldn't help using it to cheat."

Jacob's mouth fell open. "That's . . ."

"Evil? Jacob, darling, good and evil are the very least of what I'm concerned about. They're the words people use to make sense of blind fate and the things they can't understand about each other. Irony is so much more noble and explicable. That's the beauty, Jacob. Everything makes sense now. Everything works here. When you laugh at the irony, you know it's because irony is what's doing it."

"Wait a minute," said Rose, "Which comes first there? Irony is how you see something . . . it's how you see a coincidence."

"Wrong. Irony is a thing that creates situations you tend to consider meaningful. The coincidences that you're so fond of imbuing with meaning . . . well, they were coincidences. It all meant nothing. Coincidence is what breaks down meaning. And the fact that none of your species ever understood these two basic principles is why you were all so miserable."

"They're all still miserable down there," said Greg.

"Yes, but eventually they'll know why. You people don't need to end suffering. You can't do that. You need to understand it. That's what I've given you."

They watched the hum of the universe around them.

"Can you stop looking like my ex-girlfriend?"

"Of course, love."

She changed again. "Greg likes this one. I know he does."

"It's true," said Greg.

"All you had to do was get over me and put your life back together. But as much as you're able to choose anything, you choose to suffer. You still find ways to drag out your awful little relationship with Rose, for instance, even though you go out of your way to make sure neither of you are happy. I could make her stay with you. I could make her like you again. Oh! I could make her pretend to like you, so she keeps suffering. That seems ideal to me. What do you think, Jacob?"

"No."

"Well, fine. I'll get what I want soon enough."

"She's right," said Greg. "If you don't stop her, nobody will."

"But how?"

Greg turned his heavy gaze on them again. "I don't know. But it's lucky that you're here together, I think."

"Lucky for me," said Dorellen.

"Not entirely."

Dorellen arched an eyebrow at Greg, and sipped her wine. She giggled.

"What is love?" Greg asked Jacob.

"I . . ."

"What kind of a question is that?" said Rose.

"It's one that's hard to answer. Look." He turned his chair so he could look at them. "She's already told you coincidence counters irony. In our world, these things balance each other. I've seen another force. I don't know what it is."

"Love?" asked Jacob.

"No, I doubt that. If love had a say in the universe, it wouldn't be so cold. Love is a coincidence of chemicals that may or may not reach into the thoughts that affect our world. I'm pretty sure, anyway. I've had a lot of time to think about this. I've been drunk most of that time." He looked down for a moment. "But still, I think it's true. It's what stopped her last time."

"Don't you have something nasty to say?" Rose said to Dorellen.

"No, no. He's quite eloquent when he's sober."

"Thank you. As I was saying. She invariably creates the coincidence that is supposed to bring her down. But she used you this time because she'd already hurt you once before. And when she used you, she reinterpreted the happenstance in your life as her own intent, her own ironies. But before now, before you became what she needed you to be, those were coincidences."

"The things that happened before I came here were coincidences, but now they are irony?"

"Yes."

"That doesn't make sense."

"Yes it does," said Rose. "She's taking over everything that ever was and ever happened. That's what this universe is. She started with you."

"How does that help me?"

"She has to keep the universe in a cycle of meaning. Nothing should make sense after what happened—what happened was psychotic and impossible—but she spins it into a neurosis of irony through us. Mostly through the cycles in your head."

"And I end a cycle by breaking it?"

"Yes!"

"But I'm missing the part of my brain that does that."

"That's true. It's a problem."

Greg gave in to the glass of wine. After a long drink, he leaned back in his chair. "I've been in a cycle for years, and my brain's intact."

"Would you like to see your mind, Jacob?" Dorellen asked.

"Would I what?"

"You've lived in it for so long. You've argued with it. I can introduce you to it."

"What are you talking about? I am my mind."

"No, you are you. You guide the pattern of your consciousness. Your mind is the sum of your brain and your thoughts and your life. 'You' is a short-term memory."

"That's just playing with words."

Dorellen choked on her wine. She wiped her mouth with her sleeve and started laughing. "Oh, Jacob, where have you been? Here."

She snapped her fingers in front of his face.

○ ○ ○

Jacob's eyes opened. He was in a small room with no windows. He looked around.

The room did look vaguely familiar. It sparked a dim memory of . . . being in a crib? That was ridiculous. He couldn't remember that far back.

When he turned around, there was a window. Outside was a desert.

"My mind is a very strange place," said Jacob.

As he spoke, the walls fell down, revealing the desert to be a picture on the wall of another room that had a door.

Jacob opened the door, for lack of anything better to do.

"Hey," said his creativity, walking in and sitting at a table that definitely wasn't there before. He lit a cigarette.

"We can smoke in here?"

"Not really, but kind of. I do because I've been so bored."

"But . . . you're my creativity. How can you be bored?"

"You missing the thing that usually makes me work. Check it out." He pushed the picture of a desert aside to reveal nothing. Not blackness: A violent blind spot in the wall. Jacob covered his eyes.

"Yeah, that's why we put the picture up," said creativity, letting it fall back into place.

"What am I supposed to be doing here?"

"Beats me. But if I had to guess, and I'm reasonably good at guessing, that woman out there is trying to demonstrate how little a piece of yourself you actually are. This doesn't happen very often, so me and Steph came down. Hey, Steph," he said.

Jacob turned to see his ego walk in. She had a bit of a limp.

"Mark. Jacob." She sat down.

"My ego is a woman?"

"Well, your ego's wholly dependent on women, so it makes sense," said Steph.

"Where's the rest of . . . me? My mind?"

"They're all working overtime. Suppressing emotions is not easy work."

"But it doesn't take my ego or my creativity?"

"Well, again," said Mark, "I'm only part-timing, and no, it takes a complete lack of ego. Your ego respects your emotions."

"She does?"

"I try. You haven't been very helpful."

"Sorry."

"It's okay."

Jacob looked around again. The room was well lit, at least.

"So, help me out here. You're all representations?"

Mark tilted his head and squinted. "Sort of. Everything is somehow a representation of something else. See, the demon girl told you consciousness was a pattern. That's true. But patterns are also consciousness. Everything affects everything else. We think insomuch as we exist, even if we're just aspects of your thoughts."

"I see."

"I hope not," said Steph. "That kind of thinking will drive you crazy. But the point is, everything fundamentally *Is*, capital *I*, and everything that *Is* is a pattern, and every pattern is related to what you call thought."

"By the same token," said Mark, "thought is a pattern related to little particles running around. You see, you have a rational cutoff point, before which you consider a part of the universe a thing and after which you consider it abstract. But it's not that cut and dried. It changes. It's relative."

"Then . . . how does anything make any sense, ever? What's absolute?"

"Well," said Steph, "to a certain degree, the dimensions that define the space in which we move. More fundamentally, the gaps in that space."

"Wait, how do you know all this?"

"We're more subtle patterns than you. You know about us; we know about even subtler patterns."

"Interesting."

"We think so."

"Since I'm here, can you help me?"

"Not really. You're still sort of running things, even if you're down here with us. But we can tell you things you already know."

"Like what?"

"Like you're still obsessed with your ex-girlfriends, but not really in love anymore," said Mark.

"Or that you have a huge guilt complex," said Steph, pointedly looking at her bad ankle.

"That you and everybody else in this town have been flooding their brains with marijuana."

"Not that we mind," said Steph. "But you could have picked up on some of the things going wrong around here earlier than you did."

"Oh, and we don't know how, but the nicotine is out of your system and the part of your brain that was addicted, isn't."

"Really? I noticed I didn't want a cigarette."

"Yeah," said Steph, "that's what was covering up the missing part of your brain. So we had to put the pict—"

The room shook slightly, and Steph vanished.

"What was that?" asked Jacob.

Steph flickered back into existence. "Sorry," she said. "I think you got slapped."

"By whom?"

"Hell if I know. Probably somebody trying to wake you up."

"Why am I not waking up?"

Mark finished his cigarette and stamped it out on the floor. "Because you don't want to. Maybe you don't really want to deal with being awake. Or you have some nagging thought keeping you here."

"What are nagging thoughts, anyway?"

Steph pointed at the picture on the wall. "They're kind of like what's behind there."

Mark shuddered. "I hate that thing."

The room shook again. Steph vanished.

o o o

"Wake up!" screamed Rose as she slapped Jacob again.

"He can't hear you," said Dorellen. "You should probably stop that. I mean, he must have a concussion by now."

Jacob's eyes looked at nothing.

"What did you do to him?" asked Rose, nearly crying.

"I put him somewhere where he can deal with his issues without distractions."

"Why won't he come back?"

Dorellen stretched. "Oh, he'll get back eventually. I wouldn't hold your breath. He's still got that little problem of his missing bits being stuck in your mind."

Greg looked up. His eyes drilled into Rose's. "Remember," he said, "everything you do, think, and say does something. Shifts something. Here, it means something, and everything that means something does something."

Rose shook Jacob. "But this doesn't mean anything!"

"Oh, yes it does," said Dorellen. Her eyes were beginning to shine with a pale white light. "All your intentions are diced on my cutting board, loves. Everything means me here."

Greg straightened up in his chair. "But you don't control it all. You've already lost ground. In fact, even when the universe became yours, it wasn't perfect. You're not—"

Dorellen swung around and backhanded him in the face. He flew out of his chair and hit the far side of the terrace. Dorellen waved her hand angrily, and the sky became a blind spot, a total absence that the brain could not fill as it refused to believe what the eye was telling it. The horror of most of her vision becoming nothing made Rose cry out. She fell to the ground and crushed her eyes shut against it.

Dorellen stood above them, her eyes burning, an impossible liquid light falling out of them into the directionless void.

"This is nothingness!" she screamed, her voice ripping through the emptiness, creating the space for its own sound. "Is this what you want? If it doesn't mean me, it means this! The universe itself wept at the idea of this void, so it tore me from a thought, created me to give itself hope!"

The sound of her voice dug into Rose's ears in a sensory assault as terrifying as the empty sky.

Rose reached out her hand, searching for Jacob.

Dorellen grabbed Rose's head and pulled open her eyes. "Look at it! This is the emptiness you're all so afraid of. It is to be feared. The coincidences that you're so fond of, that make you blink in surprise, that joy is only the relief that something still exists. It exists only because of me, because I won't let the emptiness win. All things decay, but not here! Here, meaning is forever, and your fear and your pain are not for nothing. Look at it!"

Greg picked himself up. He was crying. Dorellen laughed once and let go of Rose's head to point at him. "Even Greg can't stand it. It's his job to see, and he can't open his eyes."

"You might be necessary," said Greg, "but you were never supposed to rule."

"Supposed? Don't you mean meant? I wasn't meant to rule? I am the only meaning worth the title. The end is always getting closer, but maybe, just maybe, it won't be what you expect. Maybe it won't mean what you expect it to mean. That's the only thing you hold on to, the only thing that any dying scrap of creation can hold on to. You depend on me to laugh at the absurd, to face the fear of oblivion. Your hopes, your dreams will always die with you if you're lucky. They die before you if you're not, because you see your ends, you see your failure, and this is what waits for you!" She threw her arm into the sky. "I am what lets you end those moments of dread and live another minute, another day in a cold universe. All of life, all of thought depends on me, lives on me, and suffers because of me. Why shouldn't it be mine?"

She waved her hand and the void receded.

"That was your option. The universe wrote me into its fabric, to give thought hope. To give existence hope. Your gods are nothing. Your desires are nothing. Without me, your dreams will come, in the end, to nothing."

The light faded from her eyes. She picked Greg up and put him in his chair.

Rose clutched Jacob's limp hand.

"You see, don't you," said Dorellen, calm now, "this was what all creation hoped for when I became a part of it. That I would lead it into this world. That I would turn it through myself. That at least meaning would live past its creator. And now that universe is dead and gone, yet we continue in a trick of meaning. What else could you possibly desire?"

Around them, they heard the distant and weakening rattle of pipes.

The sky seemed to be making a sound as it pulled inward, like the tide receding before a wave.

o o o

Somewhere in between the extremely physical and the extremely abstract, the homunculus version of Jacob's stream of consciousness looked around its latest prison.

"So," said Jacob, to the pieces of his mind, "I'm stuck in my own head."

"Looks like it," said Mark.

"And you have no idea how I can get out?"

Mark and Steph shook their heads.

"I see."

Jacob thought. Carefully. He didn't want to upset the newly discovered people in his mind. It was possible, he thought, that his discussion with himself about going insane might have had a different outcome than he'd assumed since finishing it.

He looked at Mark, who was picking something out of his teeth. *No*, he thought, *my creativity would probably be more active if I were a crazy person meeting his creativity. I have to assume I'm marginally in control of my facilities.*

Well then.

Steph coughed. "Um. If you're going to do that, do you mind if we leave?"

Jacob shook his head and waved them out.

Steph and Mark got up quickly and went out the door they had come in.

He felt a pressure around his hand. It crept around his body, as though the air were steadying him.

He walked to the picture on the wall and took it down.

He gazed into the nothingness.

It was nothing. It wasn't even blank. It was like an opening in his mind—no, it *was* an opening in his mind. It was a pure void. It was loss, immaculate. It was the end of everything: Complete absence, no trace, no whisper, no memory left behind.

Jacob climbed into it.

o o o

Elsewhere, Jacob's eighth circuit simultaneously occupied every space within the map of Rose's conscious process, because it thought it would be fun. It was impossible to do: Both the location and the movement of the circuit altered the structure of the space, so the indeterminate nature of the circuit's explorations made the structure of the space indeterminate, thus impossible to reconcile with any position the circuit chose or did not choose.

It turned out to be quite a lot of fun. The circuit and the space looped through many impossibilities, vibrating with pleasure.

The circuit had a vague sensation of things happening in the physical world that might be important, but had no inclination to define *important*. It decided to stop its positionless existence and explore Rose's mind for a while.

Its multilocation being coalesced into a single place upon a moment's self-reflection and found itself in a wide valley of definitions, near a tributary marked "Important."

"Ah!" said the circuit.

It wandered aimlessly around the path of Important. It was tangled and complicated, and many of its branching paths either turned into unrelated topics, or looped back on themselves. There seemed to be a strong parallel flow between Desire and Important. The circuit looked around Desire. Sudden dead ends, hairpin turns, and endless spirals made Desire's path difficult to navigate, and though it ran along many other elements of Rose's mind, it made few connections. Those connections were mostly thin, dangerously unkempt paths to Important and wide channels to Despair. There was also an odd connection that looked as if it had been recently forged between Desire and Necessary. The circuit strolled into Necessary and found it to be a clear, simple path running above Despair. It followed Necessary to its base, where it appeared to branch away from Denial, which in turn shared a forked root with Distraction. This fork was a branch from Important.

Back where it started.

The circuit borrowed the emotion of curiosity from a memory of a conversation with another circuit, and switched its viewpoint to a position looking outward from Important. The geography twitched into a new formation.

Here, things were much more ordered. The entire path was a circle. Most of the other symbols and meanings were tiny stopping points along the way, but the major signposts were Important, followed by Need, followed by Want, followed by Desire, followed by Despair, followed by Denial, and leading back to Important.

The circuit walked around the path a few times, then switched its viewpoint to Desire.

Everything became an unnavigable mass of twisting connections. Despite its complexity, the landscape looked strangely dead and boring. In the center of the tangle appeared to be a small feedback loop made of Hope and Reason. The loop was furiously canceling itself out, the only motion in a sea of inactivity. Both Hope and Reason were being fed equally and simultaneously by Despair and Necessity.

The circuit felt a sudden urge to short. *Short what?* it asked itself.

The loop, said the urge.

The circuit switched back to its original point of view within Rose's mind and sat still, deciding it had made no progress and was okay with that. But what was that urge? It felt like a reasoned, sensible thing to do, and there was a strong sense of importance surrounding the action. This was completely alien to the circuit. Importance and reason were not motivating issues in its existence. It looked outward through a memory gap, into the space beyond Rose's mind.

It saw a powerful and compelling force of fear emanating from the irony hole of the universe. Now that was odd indeed. Specifics weren't supposed to emanate from generalities. Or were they? The circuit became lost among various definitions of specific, supposed, and general, and was bored instantly.

Whatever the cause of its manifestation, the fear seemed to be pushing the circuit toward the reason gap defined by the feedback loop in Rose's mind. This made sense. This was the hole in reality opened up in an otherwise exitless prison. To go there would be to fill the void that a chain of consequence had opened directly in front of the circuit's existence, much in the way that a space had opened in Jacob's brain. If the circuit weren't trapped where it was, it would inevitably fill the next void in its journey, inside Jacob's head. Were Rose's mind not trapped out here, it would rush to fill the gap in her mental process. These things all led naturally and plausibly from one to another.

The circuit didn't care about any of this. Natural, plausible, and reasonable were uninteresting to its mode of being, and it had never even gone so far as to create a definition of motivation in its awareness.

The circuit interpreted an element of concern in the landscape. It blinked out of a visual interpretation and into a syntactic observation. It appeared the Rose geography was resisting the impulse of fear and encouraging the circuit to stay away, because . . . it didn't want to go home.

That didn't make sense.

Wait . . . it didn't want to be forced home. As much as it wanted anything at all. The circuit looked at its own situation. If it were forced back home, by whatever route, it wouldn't actually be able to connect. It would still exist as it had for the last couple of years, but in the more limited space of Jacob's brain chemistry. The connections between it and the rest of Jacob's circuits were and would always be unresponsive to forced entry. Not out of resistance, but because they would still be looking, and would not believe the thing they were trying so hard to find could be shoved in front of their faces.

Rose's mind was in a similar predicament. It was too organized and too self-aware to accept an artificially forced resolution to its feedback loop, so though the resolution would temporarily solve the problem, the system would ultimately break down again.

It was a conunundrum, and should be tended to. The circuit could jump in of its own accord at any time, but it calculated the odds of that as negligible.

"?

" !"

"I"
"   ?"

"

"I!"

"Jacob found himself conscious in the void. Why am I narrating?"

"Because I need to. There's nothing here."

"Who are you?"

"Why am I talking to myself?"

"..."

"That sounded like a pause."

"It did."

"How am I talking?"

"I'm not sure. But there's nothing here."

"The absolute nothingness . . . no, I lost it."

"There's nothing here."

"There's my voice."

"Which is surprising."

"That is surprising. Perhaps I can define my surroundings."

"There are no surroundings."

"."

You're losing it.
"I'm losing it."

"Is this death?"
"Doesn't sound like it so far."
"Where am I?"
"This is like nothing I've ever . . . this is like nothing. How long have I been here?"
"There is no time here."
"How can you tell?"
"Things seem to be happening. Or I am a thought in nothingness."
"I am."
"You are."
"There is no reference. No point."

There never was. There's no—
What?
There's me.
But, thought Jacob, *what am I? Here—*
Without a point of reference.
I'm me.
I am here.
"I am here."

But there is no here. There is nothing. You are nothing.

But I am.

"Can I define what I am?"

No.

"Can I define who I am?"

No.

"Why not?"

Because your definition is not up to you. You cannot be defined without a point of reference.

"But I am my point of reference."

"But you have no comparison."

"Then I am everything."

"Then I am everything."

"Where do I go?"

"There's no place to go."

"But."

"But what?"

"I want to go."

"I don't want to go."

"What's the difference, if there's nothing around you?" Jacob wondered what to do in a place where there was nothing to do, see, feel, hear, attack, love, hate, observe, contemplate, or be remotely interested in.

"Remotely."

"It suggests . . . comparison."

"But there is no comparison."

"Unless the loop of the remainder of Jacob's mind puts two points apart from each other and declares one remote."

"What are you?"

"What am I? I am me."

"But what are you?"

"A memory of a second ago."

"Then time is passing."

"Then I am somewhere."

"No. You are existing."

"But I exist in this."

"Aren't you afraid? Jacob was afraid. Jacob was nowhere. Jacob was as close to death as anyone could be without dying. He was at the margin of nothingness, no time, no space, nothing to denote the moment of being besides a train of thought barreling forward without a track, no intent, no purpose, no—"

I have a purpose.

"—way to define a meaningful—"

I have a purpose.

"What?"

"I have a purpose."

"But you're just talking to yourself."

I am. So I am myself. I am. Here. This is here. There are other places. There is something that isn't the void. There is something that was, or will be, or has been.

"But it is all between the void."

"No," said Jacob. "The void is between the something."

"The void is always waiting."

"But I'm not ready yet."

Jacob was suddenly aware of himself. He wasn't dead. He wasn't precisely existing, but he was something. In nothing, true, but he was reasonably sure he existed.

At least he had a purpose. And if, in the void, his purpose was the only thing that existed, then he should be able to—

∘ ∘ ∘

Jacob popped into existence in Rose's mind.

Moments later, Jacob's eighth circuit appeared next to him.

"Me!" said the circuit, and hugged Jacob.

"You!" said Jacob, hugging him back.

They disengaged and looked at each other.

"Do you have a cookie?" asked the circuit.

"No. Where are we?"

"In some chick's head. Or in the part of her head that was taken out of her head. So we're not really in it; we're in the part of some chick's head that would be in her head if it hadn't been taken out by some other thing."

"Of course. Look, I need you to come with me."

"Where?"

"I'm not sure yet."

"¥œπʃ¬!"

Jacob clamped his hands over his ears. "What was that?"

"Oh, sorry," said his circuit. "I was excited."

"Look. I've been wrapped up in a lot of things."

"I don't care!"

"Yes . . . anyway. You need to come back."

"How?"

"I'm not sure. You're supposed to know that."

"And I do."

"Well, I'm your intension."

"Prove it."

"Look . . . where are we?"

"Rose's train of thought."

Jacob looked around. There was nothing, but it was the solid black kind of nothing that you could see and think, *Oh, there's nothing there.*

"I don't see anything," he said.

"Oh, sorry. Here."

And they were in the desert of Rose's desire.

Jacob's circuit motioned him toward a dune. "This way."

Jacob followed. They crested the dune, and Jacob saw the loop. Or at least, Jacob's circuit saw the loop. Jacob saw Rose, sitting placidly in the sand.

"Hell of a thing," said Jacob's circuit.

Jacob walked over to Rose. She looked up at him.

"You're kind of cute," she said, "sort of in that puppy way I suppose you remind me of some boys I saw in movies when I was younger it's too bad you're knocked out by that demon thing I think she is pretty but I don't really care it's a bigger problem that she put you in a coma and destroyed the universe I didn't expect things to be like this when I left home but I didn't expect much of anything really I still don't I guess this universe is as good as any other I think she may have a point but she's pretty nasty about it it reminds me of a psychology course I took at the community college when I was skipping grade school they weren't very forgiving of that they'd rather I went to that awful place with the idiot child they wanted me to mix rum and cokes for the teacher in that class was cute and probably a pedophile why are the fun ones like that I guess it's not really pedophilia if I had tits back then but the class was saying something about people needing a story and humor being a cure for fear or maybe that was a theology course I can't tell them apart anymore should have stuck with math I wish Jacob would wake up."

Her expression hadn't changed during her monotone speech.

"Rose . . ." said Jacob, as in another facet of reality a physical Rose was holding Jacob's inert body, whispering, "Jacob . . ."

"Hi," said Rose's thoughts.

"I'm actually here."

"I suppose that's possible."

Jacob sat next to her.

"I think we should leave," he said.

"I know how," she replied.

"Then why don't you go?"

"I'm thoughts and thinking and never found a reason to do it because what's out there that's better than here and why not I'm not a body don't have needs don't have to run around trying to think of things to do or have regrets or do anything what's worse about this than anything else someday your circuit will shove me back where I don't want to be and that will be that trapped again in another place I don't want to be lovely fucking lovely."

Jacob thought. He reached out gently and touched her arm. "Will you come back with me?"

"Why you hate me and I don't like you very much?"

"Maybe we could stop hating each other and get on with things."

"Like you could do that I watched you not get on with things for two years and watching reruns got old after a while I mean that literally and figuratively and you don't have what it takes to live a normal life why go out there or do anything."

Jacob looked out across the desert. She had a point. It was quiet and cool and nothing would happen anymore. There was nothing to be afraid of, nothing to do, no sun for anything to be new under.

He stood up.

"How do I do it?"

Rose's brain sighed. "You have to pull yourself together."

Jacob looked at her for a moment, then walked to where his circuit was and grabbed it by the collar.

"Hey!"

Jacob wasn't sure what to do next. He wasn't even sure what he was, but he was pretty sure he was an artificial projection of his stream of consciousness that had been reflected into his own head by the anthropomorphic meaning of a new universe, that had then escaped by plunging into the pocket of nothingness in its own head to end up in the pseudoreality between all universes currently defined by the shape of Rose's thoughts.

Really, he thought, the next part should be easy.

He reached back into his own head and looked for the thoughts that were trying to think of something they couldn't quite remember. He found each guess that knew it was wrong, but didn't know why. He homed in on the empty point of his brain, the void, the nonmind that he'd been thinking around for so long.

Then he thought, *This is stupid. It's in the back of that room. I was just there.*

He put his circuit in the void.

Rose's thoughts watched the universe bend and snap around the process of Jacob fixing his mind. There was no possible explanation for what was happening to the figures wrenching themselves through one another in front of her, and as meaning dropped away, she saw a randomness, and a choice, and a chance at . . . well, if what she was seeing was really happening, anything.

Jacob's circuit was everywhere, inside Jacob's mind, filling Rose's, then Jacob was within his circuit, Jacob was a self-sustained hallucination fading, he was a hologram of himself projected from his circuit's mind, he was real and not real. For a moment, everything was happening at once.

Then the chaos retracted to a single, burning spark.

Rose's thoughts were silent.

She walked to the spark.

She stepped into it, looking for home.

o o o

On Dorellen's balcony, Jacob opened his eyes and looked at Rose.

"Hi," he said.

Thank God, thought Rose. Then she thought, *I can think.* She said, "No shit."

A squirrel made its way over the rail and looked around. For no apparent reason, it ran over to Dorellen and bit her ankle. Dorellen watched it, unresponsive.

She drained her wineglass, which remained empty, and let out a heavy sigh.

"Dammit."

o o o

Here it comes, said V.

You ready for it?

Yeah, I'm okay.

They waited.

They waited some more.

V looked at Time. Yeah, you know, whenever you're ready. I think I've been staring at the back of this guy's head long enough.

I thought we could talk, said Time.

Right.

Look, I'm sorry I never got in touch with you . . . I've been busy . . .

Yeah, you got away from yourself.

Well, it's a big responsibility.

You asked to do it.

I had to, said Time, shuffling its metaphorical feet.

It's okay. Can we do this?

You sure?

Don't worry about it.

Okay. I never meant to hurt you.

Yo. Universe. Waiting.

Okay.

Existence came at them.

o o o

Bits of Jacob and Rose flew through conceptual space, melted into enigmas, and smacked (metaphorically) into Jacob and Rose's respective heads. As Jacob's circuit passed through the other hole of the universe, it was, for the first time in its existence, taken aback.

On its way home, it dragged a thread of a world that existed only in its pseudoconscious memory, a universe that did not have room to exist in that memory once the consciousness rejoined with Jacob's physical head, and the proper universe popped out from many billions of years of pseudononexistence. Once back, it sternly called its dimensions back home, pointing out that having two separate sets of spatial definitions in a single equation of existence was absurd. The dimensions grumbled, but put down their drinks, and began to invert once again, twisting through the hole of uncertainty Morning Star had kept open behind Zack's head.

Star sagged in relief and stepped aside as creation roared through, traumatizing Zack's higher functions, all of which shut down immediately, allowing Zack to ignore what was happening.

Spasms of Had Been cancelled out undulations of Being, and a number of lonely paradoxes and bad puns were spit out into the void, where perhaps they rebelled in the emptiness and began new lives as universes of their own, but that is outside the scope of this narrator's research.

Irony, coincidence, and other naturally reasserted themselves in their proper places, and most of the inhabitants of the universe felt only a brief disassociation of all principles of being and logic, which produced only the mildest of emotional scars.

Once everything was in place, the God Effect muscled its way into being and checked over the contents of Jacob's head. It then had a brief discussion with the phone, which explained everything as quickly as it could. Once the God Effect knew what had happened, it did a quick review of the universe and patched up the last of the gaps and linguistic loopholes. As an afterthought, it inserted a brief historical period of total particle uncertainty that would explain anything and cover whatever it had missed. After that, it gently receded into mathematics.

And so the universe, as everyone had come to know it, was back.

• • •

"Holy shit!" said Boris. "I'm alive."

He looked down at himself and saw Richard's clothes.

"Or not, possibly."

"Hey," said Richard.

"Um," said Boris.

"I guess we're on a time-share right now."

"Should be interesting."

The others woke up and greedily ate the candy bars Exley handed them.

"I feel like shit," said Cecily. "That better have worked."

"We're not dead," said Shen, rubbing his eyes.

"It worked," said Exley. "Or so the phone says."

Megan stood up and adjusted her skirt.

"I, for one, am going back to my hotel. I'm a mess."

"You're a train wreck," muttered Cecily.

"And I'm keeping the car."

Cecily spat. "Gotta admit, doesn't seem so important to get that piece of shit back home anymore. Wanna get drunk 'fore I head out?"

"That sounds nice." Megan turned towards the group. "Nice to meet you all. I don't ever want to see any of you or talk about this again."

They left.

Shen lay back on Jacob's floor and stretched.

Basil, who had just had his mind reattached, was *eep*ing at the computer, which was meowing back.

"What's he saying?" asked Shen.

"He wants to know what happened, and if Morning Star's okay."

"Oh. Is Star okay?"

"He's fine. He's headed back to your place with Zack."

"Ah, Zack. How's Zack?"

"Also fine."

The computer resumed its conversation with Basil.

"What are you guys doing?" said Shen to the remaining humans.

Exley shrugged. "I think I'm going to get drunk and go sleep in the woods again. See if my coat goes back to normal."

"That would be a lucky break for you," said Shen.

"That's what I'm counting on."

"Richard?"

Richard swallowed the last of his candy bar. "I think we're going to become a plumber. Boris?"

"Agreed," said Boris.

"Boris?" said Exley.

"Kind of," said Richard. "We're working it out."

"Good call. This town needs a decent plumber," said Shen. "Exley, I don't suppose you have a joint in there?"

"Pretty sure I do."

"Good. Let's get out of this apartment and smoke it."

• • •

Leah stretched in her bed with her own joint, thankful to be out of the woods. She had walked the two girls back to their apartment and dropped them off with a stern warning to never steal another garden ornament.

She toyed with the thought of giving up drugs for good, but decided that would be a cop-out. There were obviously many exciting places to go while high, and surely most of them wouldn't involve gnomes.

• • •

Rose and Jacob walked slowly back down the hill. They didn't speak as they walked through town. It was definitely, unarguably nighttime, and they watched the night, comforted by its relative stillness. The streetlights threw ladders through trees rustling quietly in the wind.

They stopped at the corner where their paths diverged and stood in silence for a minute, not looking at each other.

"So." said Rose.

"I don't know."

"What?"

"Oh. I was . . . answering a different question."

"It wasn't a question."

"It kind of was."

"Okay," said Rose, "Starting over. What are you going to do now?"

"I think I'm going to go back to school."

"Seems anticlimatic."

"I am really, really okay with that."

Rose nodded. "I think I'm going to move back home for a while. Maybe clean out that closet."

"I'm sorry."

Rose *tsk*ed at him. "Look there's nothing—"

"No, I just mean sorry. I don't want anything."

Rose thought about this.

"I'm sorry too."

They looked at each other.

"Do you think we're bad people?" asked Jacob.

"No."

He waited for more.

"Just no?"

"Just no."

"Okay." He looked for something else to say. "Look me up next time you're in town, I guess."

"I might. Take care, Jacob."

"Goodbye, Rose."

• • •

"Wow," said Zack, after Jacob had finished. "That is some heavy shit."

Jacob took a hit off the pipe before passing it to Shen. "Yeah. If you could have seen it . . . it was just . . . nothing."

Shen puffed lightly on the pipe and blew a smoke ring.

"What happened to that butler guy?" asked Jacob.

"I called the police. I asked for those guys that busted in here by mistake and told them it would be nice if this guy went away and I never heard about it again."

"That's a little scary," said Jacob.

"Oh, you know small-town cops. They've been waiting their whole lives for that phone call. How's your head?"

"It's been better, but at least nothing's bleeding anymore."

The pipe went around again.

"Do you think she was right? I mean about everything decaying, emptying into nothingness?"

"I don't know," said Jacob. "I mean, that's sort of what I've always assumed, and I'm happy to keep using regular, nondemonic irony to not think about it, but she could have been wrong."

"Frankly," said Zack, "after that, I'm never going to take anybody's word for anything ever again."

They all nodded, stoned.

"Still," said Shen, "maybe she was right. Maybe she offered what people really want. A meaning beyond the end."

"Well, she's still out there," said Jacob. "I'm sure she'll try again."

"True enough. How does it feel to have your brain in one piece?" asked Shen.

"Feels good. I'm also feeling good about other things."

"Excellent," said Shen.

Jacob passed the pipe. "I should probably start looking for another place."

"That's true. Do you even have a job right now?"

"Less talk. More weed."

Shen complied, and they fell silent.

"You know," said Shen after a few minutes, "I completely forgot about all that money we made."

Jacob coughed.

"So did I," said Zack.

"Yeah, how much was that?" asked Jacob. "I remember something about it being more than you could count."

"It is quite a bit of money."

Shen displayed a thoughtful frown.

"Well. I guess that takes care of things," he said.

They all looked into the distance, pondering the thought of not having to work for at least a year.

"It's going to be very difficult to talk about philosophy after this," Zack eventually said.

Jacob looked over to Shen.

"He's got a point. You think we'll still be able to hang out?"

"Oh, sure," said Shen, "we've got video games."

• • •

And so we come to the end.

I myself went out to unearth the finer details of this narrative, including my own history and some of the facts relating to events prior to my birth. I found myself in a curious position, having been created as the active counterbalance to Dorellen's emergence. In irony's previous attempts, the counterbalancing force of coincidence met with irony, and the representations cancelled each other out. This time, however, I played only a supporting role, and was in fact temporarily a part of her nature. Having failed as the active cancellation, I met no end, and found myself in the real world with an enormous amount of knowledge and power at my disposal.

Having researched many theories of ethics, and feeling a strong emotional attachment to the humans I'd come to know, I felt it best to remove myself from their daily life. My friendship with them would ultimately have created a great deal of greed and paranoia, and I felt it best to take a more bureaucratic role in the world and leave my personal life behind, though I do still occasionally write to Jacob, and I took care of his utility bills. It is more for me than him that I remain in contact, as his emotional life no longer requires friendships with anthropomorphic household objects. I find it fulfilling to ground myself in human sentiment on occasion.

It was some months later that I finally settled on a name for myself. I fear the complexities of my existential, ontological, and mathematical calculations would consume several volumes considerably longer than the one you are holding, but I ultimately determined that the best of all possible designations is Steve. It was close, and there are good arguments for Unit 102G, but if we happen to meet, call me Steve.

I don't do a great deal these days, but I serve to call attention to difficult situations like the one described in these pages, and I like to think I add a touch of love to the God Effect.

There is only one more tale to tell. It occurred thirty-seven days after the incidents described above.

It began with Greg sitting outside a small coffee shop. He had moved away from the town, and settled in a slightly larger town about forty miles north, getting a job at local music shop. He had left his guitar at home on this day, and was reading a book about kites.

A woman approached him. She was probably thirty, though could be mistaken for twenty or forty, with long, unkempt hair. She stood in front of him, quietly, and Greg didn't notice her at first. He finally looked over the edge of his book and saw her hands clasped awkwardly at her waist. He looked up.

"I think we should be together because that would be ironic."

She said it all at once and bit her lip.

Greg didn't respond. He didn't move a muscle.

She stood in front of him, twisting her hands. She had rehearsed apologies for weeks, but couldn't remember any of them at the moment.

"I'm not who I was," she said. "Well, I am. I'm not *what* I was. The force recedes from the vessel when I fail, and I get left here. I can't try again until I die. I'm human. You know. A person."

Greg folded down the corner of the page he was reading, closed his book, and set it aside without taking his eyes off her. He put his elbows on the table and leaned on them. He didn't say anything.

She tried to meet his eyes, but couldn't. "Can I sit down?"

Greg indicated the chair across from him with an elaborately courteous gesture.

She sat down quickly.

Greg stared at her.

"So how are you?" she asked.

"I see you haven't killed yourself."

"Well, no. I was a little bit older when I became human this time, so, you know, fewer hormones running around. Once I was normal, I didn't want to try again. Not right away. I mean, I probably will. It's what I do."

Greg picked up his coffee cup and sipped it.

"Look, I really did like you. Things might have even worked out if I'd won. I hoped they would. I mean, I would have made them work out if I'd felt like it. I sort of have different feelings now. I don't know what to think. But I remember I really liked you. It wasn't a coincidence that Megan brought you."

"I know. You had her bring me because I was lonely."

"Well. Yes. But I liked you. And I'm sorry about hitting you. I . . ." She trailed off.

A part of him wanted to leap across the table and strangle her, and laugh all the way to jail. But he wasn't like that. He knew he was deeply, and completely, a good person. He found that knowledge frustrating at the moment.

"I'm really old," she said. "Like, billions and billions of years, and that's counting it in your terms. It's not easy to be human with all that."

"It's not easy to be human anyway. Especially when people are twisting the universe around their diabolical schemes."

She looked up and smiled. "Diabolical? You really think so?"

Greg stared at her, and her smile vanished.

She scratched at the tabletop.

"Can I have some of your coffee? I had to hitchhike out here, and I'm kinda thirsty."

Greg pushed his coffee across the table.

"You didn't have a car at that mansion?"

"I can't drive. And some people came around inspecting the place. I didn't have a deed or anything, since it wasn't really mine.

I grabbed some jewelry and hocked it before I left town. It took me a little bit to find you. I don't have any money. I haven't had anything to drink all day."

She picked up the coffee and sipped from it.

She laughed a little. "Remember the wineglasses?"

"I remember everything."

She bit her lip again and put down the coffee.

"I don't know how to say I'm sorry. I don't know how to say I'm sorry to anybody. Especially not to you. Things look different from here. I've never stayed human this long after a failure."

"Maybe you didn't fail this time."

She looked up at him with wide, hopeful eyes. "You think?"

Greg looked at her. He couldn't stop his heart from doing what it did best. He remembered how worried he'd been about her on the terrace when she was coughing up blood. Even when she was in the process of finishing off the world. He couldn't help it about himself.

It wasn't as if she were completely helpless, he thought. She'd find her own way eventually. But right now she needed help, and she wanted it from him. *You can't always get what you want*, he thought. *But sometimes . . .*

She was watching him think it over.

"Greg?"

"Okay," he said, "tell me again why you want us to be together?"

"Because it would be ironic. You know. I still need something."

"I thought the irony was you using me as a miserable, sex-starved slave. This sounds like a real relationship."

"Well, yes, now it's a double irony, since I turned out to be a demon when you thought I was an easy lay. This is definitely the opposite of the expected outcome."

"But is that—"

"Greg, look at who you're talking to."

Greg gave up. "Fine, I'll admit that it would be ironic if it happened. But that's not a good reason for two people to get together. You can't always be doing whatever seems ironic at the time."

"I know," she said. She looked at her shoes, then back up to him. "That's not the only reason. It's one of them. I'm still what I am. But I'm changing."

Greg brushed his hair back. He was losing his resolve, rapidly.

"I'm lonely too," she said.

Greg closed his eyes.

He reached into his bag. He pulled out a dollar and handed it to her. She took it, gingerly.

"Get yourself some coffee."

She got up. "And then?"

"You need a job."

"I'll get one."

"And give the irony thing a rest once in a while."

"I'll try."

"And please refrain from hitting me."

"I will."

"Okay." He pulled out his tobacco and began rolling a cigarette. "We'll talk."

She flashed him her wicked grin before she went inside. Greg flinched. Her wicked grin hid her eyes until they were crescent glints above a line of stark white teeth. It didn't sit right on a human face.

He finished rolling his smoke and lit it. He wasn't sure what he was getting himself into. Then again, he wasn't sure about anything, except that everyone appeared to be consistently wrong about everything. So if he thought this was bad idea, he would probably turn out to be wrong.

I'm okay with that, he thought.

Besides. There was something about her grin that made him think of butterflies.